SWORD OF THE RONIN

THE RONIN TRILOGY: VOLUME II

SWORD OF THE RONIN

Travis Heermann

Bear Paw Publishing
Denver

Illustrators: Alan M. Clark and Drew Baker
Calligraphers: Midori Maruoka-Buchanan and Naoko Ikeda
Cover Designer: jim pinto

PAPERBACK EDITION

ISBN 978-1-62225-402-6

Bear Paw Publishing
Denver, Colorado, USA

www.bearpawpublishing.com

ACKNOWLEDGMENTS AND THANKS

The author wishes to thank all the folks who made this book possible, from early readers to final proofreaders, Odfellows, Codexians, Kickstarters, No Name Heroes, and friends. Jared Oliver Adams, Jason Allard, Scott Barnes, Eytan Bernstein, David Boop, Arthur "Buck" Dorrance, Susan Ee, Philip Harris, Lorraine Heisler, Chanel Helgason, John Helfers, Rahul Kanakia, Sam Knight, Amanda Lang, Peter Mancini, Mistina Picciano, Daniel Read, Josh Vogt, and Peter Wacks.

Also deserving of thanks are the calligraphers who lent their art to this volume, Midori Maruoka-Buchanan and Naoko Ikeda.

Any omissions are purely the author's fault. He will gladly commit figurative *seppuku* to rectify the grievance.

For all the people who made this book possible.
You know who you are.

PART 1: THE THIRD SCROLL

"Call me 'Brown Leaves.'"

To be truly happy, a man must forget the past and the future.

— *Zen proverb*

K en'ishi's wooden sword *clacked* against the crown of his practice post over and over. The wooden post, hardened by endless multitudes of blows over the past three years, felt like a stone pillar. Hot summer wetness thickened the afternoon air, and sweat slicked his callused palms and naked legs, made his loincloth sag low on his hips.

Then a loud *crack* from the end of his *bokken* made him pause as the tip splintered.

With a sigh, he tossed it aside. With only one remaining, he would have to ask the village woodcrafter to fashion another set. In a time of peace, with his teacher so far away, this was his only way to maintain his skills.

The music of the nearby forest whirred and sang and droned, here on the outskirts of Aoka village, where he went for quiet practice. The conversations of the birds fluttered past his ears, echoing up into the forested mountainsides that flanked the expanse of Hakata Bay. Many of their nests were empty at this time of year, with the parents teaching their hatchlings to fly. They had little use for the activities of humans in any case, except to scrounge thread or steal thatch or scavenge bits of detritus for nest-making, or to pilfer food.

Ken'ishi ignored them, too absorbed with practice today to speak to such small-minded creatures.

He suspected Little Frog was nearby; the boy always seemed to be when he was practicing. Perhaps someday he would teach the boy to speak to animals, as Ken'ishi's old teacher had taught him.

Ken'ishi raised his voice, "I'm certainly glad no one is about. I could not possibly practice with anyone watching."

A rustling bush nearby, then a hoarse, stifled giggle. He caught a glimpse of a tiny topknot peeking above the foliage.

Ken'ishi smiled and reached for his last *bokken*, propped next to his sword, the *tachi* named Silver Crane. The two cranes engraved into the circular guard glimmered in the sun, ever in pursuit of each other. Even the old, battered scabbard seemed freshly polished today.

Hearing his name called, Ken'ishi glanced up to see Norikage running toward him, robes flapping like sacks on a scarecrow, his face red with alarm.

Ken'ishi faced him. "What is it?"

The small man puffed, his narrow cheeks flushed as he halted before Ken'ishi. "Trouble ... on the docks ... A brawl!"

Ken'ishi snatched up Silver Crane and ran toward the village docks.

Norikage tried to keep up. "You know ... I cannot fight ... I could not ... stop them."

As they neared the village center, shouts rose from the direction of the docks. Faces peeked out of the doorways. Children ran toward the noise. In the three years Ken'ishi had lived in Aoka village, he had never heard such a ruckus—part shock, part cheering, part pleading. The villagers were generally peaceful, except occasionally on festival days when an excess of *saké* or the eye of a maiden brought a pair of young men to fisticuffs. This sounded serious.

He rounded the corner of the inn, trotting down the slope toward the docks. A gathering crowd obscured the fight. Reaching the ragged edge of the throng, he used Silver Crane's scabbard to thrust between bodies and pushed himself through. "Out of the way! Make a path!"

The throng ringed not two, but a handful of combatants grappling in the dirt, one wrapped in a headlock, others with punches flying. When Ken'ishi saw who they were, his heart sizzled. Three distasteful brothers—fishermen—versus three honest, upright brothers—woodcutters. A club and a knife lay in the dirt. Blood covered the face of one sprawled combatant from a gash above his ear; he struggled to right himself and rejoin the fray.

Ken'ishi gathered a great breastful of air and blasted it like a war cry. "STOP!"

The crowd drew back at the force of his voice. Two of the combatants relented their grips. Two others continued pummeling a helpless, nearly unconscious third, and the last staggered to his feet, blood streaming from his chin.

Ken'ishi leaped forward and dealt a sharp blow to the back of one's head. Chiba the fisherman bawled in pain and collapsed into a ball like a caterpillar.

The man being pummeled shrugged off his attacker, shoved him away, and turned to attack, but Silver Crane's scabbard against his chest stopped him.

As the combatants stood apart, their faces bruised and swelling, blood dripping from lips and noses, Ken'ishi's nostrils curled at the odor of blood and rancid fear-sweat.

Ryuba, the eldest of the three fishermen brothers, helped Chiba to his feet. The third, Shota, kicked his distracted opponent hard in the belly, then joined his brothers, the deep sneer never leaving his face. The three gathered as a glowering mass, their demeanors spilling contempt upon their younger opponents. These three were older than Ken'ishi, in their late twenties and early thirties. He was only twenty summers.

The three woodcutters—Daiki, Shun, and Sho—were all roughly Ken'ishi's age. Sho, the youngest, with the gash above his ear, was only seventeen, the same age as Ken'ishi when he had arrived in Aoka, the others were twenty-one and twenty-two. All three were strapping young men, but if not for Ken'ishi's arrival, their bruises and scrapes might have been worse. The fishermen had a well-deserved reputation as the roughest men in the village.

Ken'ishi held the curved, black finger of Silver Crane's scabbard between them all. "What is the meaning of this?"

Ryuba stepped forward. "What are you doing interfering? We were just bringing in our catch, and these three jumped us! They deserve worse than they got!"

Chiba rubbed the back of his head, his fingers coming away wet with blood. "You bastard! That wasn't fair!" he slurred at Ken'ishi.

Years of sun and salt spray had leathered Chiba, and had not made his disposition any more pleasant. When Ken'ishi had first encountered these three miscreants, he had killed a man named Yoba, their wicked, drunken father, for stabbing the village's samurai constable in a tavern brawl. Ever since, the family bore him naught but ill will.

Daiki, the eldest of the woodcutters, wiped bloody spittle from his mouth and shouted back, "If you touch my sister again, I'll kill you!"

Ryuba spat. "A lie, constable." The last word dripped with contempt. "None of us has the slightest interest in their sister. She has a face like a horse!"

Daiki lunged forward, but his brothers held him back. "Filthy bastard!"

Norikage stepped into the ragged circle. His voice was ragged from exertion, but he still managed a deep outrage. "This is disgraceful! Somebody speak up, or you shall all find yourselves under arrest!"

Tears of rage glistened in Daiki's eyes. "My sister was gathering *ayu* from our nets at the river, near nightfall yesterday. Somebody … attacked her."

"Where is Miwa to tell her story?"

Daiki's face fell. "She is home, weeping for shame. She is only fifteen. I will speak for her, if it please you, Norikage-sama."

Norikage said, "Let us hear the tale, and we'll decide whether we must investigate further."

Chiba snorted. "Investigate."

Ken'ishi pointed the butt of his scabbard. "You. Shut up. You'll give Aoka's administrator his due respect."

Chiba averted his eyes, chewing on unspoken words.

Daiki said, "As I said, Miwa was fishing for *ayu* in the river. Somebody jumped her, tore her clothes, tried to—" His voice choked. "She pulled free and ran away."

Ken'ishi said, "Did she see who it was?"

"He had a cloth over his face, but she knows who it was. It was him." Daiki pointed at Chiba.

"She's lying!" Chiba shouted.

Daiki kept his eyes downcast. His voice quavered with restraint. "Miwa is a good girl. She doesn't lie. She recognized his eyes. And his foul stench."

"Another lie!"

Ken'ishi sniffed. "I can smell you from here." Quiet laughter rippled around the throng.

Chiba's face reddened. "You don't know what you're talking about! You think you're a big man with that sword? You're not even *from* here."

Ryuba sneered. "Where *are* you from, anyway? Maybe you're not even samurai! Who is your family? Maybe you're just a bandit with a pretty sword!"

Chiba said, "Aren't real samurai supposed to wear something besides a ponytail?"

Their words burned into Ken'ishi's patience, chipped at his restraint. The truth was that he did not know who his family was, except that he had been born the son of a *ronin*, a masterless samurai. Silver Crane was all that Ken'ishi knew of his father. The sword was all he had to establish his status as anything but a beggar or a bandit. Without it, who was he?

Having a man like Chiba ask that question was like pouring salt in a gaping wound.

"Oho!" Chiba grinned like an eel. "Touched a nerve, have I? Sensitive about your hair?"

Ken'ishi's hand clasped Silver Crane's hilt. In a blur, the butt of

7

the lacquered scabbard flicked out and struck Chiba squarely on the forehead. Chiba dropped as if his legs had turned to noodles, and the crowd gasped. Ken'ishi pointed his scabbard at Ryuba. "You and your brother go. Leave this trash."

Ryuba stiffened. "You're going to kill him!"

Norikage stepped forward. "No, we're going to arrest him until we can speak with Miwa and determine the truth of things."

Chiba lay at Ken'ishi's feet. Silver Crane's hilt throbbed strangely in his hand, writhing in his grip as if it wanted to be drawn, to taste the blood of Chiba's wickedness. The distrustful eyes of the villagers touched him like fingers, probing for weakness.

Norikage raised his voice. "It's over. Go."

The crowd began to disperse.

Chiba began to stir. Ken'ishi said to Norikage, "I'll truss him up and take him to the office storage closet."

Norikage scratched his chin, pursing his lips in approval. "I shall go and converse with young Miwa."

"Do you want me to accompany you?"

"You take care of this ruffian. I shall hear the truth of this from her."

Chiba's hands were well trussed behind his back when Ken'ishi dashed a bucket of water in his face. He rolled onto his side, spluttering and spitting. A bloodshot eye glared sullenly up at Ken'ishi. "What are you going to do with me?"

"We will keep you locked up until we determine if the accusation is true. If it is, we'll turn you over to the government offices in Dazaifu for punishment. If not, you will be released. Now—on your feet!"

Chiba struggled to his feet, grunting. A great yellowish knot, like a chicken's egg, swelled on his forehead. "Can I have some water?"

"I just gave you some. Now, to the constabulary."

Chiba shuffled ahead. "I've been out on the boat all day. Thirsty work."

"Very well. When we reach the constabulary." Having to accord

Chiba even simple kindness chafed at Ken'ishi. He would prefer an excuse to cut him down. The man was ugly and mean, and was often heard in the inn lamenting that Kiosé's services were no longer available. Rape was doubtless not beyond his capacities.

"I haven't done nothing," Chiba mumbled. "She's lying. And you're gonna believe *her.*"

"Shut up. I'll wager your head hurts." He raised Silver Crane.

Chiba bit down on something and kept shuffling.

Some of the villagers had gone back to their business, but some watched with interest as Ken'ishi followed Chiba to Norikage's office.

The birds in the thatched roofs sang the songs of summer, but Ken'ishi did not listen to them. His attention wandered from Chiba's dark, wiry back, hunched shoulders, and bound hands to the scent of wood smoke on the air from evening cookfires. Somewhere, a baby cried, likely the *saké* brewer's infant, only a few weeks old. The gray feathers of a sparrow ruffled as it preened itself on the roof of a nearby house.

Ruffling gray feathers.

An image scratched at the inside of his memory. *The point of a sword ... Smoke ... A dark, muscled back disappearing through a smoky doorway into the light ... The gray feathers, as of an enormous, long-legged bird alighting before the man, a figure he recognized as Kaa, his old teacher ... The flash of steel and spray of blood ... The man, falling ...*

Ken'ishi stumbled and blinked, shaking his head with a sharp intake of breath. Chiba plodded ahead as Ken'ishi regathered his scattered attention.

It had not been a vision. It was a memory.

In an uncharacteristic manner, Chiba wisely held his tongue when Ken'ishi threw him into the closet of Norikage's office. It was not a proper cell, but it would have to suffice. Ken'ishi looped a rope over a rafter, tied Chiba's bound hands, and shut him inside.

Chiba demanded water again, but Ken'ishi ignored him and sat outside, feeling for the memory again. He knew there was more, but the memory was so old that he had no further sense of what he might have forgotten.

He settled his body, his mind, breathed deep, allowing his conscious thoughts to float away into the Void—the realm where the struggles, suffering, everyday thoughts, and flotsam of the world floated into nothingness, the realm where true thought became clear and empty.

The realm of the *kami*, the spirits of the wind and earth and sky, the trees and stones and sea, spoke to him, as they often did, as Kaa had taught him to listen. The *kami* sometimes warned him of danger. When he listened properly, they would speak to him as long as they favored him. He gave them reverence, and they gave him favor, but they were a capricious lot.

The scratching had worn an opening in the seawall of his memory, and more images trickled through. *The shouts of the men who had come with blood in their voices … The screams of his mother as they dragged her from the house*—and he knew they were the screams of his mother. In the seventeen years since, he had never heard or recalled her voice, but he knew it now.

To recall his mother's voice only by her screams brought tears to his eyes, cooling as they slid toward his chin.

He stood in the center of a room, and the walls were burning, the tatami *was smooth on his bare feet, and the smoke made his eyes water. His father's voice, fueled with rage and grief and struggle. The pretty, black-lacquered scabbard with the cranes inlaid in mother-of-pearl, flying toward a silver moon, lying there near the doorway. A glimpse of the blade, flashing orange in the light of the fire, wielded by his father's hand. Dark red stains on the steel, on the hand. And then a storm of dust and feathers flitting past the open doorway. The smoke burned his eyes. Suddenly he couldn't breathe. A dark man with angry eyes, sword in hand, coming for him through the door. He ran, but he was little, and the man was big, and there were two of them now, chasing him. A rough hand snatched his upright topknot, jerked him off his feet. He was crying.*

A rush of wind, and the smell of dry feathers. The hand released him. Warmth sprayed the back of his neck, and something fell onto the tatami *like a slab of meat. A cry of pain. Another rush of wind and the man fell. The second man with his tanned, muscled back fled for the square of smoke-hazed daylight. The bird—or was it a man?—suddenly in the man's path. The man's head tumbling from his shoulders.*

The tall, gray-feathered bird, with its thin body and spindly limbs, crimson beak and beady eyes, looking at him. And the sword in its ... hand. *So swift he could barely follow the movement, the creature sheathed its weapon, stepped out of sight for a moment, then returned with another sword in hand, his father's. It picked up the pretty scabbard and put the bloody sword away. A great wind cleared the air of smoke. The creature stood over him, reached down and took the boy's hand in its own long fingers. Knuckles covered in soft gray down ...*

Ken'ishi's eyes opened again in the present. These memories had been from the day Kaa, a *tengu,* had shown mercy to a human child, saved his life, and taken him into the mountains to raise him and teach him the ways of the warrior. These memories had never before crossed his thoughts, but he knew them to be true.

A chill whispered over his shoulders and neck and took a long time to go away.

Fever-felled
  halfway,
My dreams arose
  to march again
Into a hollow land
  — *Basho, Death*
        Poem

en'ishi was thinking about these strange new memories, even as he returned to his house that evening.

As he climbed the steps to his door, a stick darted between the steps and whacked the side of his ankle—not hard enough to be painful, but enough to startle him out of his reverie. He leaped back, hand on his hilt. A muffled giggle sounded from under the steps, and he smiled.

"How unfair to strike from ambush!" he said to the dirty little face hiding in the shadows. "Show yourself, ruffian, and let us duel like men!"

Little Frog darted from under the steps, topknot bobbing, twig clutched in both hands like a sword. He swung the sword and struck Ken'ishi across the knee.

"Oh, well struck!" Ken'ishi allowed his leg to collapse. "You are victorious, sir! Spare me my life, and I will be your faithful servant forevermore."

Little Frog put the point of his stick victoriously to Ken'ishi's chest and sniffed nonchalantly.

Ken'ishi stood and swept the boy up into his arms and onto his shoulders. "Allow me to carry you, my lord. Where shall we go?" The boy pointed toward the inn. "Mama!"

"Very well."

Ken'ishi carried him to the inn where Kiosé was doubtless still hard at work. Naoko was a kind enough employer, but the duties associated with an inn often went late into the night, even with as little outside traffic as Aoka village received.

Reaching the entrance, he took Little Frog down and led him inside.

Naoko spotted them from the door to the kitchen, and her face softened into webs of happy wrinkles. She called into the back for Kiosé.

Moments later, Kiosé came out, wiping her hands on a towel. Her haggard face beamed like a warm dawn when she saw Ken'ishi and Little Frog together. She saw Ken'ishi noticing this, and averted her eyes.

She bowed to Ken'ishi and then held out her arms to Little Frog. The boy leaped into them. "Thank you for bringing him," she said. "He has not eaten today, and I just made some rice balls." She wiped at the grime on the boy's face. "Are you hungry?"

The boy nodded vigorously.

A few other villagers, all of them men without women at home to cook for them, sat in the large *tatami* room at little tables, where they ate their evening repast.

Ken'ishi noticed that her clothes looked particularly threadbare today, but the happiness on her face warmed him. Perhaps he would speak to the village seamstress about a new *kimono* for her.

She said, "It was good that you stopped the fight today. Those poor woodcutter boys might have been hurt very badly, or killed."

"That was the worst brawl since ... since I came. And somehow that family is always involved." It was in this very room, on Ken'ishi's first arrival in Aoka, that his life had been changed from wandering *ronin* to respectable constable. And it had all started with Kiosé. Back then, she had been a whore indentured to the inn. In a drunken frenzy, Yoba had threatened to kill her, only to be stopped by Hojo no Masahige, the administrator of the village, Norikage's former master. In the ensuing brawl, Yoba stabbed Masahige to death. To avenge Masahige and save Kiosé's life, Ken'ishi had drawn steel and cut Yoba down. Norikage had subsequently hired him as assistant constable.

Chiba and his brothers had once cornered Kiosé behind the inn and beaten her in revenge for Yoba's death. Perhaps those were the memories behind her eyes as her expression went cold. "You can believe Miwa's story. She is a very nice girl. She doesn't … treat me the way the other women do. She's kind."

Ken'ishi nodded. Because of Kiosé's history as the village prostitute, she would never be accepted among the other women. He had bought Kiosé's contract, freeing her from indenture, but such prejudices died only with the passing of generations.

"I am certain Norikage will have the truth of it from her, and if it's true, he'll hang for it in Dazaifu."

She shuddered, and her mouth hardened. "Few men deserve it more than he does." Her eyes turned back toward Ken'ishi and a flush appeared in her cheek. "May I—may we come tonight?"

They had not lain together for several days, as she had secluded herself in the inn's storage hut until her moon's blood had passed.

"Yes."

Ken'ishi had bought her contract, but he had not married her. Whisperings of their relationship were never kind—"How fitting! A *ronin* and a whore!" Sometimes he refused her requests for a visit. She never refused his.

She put Little Frog down and bowed to Ken'ishi, bowing her son's head as well. He bowed in return.

They sat together quietly after Little Frog had been tucked into his *futon* under the great gauzy mosquito net. Bowls lay picked clean of rice, fish, and fresh *daikon* radish.

Ken'ishi waited until Little Frog lay sound asleep, which did not take long, as the three-year-old spent every day exhausting himself at untold adventures around the village and its environs.

14

Then he took Kiosé in his arms, pulled her to him and kissed her. The angles of her bones were little padded by softness, but her breasts were still full with milk, her lips soft and hungry, and the fervor of her grip arousing in its intensity. She wanted *him*. Her arms and legs clutched him with a wanton, desperate heat, and every dozen, close-packed heartbeats, her body convulsed as she bit back cries of ecstasy. And when he spent his seed within her, she clutched him tighter and tighter as if desperate for it to take root.

Rolling off her, their bodies sheened with sweat and musk, Ken'ishi lay naked in the wet summer night, letting himself dry.

She sidled up to him, still gasping in the afterglow of pleasure. "Again?" she whispered.

"Perhaps later. Sleep now."

She fell asleep against him.

As the sweat dried on him, his thoughts trailed off into nothingness—

Until suddenly the *kami* awoke him with words he could not hear, not words at all, but flashes of perception, stabs of emotion that were not his own, not even those of a human being, but the silent spirits that permeated all things, the spirits of the air and earth, of fire and sea, of trees and bamboo and grass, of life itself.

He had been asleep, but did not know how long.

Starlight trickled through the window slats, across the floor toward the rack where Silver Crane rested. The ephemeral glimmer turned the mother-of-pearl inlays on Silver Crane's scabbard into daubs of moonglow, like a pearl amid lava stones, painting the mosquito net overhead into silvery gauze. The light grew so bright, even the black-lacquered stand caught the gleam. His modest, one-room house echoed with the sounds of night under the dark canopy of the thatched roof, the sounds of breathing near him, against him. Outside, night creatures sang among the silent houses of Aoka village.

Kiosé lay in the curve of his arm, her breathing quiet, snuggled up to his chest, the softness of her breasts pressed against his side, her leg on top of his. Whenever he pushed her away, she

15

whimpered in her sleep until she could cleave up beside him again. With a sigh, he allowed it. Nevertheless, it was a distraction.

His thoughts turned immediately to Miwa's accusations against Chiba, who still sat tied up in Norikage's office closet. Norikage had not been able to speak to Miwa. Her brothers said she was hiding in the forest for shame. Norikage would try again tomorrow. How sweet it would be for justice to find a reprehensible bastard such as Chiba.

He lay still, hoping sleep would return, but anger at how Chiba and his brothers had treated Kiosé—and anyone else in town who crossed them—drove any relaxation away. Strange how memory was such a malleable thing, like clay. His memories of the night he had killed Yoba were as solid now as kiln-fired pottery. And yet, he considered these strange new memories. Where had they come from, so half-formed they hardly felt real? Even as they slipped away, his thoughts clung to them, sifting them for images of his father, but found only blood and fear, smoke and screams. Why had they opened to him now?

On nights like this, when the moon waxed round and the sky was clear, Silver Crane's voice whispered at its loudest, but even then it was only the merest suggestion of a voice, like trying to pick out a murmur amid a typhoon. Had the sword whispered to his father so? The *kami* residing within Silver Crane seemed to have something to say, if only he could learn to hear.

Perhaps if Kaa were here, the old bird could teach Ken'ishi how. Whenever he felt the sword's silent touch, he reached for it, but it retreated, and each time his frustration redoubled.

It seemed the closeness of the sword's voice increased on the nights after he had coupled with Kiosé, and the hard spike of guilt lay coldest in his belly, a guilt he would never express to her. Her presence sometimes added another layer of the world's distraction that he had to push aside, to quiet the typhoon.

Other flashes of memory flitted through his mind, moments of passion with her, bursts of emotion that inevitably led his thoughts toward guilt, toward memories of another lover who had made his soul sing as Kiosé never would.

16

He sat up, pushed the mosquito net aside, and stood naked. His thigh ached as he stretched, and he pressed his thumb against the dimpled puncture scar there, given to him the night that Little Frog had come into the world. Little Frog lay there now, at rest on his own small sleeping pallet a couple of paces away, the only time when he was ever at rest. The sleeping boy was like a ball resting at the top of a mountain; at sunrise the ball would roll and bound and bounce down the mountain with such energy it was exhausting to watch.

Thoughts tumbling into flashes of the two *oni* he had slain, the demon-bandit Hakamadare and vengeance-crazed Taro, and then the soft musky richness of ... her. She whom he had saved from Hakamadare's lust ... She who had taken his heart and never given it back ...

Frustration tightened his jaw, and he got up and paced the room. Would he ever have peace in his own mind?

Then an idea came to him. Silver Crane's voice had been most accessible when he was in battle. He must find a way for it to speak to him at his own choosing. But how could he recreate those moments when the sword had awakened? Must he be near death? Perhaps if it finally spoke to him again, it might give him more clues to the identity of his father, knowledge of his ancestors—a place in the world where he might belong.

He crossed the room to kneel before the sword on its stand. The silver fittings of the *tachi*'s curved scabbard glistened brighter than they should, leaving an afterimage behind his eyelids. He took a series of long, deep breaths, allowing his mind to go still, gently pushing his thoughts away. Kaa had taught him to seek the Void, the timelessness between moments where true clarity lay hidden like the secret treasure of the universe. Perhaps in the Void, he would find respite from the typhoon of the everyday world.

Frogs sang outside to the music of the crickets. An arrow-shot away, the rumbling sea stroked the shore with gentle fingers. A shutter down the street *clunked* once in the faint breeze. A neighbor's tom cat yowled its loneliness at the moon.

Amid these external noises wandering past his ears, a presence.

His awareness snatched for it, and it swirled away like a butterfly.

His nose caught the sudden scent of blood. Thick. A river of it.

His eyes snapped open. He looked about him in the dark, down at himself for the source of the smell, at Kiosé and Little Frog to check that they were still sound and whole.

The scent was gone.

He had not smelled such a profusion of blood since the last time he had killed, almost four years ago, a long time for a man of only twenty summers. His body was whole. No blood on the floor or anywhere in sight.

He sniffed deeply. Only the smell of wood, *tatami* mats, and a wisp of smoke from the fire pit.

A chill brushed the back of his neck.

Kiosé moaned in her sleep like a lost soul.

The chill had not been the warning of danger. More like the touch of winter, an imminent frost. He frowned.

Kiosé moaned breathlessly again, "… touch … me." Her hand blindly cast about the bed for him.

Ken'ishi often sought the pleasures of her flesh, but her yearning for him sometimes felt so needful that he found himself drawing away.

"Don't … touch me!" she groaned.

His annoyance evaporated into pity for her. What must it have been like for her to lay with so many of the village men?

He crossed to her and knelt at her head, reaching under the mosquito net to stroke her hair. She quieted with a deep sigh. He waited a few more moments, then stood up and left her asleep, taking Silver Crane with him out into the night.

The moon had just risen like a gleaming coin. A hum vibrated through his left hand, the hand that gripped Silver Crane's scabbard, up through his arm, becoming a spreading warmth across his chest. His heart sensed the warmth and sped its rhythm. The shower of celestial light cast black shadows at the feet of nearby houses, the inn down the street, the constabulary office. Beyond the houses, the white froth of Hakata Bay washed across

18

the beach, around the legs of the docks where the villagers' fishing boats floated against their moorings.

Aoka village lay as silent as a sleeping dog. Larger villages or areas threatened by *ronin* bandits often employed night watchmen who roamed the streets with lanterns, but Aoka was too small. A mere two hundred-odd fishermen, tradesmen, and townspeople comprised the village, and Ken'ishi the only samurai.

The hum intensified, and the smell of blood crept back into his awareness. He raised his nose into the breeze, but no matter which way he turned, he could not discern the source, as if a great slaughter had been wreaked here. The scent subsided again, maddeningly. Out here, bathed in the glimmering quiet of night, the whisper brushed closer against his mind.

The sand of the moon-frosted beach *skritched* under his feet until he found a suitable spot a hundred paces or so from the village. He knelt, resting the sword across his knees. A deep breath. Reaching for the Void.

Crabs scuttled around him, sidelong blurs of motion along the pale sand. For a moment several of them looked as if they were moving *en masse,* like warriors to a battle.

And then—

Blood. Gore so thick and heavy and drowning it flooded over him like a hot waterfall.

He gasped against it, through it, sucking its coppery stench into his nose.

It filled his ears like warm water, spilled into his mouth, choking him, washed a deep, crimson haze over his vision. He coughed, retched, gasped for air, confusion crashing through him. Muffled by the unclean deluge, the whispering became a murmur.

He snatched Silver Crane free of its scabbard and whirled into the high guard stance, wiping at his eyes with his wrists, but feeling no wetness.

Something bowled into him, a heavy weight smashing into his back, driving him forward a step. He spun and slashed, but the feathery blade sliced only empty air. Another blow, this time from the front, like fists plowing into his ribcage, drove him back two steps. He slashed again, unable to glimpse any attacker.

Another blow from the side.

He bit back a cry of pain.

Another blow.

Another.

Another.

Pounding.

Pounding.

He thudded onto the sand, all breath expunged from him.

His mouth and nose full of blood that was somehow not his own, as if it were pouring into him from outside.

His eyes burning.

Like a pure, clear temple bell, a thought reverberated through his mind.

My life.

He slashed blindly.

He caught a glimpse of a wispy shape streaking toward him, an instant before he felt another blow. A wispy shape with a contorted face, the embodiment of rage and blame.

My history.

The hilt in his hand had become a thrumming vibration. More ghostly shapes pummeled through him, pale faces barely glimpsed.

Honor. Courage. Slaughter. Glory.

Ken'ishi's body suddenly was made entirely of hard, sharp lines. No more softness of mortal flesh, or even of bone. Only steel. With a single, supple razor-edge. A thing—a being—created for the sole purpose of taking life. Infused with the power of those whose lives it had taken. And through those lives, to bring power to the man strong enough to claim it. A man of honor, of courage. Of lineage.

Through lakes of blood, I glide.

He stiffened, his body curving painfully backward, his legs feeling as if they were bound tightly together with thick silken ropes.

Through halls of power, I pass.

The sensation of his hard edges and contours gouging into the sand, scoring the surface of a nearby rock with his edge undulled. *Through screams of the dying, I conquer.*

The memory of his razor-sharp edge slicing through untold mountains of muscle, forests of wet bone, rivers of pungent entrails. The courage of a man holding firm his hilt, courage flowing like *ki*, lifeforce itself, strength, into the man, out of the man, into the sword, out of the sword, in a rhythm that fed upon itself.

Through countless generations of men, I journey.

How many men had claimed this hilt? Some of them wise, strong, brave; some of them ambitious, vengeful, petty. How many more would try to claim it, after (Ken'ishi's?) bones had long become ash and dust? Who was this mere mortal man who now thought to possess such power? Who *dared?*

Rivers of blood spill behind me, before me. It is destiny. A river of death unto the end of the world.

His mind snapped free of its brittle confines. He looked down at the fragile body of a young man, alone on a moon-bathed beach, clutching the hilt of a sword in both hands. The point back against his throat. A deft twist, a tiny thrust, a little pull. So effortless to lay the man's throat open like a butchered pig's. And then, perhaps it would find a more worthy master.

"No!" The raw sound of the young man's voice crashed through the walls of time.

The rumble of ebbing tide vibrates through tempered rigidity. The waters of the man's life recede into the vastness of time. A rigid razor-edge touches the most vulnerable of points. How many throats have I laid open with the slightest touch?

"No!"

Ken'ishi became a man again, had hands again. He strained against the pressure that held the point of the blade to his throat.

Who are you to claim my power?

"I am Ken'ishi! Son of a great warrior!"

A great warrior.

The thoughts came without words, only perceptions, emotions, images. Ken'ishi sensed careful neutrality, without any hint of mocking. "You have served me this long! You belong to me now!"

Amusement. Perhaps the man belongs to me.

"Many times, I have sensed you sleeping. You helped me once, in a moment when I would have died otherwise. Why turn on me now?"

Because time means nothing to the spirit of steel. Perhaps you were worthy then. Perhaps you will be worthy then. Are you worthy now? Death is coming. Death is past. Death is now. I may soon have an old master. I may earlier have a new one.

"What must I do? You *know* the story of my family! Tell me!"

Amusement at foolishness. The man knows nothing. I follow the bloodline.

"What bloodline?" The long-sought answer to Ken'ishi's greatest question—who was he?—seemed to taunt him, just out of his grasp.

The man will know. In the endless river of time, he may already know. But not from me. It is destiny.

"When will I know? How?"

The future and the past are meaningless. Only this timeless instant matters. It is all that exists.

Just as quickly, the voice, the hum of power, the stench of blood, all gone.

Ken'ishi lay with Silver Crane in his hand, clean and dry, the sand gritty against his back, the stars in the heavens—perhaps his ancestors staring down upon him—cold, aloof. The sword was quiet now, but quiet like a new-discovered mountain path. The path was shrouded in forest, perhaps still difficult to find, but he knew it was there.

The rivulet of real blood trickling down the side of his throat told him this had not all been just a dream.

The *kami* of the sword had spoken to him. He would never be the same again.

Hell is not punishment;
it's training.
— *Shunryu Suzuki*

The bound ronin snarled and spat a bloody wad at Yasutoki's feet. The deck shifted rhythmically under them, scents of wood, resin, rope, and stagnant brine filling the hold of this Koryo vessel. The hull creaked and brushed against the pier as the tide came in. This particular dock of Hakata Bay was far enough removed from the trafficked areas that no one would hear any screams. Besides, at this time of night, even sailors were mostly asleep.

Under the voluminous basket hat that obscured his face, Yasutoki teased his mustache. Loose dark robes, worn Chinese-style, obscured the profusion of deadly weapons secreted on his body. "I am considering having you sliced into chum."

"So kill me then!" the *ronin* gasped. His hands and elbows were bound behind him to a stout wooden club wedged between his elbows.

Yasutoki glanced at Fang Shi. "Perhaps we should oblige his wishes, Fang Shi. Tenderize him for the sharks."

The enormous brute loomed over and laid a powerful kick against the side of the *ronin*'s head. The man slammed into a stack of barrels before sprawling onto his back.

Fang Shi looked back at Yasutoki. "I kill, Master?"

Yasutoki shook his head and stroked his narrow beard.

The *ronin* had restrained any cry of pain. His one unswollen eye blazed with defiance as he glared at Fang Shi and Yasutoki. "Cut me free, and let me die like a man!"

Yasutoki hovered as still as a cobra waiting to strike. "No one steals from me and lives."

The *ronin* snarled, "How was I to know that money-changer worked for Green Tiger?"

"So you know who I am."

"Who else could you be? Green Tiger, the Lord of the Underworld!"

The level of fear and reverence given to Yasutoki's secret identity, Green Tiger, always pleased him. He smiled inside his basket hat. "What is your name?"

"Why do you care?"

"I once had an *oni* in my employ, until some unwashed *ronin* with too much fortune for his own good killed my poor Hakamadare. Ah, you've heard of him, have you? Then you know I am not a man who forgives. Tell me your name so that when you die, I can send an *oni* to hound you into Hell."

The *ronin* laughed. "I already walk the road to Hell. Perhaps your *oni* and I will bow to each other, have some *saké*, and go whoring."

Yasutoki studied the man again. Unshaven, unkempt, filthy, stinking of old sweat and piss. The man had long ago abandoned the samurai topknot and let his hair fall in bedraggled strings around his face, crusted with blood and the detritus of his week-long captivity. But there was also a suggestion of pride long lost. He had not always been a bandit, but what else could a warrior do with no master and no wars to fight? After fifty years of peace, what were all those bored warriors to do except fight among themselves or prey upon the weak?

"How did you do it?" Yasutoki said. "The guards saw nothing."

The *ronin* laughed, a harsh, ragged sound. "Would Green Tiger give up *his* secrets?"

Fang Shi buried his meaty heel in the *ronin*'s belly. There was a muffled crack of bone.

The *ronin* curled into a ball, gasping, hacking.

"That was a rib." Yasutoki waited for the *ronin* to regain the ability to speak; he was nothing if not patient. When the man's gasps subsided into ragged breathing, Yasutoki stood over him. "What did you do with the gold?"

"Spent ... it ..."

"All of it?"

"Debts ..."

Yasutoki laughed. "You stole from *me* to pay debts?"

"Not all of it. I had a good time."

"You must have had a very good time."

The *ronin* was regaining control of his breath. "I made many a whore smile and many a *saké* brewer re-count his stock."

"You didn't gamble it away?" If he had, then Yasutoki might have at least have already reclaimed some of it through his gambling dens. Most such men, in the depths of such a binge, spewed money like blood from a severed head.

"Gambling is for fools. The house always wins."

Yasutoki found himself not wishing to kill this man anymore. At least for now. "What is your name?"

"Call me Masoku."

"Who was your family?"

"It doesn't matter."

Yasutoki nodded. This *ronin* did not appear to cling to his past. Such entanglements could create mixed loyalties.

Fang Shi fidgeted and cracked his thick knuckles. "I kill, Master?"

Yasutoki shook his head. "You see, Masoku, how eager my man is? I can scarcely restrain him."

Fang Shi sighed like a child denied his favorite game. His broad, naked brow furrowed.

The *ronin*'s voice dripped with sarcasm. "I'm in your debt for such boundless restraint."

"My, but you do have a serpent's tongue. And you are, indeed, in my debt. For quite a sum."

"How long was I in that barrel?"

"A week. Does it matter?"

"Let me stand on my feet like a man before you take my head."

"What makes you think I'm going to take your head?"

"Why should I think you won't?"

"The taking of heads is a warrior's business, a pleasantry exchanged by 'honorable' men. I could just as easily gouge out a couple of loops of your entrails, hamstring you, and leave you in the sun. Bury you to the neck in a cistern of shit. Slice you into fish bait and salt the cuts. Let Fang Shi here pound your arms and legs flat with his hammer, one extremity at a time. Stuff your mouth with fetid—"

"I get the idea!"

Yasutoki knelt before him in an instant. The needle that had been concealed in his palm hovered a finger's breadth from the *ronin's* good eye. Even in the dimness of below-decks, the black stain of poison was evident on its tip. "Listen to me, Masoku. You are correct that you already walk the road to Hell. I *own* the road to Hell!"

Masoku did not flinch, did not blink. Most other men would have quailed in fear.

"Perhaps you would like the opportunity to walk this road a bit longer, put off the inevitable a bit longer. I have plans coming to fruition, you see, and I need swords. Yours was a passing fine blade. Of course, I examined the make of it during your stay in the barrel. Saburo Kunimune was a renowned swordsmith in Bizen. The Shimazu clan would not entrust such a weapon to a man of no ability. Unless you stole the blade from someone more worthy." His gaze bored into Masoku, drilling for truth, but the *ronin* said nothing.

"At this moment, I am inclined to give you the opportunity to repay what you stole from me. It was a sizable sum, so by my calculation, I now own you for the length of your stroll to Hell. I would prefer to regain some value over time, but I would also be content to take a one-time repayment from your guts. What say you?"

The *ronin*'s eye flickered with surprise, and with calculations. His breathing slowed. He licked his lips, crusted with old and fresh blood. "I would say, let us go drinking and whoring on this road together. Master."

The season's first melon
Clutched in its arms —
The child sleeps

— *Issa*

The afternoon rain sprayed the world in sheets, turning the streets outside into a morass. Ken'ishi settled himself onto a cushion on Norikage's rear veranda overlooking the modest garden. The emerald moss coating the stones seemed to grow richer with every passing moment, the grasses to open their throats. It was the end of the summer rainy season, and there was little respite from the humid air, even at night.

Norikage settled his reedy form nearby, brushing his robes around his feet, then stroked his thin beard with a bony hand. "I am fortunate to have returned from the woodcutters' house again before this awful rain. Is Chiba still trussed up in my office?"

"Yes."

"Then we should let him go."

Ken'ishi stiffened. "What?"

Norikage sighed. "Poor Miwa is terrified. She will not speak against him. She is afraid that if Chiba is punished, his brothers will kill her or her brothers."

"You know as well as I that he is the likely culprit."

"Indeed, but if she will not speak publicly against him, we may as well let him go. There were no other witnesses."

Ken'ishi shook his head with a sigh. "I will release him later."

Norikage smiled. "Oh, *do* take your time about it. Stay a while. Hana will be bringing refreshments momentarily. She made some tasty bean cakes yesterday."

Rainwater sluiced over the eaves. Ken'ishi breathed deep of the scent of rain-washed foliage. With thoughts of Chiba melting away at the sound of the downpour, his mind turned to the visions of blood and violence of the night before. His body still ached as if he had been beaten with clubs, but his skin was free of bruises.

Norikage said, "You have the look of something troubling you."

"My master from when I was a child taught me many things. The ways of the sword and the bow, how to speak to the animals of the earth and sky, how to listen to the voices of the *kami*."

Norikage leaned forward, cocking his head.

"Last night, the *kami* of Silver Crane spoke to me. It has never done so before."

Norikage raised his eyebrows. "What did it say?"

"It was unlike any *kami* that ever touched me before. Most *kami* are thoughtless, capricious things, flowing over the earth, through it, around it, moment by moment, like pinpricks of thought. This was almost like speaking to another person, but not a person, something with thoughts that go far beyond, travel farther than a human being can, as if it sees the past and the future. I couldn't understand much of what it said."

Norikage studied him. "Fascinating."

"It was cold and cruel, but powerful. Have you ever heard of such *kami* within a sword before?"

"The Imperial Court's augurers, the *onmyouji*, speak of such things, but only in the quietest of whispers. I never pursued such knowledge. My attentions were more base than those lofty realms—the under-robes of princesses and such things."

"I felt this sense of its history, bigger than the world itself, or so it seemed, but that history was hidden."

"I heard those in the court say that many of the ancient, sacred Imperial regalia possess such spirits, growing in power from their long march through the hands of many emperors. There are few realms more charged with lust, intrigue, and cruelty than the Imperial Court. Perhaps some *kami* feed on such feelings."

Norikage's serving woman appeared through the rice-paper door and knelt beside them with a tray of tea and cakes. Hana was a bit older than Ken'ishi, in her mid-twenties, with a solid, working woman's carriage and a pleasing face. With deft hands, she poured them each a cup. Just as silently and efficiently, she withdrew into the house. Norikage cast a lascivious glance after her.

Ken'ishi lifted a cup and took a deep breath of the earthy steam. The green tea from nearby Mount Takatori was exceptionally aromatic. "It was good of you to offer her a position after Yuto's death."

Norikage sipped his tea and shrugged. "A man gets tired of living alone."

"She is pretty."

"She is passing acceptable."

"What about her family? Can she go back to them?"

"I have asked her about them, but she is tight-lipped. She mentioned her father briefly, but ..."

"You haven't yet bedded her."

Norikage frowned. "She'll eventually bow to my will. Yuto's death remains too fresh for her, I suppose."

"Your patience is gracious."

"Indeed. I even bought Yuto's fishing boat from her."

"Wasn't it damaged in the storm?"

"Not badly. It is perfectly serviceable."

"What do you want with a fishing boat?"

Norikage shrugged. "A man never knows the vicissitudes of life. Recreation, perhaps. Perhaps I shall one day give up the luxurious life of Aoka's administrator and become a fisherman."

Ken'ishi chuckled. "You have never lifted a fishing pole, much less hoisted a net." His gaze was drawn to movement outside the wooden fence opposite the veranda, a faint scrabbling in the corner.

"Perhaps I'll have slaves, or at least henchmen. They can hoist the nets for me. And Hana can manage my pole."

Movement across the garden snagged Ken'ishi's eye. A small arm reached under the garden fence, questing.

Norikage followed Ken'ishi's gaze. "What are you looking at?"

"A visitor."

Norikage squinted. "My eyes are not so good. A *tanuki*?"

Ken'ishi smiled. "I hardly think we would see a *tanuki* during the day. At least not in its everyday shape."

"A fox?"

"No, this is not an animal."

A round pink head tufted with black fuzz thrust itself into the hole under the fence. Small, hoarse grunting noises. The child's brow wrinkled as he wriggled. Two arms now, grabbing for purchase at the fence.

The little boy's progress halted. His lips pursed as he realized that he was stuck, but he redoubled his efforts.

"Is that Little Frog?"

Ken'ishi smiled.

"In this rain!"

The diminutive body squirted through the opening with a wet *slurp*. Little Frog rolled over and stood, his meager clothes drenched and muddy. The little black tuft of topknot on the crown of his head looked like the withered stalk of a melon. He took a deep breath and wiped the rain and mud from his face. When he spotted the two men on the veranda, his eyes lit up and he jumped up with glee. "Da!"

Ken'ishi's smile faltered only for an instant.

Little Frog toddled through the puddles, giggling his hoarse giggle at the splashes.

Norikage said, "Is his voice getting better?"

Ken'ishi shook his head. The boy was stricken with a croak for a voice, and he loved to splash through puddles, hopping like a frog.

Little Frog threw himself against the edge of the veranda, thrust his little body up onto it, then hoisted a leg up. Water splashed off him. Ken'ishi grabbed the boy's arm and pulled him up. Little Frog's face was absurdly serious as he sat beside Ken'ishi and reached for his teacup with an expectant expression.

Norikage laughed. "Some tea to warm the belly, little man?"

Little Frog nodded once. "Mm."

Norikage called into the house. "Hana, one more cup, please!" Then to Little Frog, "Does your mother know where you are?"

Little Frog nodded again, once. "Mm."

"Somehow, I am skeptical." Norikage smiled.

Little Frog looked up at Ken'ishi, beaming, assuming his posture.

A look of pity flickered across Norikage's face. "Are you going to teach him?"

"Teach him?"

"Samurai ways."

Ken'ishi frowned. "And make him *ronin* like me?" He had been the constable of Aoka village for almost four years. He thanked the gods and Buddhas that no one had ever questioned his and Norikage's arrangement. Norikage was not Ken'ishi's lord, just a bookish man who needed a sword to back up his position, a man who had given Ken'ishi a place to exist.

"Would that be worse than the lot he's been born into?"

"I'm not ... I don't ..."

Norikage's eyes narrowed, warning Ken'ishi not to say it in front of the boy. "Look at him. Some boys need a man to teach them, some more so than others, such as this one. You said you had a teacher, someone who taught you warrior ways. And you were a stripling like Little Frog once. Who was this teacher of yours?"

Ken'ishi's earliest memories were of the lonely mountain cave, long-fingered gray hands giving him bits of raw fish to eat, and rice balls and wild plums. Curling up on a straw mat as the daylight diminished in the mouth of the cave, where Kaa's tall, spindly form sat silhouetted by the sunset, deep in meditation.

Little Frog reached for a teacup again. "Da, tea please."

Ken'ishi handed his teacup to the boy. Little Frog took it in both hands and sipped in perfect adult style. Ken'ishi did not know if the boy was his son. He could be the seed of half the men in the village.

Little Frog slurped his tea and grinned.

Ken'ishi said, "My teacher was a *tengu*. He raised me from a child smaller than this."

"A *tengu!*"

"I stopped telling people that when I grew tired of that reaction. Most people think I am either mad or a liar."

"My uncle said he saw a *tengu* once, on a pilgrimage to Mount Kurama. It tricked him into believing it was a mendicant monk, and then stole his food. There were legends of a whole tribe of *tengu* living atop Mount Kurama. It was a holy place."

Hana came out with a fresh cup, poured tea from the pot for Ken'ishi, and hurried back inside just as quickly. She gave Little Frog a quick smile before she departed.

Norikage said, "It is a harsh thing for him, to be born under such bad kharma."

Ken'ishi frowned. Was it any worse than being an orphan with only one clue to his real past? Or being raised by a teacher whose chief instrument of instruction was a bamboo switch? Kaa had been wise beyond Ken'ishi's young understanding, unfathomably skilled with a blade, and crafty, but a *tengu* was not a human being.

He looked at Little Frog and thought of Kiosé, then back through his journey from the north, to the days when he and Kaa had spent enough hours with a *bokken* to turn a young boy's hands raw with blisters. He studied Little Frog and considered teaching the boy as Kaa had done. But Ken'ishi was not ready to be a teacher. There was still too much for him to learn, and he could not learn it here. He had a position. The village needed him. Norikage needed him. Kiosé needed him.

Something stung him inside, and he felt Norikage's gaze.

Ken'ishi said, "Even a shogun cannot control the circumstances of his birth."

Silver Crane's presence, resting in the sword rack inside the foyer of Norikage's house, suddenly reached out to him. *Is it worse to be born into expectations and fail to meet them, or to have none at all? To have hope and lose it, or to have never felt the sting?*

Ken'ishi's frown deepened. He sometimes wondered what sins Little Frog had committed in a previous life to be born the bastard son of a common whore, or the bastard son of a penniless *ronin*.

Little Frog's threadbare rags dripped a puddle around him, but he didn't shiver. As a boy growing up with his teacher on the side of that far northern mountain, Ken'ishi had learned to tolerate cold. Little Frog had the same grit. Hana came back outside and draped the boy in a blanket. The boy allowed it, and bowed his head to her in thanks, grinning.

They sat in silence for a time. Little Frog slurped his tea and sighed with satisfaction. Ken'ishi cradled the warm earthen cup in his hands.

A distant knock echoed through the house. Ken'ishi could hear Hana shuffling through the house to answer the knock. Kiosé's voice, quiet but half-frantic. Hana's reassurance. Kiosé's sigh of relief. Two sets of footsteps shuffling through the house.

Kiosé came out onto the veranda, bowing effusively. Rain dripped from strings of her hair, plastered her ragged trousers to her legs. "Excuse me, sirs."

Little Frog grinned and waved. "Mama!" He held his cup high.

Her shoulders slumped with relief. She bowed again to Ken'ishi. "Thank you for bringing him with you. I was too busy working and he just disappeared, and ..."

Ken'ishi said, "It's no trouble."

"He loves going with you." A lilt to her voice, a subtle yearning. "He's no trouble."

Kiosé held out her arms. "Come."

Little Frog jumped up, shedding his blanket, and ran into her arms with a happy croak.

"You're soaking wet! I have some fish soup at home. You like fish soup."

The boy twisted like a monkey and reached for Ken'ishi. "Da!"

Ken'ishi smiled as best he could. "I'll see you tonight."

Kiosé's face brightened. "We can come again tonight, then?"

He nodded.

Joy bloomed in her face, making Ken'ishi squirm.

She bowed to Norikage. "I'm sorry for your trouble. Excuse us."

Norikage smiled. "It's no trouble at all." He waved to the boy.

Little Frog waved over his mother's shoulder as she disappeared back into the house.

Ken'ishi's gaze fell to the floorboards and meandered along the wood grain. When he glanced up again, Norikage's expression bore a strange mixture of pity and reproof.

"She certainly behaves as if the boy is yours," he said.

"She wants me to claim him. I know that."

"It is more than that. She believes it to be true."

"I don't see how she can know."

Norikage pursed his lip and stroked his chin. He sighed.

Ken'ishi said, "What is it?"

"Forgive me if this stretches the bounds of our friendship, but ... you don't love her."

Ken'ishi stroked his cup. "I am fond of her."

"She is so much happier these days, since you came to the village."

"She's not a whore anymore."

"You forget that I was raised in the Imperial Court. Survival there depends upon the ability to read people like a scroll, to perceive what is underneath the ink of the characters. She's not yet twenty, but there's something of an old woman's gaze in her eyes."

"Perhaps we should be drinking *saké* instead of tea."

"I shall say this, and then we shall never speak of it again unless you choose to. I see the way she looks at you, the way her eyes follow you, the way she sighs. And I pity her, because there is something of you that she'll never have. It is as if you wear armor, even when you're out there on the beach half-naked, practicing your sword techniques. Your spirit is closed and hard, like the shell of a clam."

"It doesn't do for a warrior to oblige his heart. It distracts from discipline."

"Ken'ishi, you and I have known each other for almost four years. Why have you never mentioned anything of your life before coming here? Only a few vague comments. Nevertheless, I am certain there was a girl."

The earthen teacup withstood Ken'ishi's tightening grip. Some memories he clung to like an old pair of trousers, habitually slipping into them, but they were trousers too soiled and fraught with holes to be useful or proper. Memories of someone else, who had once stoked his heart to a brighter fire. How many nights had he lay here on his *futon* beside Kiosé and stared into the rafters with another's name a mere half-breath from his lips? And that name turned to a half-snarl, turned his guts into a roiling pit, when he thought of the hands of another man upon her, a man who was, long since by now, her husband. How many children had she borne him since? Two? Three? Had she accepted her duty with happiness and forgotten the penniless *ronin* who loved—

His exasperation with his own thoughts trod its familiar path.

"Some people can let that kind of pain go," Norikage said, "but you do not. You clench it tight around you like a breastplate."

"You overstep."

"Hear me out. Priests and monks have a saying: the past and the future make men suffer. I saw people at court play at love like a game of *kemari*. The anguish of broken hearts ran in runnels down those sacred corridors tainted with the scent of lust. I played the game with the wrong girl, and it landed me in exile."

Ken'ishi's shoulders tensed, and his belly clenched as if drawn tight by the same spring. "It is not a game. Do you have a point to make?"

"Do not cling to it forever. As long as you wear that breastplate, you do not have to look at that pain."

"Why would I want to look at it again?"

"If you do not look at it, and choose to let it go, it will fester. And you will destroy the spirit of someone who cares about you. Her spirit is already fragile."

"Such words surprise me from a man who has at times claimed

to have no heart, a man who aims to have a helpless widow in his bed."

"A man can lament his own folly. And as for Hana, it is not just my little warrior doing the thinking."

"Are you saying that I should marry Kiosé?"

"Not at all. You have nothing of wealth or position to gain. But the way you embrace her with one arm and keep her at arm's length with the other hurts her. That is cruel. She dotes on you because she loves you. It is wrong to accept that with coldness."

Ken'ishi looked off through the rain, wishing that the wetness would not ruin his bowstring or rot his scabbard. Practicing weapons came easier than understanding people. "Thank you for the tea."

Before Ken'ishi could stand, Norikage said, "Think about what I've said."

Ken'ishi nodded.

"Have you finished reading the book of poems by Ri Haku?"

"Fear not, I have been studying. I must say that sometimes you surprise me, Norikage. You have never struck me as the poetic sort."

"The Chinese classics have long been out of favor at court, but there are still schools in Kyoto that teach them. Of course, a randy lad must master the tools of love, so I applied myself with vigor. There are few things that make a woman swoon and moisten with desire faster than poetry.

"For a poet, Ri Haku lived a life much like a *ronin*, using his brush for a sword. But he loved wine too much. My master always said that one should not love anything in this world too much." Norikage paused, looking out at the rain. "Perhaps you should take his advice."

Ken'ishi opened his mouth to speak, then closed it again.

In the park a crow
    awakes
And cries out under
    the full moon,
And I awake and sob
For the years that are
    gone.
        — *The Love Poems of*
            Marichiko

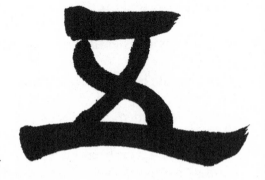

L ady Otomo no Kazuko sighed as she smoothed her soft robes over her legs. Morning birds trilled just outside her window, along with a chorus of higher, smaller voices, a clutch of hungry hatchlings with their throats upraised for their attentive mother. The nest had been built among the eaves of the tile roof, outside the highest chamber of the castle. For a week now she had listened to the hatchlings crying for their sustenance, and the songs of the parents as they came and went, while she sat here in her chambers, often alone after her husband's departure.

Her handmaiden, Hatsumi, had wanted to "knock the filthy, noisy things out of there," but Kazuko had refused. Perhaps they were an auspicious omen.

Kazuko had done her duty for today. Her husband's seed lay deposited within her. The sweat on her skin cooled, along with the memory of his hands upon her.

The cup of special fertility tea cooled in her hands as the squawkings of naked, blind swallow children filled her reverie. This was a new kind of tea, commissioned from a renowned midwife who served the Hojo clan in faraway Kyoto. It was said that if anyone knew the secrets of conceiving a healthy heir, she did. Kazuko sighed again. This tea could hardly be less effective than everything else Lord Tsunetomo had tried.

She heard movement just outside the door, moments before it slid open, and Tsunetomo's face appeared. His eyes darted from her face to the cup in her hands; then, the slightest expression of relief disappeared behind his stoic features. Putting down her cup, she turned on her knees and bowed to him.

Although she would not call him handsome, he was far from ugly, and his eyes were deep and insightful—gentle at times, hard and unyielding at others. Her father, Lord Nishimuta no Jiro, could certainly have found a worse husband for her, even though she had been too sick with love for another to appreciate Tsunetomo at the time. "I am sorry to intrude upon your tea, my dear. I have received a letter from the Governor. He has invited all the lords of Kyushu to attend the naming ceremony of his son next month in Dazaifu."

She maintained her composure, and even managed a bit of happiness. The chance to leave the castle and visit the island capital was a welcome one. She often felt like a cloistered Buddhist nun, shut up within this stone prison. Summoning her best smile, she said, "That is wonderful news, Husband."

Tsunetomo's face flushed, and his gaze lingered on her face. "You and Lady Yukino will see to the arrangements, yes?"

"Of course, Husband. I will speak to her as soon as I can. The arrangements for the trip will be made with all speed." Perhaps she might even indulge in a game of *Go* with Yukino as a respite from worries about quickening her womb. Lady Yukino was ten years older than Kazuko, but had married the younger brother, Tsunemori. Kazuko's position as wife of the elder brother, a man more than twenty years her senior, sometimes created tensions of etiquette and status, but in almost four years, she and Lady

Yukino had always handled matters amicably.

"Of course, of course, I trust you to handle it." He glanced overlong at her teacup again.

A sizzle of anger, a dash of despair.

In almost four years, her womb, chosen for its youth and her father's influence in central Kyushu, had yet to grant him an heir. She bit back a stab of recrimination upon herself. Perhaps this was the will of the gods, punishment for the fact that she had not been a virgin on her wedding night. She had desecrated herself. How many endless nights had she lain beside her husband, wishing that it had been another man who had just bedded her? How many nights had she yearned for those moments of ecstasy she had only experienced with *him*? Certainly, her husband's lovemaking was gentle enough, strong enough, frequent enough to give her some pleasure, but never the flaring, flaming convulsions of bliss that had torn her apart on one single night so long ago.

The young *ronin* still haunted her dreams, so handsome, so strong, with his wild hair, the strange mixture of innocence and earnestness in his eyes, fierce one moment and kind the next, and the deep devotion between him and his rusty-red dog.

As she did every day, she wondered briefly of Ken'ishi's whereabouts. Was he alive? Had he been killed in some meaningless brawl? Starved in the wilderness? Or had he found service with a samurai lord?

So many regrets.

The rigid mask of control on Ken'ishi's face at the banquet where her father had announced her betrothal to Lord Tsunetomo. The expressions of surprise and ecstasy on his face that night she had stolen out of her father's house and come to him. The forlorn despair and anger as he fled before sunrise, on pain of arrest.

How many days had she spent lost in yearning for him, worry for him, regret for him?

And her womb would not take seed and quicken with her husband's heir.

Tsunetomo awkwardly shifted his blockish shoulders and cleared his throat, opened his mouth to say something, glancing at her tea, then simply bowed to her and backed out of the room, sliding the door closed behind him.

Kazuko sipped her tea. If only she could speak to birds, as Ken'ishi claimed he could—she had practically called him liar then, another regret among many—if she could, perhaps the swallows might tell her the secrets of bearing children.

The cicada's cry
Foretells no sign of
How soon it must die.
— *Basho*

Yasutoki leaned back and stroked his chin, concealing his pleasure at his dinner companion's discomfiture. The serving maid had already brought small bowls of fish soup and rice, with several courses still to come. The Bamboo Snow was one of the finest inns in Hakata—and one of the most private. This quiet third-floor dining room overlooked a pond and beautifully manicured garden, where a nightingale's melody echoed from one of the meticulously trimmed trees.

Such a conversation as the one coming would have been impossible unless he owned the entire establishment and everyone in it.

The Mongol sniffed the fish soup and grimaced. A creaking boulder of twisted leather and horsehair, taut with muscle and distrust, he never let his glance slide too far away from Yasutoki. "When is the meat coming?"

"Fear not, my friend, there will be blood and flesh aplenty. How long has it been since we last met? Three years? Four?"

"Not long enough. Count yourself lucky I haven't already taken your narrow head."

"Is that any way to treat a fellow servant of the Great Khan?"

The Mongol grunted. "I fail to fathom why the Great Khan covets these islands. The women are too skinny, the liquor makes mare's piss taste like honey nectar, and there are no open places to ride."

Yasutoki slid his hands into his sleeves, restraining his smirk as the Mongol tensed. Memory of their last meeting—when his deftly thrown poison needle had left the Mongol in a somewhat ignominious position—doubtless made the horse warrior more civil than he would otherwise have been. Yasutoki hoped the Mongol was wearing different trousers than those in which the poison had caused him to empty his bowels. "Nevertheless, we have a task, don't we? We are loyal to the Khan."

The Mongol tossed the bowl of fish soup out the window. "I estimate that you're loyal to the thought of the gold and women he promised you when he finally claims these pitiful islands for the Golden Horde."

Yasutoki's heart thumped. "I have my own reasons." He was loyal to his desire to see the heads of every last member of the Minamoto clan, all nicely cleaned and powdered and mounted on boards placed at his feet. He picked up his bowl and sipped the broth. "So, my fragrant friend, in the three years since my last report to the Great Khan, I have heard only vague rumors from across the sea. I hear that he is now the emperor of all of China, and that the Koryo have been, shall we say … convinced to aid in the Khan's venture."

"Beaten into submission, more like, and held in yoke by the crown prince's marriage to the Khan's daughter. But yes. The day will come soon. The Koryo are building for us a fleet that will stretch to the horizon. And tell your man in the next room that he farts louder than a horse." The Mongol tilted his head toward the rice paper door behind Yasutoki.

Yasutoki concealed his annoyance. Best not to underestimate the Mongol's perceptions. Masoku and Fang Shi occupied the next room as protection. He would have a word with them about discretion. "No doubt his odor exceeds a horse's as well.

Unfortunate that he is only slightly more intelligent."

The Mongol grunted.

"When will this massive invasion fleet launch? When you say 'soon', do you mean this year? Next year?"

The Mongol sneered. "I mean 'soon'. The Great Khan sent me to this hell-pit to request information from you, and to secure further cooperation. He said nothing about supplying any."

"I am at the Great Khan's disposal."

"You will receive a message here on the eve of the Golden Horde's coming. The message will come with instructions."

Yasutoki suppressed his frown. "Your words are meaningless. Of course, the Khan will have instructions for me. Why are you here?"

The Mongol bared his cracked, yellow teeth. "After we have sent your warriors to rout and taken all the women for slaves, we will have need of political aid to mortar the bricks of our empire."

Yasutoki nodded.

"The Khan knows that your treachery to your own kind flows from your hatred of the Hojo clan and their Minamoto shogun puppet."

"I have made no secret of that with the Great Khan."

"Let us say that he believes your ties to more of such people are … extensive. Many more such people."

Yasutoki froze. What was this unwashed horse-stinking lout implying? To this man, he was only Green Tiger, Lord of the Underworld. No one knew Green Tiger's identity in the world above. No one. A chill touched his shoulder blades. The idea of someone spying on *him* set his teeth on edge. How could the Khan know that Yasutoki was descended from the Taira clan, who had fought against the Minamoto in the Great War? His upbringing in one of the "lost" houses of shadow provided him with just such a web of contacts and spies. But how could the Khan have learned of that?

The Mongol smiled faintly, apparently at something in Yasutoki's face. "The Great Khan expects your influence among such people to be profound. At the proper time, of course."

Where had this barbarian learned such pregnant speech? He practically sounded like a courtier.

The Mongol grinned smugly, as if to say, *Don't underestimate me.* "Are you able to fulfill the Khan's wishes?"

"I may have connections with such people. My influence is significant, but not without limits. I am merely the Emperor of the Underworld. The world above is another matter."

"Once we start burning your villages and presenting your women to the Khan for his pleasure dome and house of concubines, your influence may increase." A sudden scuffle erupted from the room behind Yasutoki. The Mongol ignored it. "Words of supplication from your own countrymen will make our conquest move more smoothly."

Yasutoki felt a weight thump through the floor, heard a suppressed grunt. He reached out with his awareness. He reached into his sleeves—a dagger in one hand and a *shuriken* in the other. "You want puppets."

"We want allies. Loyal allies. In Ningxia, we put an entire city to the sword for their disloyalty. In Nishapur, we laid such waste upon the town that afterward the land could not be plowed upon, not even a cat or a dog left alive. In Kyiv, we made a mountain of skulls that rose near to heaven. In Zhongdu, the earth is still greasy from rendered human fat. But we can be merciful and generous to those who are loyal."

Yasutoki clenched his teeth. Such boasting was to be expected at times like this, but he wanted to point out that most of those infamous barbaric exploits had been accomplished in the time of Khubilai Khan's grandfather, the man known as Genghis Khan.

The Mongol either missed Yasutoki's sudden tension or ignored it, placing a leather bag—made from the jewel sack of a stallion—on the table. The bag tipped onto its side, and the blue gleam of a sapphire peeked past the drawstring. "A token of his faith in you, misplaced though it might be."

Yasutoki leaned back and nodded. "Tell the Great Khan I accept his generous gift. I will turn my efforts toward gathering support among the scattered shadows of the underworld."

A board sang a warbling note on the nightingale stairs, warning Yasutoki of a servant's approach. He remained silent until the serving woman brought a platter laden with pork skewers, mountain potatoes, grilled chicken skin, thin-sliced horse-flesh boiled in broth with noodles and onions. She placed it all before them, arranging each bowl with exquisite care. Yasutoki admired her precision, her delicate hands, and the elegant curve of her neck. Without a word, she departed.

The Mongol grunted again. "I see no need to continue in your presence. The Khan's message has been delivered."

Yasutoki stiffened at the insult. He let the anger flare through his eyes.

As the Mongol stood, his cold smile washed over Yasutoki. Leather creaked as his muscles rearranged themselves beneath. "Do not let the Great Khan be disappointed. He lavishes suffering on those who fail him." The Mongol turned and strode out of the room, leaving Yasutoki to clench his teeth and steam.

Taking a deep breath to calm his burgeoning rage, Yasutoki stood and turned toward the door. He slid the door open to reveal Fang Shi's scarlet face pressed against the *tatami*. Masoku knelt with one knee between his shoulder blades and held Fang Shi's wrist behind his back in a painful joint lock. Yasutoki appreciated the skill of Masoku's technique. Just a little more pressure on Fang Shi's hand and the wrist would snap. Fang Shi knew it, too.

Masoku's white-toothed grin split his scruffy beard as he peered up at his master through tendrils of greasy hair. "The lad nearly barged into your meeting, Lord. I thought it best to restrain him."

"Our guest is gone. Let him up."

Masoku released Fang Shi's wrist and leaped back out of any harm's way.

Fang Shi collected his dignity and lumbered to his feet, rubbing his wrist. He cast a look of wariness laced with bile toward Masoku.

Yasutoki moved nearer to Fang Shi. "Explain."

Fang Shi's smooth brow creased. "My village. Mongols come and take women as slaves, kill everyone else. I hide in shit pit, seven years old. They take my father's head, shoot my brothers with arrows. I get away, become a beggar in Shanghai, a dock worker, come to Kyushu, work for you. But I twist off Mongol heads."

Yasutoki stepped up and backhanded him across the face. It felt like slapping a bridge pile. "You work for me. Your life before now matters less to me than a speck of flea shit."

Fang Shi's face flared red, and his body tensed to lash out, until he spotted the gleam of the dagger in Yasutoki's other hand, with its point resting against his crotch. The flare diminished.

Yasutoki purred, "Now, I do appreciate your hatred. It can be useful, and you are certainly justified. But if you ever disrupt my dealings—ever—I will string your guts from here to Hakata Bay. The crows will feast upon your balls."

Fang Shi swallowed hard. "Yes, Master."

He gestured to the table. "Now, sit and eat. There is much to do yet tonight."

The two ruffians fell with relish upon the meal.

Yasutoki sat silently, his fingers intertwined in contemplation. Throughout the islands of Japan, in forgotten crevices and shadows, the remnants of the once-proud Taira clan waited like shreds of a torn banner. For them to rise amid the ashes of the Mongol conquest, they would need something to rally them, a powerful symbol of a once-great clan. Many of those scattered remnants had found refuge across Kyushu, for centuries a Taira stronghold. Iki Island, which lay northwest of Hakata Bay toward the Koryo peninsula, was governed by Taira no Kagetaka. Only through swearing fealty to the Shogun and the relative difficulty of reaching Kyushu's remote areas had lords of the Taira clan been allowed to keep any holdings. Small pockets of Taira were scattered around Kyushu, but those existed only at the sufferance of the more powerful Otomo clan in the north and the Shimazu clan in the south. For Yasutoki, the relegation of his clan to a tiny backwater island like Iki was like a slap in the face.

His thoughts turned toward the great symbols of the Taira clan. So much had been destroyed during the Great War. But he knew of one thing that had been recovered. The sword known as Silver Crane. Yes, if Silver Crane were back in the hands of the Taira, he would be able to reignite the fire of his kinsmen's hearts. Over the last few years, he had allowed his search for the sword to languish in favor of more immediate interests. It was time to refocus his efforts.

[T]he accomplished [martial artist] uses the sword but does not kill others. He uses the sword and gives others life. When it is neces-  sary to kill, he kills. When it is necessary to give life, he gives life. When killing, he kills in complete con- centration; when giving life, he gives life in complete concentration. Without looking at right and wrong, he is able to see right and wrong; without attempting to discriminate, he is able to discriminate well. Treading on water is just like treading on land, and treading on land is just like treading on water. If he is able to gain this freedom, he will not be perplexed by anyone on earth. In all things, he will be beyond companions.

— *Takuan Soho, "Annals of the Sword Taia"*

Ken'ishi enjoyed eating his evening meal on the inn's veranda. The sun cast petals of camellia and chrysanthemum across Hakata Bay as the fishermen sculled in their boats with their day's catch.

As always, there was wrangling for places at the docks among men too weary to be diplomatic. Weathered faces grimaced at the weight of their catch, callused hands slinging silvery shapes into baskets and barrels. Even though they were already weary, their work was only half done; more hours would be required to gut the fish, after which the fish would be hung on racks to dry, or be smoked, or be salted in barrels. Every evening, the stench of offal hung thick in the air, until the sea breezes finally dispersed it. The docks and smokehouses nearby became a flurry of knives and nets and heads bowed with effort. That Chiba was free again irked Ken'ishi, but there was nothing to be done if Miwa would not publicly accuse him.

The setting sun turned the fishing boats and men into silhouettes, the sounds of their effort echoing across the tranquil evening waters.

Naoko, the innkeeper's mother, cooked the inn's meals, and she always favored Ken'ishi with an extra rice cake or portion of smoked sweetfish, *ayu*. Kiosé always served him, and her understated presence and hooded smiles gave him a feeling of contentment—for a while, until it became too much and he found himself wanting to go off and practice sword drills and archery.

Lately, after almost five years without his teacher, he had sensed his technique stagnating. He could practice and practice, always seeking the simultaneous emptiness and wholeness of true perfection, but he missed Kaa, harsh though the old bird might have been. He missed the discipline forced upon him, the relentless push toward perfection. Ken'ishi knew well his own techniques, but he knew there were others out there, so much more to learn. At some point in the last three years of life in Aoka, he had passed through some invisible partition, and suddenly felt as if he were nothing but a rank novice, like the first day that Kaa had ever placed a wooden sword in his hand. Somewhere out there was a world of study of the way of the sword, but he could not touch it. He had seen sword schools during his brief time in the capital, even in Hakata, but not here, in this small village.

A gruff voice and the thump of a sloshing bucket brought him out of his reverie. "Hey, Gonta!"

Through open veranda doors where Ken'ishi sat enjoying the sea breeze, he saw Chiba standing in the foyer, looking around expectantly, letting his eyes slide over Ken'ishi's presence. A bucket full of water sat at his feet. A lone tentacle snaked out of the water, suckered against the side of the bucket as if holding on to life itself.

Chiba yelled, "Hey, Gonta! Where are you?"

Kiosé came out of the kitchen, and her face stiffened when she saw who it was. She kept her gaze down, clutching a washcloth to her chest. "Please excuse me, but Gonta-sama is not here, sir."

Chiba's wind-leathered brow furrowed. "I don't want to talk to you, whore." A boning knife was thrust into his waistband. Ken'ishi wondered if it was the same knife that Chiba's father had used to kill Hojo no Masahige.

Kiosé flinched. "I'm sorry, sir. Gonta-sama has gone to Hakozaki today. He will come back tomorrow."

"Idiot." Chiba could have been referring to Kiosé or Gonta, or both.

Ken'ishi tensed.

"Would you like me to fetch mistress Naoko for you? She is upstairs."

"I caught an octopus today. I thought Gonta might want to buy it. I can't stand his mother any better than I can stand you. You're both thieves."

Kiosé flinched again. "I'm sorry, sir."

He snorted in disgust, pointing at his bucket. "What am I supposed to do with this? Idiot."

Ken'ishi put down his teacup and turned his gaze full upon Chiba. "Abuse her with one more word, and you'll answer to me."

Kiosé paled. Threat of violence hung in the air like a silent ghost.

Chiba sneered. "Still taking her side, eh? I suppose that's easy since yours is the only cock she moistens these days."

Ken'ishi eased his table away from his knees. "Perhaps your

father misses you. Would you like to meet him again? He would be proud."

A vein bulged on Chiba's reddening forehead. "A dirty bandit and a dirty whore. You make quite a pair." He picked up his bucket and upended it at Kiosé's feet. Seawater sloshed across the floor. The octopus landed with a wet *plop*, its tentacles sprawling like seaweed in an ocean current, then suckering to the floor, its body a limp sack the size of Little Frog's head, gasping. "Tell Gonta he owes me for the octopus."

Ken'ishi had closed the distance between them by half before Chiba reached the door.

With the lightest touch on Ken'ishi's arm, Kiosé stopped him. "Please."

Chiba disappeared outside.

Ken'ishi ears pounded with Chiba's insult. "Why?"

"Because I don't want anyone to die because of me. Because of who I was."

He threw her arm off. "Why don't you get angry?"

She flinched again. "They are just words. I am not a whore anymore. I am a mother."

"Stand up to them! Half of the village doesn't even see you as a person! You'll always be a whore to them!"

Her eyes teared, and her lips turned down with a rising sob. She opened her mouth, but no words came out, her gaze flicking right and left as if looking for something.

His anger pushed him closer to her. "And why should I let you stop me? He insulted me. You're just a woman."

She collapsed to her knees, looking up at him with a kind of pain, and a strange surprise. He saw something crack inside her, something fragile that he had not recognized before, the shards of something that would cut her inside. She covered her mouth with the back of her hand.

As the runnels of water glistened all around her on the polished floor, as the octopus gasped its last breaths against the wood, her voice quavered. "I hope that octopus bites your balls off." She jumped to her feet and dashed into the kitchen, a single sob

52

echoing in her wake.

Stunned, he could only watch her go for a moment, until his anger swelled again, and he ran outside after Chiba. In the evening coolness, Chiba was already gone, but it was just as well. The blind heat of his anger drained away, with something else taking its place, something cold and bitter and confused.

Mountain pheasant,
Is that your wife's voice
Calling, calling

— *Issa*

Τhe little boy who would become Ken'ishi walked through the forest, up the rocky mountain path he knew so well. Angry, ancient, harsh-voiced Kaa waited at the top of the mountain for him to return. It would be five more years before he had a name besides Boy. The bucket of water weighed as much as a boulder to his ten-year-old arms, but he did not complain, even though it was half a day's trek up the mountain. The bucket was a part of his life, as much as the wind and the sky. He had been carrying it for as long as he could remember.

Birds sang out of sight, calling to their mates, or trumpeting the discovery of excellent nest-makings, or quarreling with their neighbors, or warning their friends of hawks or foxes.

He had been listening to those songs for as long as he could remember, too. Every day Kaa would smooth his feathers, close his beady black eyes, and sit with the boy, and they would listen to the birds together. Speaking to the birds was as natural to the boy as carrying the bucket. Sometimes his teacher spoke to him in the language of the birds, sometimes in the speech of men when the bird-words were too limited. Sometimes they spoke in both, saying things easier to express in one language, then shifting to the other. The boy marveled at how his teacher was so much like birds, with his pretty gray feathers, but so much more, almost like a man sometimes.

The boy happened to be passing through an area where the slope was less steep than the upper reaches of the mountain where the cave lay hidden. The grass had grown long over the summer, and its long flat blades waved at the same height as his head. He knew this meadow like he knew his own hands.

As he retraced his earlier path through the grass, faint whispers filtered through his awareness. The whispering sounded tense, fearful. A cock pheasant and his wives lived on this slope, hiding in the long grass. Perhaps it was them he heard.

One voice clucked, "Is it gone?"

"I don't know," said another.

"Don't move," said another.

"Hush," said the cock. "The man-chick will hear us."

"It was angry," said another.

The boy could not distinguish the voices of the hens from each other.

"Maybe it will come back," said another.

"Should we warn him?"

"Maybe he sees it."

"That's why he stopped."

"Maybe he heard us."

The boy asked the pheasants, "What are you talking about?"

"Shut up, you hens!" snapped the cock. They all fell silent. The hairs on the boy's neck stood on end, and chicken skin rose on his arms. He froze.

Something moved near the bushes at the edge of the patch of grass. Something much larger than a bird. The hens whispered, "He should hide!"

"It will kill him!"

"He cannot hide."

"It will smell him!"

Fear rose up in the boy's breast and shot back down into his legs, turning them to wood.

"He should run!"

"He should hide!"

The rustling at the edge of the underbrush grew louder, along with a breathy huffing, snorting. The thing's head emerged from the bushes, its snout raised to sniff the wind, yellowed tusks bright against the bristly, dark hair of its face. Then it turned its snout toward the boy and snorted a challenge. He should run, but he could not. The boar snorted again, tossing its head, tensing itself to charge.

"What can we do?"

"Should we help him?"

"If we fly away, it can't hurt us."

The boar threw up its head and lunged straight at the boy, its beady, bloodshot eyes blazing with rage, its body an undulating knot of solid, wiry muscle. The boy flung his bucket at the boar and fled for the nearest tree. The boar was closer than the trees, tearing the grass into pulp as it came. Terror lent wings to the boy's feet, but the boar was too close. If he could only reach that tree. But it was too far. The boar's heavy, snorting breaths warmed his naked back.

Then a furious, fluttering, clucking commotion burst out of the grass. A flurry of rainbow-colored wings, tails, and grass leaped into the air directly in the boar's path.

The boar swerved away like a diverted boulder.

The boy strove for greater speed. This was his only chance.

The flock of pheasants rose toward the treetops. The boar remembered its prey and charged again, shocking in its speed. How could such a big, clumsy-looking animal be so fleet of foot? The beast was upon him. Its cloven feet tore through the sod and grass.

The boy reached the tree, leaped up, caught a branch with both hands, and swung up onto the lowest bough. The boar snapped at his dangling ankle, its hot spittle spattering his bare foot. He jerked his foot up out of reach and stared down into the boar's fierce eyes. His heart hammered in his chest like a rabbit's, and his limbs quivered like grass in a breeze.

The boar snarled up at him, then gave a snort as if satisfied that it had proven its superiority, and began to root through the earth around the base of the tree. It cast him the occasional contemptuous glance. The boy climbed higher. After a time, the boar seemed to grow bored, looked up at the boy, and snorted again as if to say, "And stay up there!" Then it wandered off into the bushes.

The boy stayed up there for a long time, waiting for the sounds of its passage to disappear. Then he waited some more to be sure it had gone. The shadows had grown long when he warily climbed down and retrieved his bucket. It was empty now, so he had to refill it, but he did not mind.

Every day after that, for a long time, he brought a handful of rice to the grassy mountainside for the pheasants.

Ken'ishi let the evening fade around him. As the sky deepened to purple through the open patch of sky above the pond, a pheasant cock crowed for his wives. A hen somewhere clucked back.

Something about their exchange bothered him, but other thoughts shoved consideration of it aside. He had wanted to wipe Chiba's blood from his sword. He had killed men before. Why should it bother him now to cause pain? Was his heart not hardened to such things as ending a man's life? Why would causing a bit of inadvertent pain to Kiosé bother him so?

The night air cooled his skin. Moonlight dappled the pond's misty surface. Night creatures scurried and *skreeked* and sang around him as he sat on the bank of the pond. Frogs bubbled and hopped in the waterside reeds.

Anger splashed inside his belly, mixing with guilt for having hurt Kiosé. He had hurt her worse than Chiba had, and that had been the opposite of his intention. He had never heard her speak with such venom to anyone. He felt like throwing something, but the bank was empty.

His old teacher's words floated out of his memory. *Master oneself above all things.* They sounded hollow to him just now.

The sound of ruffling foliage disrupted the chorus of night

creatures.

A plump old man with a straw hat hanging down his back shuffled into sight. A tuft of white beard sprouted from his chin, with two like tufts sticking out from around his ears. His eyes squinted in the darkness toward Ken'ishi. "What's this, old sot?"

Ken'ishi's eyebrows rose. "Eh?" He found himself annoyed at the intrusion into his foul mood.

The old man tottered out with a strange, bowlegged gait and plopped down onto the dirt with an explosive sigh, settling his paunch between his thighs. "I said, what's all this, old sot?" The man gestured around Ken'ishi's face, his own face an exaggerated, exasperated grimace. "Kill someone you didn't mean to, samurai?"

"I failed to kill someone I should have long ago. He still causes me trouble."

"People do that sometimes. Life would be so much simpler without other people, yes?" The old man smiled and winked.

"I have never seen you around here, Uncle."

"Oh, I have been around these parts for some time."

"Doing what?"

"Oh, most things I please."

"Where is your village?"

"Oh, here and there."

"Are you a monk?"

The old man laughed one long, airy guffaw. "Hah! Hardly. Although I do pretend from time to time. Perhaps I should ask you what you do. Not much call for warriors these days, especially not alone in the forest."

"This place ... I like it." In spite of the horrors Ken'ishi had once uncovered in this pond, he did like this place. Here, a predatory *kappa* had killed the old innkeeper, Gonta's father. The same *kappa* had almost slain Ken'ishi and Norikage, until Ken'ishi had managed to drive it away. In the three years since, Ken'ishi had visited this pond often.

"A long walk back to your village in the dark, samurai."

A whisper of warning raised the hairs on Ken'ishi's neck. The *kami* were speaking to him, warning him. But how could this old man be any kind of threat? "I might say the same to you, Uncle."

"Oh, I'm quite at home in the dark. These old peepers still catch the moonlight." He bulged his eyes, then grinned.

Ken'ishi frowned.

"So tell me, old sot. Why the face like a beaten dog? It can't be just an old grudge."

"Why do you want to know?"

"Because people have problems. You have problems." He stood up and bowed with exaggerated aplomb. "Allow me, old sot, to lend my wisdom to your problems."

Ken'ishi sighed. "Your wisdom is much appreciated, Uncle. My dilemma is this. I am a warrior. I have been trained to kill. I would kill at the command of a master, or to end the life of an evil man. I have looked evil in the eye and slain it. But how can I, knowingly, in good conscience, cause pain to a person who has never done me wrong?"

"A woman. I knew it."

"The weight of her feelings for me bears me down like a yoke full of river stones. And yet, she is a good woman. I bear her no ill will. I am fond of her, and yet—"

"Foolish, old sot, foolish. You are too attached to outcomes, too attached to the future. Samurai are not supposed to worry about love and such nonsense. To be truly happy, a man must forget the past and the future."

Ken'ishi raised an eyebrow. "What does that mean? How can a man forget the future. It hasn't happened."

The old man shrugged. "How should I know? I'm just spouting monk-drivel."

"Are you a monk?"

"Sometimes."

Ken'ishi stood, scowling. "You're toying with me."

"Sorry, old sot. Sit down. Sit. Sit!" The old man patted the ground.

Ken'ishi sighed and sat.

"Some creatures were just not meant to mate for life. So it is with human beings."

"But men and women marry."

"But they hardly marry for love! There are many reasons, but never for that. Families trade children to cement alliances, keep family names and bloodlines growing on down through the lifetimes, yes? Love comes later, so they say. Marriage getting in your way, is it?"

"I'm not sure what you mean."

The old man clucked his tongue. "I, on the other hand, have been 'married' many, many times." He winked and elbowed Ken'ishi. "Usually because she has lovely eyes, or because I like the way her backside sways." Ken'ishi noticed that the old man's trousers bulged under his paunch, as if he carried two small melons between his legs. How peculiar.

"So, have you given me any wisdom?" Ken'ishi blinked and shook his head. His thoughts were suddenly muddled, unfocused.

"Of course. You become wiser simply by being in my presence."

Ken'ishi yawned. "Then I should thank you, Uncle, but I don't even know your name."

"Call me Hage."

"I am Ken'ishi." His eyelids were growing heavy. He rubbed his eyes.

"Sword-stone, eh? I must be careful not to cross you." With a grunt and a sigh, the old man climbed upright on his walking stick. His legs were bowed apart with the weight of something hanging between them, bulging his trousers. "I must be off, old sot."

Ken'ishi put his hand on his knee to lever himself to his feet. "I should go back."

"It's all right to rest for a while."

"Oh, I suppose it is." A profound weariness filled Ken'ishi's limbs. He sank back down.

Hage turned and waddled into the forest.

Ken'ishi lay back, and the earth felt like the softest bed he had ever slept in. Frogs and crickets sang him to sleep.

If we observe phenomena closely, it cannot be thought that anything between heaven and earth is really different. If we see differences, it is due to the narrowness of our vision.  This is like Mount Fuji's being concealed by a tree trunk with branches and leaves, and my not being able to see it. But how can Mount Fuji be concealed by a single tree? It is simply because of the narrowness of my vision and because the tree stands in the way of my vision that Mount Fuji cannot be seen. We go on thinking that the tree is concealing Mount Fuji. Yet it is due to the narrowness of my vision.

— *Takuan Soho, "The Clear Sound of Jewels"*

The sun seared the Hakozaki docks like a hovering red coal. Chiba mopped sweat from the back of his neck and ignored the ever-present stench of fish, filth, and livestock. The fish-merchant had cheated him, as always. His catch was worth half again what the merchant had given him for it. Nevertheless, the weight of silver in the coin purse against his leg lent a jaunt to his step.

He wanted some cold *soba* noodles to dampen the oppressive heat, so he followed his nose and went off down a side street to look for just such a meal. On his way, he passed a house of ill-repute of which he had occasionally availed himself. It was a lone, narrow door with a red lantern that read "Pink Orchid Dream." He paused a few paces beyond the lantern.

A woman's laugh echoed out, muffled by wooden walls.

Little bitch Miwa should not have laughed with contempt as he thrust her down onto the riverbank, should have been happy that he wanted to pleasure himself on her. If her flailing knee had not slammed into his jewels, he might have gotten his little sword inside her. How she must have laughed at *that!* And Kiosé, that filthy whore, laughing smugly behind his back. She would not be so smug without her filthy *ronin* protector. Chiba should have shoved her down on the *tatami*, rolled her onto her belly, and taken her right there in front of him. Chiba had envisioned dozens of delightful ways for his knife to end up in the *ronin's* guts. A sudden, passing attack perhaps, or a knife in the back at night, or filleting him like a yellowtail. Chiba would kill the *ronin*, and then he would grab the whore, throw her down, shove his little sword deep, and teach her who the real man was.

His encounter with Kiosé last night in the inn had given him an itch that needed to be scratched. He had awakened this morning with his little sword standing erect, and it had ached with need all day. He needed to spew his seed into another whore, pound it deep, pound it hard. That would show her.

He hefted the weight of silver in his purse. He did not have enough to buy the supplies he needed *and* pay for a whore. If he came home without the supplies again, his brothers would beat him more severely this time. He would rather relieve his little sword himself than suffer that kind of punishment.

But maybe there was a way that he could make that weight of silver grow. Maybe he could buy the supplies *and* a whore.

At the end of a dead-end alley, Chiba waited for what seemed like hours, pacing, pacing, leaning, pacing, the throbbing ache in his loins growing more persistent with each passing breeze. The sun sank, and the air cooled. The chirp of sparrows gave way to the skreeking of crickets nestled in the nooks of the close packed buildings.

Finally the narrow door creaked open. A spare little man came out and hung a single red lantern like a bloodshot eyeball above the door. He gave Chiba a bow. "Welcome! Come in, come in!"

Chiba grunted and followed him inside, down a narrow hallway, into a large room filled with four square tables. He hovered in the doorway.

The little man's teeth appeared in a flinty grin, eyes flashing. "Come in, sir. Someone always has to be first. Something to drink?"

"*Saké*, of course."

"Of course." The little man bowed and withdrew through a curtain.

Lamps lent a smokiness to the warm air, still stuffy from the heat of the day. The air smelled of spirits and his own rank sweat.

Chiba called, "Can't you open a window in here?"

The little man came out with a large earthen cup. "I'm sorry, sir, but no. We don't like prying eyes. Please, sit!" He gestured toward a table. "I have seen you before, yes?"

Chiba grunted and wiped his mouth. "Maybe six months back. Fortune was not with me that night."

The little man's eyes were too shrewd by half. "Welcome back. Perhaps fortune will smile on you tonight. I am Shozuki, at your service. What shall I call you?"

Chiba grunted at his own pun. "Call me Brown Leaves." His name sounded like the word for "leaves."

Shozuki grinned, too widely. "A pleasure, Mr. Brown Leaves. You have plans for the money you'll win tonight, yes?"

Good fortune swelled like a wave in Chiba's chest. "You can fleece all the others, but tonight, fortune is with me."

Shozuki's eyes flashed as he bowed. "See, more patrons already."

Two sweat-stained dock workers shuffled in, arms like ships' masts and shoulders like boulders. Their eyes were dull, empty of the slightest spark of cleverness. Beating them in a few rounds of Ya Pei would be easy.

Shozuki beamed. "Welcome, gentlemen! Please, sit. We have enough to begin a game now."

The three players sat at a table, and Chiba gave his opponents his best defiant glare while Shozuki disappeared to fetch more drinks. Chiba took a swallow of *saké* and let the clear, pungent warmth descend into his belly.

Shozuki produced a pack of thick rice-paper cards and shuffled them. Chiba fidgeted where he sat. His little sword throbbed in his trousers. He could already imagine a whore's musky scent. "Let's get to the game. Enough waiting!"

Shozuki's mouth drew into a neutral line as he dealt with practiced skill. His fingers stroked and snapped the cards. The first game was on.

Chiba's good fortune proved true, and he defeated both opponents and the house, winning a sizable sum. Two more rounds like that, and he would have enough for the whore. Perhaps only one more round would be necessary if he could win some side bets. Fortune was with him; he would ride her with relish.

Chiba made some sizable side bets, and Shozuki raised an eyebrow. "Oho! Bold is the man who seizes fortune!"

Chiba laughed. "Grab her by both hips and thrust home, I say!"

The dockworkers glowered at him and accepted his bets.

The next round proved less lucky. He beat the other players but not the house, resulting in only a modest gain. He frowned. At this rate, he would be sitting here for hours. His hulking opponents grumbled and scowled.

Shozuki smiled at them. "I'm sure your fortune will soon turn, sirs."

"Hah!" Chiba snorted. "Not if I have anything to say about it!"

One of the dockworkers spoke with a voice like gravel on a barrelhead, with a thick Yanagawa accent. "You're loud."

Chiba leaned back and fingered the wooden handle of his knife under the table. "Care to make another side bet?" He had won the last one.

The man gripped the table edge. "Just shut up and play."

By this time, the room had filled with other players. Other dealers played games of Sticks and Leaves or Hanging Horse, but Chiba preferred Ya Pei. It was a bold man's game.

A man with a sword stood behind Shozuki now. He looked unkempt, hairy like a *ronin*, with a thin scraggly beard. The silken wrappings of his katana hilt were darkened with use. Another thinking himself a big man with a sword, probably a *ronin* in the employ of the *oyabun* who owned this establishment.

Chiba's teeth clenched. He downed his third cup of *saké*.

In the third round, Chiba found himself with most of a Jade Gates spread collected in his hands. He only needed one more card to complete the set, which would defeat everyone else at the table and win him all the side bets. The whore was as good as his. Sweat that was not from the heat beaded his forehead. The gamble was that if he did not complete the set, he would beat no one. But he could still feel Fortune's warm flutter on his back, spreading into his chest like a golden butterfly.

Suddenly one of the dockworkers hooted with victory and laid down his cards, revealing a set of Imperial Gardens, ending the round and claiming all the wagers.

Chiba threw down his cards. "Shit! Idiot!" Having lost all his side bets, he now had less money than he started with.

The winner's eyes narrowed, and he leaned forward. His lips peeled back into a mirthless grin. "Didn't somebody tell you to shut up?"

"Idiot," Chiba muttered, then emptied his *saké* cup. The gazes around the table fell heavy upon him.

The *ronin* edged forward. Chiba's vision swam.

"Hey!" He pointed a wavering finger at the sword. "You know how to use that thing or is it just for show?"

The man crossed his arms and pursed his lips.

Shozuki smiled like a shark. "I'm sure your fortune hasn't turned completely, Mr. Brown Leaves."

Chiba tapped his empty cup on the table. "It's still there. I can feel it." The fluttering of Fortune intensified the yearning in his loins. A serving girl refilled his cup from a heavy earthen jar. He eyed the sensual curve of her neck as she knelt next to him. His ears burned as he wondered how much her favors might cost.

Shozuki dealt the next round, his fingers dancing, and the players placed wagers and side bets.

Chiba clamped his lips between his teeth. There in his hand was a nearly complete Jade Dragon. He only needed one more card to quadruple his winnings, a card that no one ever wanted. It would come up soon or be discarded. He pushed the rest of his silver forward, suppressing the smugness of his grin as best he could.

Shozuki's eyebrows rose. "Oho! A bold move so early, Mr. Brown Leaves."

Chiba did his best to keep his face neutral. The watchful gaze of the warrior awled into Chiba. Chiba waited for his card to come. He would have the supplies, a whore—perhaps two!—and coin left to spare. His brothers would be pleased.

Abruptly, Shozuki revealed his hand—the Heavenly Serpent, part of which would have completed Chiba's own hand—with an apologetic look. "I'm very sorry, sirs. The fortunes favor the house this round." His arms arced out and swept up the coins in the center of the table.

Chiba lurched to his feet. "Shit! You cheated me!" He clutched the hilt of his knife.

Shozuki's eyes narrowed. "Now, Sir Brown Leaves, I'm sure you don't want any trouble."

Chiba threw his cards onto the table. "You stole it all!"

The warrior's sword came half out of its scabbard.

Shozuki's voice grew low and grim. "Now, sir. I'm sure you don't want my friend's blade to see the light fully. If it does, it must drink blood."

Chiba pointed a wavering finger at the warrior. "You don't scare me!"

The warrior took a step forward, hand on his hilt.

"Think you're a big man with that oversized fillet knife, do you? Think you can back me down, do you? Back in my village, there's a filthy *ronin* who's a lot like you. Thinks his big, fancy sword makes him a constable! I figure the wretch found it on an old battlefield or something."

"Whatever, lout. Now get out." The warrior took another step forward.

"Filthy *ronin* got to stick together, eh? You got cranes on your scabbard, too? Maybe you stole yours from the same place!"

Even through his blurry vision, Chiba saw the warrior's expression change from barely restrained rage to suppressed surprise.

Chiba staggered toward the door, rage sizzling in his gut like a hot coal. "Bah! Listen to me, all of you! Nothing but thieves here, stealing honest men's money." He spat on the floor and backed toward the door.

The glint of steel disappeared back into its scabbard as the warrior and Shozuki exchanged strange glances. Chiba's rage drove him on hot, wobbly legs out into the night.

Chiba did not remember the alley being this long, but there was only one way out. He would have to sleep in the boat tonight and leave on the morning tide. The beating his brothers would give him would be painful, but he would survive. It would be a long time before they let him come back to Hakozaki to sell the fish. He kept looking back over his shoulder to see if he was being followed. That *ronin* in there might not take well to insults.

The only living creature behind him was a dark, rag-eared tomcat yowling his lust into the indifferent world. A nice, heavy stone would silence the noisy bastard.

The sound of a foot shifting against the earth ahead stopped him. He turned back just in time to see the board before it slammed into his face. Something snapped in his nose, shooting blinding pain into his eyes, exploding through his head. The ground rushing up smashed the breath out of him.

Through tears and pain he glimpsed a shape standing over him, board in hand.

Chiba blubbered through smashed, bloody lips. "I have nothing! No money!"

Stars blurred behind the black silhouette. "Who are you?"

"Why do you care? Are you going to kill me?"

"Answer my questions, and maybe I'll let you live." A mask muffled the man's voice. Steel glinted with starlight in the man's other hand. "Who are you?"

"I'm Chiba, from Aoka village! Just a simple fisherman!"

"A *ronin* with a sword and a crane motif. Do you know any such person?"

"I know such a man." Chiba smiled through teeth that tasted like blood. "Are you going to kill him?"

"That is none of your concern."

"If you're going to kill him, I'll tell you anything you want to know! I'll take you to his house! I'll hold him down while you put a blade in his guts!"

The figure sniffed. "I doubt that will be necessary."

This lonely moth saw
 brightness
In the woman's
 room—
Burnt to a cinder
 — *Issa*

The earth seemed to pull at Ken'ishi's flesh as if he were embedded in it. Dew moistened his clothes, a single droplet glistening over his eyes on an unruly strand of hair. He blinked. An *uguisu* warbled somewhere overhead. The light filtering through the forest canopy was dim and gray.

Could it be morning? Had he slept here all night?

He sat up, shivering, rubbing his arms. The dew on his clothes wet his hands. He would give much at this moment for a cup of fresh tea and a bowl of warm rice. Low mist ghosted the surface of the pond. The forest echoed with the sparse call of morning birds. He groaned with the stiffness of his muscles and stood to stretch. A great fuzziness filled his mind, like wads of unraveled linen stuffed behind his eyes, as if he had just awakened from a night of too much *saké*.

A few more moments of stretching, eye-rubbing, and a splash of water in the face helped dispel the confusion.

The *uguisu* chirped again.

Ken'ishi found the bird on a branch as it watched him warily. "Good morning, Mr. *Uguisu*."

The bird chirped at him.

Ken'ishi froze. He swallowed hard before he spoke again, and concentrated on speaking with as much precision as he could in the tongue of the small birds. "Are you energetic today?"

The bird chirped again.

"Can you understand me, Mr. *Uguisu?*"

The bird leaped off his branch and disappeared into the trees.

Ken'ishi could not understand the bird. The bird could not understand him. He sank to the earth again, crosslegged, scratching his head. He had spoken the tongues of birds and animals for as long as he could remember, and now ...

He realized that what had disquieted him about the pheasants last night was that he had not understood their speech, and worse, he had not paid enough attention to notice the loss.

How long had he simply failed to pay attention?

He stood again, brushed the soil and moisture from his clothes, and turned his feet back toward the village. As he walked now, he paid close attention to the sounds of birds filtering through the forest. *Komadori,* starlings, the screech of a distant sparrowhawk farther up the mountainside. He understood none of it, even when it came into his ears as clear as a wind-chime. The more utterances went past his ears, ungrasped, the heavier the stone in his belly became. He imagined this must be how it felt to go deaf or blind. Except that he had been deaf and blind for some time and not bothered to notice.

What a fool he was!

He exhausted his mind trying, but the understanding had evaporated like the dew. Perhaps the strange old man had enchanted him somehow ...

But no. The more he thought about it, the more he realized that he had not understood any bird-speech for some time. He had not bothered to listen either, too preoccupied with his own longings, wishes, and worries.

He puzzled over it all the way back to the village.

When he reached the village, the fishing boats were already out. People were doing their morning chores. Kiosé would be cleaning up after the inn's breakfast patrons. He found her busy wiping down a table. When she saw him, she tucked away the rag and approached him. "Would you like to eat something, sir?"

"Kiosé, you won't believe this!" It all came out like an expulsion of held breath. He explained to her how he could not understand the birds anymore, perhaps not even animals. No matter how he tried to control his voice, to keep it calm and even, a strange sense of panic welled up in him.

Throughout his exposition, she glanced up at him with a different kind of confusion. When he was finished, she said, "I'm sorry to hear this has happened to you, sir. Would you like something to eat?"

The stone in his belly grew colder. She was still angry with him. Perhaps if he just explained things, she would understand. "I went out in the forest to think about ... I met this strange man, and we talked about life and things. I don't know what to do yet. You're very good to me."

She stiffened, a frown on her face. "Thank you, sir, but—"

"First, I must figure out why this has happened—"

"Sir—"

"—and then we can talk about what to do about—"

"Sir—"

"Yes?"

"Um, I don't understand why you're telling me all this. Would you like something to eat?"

She had never been cruel to him before. He had never imagined that she could be, but her words struck him like a cold fist in the stomach. "Kiosé!"

Her eyes bulged up at him, then she drew back. "Do you know me, sir?"

He grabbed her shoulders. "Kiosé, don't joke with me. I'm sorry for what I said."

She shrugged off his grip. "I don't know what you're talking about, sir. And I don't ... I don't do *that* anymore, in spite of what you may have heard."

Ken'ishi stepped back again. He searched her face. There was

71

no recognition in it.

"Would you like something to eat?"

"No, I ... I suppose not."

"Then please excuse me." She bowed and hurried away into the kitchen.

Ken'ishi's mind reeled as if he had been struck with a *bokken* over the ear.

Ken'ishi sought Little Frog in the boy's favorite places to play—there were many—until he ultimately discovered the boy alone, arranging concentric rings of sea shells along the beach near the docks.

Ken'ishi found his mood lifted by the sight of the boy. He waved. "Good morning."

The boy glanced at him but a moment before returning to his work.

Ken'ishi approached him. "What are you making?"

"Shells," Little Frog said.

"Many, many shells."

Little Frog grunted the kind of assent that children give to adults with whom they are not particularly interested in speaking.

A cold hand touched Ken'ishi's neck. "Little Frog, do you know who I am? Do you know me?"

Little Frog stuck a dirty finger in the corner of his mouth and looked at Ken'ishi for a long time.

"Do you know me?" At no point in the boy's short life had Ken'ishi wished more for Little Frog to smile at him and say, *Da.*

Little Frog picked up a shell and gave it to Ken'ishi, then went back to his work.

All Ken'ishi could do was thank him and walk away, his throat tight and his brain spinning.

This flesh you have
   loved
Is fragile, unstable by
   nature
As a boat adrift.
The fires of the
   cormorant fishers
Flare in the night.
My heart flares with
   this agony.
Do you understand?
My life is going out.
Do you understand?
My life.
Vanishing like the stakes
That hold the nets against the current
In Uji River, the current and the mist
Are taking me

                — *The Love Poems of Marichiko*

Ken'ishi trudged back from the beach. Had he been enchanted somehow? How could he have been erased from the memories of both Kiosé and Little Frog, like a drawing in the sand washed away by the tide? He had been enchanted before, and this was beginning to feel similar. Nevertheless, he was still in full possession of his faculties. He must explore the extent of this strange situation.

He found Norikage in his office, brush in hand, writing something, surrounded by piles of hand-bound books and scrolls.

When Norikage saw him, his eyes bulged. "Gods and Buddhas, where have you been? I had to let Chiba's brothers beat him senseless—not an unpleasant task, I assure you—but you have to keep order—"

Sweet relief punctured Ken'ishi's sack of worry, and he nearly collapsed with the release.

"What is it?" Norikage said. "You look like you've just seen another monster."

"I fell asleep in the forest. Something strange is going on."

"Such things seem to follow you. Tea?" Norikage gestured to the pot beside him.

"I would be obliged."

Norikage poured for him. "So, you fell asleep in the forest. What about the other three days?"

"Three days! How long have I been gone?"

"Four days. Are you telling me you don't remember?"

Ken'ishi ran a hand across his cheeks and felt a greater growth of stubble than he should have had if he had been in the forest only one night. "I was asleep. I talked to this strange old man. Kiosé ... doesn't remember me any more."

Norikage raised an eyebrow.

"Neither does Little Frog. And I can no longer speak to birds and animals. I have lost their tongue somehow." A spike of remembrance of a furry, rust-red face, grinning up at him, tongue lolling. Akao, slain these three years by the *oni*, Taro. If Akao were still alive, Ken'ishi might not be able to speak even to him.

The magnitude of what he had lost pummeled him again, all through his own indifference, his own negligence. To have lost something so dear, perhaps little by little, perhaps so long ago, without even realizing it was gone ...

74

Norikage put down his brush again. "You, my friend, need breakfast and a writing lesson to take your mind off your troubles."

"Not now." His stomach was too sick to feel hungry.

"You must distract your mind from the downward spiral. All those problems will still be there when we're finished. I'll wager you haven't eaten in four days. I'll have Hana bring us breakfast."

Norikage had said 'Hana,' not 'Haru,' but for a moment Ken'ishi was uncertain. His memory flashed with Haru's beautiful face, her coquettish giggle and flashing green eyes, with sensations of love and confusion, the earthy smell of a fox den, the feel of her cool, wet nose, and the succulent juices of raw rabbit flesh. Oh, yes, he remembered well how enchantment felt.

Too shaken by all of this, he could do nothing but accede to Norikage's wishes.

A commotion outside interrupted their writing lesson after only half an hour. Ken'ishi put down his brush, picked up his sword, and gave Norikage a curious glance.

Another gusting chorus, this time clearly of laughter, prompted a raised eyebrow from Norikage.

They went out together and found a throng of villagers surrounding a man who was juggling a rainbow of small balls. The juggler's rhythmic song rose high.

An acorn tumbled down and down,
And he plopped into a pond.
Out came the loaches,
"Hello, little boy! Come play with us!"

Children clapped with delight at the man's exaggerated expressions and gawky dancing. The performer made a variety of silly facial caricatures while he gamboled and juggled, made all the more comical by his enormous, prominently hooked nose, slightly reddened as if by the sun. He was garbed in a profusion of brightly dyed rags and tatters and rattles, such that he resembled a cacophonous swirl of flower petals. He moved with such preci-

75

sion and grace that Ken'ishi could only stare along with the rest of the growing crowd.

The little acorn tumbled down and down
And he had fun, but he soon began to cry,
"I want to go back to the mountain!"
The loaches didn't know what to do.

From somewhere within the mass of tatters, the Raggedy Man produced a number of wooden cups and added them to the cloud of arcing objects.

Little Frog had joined the group of children at the front, laughing and clapping along with the rest of the crowd. Ken'ishi felt the sudden urge to pick him up, hold him higher so the boy could see.

The Raggedy Man dropped the wooden cups, one by one, onto his foot and kicked them gently toward the nearby children. The children caught the cups and beamed with joy. "Now, children," the Raggedy Man said, "hold out your cups and don't move."

The children held out their cups, and the Raggedy Man dropped a ball onto his foot and kicked it into an arc that landed it directly in a cup, then another, and another, and another.

Hands empty, he back-flipped with a flourish and ended with a bow. The throng erupted with applause and hoots of approval.

A sudden tingle of unease whispered through Ken'ishi again, and he looked around. He caught sight of Chiba, arms crossed, leaning against the corner of a house, watching the affair. He met Ken'ishi's eye with a stab of flinty hatred and a smirk. Splashes of blue-black bruises darkened his entire face. He spat on the ground, turned away, and disappeared.

The Raggedy Man held out a bangled straw hat and collected the pittance of coppers the villagers carried with them, accepting the money with great humility. His eyes flicked toward Ken'ishi, appraising him, but only for an instant as he continued busking the crowd.

* * *

Crickets sang as Ken'ishi shut the door to his modest house. Clouds darkened the night, rolling in across Hakata Bay, lending the scent of incoming rain to the smells of the *tatami* and the thatched roof. A breeze trickled through the open window. The room felt chill and empty. There was no basket of food left for him, no lingering scent of Kiosé's presence. As he walked back and forth, carrying wood to the fire pit, he was conscious of grit between his bare feet and the *tatami*, dust accumulated from his several days of absence. Kiosé had always kept his floors immaculately clean without him ever asking.

He placed Silver Crane on its rack and sat before the fire. Hunger had chewed the pit in his belly deeper, but he had no food prepared. He could not bear to go to the inn where she would be working. Her indifference, appearing to not know him at all, was worse than if she hated him. The memory of her soft sigh as she fell asleep against him brought another sigh out of him.

He boiled a pot of rice and sat playing his flute quietly, trying to clear his mind of this detritus.

Hage had been strange, but some of his words recollected the way Ken'ishi's master had taught him to seek the Void, the timeless moments between instants, to forget the past, to lay no hopes or fears on the future. The Void was where all things became possible, where pain and fear and joy disappeared.

A cold, steel voice brushed against Ken'ishi's mind. *The man sees the Way. Will he walk the clear path? Or will he yearn for it from the obstacle-bound wilderness and continue to wish for things that he cannot have? Wants and wishes have no place in a warrior's heart.*

"If the warrior does not wish to serve a master, or have want of prowess, then what good is he? Does not the reaching for things then carry a warrior away from the Path?"

A warrior's duty is to serve. If he has no master, he must serve Mankind.

"Men fear a warrior with no master. The *ronin* is wild, uncontrollable, tossed by the waves of life; at least, so they believe. How can a warrior serve those who fear him?"

What is the man afraid of? The fear that others bear him?

"That fear breeds distrust. Misplaced distrust makes me angry. I have never harmed anyone who didn't deserve it." Except one. A small mercy was that perhaps she did not remember.

And with those words, the man again steps off the path.

He punched his thigh in frustration, the same thigh that ached sometimes when the weather changed. The touch of the cold steel drew away from his mind.

From Norikage's house, next door, sounds of passion burst into the night, Hana's gasping, whimpering voice, denying and yearning in the same breaths, Norikage's deep grunts of pleasure.

Ken'ishi sighed again and readied his bed. Even after having slept for four days, he was suddenly bone-weary and sick of heart.

The demon went on, "Nowadays there are many swordsmen whose techniques are mature, whose *ch'i* is integrated, who have tested their efficiency in combat, who have no doubts, whose spirits are settled, and who have gained freedom in action. Though we may say that they are like  gods of that mysterious function, if they have not been able to escape relying on something, they [still know nothing]."

— *Issai Chozanshi, The Demon's Sermon on the Martial Arts*

The boy without a name woke up one long-ago morning, thinking everything was going to be same as it had always been. It was going to be a warm, breezy summer day. The evening before had been so pleasant he had slept outside, but the morning grew chilly in the pre-dawn hours. He lay upon his crude straw mat, perched on a stone shelf above the entrance to the cave, looking out over the lush valley below. The evergreen forest lay almost black in the shadows of the mountains, except for the wandering, silvery stripe of river that reflected the fading colors of the dawn sky.

As always, the boy's first thought was to wonder where his teacher had gone. Kaa was seldom present when the boy woke up. The *tengu* never said where he went or what he did; he just appeared.

The boy spent all of his nights alone on the mountain, high above the world. Sometimes he wondered about the society of human beings, longed for it in sharp, lonely bursts. Kaa sometimes told him of the human world, but often things so vague or contradictory that the boy came to believe that the *tengu* was unfamiliar with human things. But Kaa was the master, so the boy did not press him.

The *tengu* sometimes chose to sneak up behind the boy, as if from nowhere, and rap him on his pate with his feathered knuckles, as if to test the boy's retention of the lessons with awareness of the *kami*. Since before the boy had begun training with the wooden sword, he was always calmly alert when Kaa was not in sight. In spite of the single time that he caught his master unawares, the boy could seldom detect Kaa's approach. Even though the boy had never seen any such display of magical powers, Kaa assured him of magical powers aplenty.

On one occasion, the boy had grown angry and defiant. "Show me something magical!"

Kaa had cocked his bird-like head at that particular angle that bespoke long-suffering annoyance.

The *tengu* approached a nearby pine tree and picked up a cone from among the exposed roots, hefting it in his thin hand. "Come here, Monkey-boy!"

The boy approached.

Kaa tossed him the pine cone.

The boy caught the pine cone, turned it over and over in his hand, expecting it to transform into a bird. But it remained a pine cone.

He looked at his teacher, perplexed.

Kaa pointed at the pine cone. "*That* is the child of *that!*" Then at the tree. "That little thing—so small and insignificant—will sprout trunk and needles and fingers of roots. It will explore the earth and reach for the heavens, and it will join this city of its brethren on this wind-swept mountainside. *That* is magic, Monkey-boy!"

The boy sighed, disappointed; he had been hoping for something extraordinary.

Kaa's black eyes narrowed as he stalked forward and snatched the cone out of the boy's hand. "Bah! You are not worthy." He threw the cone far down the slope. "Magic surrounds you! It sparkles in every blade of grass, every leaf, every worm wriggling blind through the earth to its own unknowable purpose. Every moment is a wonder! Not something to be endured on the way to elsewhere!"

"Yes, Sensei," the boy said, but he did not understand.

"Bah!" Kaa crossed his arms and shook his head in disgust. "I reserve *my* magical powers for enemies. You're a fool, Monkey-boy, if you wish to be anywhere nearby when I use them." Then Kaa cuffed the boy on the ear. "Go and practice with your *bokken.*"

That day, the boy had fought back the tears and pretended the invisible enemy he fought with his wooden sword was his master.

But on this day, he climbed down from his sleeping perch above the cave entrance and started a small fire to cook breakfast.

A sharp rap on top of his head made him wince.

Kaa said, "You grow lax. With senses like that, you will be dead before you are twenty."

The boy turned and faced his master, bowing. "Good morning, Sensei. Sometimes you use your magic to sneak up on me."

"Irrelevant. You still do not understand. The world itself is magic that we make with every step we take. Our dreams take the earth, our breath the air, our tears the water, and our spirits give it fire, and we make the world with magic every day. Every breath forges our destiny." There was a strange tone in his voice. "It is going to be a fine day. But a sad day."

The boy tensed. What could his master mean by such a

portentous statement? He noticed the cloth-wrapped bundle in Kaa's hands; it had not been there moments ago. The bundle was long and thin. Just the right size ... The boy's heart leaped. Could this be the day he had awaited for so long?

"Let us eat," Kaa said. "Then we will talk." His voice was strangely subdued, less shrill, his manner less urgent than at any time the boy could recall, as if a great weight bore down upon his spirit.

The boy could hardly contain his mingled excitement, anticipation, and fear. What if this was the day? What if it was not? He kept control of himself, however, as he stoked the cookfire, and boiled a pot of rice and water for tea. His gaze kept wandering to the cloth bundle.

While they waited, they watched the world coming to life below them. Every shade of color shifting with the dawn, the endless carpet of greens and browns and blues down below, the taste of the air, the breath of the breeze, the grit of the earth beneath them. A serenity settled over the boy the likes of which he had never experienced.

Kaa breathed, "Marvelous." The air warmed, fresh breezes whispering across the mountainside, ruffling his fine, silvery-gray feathers, the boy's wild shock of hair. In the distance, birds awakened in the trees, greeting the day, quarreling with their spouses or neighbors, seeking their breakfast in the earth or in the water or in the grass. The scent of pine needles, the dusty, bird-like smell of the *tengu* beside him, the smoke of the small fire. Before he knew it, an endless series of tiny moments had passed, and the rice was ready and the water was hot.

They ate in silence, and the boy savored the taste and texture of the rice, the earthy, emerald green of the tea. He suppressed the questions bubbling in his throat. Mealtime was not for questions. Afterward, they sat quietly sipping their tea.

Kaa spoke first. "You are about to burst with questions. I can feel you quivering through the earth under your arse."

"Yes, Sensei."

The *tengu* looked off into the distance. "All of my teaching, all of your training, and all of your fortunes have led up to this day. I saved you from your father's assassins because he was the first talking monkey I had ever met whom I respected. He had a blade for the ages, and he knew how to wield it. We had fought a duel, once upon a time, and he defeated me. No talking monkey had ever managed that. He was a true swordsman."

The boy had never heard even a trace of admiration in Kaa's voice before. Excitement surged through him until his entire body tingled.

Kaa squawked, "You must conceal your emotions! If you do not, you will be an outcast."

"I am sorry, Master."

"The time has come when I must move on. My own people have demanded that I return. They do not understand why I saved your life, much less why I went to the trouble to raise you, and to train you. Your father spared my life, so I spared yours, and I have tried to make you in his image. There is much good in you, Boy, and there is evil, too. Some among my race can see the future, and I have asked them about you. But they say they cannot see where your path leads. You are a strange, rare person, as if you are outside the natural order of the world. This outside-ness means that your fate is not set. My people believe that although some people have their fate decided for them before they are ever born, yours will be made as you go through life. That is a rare gift from the *kami*, perhaps even a curse. Do not squander it. You will meet many strange and dangerous people. Many of them will not like you because you are different. Humans hate things that are different."

"But aren't they just like me?"

The *tengu*'s coal-black eyes closed and his shoulders shook in silent laughter. "Oh, no, monkey-boy! Not at all! Humans are as different as you and I! They have incredible ability to imagine themselves as 'us' and some other group as 'them.' No matter what lies they tell themselves.

"You are a warrior, Monkey-boy. It is in your spirit and your flesh. Your family was bred for it. You have been trained for it.

But being a warrior does not mean that you simply take from those weaker than you. Your father was samurai, so you were born samurai. But the word 'samurai' comes from the meaning of 'servant.' To be a true samurai, you must serve. Humans do not trust samurai who serve no one—they call them '*ronin*'—because it means they serve no one but themselves. The word '*ronin*' means a man who is tossed about by the waves of fortune. A skilled warrior out for only his own gain is a dangerous thing."

"But who was my father?"

"He is gone. If the existence of his son was revealed, his enemies would come. It is better that you do not know. The best of him is here." Kaa picked up the cloth bundle beside him. "And there." He pointed the tip of the bundle at the boy's breast. "That is what is important." Then he unwrapped the bundle, and the boy stared.

Within the coarse cloth was a sword, in a scabbard old and worn, with chipped engravings of cranes with mother-of-pearl inlays. Throughout his life, the boy had imagined the sword would be encrusted with gold and jewels, things of celestial beauty. He felt a vague confusion when he saw no such thing. Disappointment shot through him, and he scowled.

Kaa stood and drew the blade. The boy gasped, because now he saw the true jewel, the hidden treasure. The long, curved sheen of polished steel gleamed in the sunlight.

"This is a fine, masterful weapon. I just had it polished for you. I have kept it safe, in hiding, for many years. Its quality surpasses any human-made blade I have ever seen, almost as good as a *tengu* blade. It will serve you well, provided you treat it with the reverence it deserves. You must keep it clean and oiled. Have it polished when you can. The scabbard will last a few more years. You must practice with it often. Its weight and balance are a bit different from a *bokken*. You must join your spirit with the spirit of the blade, let the blade become part of your body." With a lightning quick movement, he returned the blade to its scabbard.

"Listen well. Today may be the last time you ever see me. There is no one else to teach you. There is still so much that I wish to

teach you, but the time has come. I have other things for you."
Kaa waved his fingers and a pile of objects suddenly appeared at
the boy's feet. The boy jumped back, startled.

Kaa laughed again. "I told you I have magical powers." Then
he took objects from the pile, one by one. "A bedroll. A water
bottle. A pack for carrying things. A blanket. Inside the pack are
things for helping you live—fishing line, hooks, some thread, and
needles."

The boy stared. "Thank you, Sensei! But this gift is too much!"

Kaa frowned. "It is paltry little. But I cannot shower you with
riches. You have a good head and a strong *hara*. The center of your
spirit lies in your *hara*, your belly." Kaa's spindly finger pointed to
just below the boy's navel. "If the *kami* are with you, you will
prosper. And do not forget your bow and arrows."

"They are inside."

"Go and get them."

The boy ran into the cave to retrieve his bow and quiver of
arrows, and his flute. When he went back outside, Kaa had
carefully reassembled the pile of objects and put them in the pack.

Kaa stood beside the pack, holding the sword in both gray-
feathered hands. His voice was solemn. "Boy, I give you this gift.
Wield it with honor and strength." Then he bowed and offered it
to him.

The boy bowed deeply and accepted the sword in both hands.
The moment his flesh touched the smooth, lacquered scabbard,
he felt a tingle begin at his fingers and travel like gooseflesh up
his arms. After he straightened, he looked at it for a long time,
memorizing the chips in the lacquer, the old stains, and the well-
worn hilt lined on each side with the strange, rough hide of a ray.

"Now go."

The boy looked up at Kaa in sudden panic. "Where should I
go?"

"Wherever your path takes you. There is a human settlement
in that direction. You remember where the smoke came from
when the village was on fire. They have rebuilt, and they are still
there. Be careful. Be strong. Go."

The boy picked up the pack, slung it onto his shoulder, clutched his weapons to his body as best he could. He bowed deeply to his master. "Thank you, Sensei."

The *tengu* bowed in return. "Goodbye."

Then the boy turned toward the path down the mountainside, and walked away, off to make his destiny.

As Ken'ishi opened his eyes, unease misted his awareness like the gray morning fog. The *kami* buzzed in his mind. The sea lapped at the distant shore with the outgoing tide. A cock crowed, an austere, lonely sound that struck deep into his heart. Everything was as it always was, a morning like so many others. Except that he felt alone, more alone than any time he could remember.

He rolled onto his knees, rubbed his eyes, his face, went outside to make water in the privy house he shared with Norikage. His nostrils felt plugged by a strange scent. By the time he came back inside, his mind was already on preparations for his morning sword practice.

His eyes rose to the sword stand, and he froze.

It was empty.

His gaze dashed like a hare around the room.

But there was no doubt. He had placed Silver Crane there last night, just as he always did.

Silver Crane was gone.

A choked snarl leaped into his throat. He ran outside. The cold gray fog lay dim against the land, obscuring the morning sun. The sea rumbled and frothed. A fisherman ambled toward his boat. The street was empty. A myriad of footprints scuffed the earth around his house. He ran to Norikage's house and pounded on his door. "Norikage! Open up! Come out!"

Long moments later, a faint voice came from within, thick with sleep. "Yes, yes, yes. I'm coming."

Every moment that Ken'ishi listened to the fumbling within was excruciating.

Norikage finally slid open the door, his eyes red and his thinning hair tousled. "Is someone dead?"

"Worse," Ken'ishi gasped. "My sword is gone, stolen."

Norikage's bleary eyes widened. "Are you certain?"

"We must call out the village, find out if anyone saw anything!"

"Wait a moment. Come inside and let us talk."

Ken'ishi balked. Every moment wasted was a moment that the thief used to take Silver Crane farther away.

"Come inside, Ken'ishi."

Ken'ishi sighed and acquiesced, and Norikage scanned the street for a moment to be sure there were no onlookers when he shut the door. They stopped in the entry.

"We cannot tell the villagers that we're looking for your sword."

Ken'ishi stiffened and squared to face him. "What?"

"Calm yourself a moment and listen to me. You are samurai-born. A *ronin* by circumstance to be sure, but still samurai. Your sword is the symbol of your power here as constable, your authority. What happens when that symbol is gone, and we are left without the means to enforce our will? We have no other warrior weapons save a rusty spear or two left over from wars fifty years gone. Do you want to enforce your orders with a pitchfork?"

Ken'ishi thought about this for a moment. He had, at times, felt the tenuousness of his grip on authority here, just an outsider with a sword. He had become friends with a few villagers, but most of them simply tolerated his presence as someone willing and able to keep order. Most of them were good, kind people. But not all. And some of them truly resented his presence. A few might decide to cause trouble.

"You see my point," Norikage said. "We can launch an all-out search, or we can make a few inquiries. The latter seems more prudent. And accusing any of the villagers, without being sure, will only breed more ill will. Already some do not approve of our treatment of Chiba."

"For now." Ken'ishi wanted to pick up every house and shake it until Silver Crane fell out.

"Who might have stolen it?"

"There are possibilities."

"Do you remember the spy dressed as a monk, the one you

87

killed three years ago?"

"Yes. He called himself Yellow Tiger, writing a letter when we found him. That man was working for *someone*."

"Perhaps there is a new such someone about. Are there any strangers in the village?"

"There is one."

My old barn
having burned to the
    ground,
I can now see the moon.
                    — *Masahide*

"He's in his room," Naoko said, wringing a washcloth.

"Where?" Ken'ishi clenched his fists.

The hard seriousness in his eyes turned her face as gray as the bun of her hair. "The second room from the end, but—"

"Is he still in there?"

"I suppose so, but—" She raised her hands in supplication. "Please don't break anything! Every time you fight in here I have to replace the burned *tatami* or buy new crockery or mop up the blood."

Norikage bowed. "We only want to speak with him."

"You said that last time!"

"Where is Kiosé?" The last thing Ken'ishi wanted was to put her in danger.

Naoko shuffled after them as they went toward the room. "It's very early. Perhaps she is still sleeping."

Norikage raised a hand to his lips and touched her shoulder. "Please stay here. There's no need for you to be in danger. He could be a very bad man. Ken'ishi and I might have to arrest him."

She swallowed hard and nodded, bowing. "I'll be in the kitchen." She hurried away.

Ken'ishi lowered his voice. "Do you have a dagger?"

"No. How many times must I tell you I am not a warrior?"

"But sometimes you are a crafty fellow."

"I have not had my tea yet. The day is too young for craftiness."

Ken'ishi felt as if he were walking naked into a storm of blades. His fingers hurt from clenching. His bow and handful of arrows were back in his house, untouched by the thief. It would be too unwieldy a weapon in these close quarters anyway.

Gray light spilled over Ken'ishi and Norikage from the small window at the end of the hall. He reached the Raggedy Man's door. "Open up, sir."

A high, tremulous voice called back, "Who's there?"

"The village constable, sir. You must answer a few questions."

"Oh, the village constable, is it?" Shuffling, shifting bedclothes, feet sliding on *tatami*, filtering through the rice-paper door. "What do you want?"

"Some questions, sir. Open the door."

The door slid open, and Ken'ishi looked up into the hook-nosed face of the Raggedy Man. The Raggedy Man gazed down at him over a red, axe-head nose. Long nostrils flared, and small dark eyes sparkled. He stood naked except for a loincloth, his spindly body like a doll made of pale sticks. "Oh, it's you," the Raggedy Man said.

Norikage began, "We are sorry to disturb—"

Ken'ishi stepped forward. "Where were you last night?"

The Raggedy Man's eyes narrowed. "Here of course. What is this about?"

"You're a stranger here, and last night … there was some bad business."

"'Bad business.'" The Raggedy Man scoffed. "You're little more than a stranger here yourself, and you must accuse me?"

"How do you know that?"

"I am an old hand at judging men, boy. I can assure you I was within these walls from sundown until this moment."

"You should keep a civil tongue, sir. We can arrest you."

"You don't frighten me. You look rather weaponless for a constable."

Ken'ishi grimaced and looked away. "Can anyone vouch for your whereabouts last night?"

"Madame Naoko."

"You weren't with Naoko all night."

A female voice sounded from the shadows in the room. "But I was."

The Raggedy Man stepped sidewise.

Kiosé knelt beside the *futon*, wrapped in a blanket.

A stab went deep into Ken'ishi's heart. His mouth would not work.

Norikage cleared his throat and stepped forward. "Kiosé, you were with him all night?"

"Yes."

Ken'ishi blurted, "But you don't do this anymore!"

Kiosé's hair curtained her eyes as she looked at the floor, flinching at the harshness of his tone.

The Raggedy Man stepped forward and stretched his long neck. "Listen to me, constables. I didn't pay her a thing. She came to me. Never begrudge a person's chance to assuage loneliness. If you suspect me of something, tell me now, and I'll deny it. I won't have my reputation tarnished by ridiculous accusations."

Ken'ishi tensed, fists balled. "Entertainers are not known for their honor."

"Neither are *ronin*."

Norikage interposed himself between them. "Pardon us, sir. Kiosé, perhaps he could have slipped out while you slept?"

She said, "No, Norikage-sama. We … did not sleep much at all."

The dagger in Ken'ishi's heart went deeper.

Norikage turned to the Raggedy Man. "How long are you

going to be in the village?"

The Raggedy Man cleared his throat. "I intend to move on today. There are more villages down the road. Maybe in the next one, the constable won't be inventing trouble for an innocent entertainer walking life's path." He cast a contemptuous gaze on Ken'ishi.

Norikage bowed. "Very sorry to have troubled you, sir." He took Ken'ishi by the arm and led him down the hallway.

Ken'ishi stomped outside. "We should arrest him!"

Norikage drew back at his vehemence. "For what? Kiosé is no liar. How could he have taken it?"

"I don't know."

"Did you stay up late yourself?"

"No."

"Did you examine your house? Perhaps the thief left something behind."

"Nothing was out of place. Only the sword is missing."

Down the street, a figure shuffled toward the docks. Rough hands scratched through unkempt hair. Chiba hawked and spat. Bruises darkened his swollen face. He took notice of them and stopped.

In an instant, Ken'ishi remembered the strange smirk Chiba had given him yesterday. He lunged down the street.

Chiba's eyes bulged, mouth falling open. He dropped his food pouch and water gourd and ran.

Ken'ishi's fleet stride caught Chiba before he had gone ten paces. The *ronin* threw himself onto Chiba's back and bore him to the ground. A bawling cry of pain burst out of the fisherman as Ken'ishi's weight pasted him into the dirt. Ken'ishi slammed his fist into Chiba's ear, making him yelp and curse. A familiar boning knife appeared in Chiba's fist. Ken'ishi grabbed Chiba's wrist and smashed it over his knee. Something popped, and the knife fell to the earth. Ken'ishi snatched up the knife in one hand, grabbed a handful of greasy hair in the other, dug his other knee into Chiba's back, and held the cold blade to his throat.

Chiba's struggles stopped. He wept and gasped for breath.

Ken'ishi growled. "Where is it?" He yanked back hard on Chiba's hair and dug his knee deeper between his shoulder blades.

Chiba cried out in pain. "Filthy *ronin*! Kill me ... and have done! If you don't ... I'll kill you!"

"Where is it?"

"What are ... you ... talking about?"

"This is your only chance! If we find it in your house, we'll make sure the governor's executioner tortures you well before they hang you!"

"I don't know ... what the hell ... you're talking about!" A trickle of blood ran down Chiba's throat.

"You know something! I saw it in your face yesterday. You're too much of a fool to play clever."

Chiba's elder brother, Ryuba, ran toward them, carrying a boat hook. "Hey! Leave him alone!"

Ken'ishi shouted, "Stop! Or your brother dies!"

Ryuba skidded to a halt a few paces away.

Norikage caught up, coming forward, hands raised, "Ryuba, put down the boat hook, or we must arrest you, too."

Ryuba spat, "Arrest me, *too*? Why are you arresting *him*? *Again!*"

Ken'ishi said, "Put down the boat hook, or I'll take off his head with his own knife."

Ryuba slowly lay down the boat hook.

"Back away!"

Ryuba backed away.

Ken'ishi said, "He has something of mine, or knows who does."

Ryuba's face was tight. "You're saying he stole something? What was it? My brother is an idiot and a drunkard, but he's not a thief!"

Norikage said, "Were all of you home last night?"

"The three of us were in the inn until very late, drinking. We wanted to try out the latest batch of *saké*. Naoko and Kiosé saw us there! Maybe you'll believe *them*!" Ryuba spat on the ground. "This idiot was the drunkest of all. We had to carry him home.

He couldn't have stolen a kiss from a whore last night."

"Damn it!" Ken'ishi threw Chiba's face into the dirt as he stood, knife quivering in his hand. Chiba choked and gasped between his feet.

Ryuba's eyes blazed with hatred. "He's done nothing wrong. At least, not today. Let us go, or we'll miss the tide."

Ken'ishi threw the boning knife down the street. "We're going to check your tale with Naoko."

"As you wish, constable." Ryuba sneered the last word, with a hint of threat.

Ken'ishi stormed back up the street toward his house.

"Where are you going?" Norikage called after him.

As the wheel follows the
    hoof
Of the ox that pulls the
    cart,
My sorrow follows your
    footsteps,
As you leave me in the
    dawn.
        — *The Love Poems of*
            Marichiko

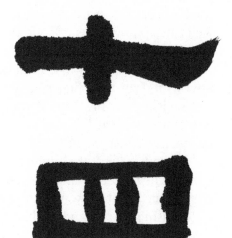

"Perhaps I was not as thorough as I should have been," Ken'ishi said, sliding open his front door.

Inside, he scrutinized the windows, the rear door, even the chimney, anywhere a thief might have entered. Nothing was out of place. He stood near his *futon*, which was still on the floor, forgotten in his earlier panic.

"The thief must have passed within two paces of me!"

Frustration coarsened his throat. Why had the *kami* not warned him?

Memory of his four-day enchanted sleep in the woods added to the sinking feeling in his gut, exacerbated by the memory of other things he had lost.

Perhaps the *kami* had warned him, and he had just been too weary, too stricken, too foolish to listen.

95

Too distracted by the past and the future.

Norikage's sharp attention scanned the room as he stepped up onto the *tatami*. He stopped near Ken'ishi's buckwheat-husk pillow. "You should dust more often."

"Kiosé ... cleaned my house the day before I left."

"The rest of the place is spotless."

"She is an excellent housekeeper."

"Even when it is not her own." Norikage knelt and rubbed three fingers across the *tatami*, examining a film of fine dust near Ken'ishi's pillow. He sniffed it, then jerked back.

"What is it?"

Norikage gestured to the all but imperceptible layer of dust, now with three faint finger-tracks through it.

Ken'ishi drew his finger across the dust and sniffed. A strange, sharp, flowery smell. The same that had been in his nostrils when he awoke. "Dust smells like dust. This does not smell like dust."

"Perhaps a kind of sleeping powder. Whoever would use such a thing knew exactly what he came for, and where to find it. And now he has spirited away with your sword."

Ken'ishi groaned and fell back on his haunches.

"Why would such a person want *your* sword, your father's sword? The world is full of swords. Your family is from the far north. Who on Kyushu would want *this* sword?"

"I don't know."

"More importantly, where would the thief take it? Dazaifu? Hakata? Across the straits to Honshu?"

Ken'ishi had no words to fill his mouth, to break the silence, to fill the cavern of his mind. Since the day Kaa had presented him with Silver Crane, it had represented everything he was. Son to a murdered father. Heir to a family name he did not know. Warrior set adrift by fate. Without Silver Crane, who was he?

He felt Norikage's gaze upon him for a long time, but could not face it.

Finally, Norikage said, "I will make some inquiries around the village. Perhaps someone saw something."

Ken'ishi did not know how long Norikage was gone before the

black miasma in his mind dispersed to allow a thought.

Silver Crane had finally spoken to him, and it happened when Ken'ishi meditated, sought the Void, then reached out to the sword. Perhaps he could seek the Void now and reach out, and Silver Crane would answer. Perhaps distance did not matter. Perhaps it did, and time was short.

He adjusted himself into *seiza* position, closed his eyes, allowed his mind to empty. Picturing the bracken and detritus of his everyday thoughts, of his pain and fear, pouring out like waste from a privy collection jar, leaving the jar empty yet whole, placing a lid on it so that passing thoughts would not tumble or splatter within.

His efforts took much longer than normal.

Only in the emptiness of that vessel could he find the timeless spaces between instants, forget the past, forget the future. From those spaces, he called to Silver Crane.

Timeless moments of silence.

Then ...

Its presence tugged at him like a glistening thread disappearing over the horizon.

Southwest.

It was moving southwest. Rocking.

A boat?

No.

A horse.

A man on horseback.

Ken'ishi reached out again.

A single idea, a lone concept, came back to him, sharp and metallic. *Destiny.*

The shock and power of it knocked him loose from the Void, and he opened his eyes.

Southwest. The thief could be headed for Hakata, Dazaifu, even farther south, depending on the road.

Destiny. Was the sword destined to be stolen from him? Was it his destiny to reclaim it? Was the sword following its own path? Did Silver Crane want him to follow?

No matter. He was going after it. If he could sense its presence now, he could do so again, and follow it.

Moments later, his old traveling pack hung from his shoulders, a *bokken* thrust into his sash, his bow and arrows across his back. It all suddenly felt so familiar, as if it had not been three years since his feet walked the dirt of the road. The difference was that now he did not look like a brigand, and even carried a bit of real money in his purse. But this time, he had no companion.

And with only a wooden sword, he could hardly call himself samurai.

No more time to waste.

Norikage's eyes bulged to see Ken'ishi in his traveling pack. "Where are you going?"

"After my sword."

"You think you can find it?"

"I must. If I cannot, there is no reason for me to be here. I cannot be constable without it, not for long."

"But, Ken'ishi! Damn you, what am *I* to do? I cannot break up a drunken brawl or arrest a thief."

"Pick one of the young men and give him a *bokken*. If I can return, I will."

"Perhaps we can commission another sword for you. It will be expensive, but—"

"Without *this* sword, I am nothing."

Norikage sighed. "I should come with you. I can hardly manage here without you."

"No. Aoka village needs you. Choose a strapping deputy to take my place until I return. And brace up, because you must. Farewell."

Naoko's face brimmed with concern as he stuffed the handfuls of rice balls and smoked fish into his pack. She even gave him a handful of sticky rice cakes filled with bean paste for the "days when life is difficult." In previous days as a man of the road, he had never had the luxury of so much food. He could walk many *ri* with this much.

He bowed low to her. "Naoko, you have always been very kind to me."

"Aren't you coming back?"

"I do not know where my path will lead. Perhaps to hell, and I must follow it even there."

Naoko bowed in return, tears brimming. "Farewell, Ken'ishi-sama. I hope you find what you seek."

"Farewell."

Naoko said, "Kiosé is out back, washing."

Ken'ishi stiffened. He bowed to her again, and went outside, wiping his nose.

He found Kiosé and Little Frog together. She was hanging linens from a drying rack. The boy was naked, stomping laundry in a tub of wash water. Kiosé was encouraging him to greater effort. "Good work! Wonderful helper! One-two! One-two! One-two!" He stomped harder and harder, grunting, grinning wider and wider, splashing water in every direction.

Kiosé spotted Ken'ishi's approach, and her body tensed. "Good day, sir."

He stopped in front of her. She bowed to him.

Little Frog ceased his stomping and hooked a finger in his mouth, watching Ken'ishi intently.

Ken'ishi said, "I'm leaving. Something has been stolen from me. I must get it back."

Her eyes remained downcast.

"Do you truly not remember me?" he said. "Kiosé?"

Her gaze flicked up for only an instant. "I'm sorry, sir. My memory must be terrible ..."

"I want to come back, but ..."

"Good fortune in your search, sir."

"Perhaps when I come back, you will ..."

She waited for him to finish, but his words simply trailed away like the trickle of retreating tide, ungraspable.

He stepped forward, took her chin in his hand, gently lifted her face to meet his gaze, cupped her warm cheek. "I hope you awaken from your dream."

Kiosé's eyes glistened with something, but it was not recognition.

Ken'ishi stepped back. "Good bye, Little Frog. Be a good boy." Then he turned and strode away as fast as he could without running.

Little Frog called after him, "Bye!"

PART 2: THE FOURTH SCROLL

When the tide receded again, the Chinaman's lumbering bulk broke the blackness to
bring another bowl of gruel.

The night is too long to
  the sleepless.
The road is too long to the
  footsore.
Life is too long to a
  woman
Made foolish by passion.
Why did I find a crooked guide
On the twisted paths of love?

— *The Love Poems of Marichiko*

Yasutoki folded his hands in front of him to keep from wringing them in excitement. "Your visit is … unexpected. It is dangerous for us to meet." His belly was doing somersaults like a court acrobat while Kage sat across the table from him. The cramped, shadowy room lay far removed from the Roasted Acorn Saké House's common room, from which sounds of revelry carried. The dark walls were stained with the smoke of a hundred years of lamps, and dim evening sunlight shone pink through the slats of the narrow window.

Yasutoki had not heard from his long-time associate, this mysterious shadow warrior, for some months. Who could say where such men kept themselves? This time, Kage had announced his coming in his occasional guise as a *saké* merchant, but the unexpected visit could only bode something momentous.

Kage's voice was as bland and nondescript as his face. "Does one so well-entrenched in Otomo no Tsunetomo's court have anything to fear from meeting a simple visiting *saké* brewer?" He gestured to indicate himself. "I always enjoy visiting Hoshiya, such a busy castle town." He sipped from his cup.

Yasutoki frowned, feeling his patience stretched thin by Kage's smug lack of urgency. "The owner of the Roasted Acorn is my man, but one never knows when a random tidbit of rumor might fall upon the wrong ear." Yasutoki fully intended that Lord Tsunetomo lay upon his death bed never having known the truth of Green Tiger's dual identity. "So tell me. What is this about? Has the drunken fisherman from Aoka village proved good to his word?"

"Indeed."

Yasutoki almost jumped to his feet. "You have it?"

A merest suggestion of a smirk. "Indeed."

Yasutoki had not dared to hope that the bundle of woven straw Kage brought with him contained a sword. *The* sword. "Show me!"

Kage untied the bundle and rolled it out, revealing a further bundle of tightly wrapped linen. The leisurely time Kage took unwrapping it whipped Yasutoki's heartbeat into a clamor. He gripped the edge of the table to keep his hands from shaking.

"It was frightfully easy," Kage said. He lifted a *tachi* with both hands from the bundle of linen.

Yasutoki held his breath as he offered his hands to receive it. The scabbard's lacquer was battered, its once-beautiful mother-of-pearl inlays of moon and cranes now chipped, its ray-skin hilt stained with sweat and blood, its circular silver *tsuba*, engraved with the shapes of cranes chasing one another, tarnished. At first glance it looked like little more than a poorly maintained relic with a pronounced antique-style curvature. A flash of anger shot through him at how the *ronin* had allowed such a treasure to decay. Was this truly Silver Crane?

He eased the blade free of the scabbard and revealed the truth. His breath caught at the glimmering polish of the ancient steel, with its exquisite, intricate temper line formed to resemble feathers.

Kage sat back and sipped his *saké* with a smug curl on his lips.

Yasutoki's mouth was dry. He had only dared hope that the *ronin* with Silver Crane would be found. And now, here it was in Yasutoki's possession. Today had been just another day in Lord Tsunetomo's court, overseeing the house and estate, arranging supplies and handling other minor matters, until Kage's urgent message arrived this morning over breakfast. In one moment, his entire life had changed.

"Well done," he breathed, "Well done. And what of the *ronin*?"

"I left him alive. I am certain he woke up that morning somewhat discomfited. I could have killed him easily, but that was not part of the bargain."

"Quite correct. He still may be of use to me alive." So many possibilities. He might make a superb ally, if he could be convinced to join forces with Green Tiger. He was also a powerful bargaining tool if Yasutoki ever chose to exert pressure on Lord Tsunetomo's stunningly beautiful young wife, Kazuko.

Yasutoki had delivered Lord Tsunetomo's marriage agreement to Lord Nishimuta no Jiro, had been at the banquet that night where Lord Nishimuta had announced his daughter's betrothal, and had noted well the heartsick agony of the young *ronin* who had saved her life. Young little Kazuko had done better concealing her pain, but the looks she gave the *ronin* spoke libraries. Yasutoki had seen her leave the castle that night, presumably for a lovers' tryst before the *ronin* had been exiled from Nishimuta lands.

Lord Tsunetomo might someday wish to know that Kazuko had not been a virgin when he married her.

Kazuko might someday wish to know that her lost beloved still lived, and what would she give for that knowledge?

So many possibilities ...

"What are you going to do with it?" Kage asked.

"First and foremost, I am going to give thanks to our ancestors of the Taira clan that Silver Crane is now in worthy hands, and entreat the gods that we can once again rise to power. What I do after that is none of your concern. You have done well. Visit my moneychanger in Hakata. He will see that you are paid per our original bargain, along with a worthy bonus."

Setting the sword down beside him, Yasutoki raised his cup of *saké*. "Let us spend a moment to celebrate. Our plans are soon coming together."

Hatsumi froze, and Kazuko nearly bowled into her, almost knocking the basket from the other woman's hands. Hatsumi squinted up the street toward the Roasted Acorn Saké House. The sky had deepened to purple, turning the buildings and the people moving between them into varying shades of colorless silhouette. The air was redolent with the smells of cooking and smoke.

Kazuko regathered her composure. "What is it?"

Hatsumi pursed her thick lips over protuberant, blackened teeth, frowning. "What is Yasutoki doing coming out of a *saké* house at this time of night? A bit early for drinking."

Kazuko tried to follow her longtime handmaid's gaze. "Where?"

Hatsumi pointed up the street. "There. The man with the basket hat and straw bundle."

Indeed, there was a man walking ahead of them up the street, wearing a woven basket hat, carrying a bundle of straw under one arm.

Kazuko said, "How can you tell that is Yasutoki? Hoshiya is a sizable town. The hat covers his features—"

"I can tell," Hatsumi snapped. "I can tell by his walk, his carriage, his shoulders."

Kazuko tried to discern the distinctiveness of those qualities in the man walking away from them, but she could not, so she tried to make a joke. "Perhaps it's just because he's leaving the *saké* house. Perhaps all men walk like Yasutoki after a few jars. He's never struck me as particularly graceful." She smiled, but Hatsumi's face grew sourer.

"He's far more … graceful than you give him credit for. Too graceful."

"Surely you're talking about something else now." Kazuko's eyes followed the man until he disappeared up the hill, around a corner.

"I don't want to talk about that. Come, we still have a way to walk."

"Oh, please, Hatsumi!" Kazuko smiled at her, cajoling. "If he's broken your heart, you must confide in me so I can help you." Anything to distract from her own morass of unpleasant thoughts that awaited every moment her mind went still.

Hatsumi's sniffle died behind a granite-hard tone. "He breaks my heart every day. I don't need any help." Then a single tear trickled. "If only he loved me."

Kazuko's heart sank. "Oh, my dear friend." She laid her hand on Hatsumi's arm while Hatsumi wiped a tear. "You mustn't dampen your sleeves for him."

Hatsumi fixed Kazuko with a mournful gaze. "It's been so long since I heard tenderness in your voice. Why today? Why now? Because you pity me?"

"I asked you on the picnic this afternoon for just that reason. We've been together for as long as I can remember." Kazuko took Hatsumi by the elbow, and they walked up the slope toward the swooping angles of her husband's castle.

"You were just a slip of a girl when your father gave you into my care. Such a beautiful child you were."

"I have been ... poor company for much of the time since we were sent here to join with the Otomo clan. You are loyal to me as no one else could ever be."

"I have spent my life being your servant, but you're like my little sister sometimes." Hatsumi squeezed Kazuko's hand. "I have not been very good company myself. I worry too much lately about that ... *man.*" She growled the last word.

They walked through the market district, which was now closed for the evening. The wide street was littered with the detritus of commerce, small scraps of food, bits of paper, like Kazuko's thoughts. "Do you mean Yasutoki?"

"Yes, of course! Who else would I mean? Oh ... him. I thought you were done thinking about *him*."

"Oh!" Kazuko felt herself blushing. "Of course. He has not crossed my mind for a long, long time." *Not since this morning.*

"He was nothing more than an uncouth ruffian, bent on stealing your honor from your family. Good riddance to such trash. But let's speak of him no more. The mere thought makes my blood simmer. We've had such a lovely day. Please, let's speak of him no more."

"Of course." Kazuko blinked away an unexpected tear.

Hatsumi sighed with contentment. "I am sure he's dead in a ditch somewhere by now. Besides, you have Lord Tsunetomo now. He is a good man, a powerful lord. Your father made a good match for you. You were lucky Tsunetomo-sama was so patient. Had he been any less kind, he could have made things very hard for you."

"I've had enough melancholy to last a lifetime. The sisters at the temple tell me I cling too much to the past." Perhaps one day, she would come to realize that and choose to let it go. Perhaps then the ache would go away.

The slope of their way toward the castle steepened, and Hatsumi began to puff. Thanks to Kazuko's endless hours of training with Master Higuchi, she felt no weariness at all. Her voluminous robes of elaborate silk and embroidery concealed how lithe and strong her limbs had become. Hatsumi would chide her as unwomanly, but Kazuko was proud of that strength.

Martial training was the only thing that had saved her through the years of aching loneliness, longing for a man she would never see again. Not her husband's love, nor her handmaid's advice, nor games and conversation with her sister-in-law, Lady Yukino, nor all the diversions available to the wife of a wealthy lord, nothing could close the hole in her heart. And Hatsumi must not know that it had never gone away, never fully. Hatsumi hated Ken'ishi with an unreasonable fervor, he who had saved both of them from the demon bandit Hakamadare and his gang, and hated that Kazuko had loved him.

"So," Kazuko said, as briskly as she could manage. "Tell me

what Yasutoki has done, and I shall have my husband scold him for you."

"I cannot understand him! He tells me he loves me, has eyes for only me, and then he beds the first low-born trollop who crosses his path! He gives me extravagant gifts, makes hints of marriage, but when I press him, he demurs. When we're abed, he gives me words of love, but these days ... his little man remains asleep. Oh, he just frustrates me."

"How can I help?"

"Send me a love potion, or send for an augurer to tell me my fate. If I'm to be forever alone, better to know now."

Kazuko's heart warmed at the news that Yasutoki's attentions had moved away from Hatsumi. Hatsumi had already been hurt by him, but whenever Kazuko was in Yasutoki's presence, she found herself tense, on edge. She did not trust him. The fact that Yasutoki and Hatsumi had been trysting for nearly three years meant that his intentions toward her were not honorable. If only Hatsumi did not pine so for him. He would never marry her.

Having tasted the feverish rapture of love herself, like a spike of lightning through her heart, through her loins, how could Kazuko blame Hatsumi for feeling the same emotions, especially after the horrors she had endured at the hands of the demon Hakamadare. The sudden, brutal attack, the sounds of dying men, the enormous crimson-purple hands that had whisked Hatsumi into the air and flung her in the bushes, the blazing yellow eyes and three vicious horns. And then ... the rape, and Hatsumi's screams.

A wonder that poor Hatsumi had ever let a man get close to her ever again. She often lamented that no man would ever want her after being so soiled.

If not for Ken'ishi, the same would have happened to Kazuko.

By the time they reached the castle gates, Hatsumi was grumbling with displeasure at the exertion of the climb. Kazuko took her by the shoulders and smiled. "Let today be the first of a new time for us. No more unpleasantness between us. No more sourness. No more melancholy. You are my big sister."

Hatsumi smiled, and tears of happiness sparkled. They went

into the castle together. Kazuko looked up and down the road for a glimpse of the man Hatsumi said was Yasutoki, but she saw nothing.

As she gazed up the castle's whitewashed walls, the massive edifice of its fortifications, the towering keep with its graceful swooping roofs, she thought about the man waiting for her upstairs. Tsunetomo would greet her with a bemused smile, and ask her if she were still drinking the special brew the temple sisters had made for her—the fertility tea—and she would smile and say, "Yes, of course, Husband," and later on he would bed her, and she would lose her sorrows in the endurable pleasure of those moments, enjoying the strength and skill of her husband's hands and body. Yes, she was happy to have Lord Tsunetomo. So much more mature than Ken'ishi's wild, hot, tortured passion. So much more measured, balanced. Calculated.

But unless she produced an heir soon, how much longer would he be happy to have her?

With a single grain of barley, the bud sprouts, and although it is endowed with the same functions as the original barley, if water and earth do not unify, it will not become barley at all.

— *Takuan Soho, "The Clear Sound of Jewels"*

The boy without a name recognized the forested mountainsides on either side of the strait, but he did not know the boats that rode the swirling waves, their decks covered in men with bows and armor, cabins filled with trembling women swathed in embroidered silks like flowing rainbows. Long, straight black hair flowed down the women's backs, their faces pale, powdered, painted, streaked with tears. He was small, so pitifully small, and the hoarse cries of the men on deck, filled with anger and tension, frightened him.

He had crossed this stretch of water once himself when he was older, or perhaps in another existence.

And he did have a name. They called him Antoku, and they all bowed to him. They were fighting about him, these men with their stern faces and hard eyes. So rough, these warriors. As his grandmother explained, his enemies all wanted his power. He wished he was bigger, so that he would know what to do. His grandmother kept a watchful eye upon him, never letting him stray too far into the throng of blades and bows.

Banners floated above, but when he tried to see the *mon* on the flapping silk, his gaze slid over it and up into the red-streamered sky. He could see on the banners that the *mon* was there, and that it was important, but the harder he tried, the more his eyelids felt weighted down, closing, half-blinding him.

He liked riding on a ship, but the sea was rough today, and the steersman was having difficulty maintaining a steady course. The boy's eyes just rose over the gunwale if he stood on his toes, and he could see all the other ships flying the same banners as this vessel, but this vessel hoisted other banners with swirling, changing images chased with gold. So many ships in every direction, some of them so close that an agile man might perhaps leap from one to the next, more ships than he could count on many, many sets of fingers and toes, like an entire tree of fallen leaves floating upon a wind-rippled pond.

And there was another mass of ships behind them, black hulls cutting the waves, bamboo-ribbed sails puffed by the wind.

The deck under the boy's feet lurched, and the steersman cursed.

He hoped he and his people would get away from the people chasing them, because if they didn't, he would die. He didn't want his grandmother to die, or the pretty ladies who waited on him. Or his uncle, who stood at the prow with his glimmering blade pointing at the sky. His uncle's sword was pretty, so sharp and shiny. His uncle told him it was special because of the pattern on the blade that looked like feathers. The morning sun turned the steel into a streak of fire. The boy reached toward it. He wanted a sword so that he could fight, too, when the bad men came, but swords were so heavy.

Samurai archers lined the rear deck, the lacquer of their armor gleaming, sparkling like eyes in candlelight, the silken laces and threads like daubs of paint. Some of them wore scary, metal *menpo* over their faces in the likeness of tigers or demons or gods.

Their bows were striped with different colors, and the feathers of their arrows fresh and new.

Distant cries reverberated over the waves, commands.

High in the sky, he noticed little black lines moving, like tiny threads, or a flock of birds, and the lines were coming closer, arcing down, and then the screaming started, and the sharp, pattering thumping of something striking the ship, tearing the sails. An arrow almost as tall as he was quivered in the deck at his feet.

His grandmother rushed out and clutched him to her. He could feel her heart beating against him, the warmth of her tears in his hair and cold rage in her voice, but not directed toward him. He loved his grandmother, but he wanted to see what was happening outside, and then, strangely, he could, as if he had become a gull sitting on the yard arm of a sail. The arrows sliced into the samurai. The archers from ships all around him returned fire, storms of arrows flowing back and forth like flocks of birds. Crimson trickled across decks. The ships in pursuit, with their own flapping banners drawing nearer and nearer. Crashing froth and salt spray surrounding the lurching ship. The steersman, bristling with arrows, clutching at the rudder with his last breath, a replacement rushing forward, only to die in the next volley. Ships meandered out of formation, their steersmen dead, sideswiping hulls, ribbed sails tearing into each other. A fleet tumbling into disarray, caught in the grip of invisible tides, pulling, surging.

His uncle roaring a challenge toward the enemy, two arrows embedded in his armor, great mane of black hair flying in the wind.

Enemy ships drawing nearer, nearer, swarms of arrows buzzing back and forth, until hulls came together and blades came free and snarling warriors charged over the gunwales.

The boy's grandmother clutched him tighter and tighter. She had a dagger in her hand, and she stroked his face with sadness in her eyes, not ferocity. The pretty ladies wept and clutched each other, and he felt sorry for them for being so scared. His fingers squeezed into his grandmother's Buddhist nun's habit. She was talking to him, her voice hard and crackling, like the blackened scales of seared fish.

Blood and brine and screams washed over the decks, spilled under doors, through cracks, dripped in tiny droplets like jewels onto the powdered, white faces of the pretty ladies.

Then, a calm settled over the ravaged ship. The clamor of battle drew farther off. The smell of smoke drifted in from afar, mixing with the immediate stench of blood and other even more unpleasant odors. His uncle stood in the doorway of the cabin. Blood spattered his face, dripped from his wild mane and the tip of his sword, caked his fingers around the ray-skin hilt. He shared a long look with the boy's grandmother. Grandmother nodded, then stood with the boy on her arm.

A terrible understanding dawned across the innocent faces of the pretty ladies. Then they wiped their tears and bowed, foreheads to the floor. Grandmother stepped outside the cabin, and the morning sea breeze was cool on the boy's face, ruffling loose a few strands from his tightly tied hair. The fleet of ships lay in ruin like leaves upturned on the waves, burning hulls and sails shadowing the sky with soot and ash, waves crested by red foam washing over flotsam of armored backs and staring dead faces, splintered banners like those on his ship tossed on the waves.

In this long war, the boy had already seen much death. It no longer sickened him. He hugged his grandmother tight, and her body felt like wood beneath her nun's habit.

Enemy vessels were converging on the boy's ship, more bows and blades on the decks ready for slaughter. Everyone here was bloody, weary, wounded. And still the enemy came.

His uncle walked to the prow of the ship, slung the blood from his blade and used it to cut through a rope from the massive coil at the prow. Then his uncle tied the rope around his waist and made a series of stout knots. Grandmother waited impassively for him to finish. The enemy was coming.

Then his uncle and grandmother bowed to each other.

Grandmother walked to the prow, squeezed him close, held his face to her chest, and stepped into nothing. He gasped as cold waves closed over his head, driving salt water up into his nose. In his grandmother's arms, they sank amid a swarm of roaring bubbles. He reached toward the light as the embrace of the sea squeezed him tighter and tighter, pain shooting through his ears. The invisible tides dragged at him. A succession of bubbling explosions above, and more figures descended through the explosions. His uncle, with the ship's massive anchor in his arms, plummeted past them in a swarm of bubbles, trailing blood. Pretty ladies with their silken robes billowing like diaphanous wings followed them toward the dark depths.

The boy held his breath until he could no longer.

Ken'ishi's eyes snapped open, and he gasped for breath, rolling onto his side with the taste of seawater still in his mouth.

As breath and uneasy calm returned to him, he felt a presence nearby, and the warmth of a fire that he had not left burning last night.

He snatched for his sword hilt, but his fingers closed around a smooth wooden shaft, not a rough, ray-skin grip. A pang of anguish. He rolled to his feet, *bokken* brandished.

Hage poked his modest fire with a stick. "You sleep like a stone sometimes, old sot."

"You!"

The gnarled little man grinned up at him, squatting nearby, his hair a wild mess, eyes sparkling. "Indeed, I am me."

"What do you want?"

"Why so hostile, old sot? I thought we were fast friends."

The fuzziness in Ken'ishi's mind dispersed like chaff in a furious wind. "Four days asleep!"

"More precisely, three nights. You must have been very tired. Much on your mind." Hage rapped his forehead with his knuckles.

"What did you do?"

"Do?"

"I came back to the village and ... everything was different."

"What do you mean, 'different'?"

"Kiosé had forgotten about me. And Little Frog. Was that your doing?" The pain in Ken'ishi's voice surprised him.

"I would say that was your doing."

"Mine? I don't have the power to make someone forget!"

"Of course you do. People come and go throughout a person's life. If you choose to remove yourself from a person's life, it will happen. They will forget. Sometimes the forgetting is immediate. Sometimes it takes longer. I merely helped you get what you wanted. Isn't that what you wanted?"

"Not like that!"

"So, you wanted to hurt her then. You said you didn't want to hurt her."

"But—"

"You can't have it both ways, old sot. Either you hurt people or you don't. You hold onto that hurt or you don't. You have your path. She has hers. Now she's simply on a path that does not include you."

Ken'ishi squeezed his sword tighter, gritting his teeth.

The old man shrugged. "The balance of pain in the world is still the same. But now you must swallow all of that portion yourself. Sit, have some breakfast, and we'll talk about where we're going."

Ken'ishi blinked as the old man's words sunk in. "We? Go? No."

"Come, sit. Tell me what we're about. Then we'll set out. Plenty of beautiful day ahead."

"I said, no. I don't need your help, Uncle."

"And what happens if you meet another *oni* like Hakamadare?"

"How did you know about that?"

"Who doesn't? Are you going to club him with your stick there, or perhaps regale him with Chinese poetry?"

"There will be fighting coming."

"Of that I have no doubt."

"I cannot drag you into that. I could die."

"You certainly could. Such is the life of human beings. You could slip on a wet stone today and dash out your own brains. A tree could fall on your head. You could catch a fever and expire in a raving delirium."

"I intend my death to serve more purpose."

"Oho! Planning for it, are you? Most deaths serve little purpose at all. What makes you think you're special?"

An invisible weight settled onto Ken'ishi's neck, and he sighed.

"Such burdens, the little mortal life." Hage scooped steaming rice into a wooden bowl and offered it to Ken'ishi. "All of which are easier to bear with a full stomach."

Ken'ishi sat beside the fire and took the bowl. "I am samurai. I must serve. If I cannot serve a lord, I must serve mankind, even with my death."

"Noble intentions. So tell me, what's the quest, old sot?"

"Someone stole something from me." Ken'ishi blew steam off the rice.

"Stole what?"

"My sword."

"Was it a nice sword?"

Ken'ishi frowned at Hage's choice of words, as if the old man were describing a flower arrangement. "When its steel is bare, it is beautiful."

"Oho, was it shiny? I like things that shine. Were there jewels on it? Precious gems? Gold?"

"No, none of those things."

"So it's not very valuable then."

"It is ... priceless. It means more than my life."

Hage scratched his stubbly chin. "That doesn't sound very valuable at all."

"Someone thought it valuable enough to go to much trouble to steal it."

"Now you want it back."

Ken'ishi nodded slowly.

"Do you know who took it?"

"No."

"Do you know where you're going?"

Ken'ishi pointed to the southwest. "That direction."

"How do you know?"

"I know."

"Oho! Perhaps you're the one with magical powers! How do

you intend to get it back?"

"Any way I can."

"Very well, then." Hage picked up his own bowl of rice and began to eat, slurping and smacking his lips with relish.

Ken'ishi took out his chopsticks and ate. The morning air was warm, pleasant, but the birdsong echoing among the trees and bamboo stung him like a chorus of incomprehensible taunts. A lump formed in his throat, blocking the passage of breakfast, until he gritted his teeth to force the regret away.

His bedroll lying atop the cushion of fallen bamboo leaves had been passably comfortable. Nevertheless, a tremendous weariness suffused his limbs. Three years since he had last lived on the road like this. A true *ronin*. It felt like falling back into a familiar bed. He had spent so many nights sleeping outside on the ground.

But now he was without his chief weapon, and he had had the furry warmth of a loyal companion for much of that time. Akao had hunted with him, slept with him, trotted along beside him, and the dog's sharp nose had rooted out many a rabbit for supper. Last night Ken'ishi had lain down, acutely aware of the cold absence of a dead friend. And the warm arms of a woman.

"Uncle, if any danger comes, I want you to run. I'll handle it myself."

"Don't worry about me, old sot. I'm quite adept at preserving my own skin. I've gotten this old, and I intend to get older. Now eat up. The day is getting on, and we have *ri* to cover, yes?"

Ken'ishi scrutinized the old man. After several heartbeats, his new companion looked up from his rice and grinned.

He uses the sword and does not kill them means that even though he does not use the sword to cut others down, when others are confronted by this principle, they cower and become as  dead men of their own accord. There is no need to kill them.

He uses the sword and gives others life means that while he deals with his opponent with the sword, he leaves everything to the movements of the other man, and is able to observe him just as he pleases.

— *Takuan Soho, "The Clear Sound of Jewels"*

The tavern keeper's wife set platters on the table, laden with bowls of *miso* soup, smoked *ayu*, and rice topped by pickled plums. Hage's eyes gleamed as he fell to without preamble. Ken'ishi's hunger was a satisfying one, product of the many *ri* that he and Hage had already put behind them today, so he savored it for a moment. At least for a while, he had money to buy food, unlike his wandering life before.

This town was much larger than Aoka village, a stopover for

travelers on the way to Dazaifu, seat of much of the government on Kyushu. The town seemed familiar. Perhaps he had passed through it during his flight from the domain of Lord Nishimuta no Jiro. Strangely, he remembered little of those days, only the pain of having something he loved, something his heart wanted, someone he longed to hold again, wrested from him, along with threat of death on his head if he tarried.

Rice stuffed Hage's cheeks and flecked his lips as he spoke. "Do you always walk so slow, old sot? I'm walking with a turtle. I thought you were in a hurry." He put down his bowl and patted his belly. "I've been wasting away from hunger!"

Ken'ishi raised an eyebrow. "You're an old man. I didn't want to overtax you."

Hage's eyes narrowed. "Don't you worry about me. I've been getting around just fine for much longer than you've been alive."

They sat in the open tavern front on a bench, bellied up to the bar, behind which the tavern keeper and his wife grilled fish and summer vegetables over a bed of coals. The wall of the tavern opened up like an awning and shielded them from the noonday sun. The street behind them bustled with activity. Crafters, tradesmen, farmers, women and children, a constable in a distinctive helmet that looked like half a clamshell. Even a handful of warriors passed by, wearing the crest of a lord Ken'ishi did not know.

Ken'ishi's attention followed them until they passed out of sight. They wore their swords differently than he did. Theirs were made in the modern *katana*-style, with slightly less curvature than Silver Crane, with hilts wrapped in an outer sheath of silken cords over ray skin, rather than just ray skin. They walked with swagger and camaraderie, and the villagers bowed to them as they passed.

A small gasp from the innkeeper's wife snagged Ken'ishi's attention from picking smoked fish flesh from its bones. He followed her gaze toward the three burly men approaching the tavern. They wore rough clothing, except for the one who walked in front with a shiny silk jacket over his robes, sword thrust into his brightly woven sash.

The tavern keeper spotted them, too, and quickly wiped his hands, his face blanching. His gaze flicked about as if looking for something, a place to run, but found nothing. Then he steeled himself and presented a wide grin to the three men as they ducked under the wooden awning.

The *kami* roared silently in Ken'ishi's mind, raising the hairs on the nape of his neck.

The tavern keeper's lips stretched, and he bowed repeatedly. "Good day, Yuto-sama. Would you like some lunch? Some *saké* perhaps? I just—"

"We would," Yuto said.

The bench creaked as the three men sat, the largest not far from Ken'ishi. The tavern keeper and his wife bustled about the tiny kitchen preparing platters, and Ken'ishi's nose wrinkled. The men stank of sweat and *saké*. Hage ignored them.

The wife tried to smile at them, but failed.

The men waited like wolves, silent, their expressions barely masking contempt and menace. Platters were set before them, bearing much larger portions of food than Hage and Ken'ishi received. The men fell to without a word.

Ken'ishi finished his meal, and let his awareness encompass the men without looking at them. Two wore swords. The largest one carried a pair of farmer's sickles thrust into the back of his sash.

An unspoken pall coalesced with the smoke of the grill. The tavern keeper's face tightened with dread.

The men ate their meals. Ken'ishi felt their eyes on him.

When Yuto was finished, he picked up his rice bowl and flung it at the tavern keeper's head. The bowl bounced high, and the tavern keeper yelped in pain. The bowl clattered to the floor. The tavern keeper turned, a tight smile on his face as he rubbed his skull. "The meal is on the house, Yuto-sama."

"You know why we're here." Yuto sucked rice from his teeth.

The tavern keeper sighed and nodded. He withdrew a small paper-wrapped bundle from under the counter and slid it toward Yuto.

Yuto picked it up and hefted it. His eyes drilled like icicles into the tavern keeper. He shoved the bundle back across the counter. "There are a lot of bad men around here. Has no one discovered why the Sparrow's Nest Inn burned down last week? That was terrible, just terrible. We don't ask for much. Imagine what would happen if bad men decided they didn't like you? What would happen then?"

The tavern keeper trembled.

Yuto picked up another bowl and threw it hard at the tavern keeper's face. The tavern keeper managed to duck just enough that the bowl only glanced off. "I said, what would happen then?"

Ken'ishi took a deep breath and settled himself. Then he stood, *bokken* hanging from his left hand. "You talk too much."

Hage whispered, "What are you doing?"

Three sets of dark, hard eyes focused on Ken'ishi. Yuto sucked more rice from his teeth. "Back off, stranger. You're not from around here."

"You've disturbed my meal. Leave now."

"Interesting. That's what I was going to say to you." Yuto glanced at his associates. The three of them stood, fingering their weapons.

Hage put down his chopsticks and bowl. "Oho! Now this could be interesting."

The big one reached behind his back and pulled out the sickles. Sneering, he pointed at Ken'ishi's wooden sword with one. "What are you going to do with that? Let the old man use it as a walking stick?"

"I'm going to use it to break both of your arms if you don't leave now."

The man's face flared red. "Idiot!"

Yuto's voice was low and oily. "You clearly don't know who we work for. If you continue this, you'll only wish you were dead."

Ken'ishi took a deep breath, released it, and switched his *bokken* to his right hand.

The big man raised a sickle and charged like an ox.

Ken'ishi side-stepped the hissing blade and brought his wooden sword down across the man's forearm. A loud, meaty *snap* tore a howl from the man's throat. The sickle fell to the earth. The howl shifted to a roar of anger, and he swung the other sickle at Ken'ishi's face. Ken'ishi caught the wooden sickle handle on his wooden blade, and with a twist, jerked it out of the man's hand, sending it flying in a high arc. Ken'ishi's *bokken* swept down across the extended forearm. A sound like a splintered sapling, the warm spurt of blood from the spear of bone tearing free of flesh. The second sickle landed several paces away.

A collective gasp rippled through onlookers, filling the moment of silence before the man screamed.

The glint of sun-brightened steel flashed in Ken'ishi's eyes and drove him back three steps.

Yuto and his other companion stepped around the wailing sickle wielder, katanas raised. They lunged toward Ken'ishi. Yuto stumbled over Hage's out-thrust walking stick and fell to his hands and knees, but the other man still came forward.

Between instants, Ken'ishi could see the rust spots sullying the glimmer of the oncoming blade. He easily batted the ill-trained stroke aside, and his return stroke slashed across the man's face. More splintering bone. The man's eye burst from its shattered socket, hanging on his cheek.

Hage swept his walking stick around and clubbed Yuto in the back of the head.

Ken'ishi's assailant dropped his sword, and his shrieks formed a horrid chorus with the sickle man's. Blood gushed from the man's face.

Yuto rolled away from Hage with surprising deftness, slashing blindly through a deluge of tears and stunned bewilderment. Hage's eyes bulged, and he dodged back. The *whish*ing tip of Yuto's blade flashed past the old man's face.

Ken'ishi leaped forward and slashed down across the spine of Yuto's blade, driving the hilt out of his grip.

The second swordsman gingerly cradled his dangling eyeball in his palm, his scream becoming a crazed gurgling.

The big sickle man staggered back to his feet, both arms

hanging at grotesque angles, a bloody splinter of bone protruding from one.

Ken'ishi kicked Yuto in the face, sending him sprawling onto his back. He stood over Yuto and lowered the point of his *bokken* to Yuto's face as the man glared up at him with hatred and fear.

A crowd of whispers and eyes had formed a wide circle around them.

Ken'ishi pressed the point of his *bokken* into Yuto's throat. "If I hear that you have given this tavern keeper any more trouble, I will find you."

Yuto spat blood from pulped lips, gurgling. "Then you had better kill me now."

"As I look around this crowd of good townspeople, I see many faces who want to do just that." It was true. The shock and curiosity of the crowd was quickly giving way to anger and threat. Eyes simmered with old hatred, glimmered with opportunity, like the desire to finish off a pack of wounded wolves. "Now, go. But leave your weapons." He allowed Yuto to stagger to his feet.

"Who are you?" Yuto said. "Who's your master?"

"I have no name."

"My master will find you."

Ken'ishi raised his *bokken* to strike, and Yuto spun and fled through the crowd.

The throng parted to let the two wounded, whimpering men stumble after him, then cheered and hallooed and threw taunts after them.

Ken'ishi stepped up to the counter and laid down a coin for his meal.

The tavern keeper's wife glared at him with mixed horror and anger. "What have you done, you fool?" she hissed. "Those men work for Green Tiger!"

"Green Tiger?"

"Lord of the Underworld!" she snapped. "Don't you know anything? He'll kill us for sure! Or burn down our place!"

The tavern keeper stepped around his wife, mumbling, "Shut up, woman!" He bowed to Ken'ishi. "Honorable sir, please accept our thanks." He grinned feebly. "Our troubles were none of your concern, but ..." He scooped up the bundled coins and bowed again.

Hage placed another purse on the counter with the heavy clink of many coins. "Think nothing of it. Perhaps this will assuage the pain of your troubles today."

The tavern keeper's eyes devoured the purse. The wife snatched it up and clutched it to her chest, her frown melting into tears.

Hage slid off the bench. "Let's be moving on, old sot, lest our departed friends send reinforcements."

Ken'ishi bowed to the tavern keeper, then picked up his things and shouldered them.

Hage said, "Aren't you going to take the weapons? You could certainly use a real sword."

Ken'ishi shook his head. "Those swords are sullied by the evil of the men who bore them. A sword should be granted, not stolen as spoils. As for the sickles, I'm not a gardener."

Hage shrugged, and they walked through the crowd, the people bowing to them as they passed. Hage said, "You are much less pragmatic than me."

Ken'ishi waited until they were out of the crowd's earshot, then frowned. "And somewhat less amoral as well. You stole his money."

"I thought it only fair to steal from a thief."

They walked through the streets for a while, away from the marketplace. They started across a bridge over a wide, gurgling river. The gentle arch of the bridge felt good against Ken'ishi's feet and raised him high enough to see over the roofs of the town's houses. The noon sun was hot on his head, the river bright in his eyes, the breeze cool on his flesh.

Green Tiger, the woman had said. Three years ago, he had slain a spy in Aoka village pretending to be an itinerant monk, and the spy had been preparing to send a message to an unknown master. The spy, Yellow Tiger, had been looking for Ken'ishi. He had always wondered if the spy had been working for Lord Nishimuta no Jiro—Kazuko's father. Perhaps Lord Nishimuta had decided that banishing Ken'ishi was not enough. This town was nearer to Nishimuta lands.

So many tigers. Could the theft of Silver Crane be connected somehow?

Hage poked him with his walking stick. "Do you know which direction?"

Ken'ishi took a deep breath, reaching out his awareness for the invisible tug. But he felt nothing. "I ... I don't know."

Hage's cheeks puffed. "What do you mean you don't know? You've been so certain!"

Ken'ishi threw up his hands. "I'm saying the sword could be in this town, within a hundred paces, and I would not know. How can I follow it this way?"

"A question you should have asked before you set out. What did you expect to do? Go house to house asking if people had seen it?"

"No, I ... I trusted that destiny would bring it back to me, or else that I would die in the search."

"That's a high cost for failure, old sot."

"Without it, I may as well be dead." Ken'ishi leaned over the rail and put his head in his hands.

"You did pretty well back there with your polished stick. Now, quit whining. We'll keep going, even if it's the wrong way. An immobile stone has no destiny but to never move."

Ken'ishi's eyes were drawn to a flash of white movement near the riverbank. Three cranes leaped into the air and with a few beats of their wings lofted over the bridge and turned toward the west. His gaze followed them until they disappeared into the west. "That way." The rightness of his words rang like a silent bell in his mind.

Hage nodded. "Glad to hear it. I just knew this would be a fun journey, old sot!" He reached up to stroke his beard and jumped with surprise. His beard now hung square-cut a finger's breadth below his chin.

"It would have been less 'fun' without your head."

Hage dabbed at the glisten of sweat on his forehead. "Indeed."

"But before we leave town, we should ask a few questions about this Green Tiger. I want to know who we're dealing with."

Now I glimpse her face,
the old woman, abandoned,
with only the moon for
    company
         — *Basho*

Yasutoki held Yuto's note in the candle flame and watched it blacken, ignite, and curl into ash. Anger flared in tandem with the burgeoning flame. Yuto would survive the brawl, but his henchmen might not. They had received a serious beating, Yuto said, and the interlopers had not only prevented the collection of the protection money, but also made off with the rest of the day's collection, a substantial sum.

The heat from the candle grew on his fingertips, but he withstood it, focusing his will. His fingertips blackened with the smoke and soot from the burning paper. This incident was a serious insult to Green Tiger's power. There must be retribution.

According to Yuto's note, five men had attacked without warning. Was another gang moving into his territory? A rival *oyabun*? Green Tiger had formed a tenuous cessation of hostilities with the Chinese White Lotus gang and their opium trade in Hakata, and the Scorpion Gambling Alliance in Kumamoto. Other smaller gangs operated in the nooks and crannies of the underworld, but they all knew better than to cross him.

In any case, his operation in Hita town had been weakened. Always it seemed that the upper world, the visible world, chipped at the edges of his empire, like rats nibbling into a sack of rice. Nothing ran smoothly for long. He would not only have to track down the perpetrators and punish them, he would also have to send a pointed message to Hita town's merchants that Green Tiger was not to be trifled with.

When the paper burned to a mere scrap, he released the rest of it into the flame, and a few final embers puffed and settled to the table. Yasutoki rubbed his blackened fingertips together. He would be much more irritated now if Silver Crane was not safely vaulted in Lord Tsunetomo's treasure room in the bowels of the castle, hidden in a nondescript wooden box with Yasutoki's personal seal. None but Yasutoki and Tsunetomo himself had access to the room, and Tsunetomo never bothered to visit it. Not even his brother, Tsunemori, was allowed access.

Tsunetomo trusted Yasutoki to handle the domain's financial affairs, and Yasutoki handled them with meticulous care; he had never stolen a sliver of copper from his lord. Silver Crane would be safe there. And if the sword was discovered by some unlikely happenstance, Yasutoki was entitled to a "family treasure" kept in safekeeping. Tsunetomo would have no inkling of the sword's true significance.

His chamber door shadowed with a presence in the hallway. "Are you in there?"

Yasutoki sighed at the sound of Hatsumi's voice. Despite his best efforts, he had not been able to maintain his illusion of interest in an affair with her. Coupling with her was like bedding a day-old tuna. Even after almost three years of their erstwhile liaisons, her body was so stiff and unresponsive that he could no longer put aside her horse-faced ugliness. For weeks he had been trying to put her off with niceties and little gifts, distractions from the fact that he did not want to see her, but she had been growing ever more insistent. It would be troublesome to have her meet with some sort of accident—she was still a useful tool in Lady Kazuko's confidence—but if her attentions became too odious, he would have to deal with them.

He mustered as much pleasantness as he could. "I am here,

Hatsumi, my sweet. Do come in."

The door slid open, and Hatsumi shuffled inside, eyes modestly downcast.

Yasutoki gave her his best smile. "So lovely to see you. Please come and sit. Would you like some tea?"

Hatsumi crossed the room in a horse's caricature of a maiden's dainty walk, her thick lips quirked into a courtesan's smile that demurely concealed her carefully blackened teeth. She sat beside him. "A lovely morning, is it not?"

"I would assume so, with the pleasant breeze coming through the window, but alas, I have been ensconced here, working on my lord's business since early this morning. While I am away in Hakata, untended business here accumulates."

"You are such a busy man. Can you not take a bit of time for some enjoyment? It has been so long since … we have had any private time together."

"I am sorry, my sweet. It has been too long. The necessities of life in my lord's service, I'm afraid."

She nodded and reached over to stroke his thigh. "Perhaps you'd like to go for a walk in the garden?"

"Alas, my sweet, no. There are duties I must perform before afternoon, or our lord will be unhappy with me."

Hatsumi squeezed his thigh. "Please, I've been so lonely." She laid her head on his shoulder.

He took her hand in his and lifted it off his thigh, squeezing. "No, I cannot today."

"Perhaps tomorrow?"

"Perhaps, if you leave me to my work today."

She stiffened and drew back. "Perhaps you would be more interested if I said we should walk to the Roasted Acorn."

Yasutoki's teeth clenched at the pregnancy of her tone. "What do you mean?"

"I saw you the other night leaving the Roasted Acorn, with your basket hat."

"Have you been spying on me?" An edge of menace found its

way into a tone that he had intended to be playful. "My lady and I were passing by, and I recognized your walk. I know you too well, dear, for you to hide from me." She pulled her hand free of his and stroked his groin. "I could recognize your little man, too, even in the dark."

"A man must have a bit of *saké* now and then. You should mind your own business!" His hand closed over her wrist and squeezed hard.

She gasped and tried to pull it away, but his strength far exceeded hers. "Why are you so secretive?"

"It is not your place to ask such questions." He dragged out each word, boring his eyes into hers, his lips drawing tight.

Hatsumi's voice shrilled like a dissonant *biwa* string. "You've been dipping your brush in some whore's ink!" She tore her hand free, drew back, and laid a stinging slap across his face.

He spurned her and leaped to his feet. "You dare!"

Her eyes brimmed with tears and rage. "You've found another servant girl who makes your little man stand at attention! Some little whore!" She rose up off the floor as if jerked upright by the claws reaching for his face. Rage boiled from her eyes like molten fire.

He caught her wrists, holding her at bay as she loosed a guttural shriek of anguish. Tears streamed down her face. She twisted her wrists and fought against his grip, but he held them fast. A deft twist of her wrists and a quick ankle-sweep sent her to the floor with a jarring thud, and he knelt on her chest, wrists still firmly in his grip. Her sour breath whooshed into his face. His words dripped with venom. "Now, my sweet. You will calm yourself and listen to me."

The door whished open again, and Kazuko stood there, chest heaving, wearing a man's practice robe and trousers. Sweat sheened her face and stained her clothes, soaked her white headband. "Hatsumi! Lord Yasutoki, what is going on?"

The faces of several wide-eyed servants peeked around the edges of the open door.

Yasutoki eased back, but did not release her wrists. "A bit of a quarrel. Nothing to concern my lady. Or the household!" He turned a pointed gaze on the servants outside, and they faded like squirrels from sight.

Hatsumi burst into harsh, wracking sobs, and the angry strength melted out of her arms.

Kazuko stalked into the room, her porcelain-smooth cheeks flushing pink that was not from exertion. "Release her!"

Yasutoki's eyes narrowed, but he released Hatsumi's wrists and slid back and to his feet in one motion.

Hatsumi lay in a sobbing pile. Kazuko came forward and took her arm, helping her to her feet, glaring coldly at Yasutoki. Hatsumi let herself be led toward the door.

Kazuko glanced back. "I'll thank you, sir, to never lay hands upon my servant again. Keep your attentions to yourself, or my husband will hear of it."

Yasutoki bit down upon his cheek at her presumption of command. True, she held higher station than him, but she was, after all, just a woman. He bowed low. "As my lady wishes. Please accept my sincere apologies."

She helped Hatsumi into the corridor and slammed the door.

In the silence, he took a deep breath and calmed himself.

Hatsumi's burst of fury had surprised him. She was becoming more volatile than he cared to tolerate. If she caused any more trouble like today, his reputation could be sullied. Lord Tsunetomo was a practical man who trusted Yasutoki, but he would not approve of anything in his court that smacked of impropriety.

Yasutoki rubbed his chin. It would be less trouble perhaps to just kill her and be done, but she might yet be useful. Perhaps he should contrive some reason to return to his house in Hakata for a while, until this Hatsumi problem subsided. He often directly oversaw the acquisition of building materials and supplies for Tsunetomo's ever-expanding holdings, new fortifications and field improvements. Such simple lies around his activities and whereabouts were his stock in trade.

Yes, perhaps Hakata's sea breezes would be a welcome respite from the heat of summer.

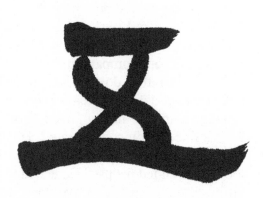

When it is necessary to kill, he kills. When it is necessary to give life, he gives life. When killing, he kills in complete concentration; when giving life, he gives life in complete concentration means that in either giving life or taking life, he does so with freedom in a meditative state that is total absorption, and the meditator becomes one with the object of meditation.

— *Takuan Soho, "The Clear Sound of Jewels"*

The castle rose against the pink streamers of sunset. Tall, sweeping walls, a stately central keep, and a prosperous town nestled against the slopes of the castle's hill.

Ken'ishi's feet ached after another long day of walking. The cool stream where he had cooled them this afternoon already felt like a distant memory. A refreshing splash to remove the road dust, followed by a quiet soak would be welcome.

He hailed a passing woodsman and pointed. "Excuse me, Uncle, but whose castle is that?"

The woodsman's heavy-laden rack hunched his back and bowed his skinny legs, but he turned and bowed politely. "This is the domain of Lord Otomo no Tsunetomo, sir."

Distant scarlet banners above the gates flapped on the breeze, caught the dusk light.

Ken'ishi thanked the woodsmen and tried to remember where he had heard that name before. The half-recollection felt like a sliver in his flesh so fine that he could not find it.

Hage poked him with the walking stick and grinned. "Perhaps you should ask him for a job, a strapping young samurai like you."

He frowned. "The last time I asked a lord to be taken into service, I was chased out of the domain upon threat of death."

"Ah, old scars I see." Hage clicked his tongue. "Why must I drag every tidbit of tale from you? Why couldn't I have chosen a more loquacious companion?"

"I would rather do than say. It saves breath. Perhaps if you talked less, you'd breathe easier coming over some of those hills."

Hage pointed a meaty finger. "You watch your tongue, boy. I do just fine for someone my age." He breathed deep of the scents on the air. "This looks like a good town to rest for the night. These look like well-fed people." Hage patted his belly, then adjusted his groin. "Besides, it's been two days, and you're still chewing on the name of Green Tiger. Is he anyone you would truly want to meet?"

The *kami* buzzed like mosquitoes at the edges of Ken'ishi's consciousness, perhaps with warning, perhaps significance. He pursed his lips and continued down the street.

"You're so serious today, old sot."

Too many things on Ken'ishi's mind, too many half-glimpsed connections and half-forgotten names, like leaves blown from his grasp by the wind. He stopped beside a *saké* house. The rich smell of grilling fish and vegetables wafted out alongside sharp tinges of *saké*.

"Oho! Your pause here makes its own merit! The Roasted Acorn, eh? I'm famished and thirsty." Hage parted the curtain over the door and ducked inside.

Ken'ishi could say the same, so he followed into the dim interior.

Hage seated himself at the counter, behind which sat rows of shelves and jars of *saké*. The bar man shouted a jovial "Welcome!" Several other patrons occupied the room and the counter near Hage, their conversations filling *tatami*-floored nooks.

Ken'ishi and Hage ordered food and shared a jar of *saké*. As they ate, Ken'ishi's mind floundered around the name of Otomo no Tsunetomo. Where had he heard that name before?

Meanwhile, Hage struck up a conversation with a neighboring patron. They spoke of the heat, the quality of the fare here at the Roasted Acorn, the general state of the town. The other patron was a leathered farmer with gnarled, callused hands, a broad, blunt countenance, and an easy manner. Soon Hage and the farmer were chatting like long lost friends.

Ken'ishi listened with half an ear, but he had never been good at affable conversation. Between when Kaa had saved him from assassins and then later sent him away at the age of fifteen, Ken'ishi had seen only one other human, a mendicant monk. Nevertheless, Hage soon tried to draw him into the conversation. Ken'ishi could only sit awkwardly while Hage's words filled every space between breaths. When Hage regaled the farmer with an embellished yarn about how they had trounced some uncouth brutes in Hita town, the farmer's eyes sparkled.

The farmer said, "Ah, it's good to hear when someone stands up to the rough element. Filthy *ronin* and foreign gangsters think they can tell everyone what to do. The country is just going to hell with all those foreigners in Hakata. The government ought to send all those Koryo and Chinese back where they came from."

Ken'ishi leaned forward. "Have you ever heard of someone called Green Tiger?"

The conversation in the room hushed for a moment. The barkeep cocked an ear and looked askance at Ken'ishi.

The farmer stiffened and looked away. "Never heard of him."

Hage chuckled amiably. "You'll have to forgive my young friend. He's a bit short on social graces. Barkeep, a fresh jar please for my new friend here."

The barkeep filled another jar from the larger barrel. "Looking

135

for someone, are you?"

At a warning glance from Hage, Ken'ishi shrugged and held his tongue.

The barkeep set the jar on the counter, and Hage held it up to fill the farmer's cup. The farmer nodded and raised his cup to accept. The barkeep eyed Ken'ishi for a long time, and the *kami* tingled over his neck.

For almost an hour, Hage drank with the farmer, and Ken'ishi did not try to keep up, only sipping his *saké*. With possible danger nearby, he would not weaken his faculties or unsteady his body. Hage, on the other hand, poured it back as if he were dying of thirst. Patrons eventually wobbled to their feet and meandered out. The farmer's eyes grew bleary and bloodshot, and Hage's cheeks reddened, words slurring. Eventually, Hage's forehead descended to the counter, and soft snores followed. The farmer finally stood, bid Ken'ishi good night, and departed, leaving him alone with the barkeep and the sleeping Hage.

The barkeep gathered up empty jars and cups.

Ken'ishi said, "What do you know of Green Tiger?"

The barkeep stiffened again, but only for a moment. "Why, nothing, sir. I've never heard of him. Why do you ask?"

"Many people in these parts seem to know about him."

"What do *you* know about him?"

"Nothing. That is why I asked."

"Why do you seek him?"

"His name came up in certain dealings."

"With a name like that, those might be dangerous dealings."

"Perhaps you would be kind enough to help me steer away from danger."

"Too much knowledge can be dangerous."

"Who is he?"

"My cousin, he ... ran afoul of one of Green Tiger's gangs in Hakata."

"So, Green Tiger, he's a big man in Hakata?"

"And other places."

"What about here?"

"Not here. Lord Otomo doesn't tolerate rough men. *Ronin*, gangsters, bandits, they don't fare well if he catches any. Perhaps Green Tiger stays away from here for that reason."

"What happened to your cousin?"

"They tied him up, sliced up his face, and buried him in shit up to his neck until he died. This was in the height of summer a few years back. So, I say to you because you have an honest face, if you start looking for such men as Green Tiger, they might find you instead."

Ken'ishi nodded. "I understand. And I thank you for your concern. Is there an inn nearby?"

"I have a room if you want it, above the storage closet. You won't have to carry *him* so far."

Hage's head bobbed off the counter. "Carry! Carry me? What?" He slapped Ken'ishi's arm with a limp hand. "Discretion, old sot! Discretion!" His words slurred oil over one another. "You can't just go around throwing a name like Green Tiger around! He must be some sort of gangster! Have you learned nothing?"

Ken'ishi said to the barkeep. "We'll take your room." He took Hage by the arm, slung it over his shoulder, and hoisted him to his feet.

Hage tried to poke his chest, but missed, whispering so loud someone outside could have heard, "Discretion, I say! Subterfuge!"

Destiny....

The word rang in his mind like a receding shout.

Ken'ishi opened his eyes with a gasp. He reached for the silver thread that had been so sharp and clear in his dreams, but it had disappeared in a wash of worldly smells and sounds and darkness. The sound of the town coming to life outside his window, the musty *tatami* and dust of the cramped room, patches of dawn gray filtering through the small window.

He sat up and rubbed his eyes, expecting to find Hage in a senseless lump, but the old man was gone. The *futon* and blanket lay neatly folded, as if Ken'ishi had not left him sprawled amid the bedding like a great, snoring beast.

The steps downstairs from the room above the storage closest were steep and narrow, and Ken'ishi wondered how an old man, likely still suffering from too much drink, could have negotiated them without making enough noise to call ancestors from the afterlife.

Downstairs, the establishment was quiet at this time of morning, and he found no Hage there, nor outside in the privy, nor in the street. With growing consternation, Ken'ishi began walking the streets looking for him. The more industrious townspeople were already about their business, and Ken'ishi passed a building where the click and clatter of looms were already underway. The smell of bean cakes baking, the unique tang of a *saké* brewery, the sharp vinegar of vegetables pickling in great earthen crocks.

For an hour, Ken'ishi walked the streets, but without any glimpse of Hage. He bought a stick of incense and a rice ball and offered them to Jizo at a street-side shrine. The kind-faced god, protector of children and travelers, smiled beneficently at him as he prayed for help in his journey.

Ken'ishi wanted a sign. Memory of that word, *destiny,* ringing in his mind made him vigilant for signs. As he prayed, he sought the emptiness of mind and in that emptiness, he listened for the voice of Silver Crane. But there was only silence.

He made inquiries in the locale of the Roasted Acorn, but to no avail. When he returned to the Roasted Acorn and asked after Hage, a deep frown furrowed the barkeep's face. "No, I haven't seen that old drunkard today."

Sensing the barkeep's foul mood, Ken'ishi asked, "Some trouble today?"

"An animal got into my storage last night, shattered a jar of *saké*, ate half a dozen apples, a week's worth of bean cakes, and half my dried squid!"

"How do you know it was an animal?"

"Claw marks all over everything. It even pissed on a sack of rice!"

"Monkey? Fox? *Tanuki?*"

"Whatever it was, it had cleverness enough to open the door.

I'll be ready for it if it comes back, you mark me."

"Bad fortune. Or perhaps you angered it somehow. I've had experience with angering a fox. They can cause no end of trouble. Perhaps if you left it an offering outside."

"I'd rather just kill it and be done."

"You might risk the wrath of its kin."

The barkeep's lips writhed over each other.

"Good day, gentlemen!" Another voice intruded on their conversation.

The barkeep rolled his eyes.

A short, rotund man with a beaming smile, cherry-pink cheeks, and long, white, dangling whiskers bowed to them. His brightly-colored silk robes were finely woven with an eye-catching pattern. "Always so lovely to be back in Hoshiya town."

The barkeep growled. "I don't need any of your trinkets today."

"Perhaps you'd like to see my new crockery. I brought it all the way from Dazaifu with you in mind. It has an acorn design."

The barkeep grunted.

The peddler pressed on, and Ken'ishi excused himself. Outside, the rear gate of the peddler's creaky wagon hung open, exposing a cargo of cloth bundles, boxes, crockery, innumerable things. A bored-looking black ox stood yoked to the wagon, swishing its tail as it chewed on something. A group of four small children ran up to the beast and stopped, their eyes wide with wonder and some fear.

The ox snorted at them. Clear drool dripped from its mouth as it chewed, and the children giggled.

"Ah, gross!"

"Icky!"

"It's not moving."

"What a strange-looking beast!"

"It smells!"

"It wants to eat you," a boy said.

"No, it don't!" a girl said.

"Yes, you're very tender. I can tell it thinks so."

"Oxes don't eat people!"

"What *do* they eat?"

"Those horns are for spearing people. See, they're sharp! Go right through somebody's belly." The boy made a stabbing motion.

The girl's eyes widened again, and she drew back.

The ox looked at her impassively.

Her eyes teared. She faced the ox and squared her shoulders. "You're not going to eat me, stupid ox!" She picked up a clod of dirt and flung it at the ox's face. The startled animal flinched back. The cart loosed a creak and clatter of wares and old wood joints.

Something fell out of the back of the wagon and landed heavily with a crack at Ken'ishi's feet.

The ox snorted at the children and lowered its horns. The children squealed and scattered like startled gulls.

The peddler ran outside and grabbed the ox's halter, trying to steady the beast. His gaze threw *shuriken* after the children, and he sighed. Then he turned to Ken'ishi with a smile. "Cute little scamps. But no harm in childish play, eh?"

A porcelain statue had fallen from the back of the wagon at Ken'ishi's feet. An elegantly cast likeness of a crane, white and smooth, its long neck broken in the fall.

The peddler clucked in dismay and bent to pick it up. "Terrible!" He shouted after the children. "You vile little bastards!" He sighed again and said to Ken'ishi, "I don't want to think about how much that cost. Made in China and brought all this way! The finest quality!" The peddler sighed again and rubbed his wrinkled forehead.

"It fell out when the wagon jounced." Ken'ishi could not take his eyes from the crane statue. *Destiny....*

"Stupid children! Scaring poor Pon-Pon."

"Where are you bound, sir?" Ken'ishi said.

The peddler twisted his mustache. "Well, I'm nearing the end of my business here in Hoshiya; then I expect I will head north. This is as far south as I usually travel."

"North to where?"

"Dazaifu, then Hakata."

"You have some valuable wares, sir. Don't you fear bandits on the road? I hear there are rough men in these parts."

"One does meet such men occasionally."

"Take me with you, and I'll act as your guard."

"That's very kind, but I cannot pay you—"

"I expect no pay. I would only ask a seat on your wagon."

The peddler shrugged. "The road does get a bit lonely. And you look like a stout, honest young man. Do you have weapons?"

"I do."

"Then load your things. Everyone calls me Shirohige."

"'White Beard?' Did your parents name you that?"

Shirohige smiled. "A joker, are you? We can have many names, many lives between one birth and one death. Shirohige is the life I am living now."

"I am Ken'ishi."

"I'm sure there's an interesting story behind that name. And we'll have time. Pon-Pon here moves at the speed of mud. You'd reach Hakata faster crawling on all fours."

The flower that would
  surrender its fragrance
  before my brushwood
  door
Does so regardless.
I, however, sit and
  stare—
How rueful, this world
      — *Jien, quoted in Takuan Soho's "The Mysterious Record of*
Immovable Wisdom"

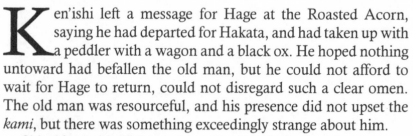

Ken'ishi left a message for Hage at the Roasted Acorn, saying he had departed for Hakata, and had taken up with a peddler with a wagon and a black ox. He hoped nothing untoward had befallen the old man, but he could not afford to wait for Hage to return, could not disregard such a clear omen. The old man was resourceful, and his presence did not upset the *kami*, but there was something exceedingly strange about him.

Shirohige said, "I have one more stop before we leave town. Lord Otomo's household may have need of some fine crockery." The two of them climbed aboard the wagon. Shirohige snicked the reins and began to sing a rhythmic ditty. Between verses, he said, "Pon-Pon likes this song. It practically puts a bounce in his step."

Ken'ishi could not discern any difference in Pon-Pon's

methodical, inexorable plod, whether or not the peddler was singing, but Shirohige had a pleasant enough voice.

At roughly noon, they reached the gate of the castle. Shirohige was forced to stop the cart at the guard post at the base of the hill because the steps built into the fortifications would not allow the passage of wheels. Shirohige went into the castle to seek an audience with the lord's housekeeper.

The guards eyed Ken'ishi while he stood beside the wagon.

Ken'ishi's gaze roved over the impervious, sloped walls of interlocking stones, the stately, white-washed central keep, the terraced tile roofs, the massive iron-bound wooden doors of the main gate, and then over the two armored guards, naginatas in hand. Their faces betrayed little emotion or interest, and sweat sheened their cheeks in the rising heat, soaking their red headbands.

After all the warriors sized each other up, Ken'ishi turned away and looked down the slope toward a well-kept orchard of cherry trees. Oh, but they would be breathtaking in spring. Among the trees, two women strolled hand-in-hand, one carrying a lacquered basket. Their faces were obscured by distance and the tangle of leafy branches, but one of them moved with a captivating grace. His gaze lingered.

The rattle of armor and the tramp of palanquin bearers turned him around. The samurai moved aside for a palanquin, carried by four stout men, coming down the path toward the gate, with four armored bodyguards walking before and four behind. Shades made of fine bamboo slats concealed the occupant. The gild and lacquer gleamed, wrought with elegant patterns of mother-of-pearl feathers. Ken'ishi watched it come, curious about who might ride in such an august conveyance.

A sudden pull dragged his eyes to the palanquin.

The *kami* screamed in his mind.

He found his hand on the hilt of his *bokken,* and at the same moment, one of the bodyguards noticed as well.

"Kneel, *ronin* dog!" the bodyguard snarled, turning toward Ken'ishi, hand on his own sword.

Ken'ishi knelt and pressed his forehead to the cobblestones.

The palanquin stopped, blocked by the wagon.

The bodyguard shouted at Ken'ishi, "Move that wagon! Make way!"

Ken'ishi climbed into the wagon, took the reins as he had seen Shirohige do, and flicked them. The wagon lurched as Pon-Pon jerked, but the wagon rolled aside. The *kami* roared in his awareness like a typhoon wind.

Destiny.

The word rang clear like the clash of blades in his mind, echoing.

Silver Crane was near, painfully near!

But where? Could it be in that palanquin? How could that possibly be?

Or was it the women that had driven the *kami* into such a frenzy? One of them moved so much like ... Kazuko.

Part of him wanted to chase after the palanquin, tear off the flap and look inside, but he would not survive an instant afterward.

Long silken hair and embroidered silk robes like splashes of rainbow floated deeper into the orchard, disappearing from view. Could it have been Kazuko? No, she was married off now to some distant lord.

He watched until the palanquin disappeared down the slope into the town, and was left with a tingling, lingering sensation that something enormous had just passed him by in the darkness of a dream.

"Excuse me, sirs," Ken'ishi said to the samurai. "Who was that in the palanquin?"

One of them glared at him with disdain. "Our lord's chamberlain."

"Do you know where he's going?"

"You ask too many questions."

Shirohige came huffing down the path, brows knit together into a single white caterpillar. Climbing into the wagon, he said, "What's gotten into you? What are you gawking at? You look like you just crossed paths with a monster."

The wooden box with Yasutoki's personal seal sat right beside him in the palanquin. It would not leave his sight until he reached Hakata. The bamboo shades kept out the sun, not to mention unwanted eyes, but they made the interior stiflingly close. He hated making the trip to Hakata in this heat, but Hatsumi's behavior had grown intolerable. With Tsunetomo's leave to acquire ore and charcoal for smithing and new horseflesh from the Kanto Plains, it was time for Yasutoki to remove himself for a while.

He had made inquiries around the castle, but Hatsumi was locked in her room, seeing no one except Kazuko. Some of the servants spoke of her wandering the hallways at night like a weeping ghost.

Lord Tsunetomo had not been happy with Yasutoki's plans to leave again so soon, but he had made a strong case, citing a contact with a horse trader, as Lord Tsunetomo was seeking always to expand his herds.

Tsunemori was, as always, delighted to see Yasutoki packing up to leave for a while. The lord's younger brother was a detestable lunkhead, but too perceptive by far for Yasutoki's comfort. Tsunemori would be buzzing with poisonous talk in Tsunetomo's ear about Yasutoki from this moment until he returned, but that could not be helped. Tsunetomo accepted the enmity between his brother and his chamberlain as a useful tension.

As soon as Yasutoki reached Hakata, he could begin contacting the scattered shreds of his clan. With such a powerful symbol as Silver Crane, they would rally again, reclaim the favor of the emperor's court, and cast down the military usurpers. The Taira would rise again.

As the wagon trundled back down the slope toward the town, Shirohige wore a sour face.

Ken'ishi said, "So you didn't sell anything."

Shirohige spoke through gritted teeth. "The chamberlain had just left the castle, and the chief handmaid of Lady Otomo was indisposed. No one would see me."

"It must be hard, living on the good will of others, making them want to buy your wares. Living by the sword seems easier."

"Words can be like swords. You can win battles or cut your own leg off. You are correct, though. People say I have a natural way of getting along with others. When someone likes you, it's easy to sell them things." The cart rumbled and rocked down the slope, jostling Pon-Pon in his yoke.

Pon-Pon's hindquarters continued their inexorable, plodding rhythm.

Shirohige continued, "A brief stop in Tanushimaru, then Dazaifu. After that, the road to Hakata. We should be there in a few days. There's a man in Tanushimaru who owes me money, and it's time for him to pay up. I would like your help with that. Just a quick stop."

Ken'ishi nodded. "Did he fail to pay for your goods?"

"Um, yes, that's it."

Soon the town lay behind them, and they passed fields thicketed by rice, stalks beginning to sag under the weight of kernels. The road meandered among the terraces and embankments. Irrigation canals channeled water from mountain streams. Hills rose on either side of the fields, shouldering closer, becoming mountains, until they funneled the meandering road into a path between a bamboo-and-pine-covered slope and a gurgling river. The cessation of summer rains had reduced the river to little more than a stream, but it was enough to cool their feet and fill their water gourds.

They reached the village of Tanushimaru in the early evening. Shirohige's demeanor changed when they entered the town. His eyes darted here and there, and he kept trying—unsuccessfully—to whip Pon-Pon to a brisker pace. A pine-swathed mountain swept toward the sky behind the village. On either side of it, terraced fields stepped up and down the slopes. Farmers toiled, backs and straw hats just visible in fields of rice, millet, and buckwheat.

"Just a quick stop," Shirohige kept repeating.

The wagon stopped before a modest house. The air smelled of smoke and baked clay, and a wooden shingle was painted with the characters for earthenware.

Shirohige stepped down from the wagon and smoothed his clothing. "Come. You don't have to do anything. Just look like a rough man."

Ken'ishi's beard had a few straggling hairs, and his clothes were of modest quality, if stained a bit by travel and dust. And he had no sword. He took his *bokken* with him as he followed Shirohige into the potter's shop. He hardly looked rough by any standards. After a few more weeks on the road, perhaps he might.

Inside the shop, shelves were lined with cups and bowls, platters and pitchers. Different colors glazed the pottery, grays, yellows, blues, and earthen browns. The smells of hot earth and smoke were stronger inside.

Shirohige raised his voice, "Hey, Saburo! Come out!"

An old woman's head poked through the curtain from the interior of the house. "Welcome, welcome!" Her face was a map of creases and wrinkles and squinting, watery eyes. Lips collapsed inward, unsupported by any teeth. "May I tell my son who's calling?"

"Good day, madam. Please tell your son that Shirohige is here to see him."

Her eyes narrowed even more, and her jovial demeanor disappeared. She bowed and disappeared without another word.

Voices filtered out from the back of the house—surprise, frustration.

After several long moments, a middle-aged man came through the curtain. He bowed nervously, his thin arms and apron and face smeared with clay. "Good day, sir." His glance flicked over Ken'ishi, the *bokken*. "Would you like some tea? Come in and relax." Shadows and blood circled his eyes.

Shirohige frowned. "You know why we're here."

Ken'ishi glimpsed the old woman's feet shuffling back and forth on the other side of the curtain.

The potter said, "Let us go for a walk." He glanced over his shoulder at the curtain. "I need a bit of exercise." He wiped his callused hands again, trembling, on his apron, his eyes downcast, flicking again toward Ken'ishi's weapon.

Outside, they walked down the street. Saburo looked as if a logjam of words were built up in his chest. He coughed, a wet, raspy sound.

Shirohige said, "So let's have it, Saburo."

"But I don't have any money right now."

"Nonsense! You're one of the best potters in this province. I've seen your work for sale in Hakata." Shirohige's voice was calm, but carried an underlying edge that set Ken'ishi's skin crawling.

"But I can't tell my mother why I've given you so much money! She's taken over the finances since Yoko died of a fever last winter."

"Do you know anyone else who sells what I sell?"

"No, but—"

"Do you want more?"

"Yes! I must have it! My pottery!"

"Then quit your mewling and simpering and give me the money you owe me. I have connections in Hakata. Even if you could find someone else who sells it, it would never be as pure."

"Do you have some with you? Can I buy more today?"

"You'll not get another *momme* until I'm paid in full. After that, I might be willing to sell you more."

"Of course, of course." The potter licked cracked lips, stretching his already drawn cheeks.

Shirohige gave Saburo a hard stare. "Here's what we'll do. We'll go back to your house, and you'll come out with the money you owe me, plus some extra for what you want to buy today. Or else my associate here will smash every bit of pottery on those shelves."

A gasp as the man's eyes bulged in horror. "No, no! You'll have it." His face turned the color of sea foam.

Shirohige's attention returned to the surrounding area, as if he were on the lookout for something.

Ken'ishi noticed the attention of several of the villagers nearby, men and women. Scowls darkened their faces as they watched.

Puzzlement fluttered in Ken'ishi's mind. What was Shirohige

selling? Why did the potter want it so badly? What could make a man's want so palpable? Worse than Ken'ishi's own want for ... a certain woman.

Back at the shop, the potter sneaked back inside.

"Stop looking at me that way," Shirohige said. He chuckled, but without mirth, then lowered his voice. "Just empty threats. I can't very well get paid if he has nothing to sell."

Saburo returned with a string of coins, a sizable sum. Shirohige skeptically counted every coin while Saburo fidgeted and wrung his hands.

Finally Shirohige nodded, "How much more do you want?"

"Six *momme.*"

"You've developed quite an appetite."

"Things are so hard with Yoko gone. So hard to work with my ..."—he struggled with the words, slapped himself above the ear several times—"... mind in such a place."

Shirohige reached into a large earthenware jar and withdrew a palm-sized bundle wrapped in paper. Saburo took and clutched it in both hands, bowing repeatedly, words of thanks pouring from his lips.

"Hey, you old bastard!" A stone whizzed over Shirohige's head.

Saburo stared at the source of the voice, eyes widening.

Shirohige spun with a red flare on his cheeks.

A boy of perhaps thirteen stalked toward them, fists and jaw clenched. The boy's clothes were dirty, face unwashed, hair a greasy thatch.

Shirohige covered his wares with a blanket and gave Ken'ishi a glance of warning. "What do you want?"

The boy stopped ten paces away. "I want you to go back to Hell and stay there. I want a horse to shove his cock up your useless arse, then stomp your hands and feet flat. I want you to choke on your own poison." The fire of the boy's hatred permeated the air of the entire street.

"Hasn't your mother taught you to pay proper respect?"

"She has, to people who deserve some. She excludes you. So you're carting around your own thug now? Think you're a big man or something?"

Shirohige scoffed back at him. "Get out of here, you little turd, before my man here has to show you what happens to bastards who don't respect their elders."

The boy picked up another stone and threw it toward Shirohige's head.

Ken'ishi's *bokken* arced like a flicker and struck the stone to the ground.

The boy's eyes widened, and he gulped. Then his jaw tightened, and he stalked forward again. He stopped three paces from Ken'ishi. "So, *ronin*. What's it like working for a slimy gangster?"

Shirohige snapped his whip toward the boy's head.

Ken'ishi caught it in one hand.

The old man swelled like a puffer fish and tugged on the whip, but Ken'ishi held it fast.

Ken'ishi said, "I'll do the fighting if there's any to be done. That's why I'm here. Boy, you should apologize. Your words have wronged my companion."

The boy spat on the ground. "He should apologize to my mother. She has cursed his name my whole life."

Shirohige growled. "Run along, boy. We don't want any more trouble."

The boy sneered at Ken'ishi. "How much does he pay you? What's your job? Beating up whores and lotus eaters? Squeezing them for coin?"

Ken'ishi's jaw tightened like a drawn bowstring, but he did not move or speak. A sense of wonder dawned in him at the boy's raw vitriol.

The boy took a step closer, his dark angry gaze chipping at Ken'ishi's composure. "Perhaps I should question *your* ancestry. Perhaps I should call *your* mother a whore, as he's called mine. Perhaps you're the son of an unclean leatherer, or gravedigger, or shit—"

Ken'ishi's slap sent him sprawling.

The boy propped himself up on his elbows. Hard, black eyes blinked back tears of pain. A scarlet handprint blossomed on his cheek. "That's the spirit, big man! Does it make you feel strong?"

"If you don't stop," Ken'ishi said, "I'll gag you and tie you up in the street. Control yourself."

The boy scrabbled out of the dirt and flung himself up, plowing into Ken'ishi's belly, fists flailing. Ken'ishi caught him by the arms until sharp teeth buried themselves in Ken'ishi's hand. Ken'ishi spurned him, but the fists flew again. The boy's strength surprised him, a bundle of taut limbs and seething rage. Ken'ishi spurned him again.

"Fight me like a man, coward!" the boy screamed.

"Why do you want to fight?"

Thoughts flickered behind the boy's eyes, a moment of confusion. Then he flung himself forward again.

Ken'ishi's fist met the boy's incoming forehead.

The boy's head snapped back, his legs crumpled, and he doubled backwards into a pile, where he lay senseless for a few moments.

Ken'ishi stood over him, shaking the pain out of his fist.

The boy's eyes fluttered, glazed, tears running from the corners. He tried to struggle to his feet, but Ken'ishi's wooden sandal against his chest pressed him down.

"Let me go, you bastard!"

Ken'ishi found the boy's anger so unnatural, so disturbing that he wished him no further harm. The suffering of life already etched his face for a boy so young. "How old are you?"

"None of your business, shithead!"

"Tell me."

The boy spat. "I'm twelve."

"Do you want to die?"

"Some days it's all I want. Some days I ... want to kill every swindler, every drunkard, and every thug I see! Starting with *him!*"

Shirohige sneered, "That'll be the day, you cur! Ken'ishi, leave him."

Ken'ishi kept his foot in place. "You think you're going to be a rough man yourself? Not if you continue. I don't want to hurt you anymore, but I'm not going to let you keep this up, and I'm not

151

going to let you try to harm my companion. Now, calm yourself and go away, or I will hurt you."

Shirohige said, "Get into the wagon. If he tries anything, shoot him for a thief and a beggar."

Ken'ishi removed his foot, and the boy glared up at him, simmering, silent. Ken'ishi backed away. "I'll follow alongside."

Shirohige snapped the reins, and Pon-Pon lurched the wagon forward.

Ken'ishi kept a close eye on the boy. The boy stood, tears streaming down his face, lips trembling, breaths choking with rage. His eyes burned into Ken'ishi until the wagon finally rounded a corner and the boy disappeared from sight.

Ken'ishi climbed into the wagon. "Explain."

"You cannot reason with such people. Bastards like him."

"His hatred for you is unlike anything I've ever seen."

Shirohige sighed a little and shook his head. "The boy's mother says he's of my seed. I say there's no way for her to be sure. She was just a tavern girl at the time. He's just another fatherless cur with too much anger in his heart."

"What about his mother?"

"She was passing pretty back then, a real squealer. But nowadays," he shrugged, "she looks like a leathery old sow. Too much anger in her heart as well. That's where he learned it, I'd wager."

Ken'ishi watched him for a while.

Shirohige's eyes glistened, softening, and he swallowed hard. "Stop looking at me that way."

The mournful calm settled over Ken'ishi's heart. Had this boy ever been the inquisitive, happy little boy that Little Frog was? Would Little Frog's life come to look like this boy's, filled with unfocused rage and pain, flinging himself against the walls of society and screaming to be heard? Ken'ishi sighed.

Moreover, Shirohige was clearly not the sort of man with whom respectable samurai would ever associate themselves. As soon as Ken'ishi felt his destiny would allow, he would leave this old scoundrel's company.

Shirohige broke his reverie. "It's getting dark. We'll camp when we're farther from the village. Wouldn't want that little bastard to chase us and cause more trouble. It would be just like him. He and his mother are a vindictive lot. I haven't heard many tales of bandits in these parts lately, so we shouldn't have to worry. Not since that *oni* bandit chieftain was killed."

"Hakamadare."

"Yes, that was him. A nasty fellow, so I heard."

"A bloodthirsty demon."

"Half the domains on Kyushu feared him. And Lord Otomo maintains a strong peace in these parts. Stringing a few bandits up by the neck discourages successors."

"You say that as if Lord Otomo is doing the wrong thing."

"I think every man should be able to carve out a place for himself. The world is full of people who aren't smart enough or strong enough to take care of themselves. Why shouldn't what the weak have be taken by the strong? The strong and the clever are more deserving. For example, that potter has a taste for the lotus. I didn't give him that taste, but I'll certainly profit from his weakness and stupidity. And why shouldn't I?"

"He looked ... strange. Half-mad with want for it."

"That's what happens when you use too much of the stuff." Shirohige shrugged. "The sensations are the closest thing to nirvana in this life, but the effects don't last. Some people are so hungry for a taste of heaven that they keep reaching for it, unable to see the illusion."

"Life is suffering, so the Buddhists say."

"I can vouch for that. So I find my pleasure wherever I can."

"Where do you get it, this lotus?"

"It comes from China. I know some people in Hakata."

"Have you ever tried it?"

"Of course. Many times when I was younger."

"But you stopped. You didn't have the same want as the potter?"

"I had one very bad night. I was in Kumamoto and had a little too much in a lotus den. Ran afoul of some trouble, evil whores and their muscle who stole all my money and left me beaten in an alley. I can't afford to muddle my brain like that anymore." He gave Ken'ishi a smile, missing a couple of teeth. "Would you like to try some? I'll give you a taste. You don't even have to pay me. It's already been a profitable day."

Ken'ishi thought about this. He had indulged in too much *saké* before, and while it made him more talkative and boisterous, he hated the next day's fuzzy mind and aching head. A taste of heaven on earth? He had never heard of such a thing before.

Shirohige said, "Lotus has a powerful effect, powerful. Like nothing you've ever experienced. That kind of power can put hooks into the weak minded. If you're a strong man, you needn't worry about ending up like that potter. Besides, you have me to watch out for you." Shirohige looked askance at Ken'ishi, calculations flickering behind his eyes, thoughts Ken'ishi did not like. "In any case, we'll camp soon before the mosquitoes devour us to the bone." He slapped his neck. "I like you, samurai. You're a simple soul. A strong one. Together we could make a lot of money."

"By taking from people. Isn't it the place of the strong to protect the weak? The purpose of the warrior is to serve."

"Samurai must serve a master, yes, but one doesn't see many samurai working for peasants nowadays, does one? Lords are strong men, they must be. If they're not strong, they don't remain lords for very long. There's much to be admired in thinking about the betterment of others. But as I said, you're a strong man. I'll wager if there's something you want, very little will stand in your way. Even an angry peasant boy."

Ken'ishi scratched his head and could not find an answer.

Whether by the strike of the enemy or your own thrust, whether by the man who strikes or the sword that strikes, whether by position  or rhythm, if your mind is diverted in any way, your actions will falter, and this can mean that you will be cut down.

—*Takuan Soho, "The Mysterious Record of Immovable Wisdom"*

Ken'ishi draped a blanket over a rope tied above his sleeping pallet to keep out the evening mosquitoes, but the summer air under the blanket was stifling. He wished wholeheartedly for a mosquito net. He got up and threw wet leaves on the fire, hoping the smoke would drive away the incessant buzzing clouds. He paced, slapping at his face and arms and legs, his frustration growing with every tiny prick.

Shirohige lay in the back of the wagon with a small net propped over him, snoring.

As Ken'ishi paced and fumed, memories flooded out of black depths. Kazuko's exquisite face, soulful eyes glimmering with love and desire, the sound of her little gasps of pleasure as they coupled, the explosion of heat as her body spasmed and clutched him, the shape of her young breasts and the feel of her skin, the taste of her mouth, of her throat.

None of which he would ever see or hear or taste or smell or feel again.

All of those memories flowed like dyes of mixed colors into similar memories with Kiosé. Both sets of memories so sweet and hot and beautiful, but both steeped with longing for what had been lost. Kiosé's eyes looking at him with indifference and confusion, unremembering their many nights together. Little Frog playing alone, indifferent to his presence. Ken'ishi's feet turning away toward the horizon, chasing an ancient piece of cold, heartless steel.

He would never see Silver Crane again. He would never know the truth of his father's death. He would never be a true samurai. He would never see Kiosé again, or Little Frog, or Kazuko. Or Akao, a friend more faithful than any human. He was a man without a home, wandering a bleak, empty road, pretending to play samurai with a stick. Blackness descended over his thoughts like a midnight ice storm.

"Shirohige."

"Mmf ..."

"Shirohige. Wake up."

"I'm trying to sleep." Shirohige rolled his back toward Ken'ishi.

"I want to try your lotus."

Shirohige's breathing froze. He sat up and rubbed awareness into his face. "Are you sure?"

"I have need of a bit of heaven tonight."

Shirohige gave him a long, searching look, then shrugged and started rummaging through his wares. "Here." He took out a small block of dark brown substance, then pulled out a dagger and shaved a piece from the block. He held the tiny shaving in his palm and offered it to Ken'ishi. "Eat this. Or swallow it. Tastes like hell. Wash it down with some water. It won't take long."

Ken'ishi took the shaving skeptically. So much power in such a little piece of what looked like resin? He thought about the want he had seen on the potter's face, the wasted, empty desperation hollowing out the potter's eyes.

Shirohige said, "Go on. It won't hurt you. If you're thinking about Saburo, you needn't worry. He's been a lotus eater for years. You're too strong to become like him."

Ken'ishi sat near the fire, even though the night was warm and humid, hoping that the smoke would keep the mosquitoes at bay. He looked at the substance again and lifted it to his mouth. The harsh bitterness almost made him retch, the resin sticking to his tongue, but he swallowed it, making a disgusted noise, and washed it down with long drinks of water. His mouth and tongue grew numb. A peculiar warmth grew in his belly. He sat on the ground, leaning back against a wagon wheel.

Tethered to a nearby tree, Pon-Pon placidly chewed his cud and watched Ken'ishi, ears and tail flicking at mosquitoes.

For a long time, he lay against the wheel, waiting for heaven to come to him. After a while, the night seemed to encroach upon the circle of trees at the fringe of the firelight. He did not feel the prick of mosquitoes now.

He caught himself rubbing his arms at a strange, tingling sensation. The firelight blurred, and sweet warmth suffused him like the moments when he released his seed, only longer, less convulsive. He slid to his side with a deep, contented sigh, his heart slowing to a deep, sonorous rhythm, his every movement as languid as oil.

Thoughts of loss and pain and longing, gone, as if they had never been. Heaven indeed.

The bamboo and pine forest hedging the campsite slid into blackness. His mind fell away, and he found himself effortlessly in the Void. There was no past, no future, only the now moment, and a pinpoint of his awareness in the vast blackness of the universe. He swam through the Void like a sea creature from the darkest depths.

From the blackness emerged a low rumble, like a growl, but deeper than any growl he had ever heard, so deep he felt it in his joints, as if it emanated from the earth itself.

Two yellow eyes, simmering with voracious cunning, emerged

from the blackness between the bamboo trunks. Great fangs the size of his finger, slavering jaws. The massive shape slunk from the blackness on striped paws the size of his face, long, striped tail writhing like a snake, the massive muscles of its shoulders and low-slung body sliding and bunching under orange and black stripes.

He looked at the tiger with a sense of bemused wonder. He wondered what that might be like, to be eaten. He picked up a handful of dirt and flung it toward the tiger. The dirt pattered, and the tiger crept forward. Its hot breath swirled through the smoke of the fire, sending embers into gentle spirals. He could smell the blood on its breath. He wondered vaguely if Shirohige would be concerned about a tiger in camp, but Shirohige's snores had vanished into the nothingness.

The flutter of wings dragged his attention to the opposite side of the fire. Stately white wings gleamed like mother-of-pearl in the firelight, a span as wide as Ken'ishi's outstretched arms, a long graceful neck, bright eyes sparkling with wisdom, its long spindly legs gangly and unsupportive. The crane danced and hopped from one leg to the other, eyeing Ken'ishi, as if performing for him. The crane steadied itself with its outspread wings as it danced.

The tiger swiped a massive paw at the crane, but the crane leaped back with a single wing flap, one leg bent. The tiger snarled and swiped at the crane again, and again the crane danced back. The crane's grace and wisdom permeated every movement. The tiger's cunning and ferocity seethed beneath every hair—and its determination.

Ken'ishi was but an afterthought, a morsel. The tiger wanted the crane for its meal.

The tiger's leap scattered coals and embers, startling Ken'ishi from his stupor. A flash of orange and black fur, a flurry of feathers, a snarl and a squawk, and the crane was in the tiger's mouth. The tiger shook its head as the crane stabbed at the tiger's eyes with its beak. The tiger disappeared into the blackness between the bamboo trunks with the crane in its jaws.

Ken'ishi stood, and the world rippled strangely around him. On unsteady legs he wandered after the tiger. "Wait," he called. The tiger's movements, the flapping of the crane's wings, disappeared into the abyss of night. He followed.

He emerged atop a mountain, at sunrise, or sunset, overlooking a great sacred river as it flowed through emerald hills toward a distant silvery sea. The scent of incense drifted up through the forest from the towers and temples along the river. Great caverns yawned on the faces of the hills, filled with torchlight and music, and at the height of the farthest hill lay a massive golden dome gleaming like the sun fallen to earth.

A raft of reed bundles awaited him beside the river, and he climbed upon it. The river took the raft in the breast of its current and swept downstream.

On either side, new sights shattered previous imagination, feasts and horrors and delights and terrors, and many things he would never see again.

A naked maiden with skin the color of black tea and a foam of long, ebony hair, strumming beatifically on a stringed instrument shaped like a cloven teardrop, raising a melody so sweet that he nearly wept.

On the other side of the river, a woman wailed for her demon lover who lay beheaded at her side. Her long, black claws raked bloody furrows in her face, her blood mixing with the streams of black tears, like the streaks on the face of Taro, the constable's deputy, who had become a demon in his lust for vengeance, who had slain Akao on the night Little Frog was born, and who had finally fallen to Silver Crane's razor edge. Three stubby horns emerged from the woman's forehead. He knew this woman, and she knew him. Hatsumi, Kazuko's old handmaid, leveled a gnarled claw at him, black eyes burning with hatred. "Beware, *beware!*"

Toward the great golden dome the river swept his fragile craft. Shadows rose from the foundations of the emerald hills, from the forests, from the bed of the sacred river.

"War," the shadows said. The word fell over him like a chill rhythm. "War. *War. WAR.*" The shadows flitted and chanted, a great chorus of discordant whispers and trembling, until the river rose to a tumult and swept the raft deep into the heart of the great dome.

Within the edifice, the sky was golden, and the air smelled of incense and the musky perfume of arousal. The banks of the river were crammed on both sides with grim-faced warriors on horseback, warriors made of horn and steel and leather, spired helmets, knots of taut muscle bristling with bows and arrows and malice.

Thousands of dark eyes watched him pass, sizing him up and finding him unworthy.

The hordes of horsemen parted, and there on a massive golden throne sat a man, knee deep in dozens—hundreds—of naked, nubile concubines, all fawning over him, pleasuring themselves and each other, hundreds of them spilling away in a moaning, writhing swell.

The man's armor gleamed golden in the sun, and his face was round and blunt, his eyes as sharp as steel arrow points, with long pointed mustaches dangling past the spear of beard on his chin. His hand rested on the upright pommel of a short, curved, broad-bladed sword, sticking point-down into a mound of human skulls. A conqueror beyond the ken of history.

Ken'ishi and the conqueror locked gazes as the river pushed the raft onward, and then out of the dome, past the last foam-flecked boulders of shoreline and out to sea.

He could not paddle, and there was no oar, but the current dragged the raft out into the vastness of the ocean, until the sky grew black, and the wind drove the waves to higher and higher peaks, cold brine sprayed his face, and he dropped to his knees to clutch the raft tight as the waves tossed it higher and higher. A terrible wind blasted over him, and then a rain, and suddenly he was surrounded by an ocean of death, untold thousands of bloated corpses flopping in the tumult like rotting, fish-eaten dolls. Splinters of shattered ships swirled through the foaming waters, and the wind howled like a lost child, and the rain fell in sheets of solid water.

A voice tore with rage and despair into his awareness. *"You bastard!"*

Ken'ishi shook his head. The roar of typhoon and sea receded.

"Get off there, you vile little bastard!"

Fishing weights held Ken'ishi's eyes closed, but he brushed them aside, struggling onto his elbows.

In the light of the scattered coals, Ken'ishi opened his eyes to see Shirohige swinging the *bokken* at something in the back of the wagon. The dark, furry shape dodged back, its eyes wearing what looked like a black mask. The sound of trickling water on paper. The creature squatted atop one of Shirohige's earthen jars.

Ken'ishi tried to shake the blurriness from his vision.

Shirohige roared and swung the wooden sword again.

The creature leaped adroitly from atop the jar and across to the other side of the wagon, its weight tumbling small pottery pieces together, shattering them, scattering everything in all directions.

The *tanuki*'s eyes sparkled with mischief, and it bared its teeth as if in a taunting grin. The *bokken* swished, and the *tanuki* danced aside. More crockery crashed.

Shirohige snapped at Ken'ishi, "Get up, you lazy oaf! This filthy beast just pissed all over my lotus supply!"

Ken'ishi struggled to his feet, wobbling, trying to blink the fuzziness out of his eyes, his mind.

The *tanuki* leaped, and Shirohige swung. The leap was poorly timed. The *bokken* struck the *tanuki*'s side—

And then it wasn't a *bokken* anymore. Handfuls of cherry blossoms exploded through the air, whiffing over the *tanuki*'s back and dispersing through Shirohige's fingers.

The *tanuki* chittered, almost like a laugh, and disappeared into the night.

"Unclean beast!" Shirohige raged after it. "Ride an *oni* to hell!" Then he turned to Ken'ishi, scowling. "And a fat lot of help you were!" He went to the side of the wagon and surveyed the damage. "So many pieces broken! Now they're so much garbage." He sniffed the large jar where he had kept his supply of lotus, wrinkling his nose at the stench. "Ruined! All of it! Foul creature!" He shook his fist at the night, then leaned against the side of the wagon and sighed. "The entire world is against me. Even the animals." He scratched his head. "Perhaps a lotus-eater as far gone as Saburo won't notice the stench or the taste ..."

All Ken'ishi could do was sit back down and watch the coals die.

Without looking at right and wrong, he is able to see right and wrong; without attempting to discriminate, he is able to discriminate well. This  means that concerning his martial art, he does not look at it to say "correct" or "incorrect," but he is able to see which it is. He does not attempt to judge matters but is able to do so well.

—*Takuan Soho, "The Clear Sound of Jewels"*

The next morning lay swathed in a foggy haze. Ken'ishi became aware of the world again as the pressure of life impinged upon his muddled senses. The morning lay dewy cool amid the rustling of bamboo leaves and the now-incomprehensible call of birds. The scattered coals of the fire had burned to ash. In the blurry haze of his vision, the entire world was ash. Shirohige lay again in the back of the wagon, snoring with a sound like a tree being felled.

Ken'ishi remembered little after the *tanuki* disappeared, but as he stood up, he spotted his *bokken* lying near the wagon. He picked it up and examined it. It was scarred by use, but whole. He scratched his head and rubbed his face.

So many images last night burned into his memory. Unlike so many other dreams that faded mere heartbeats after waking up, last night's grew sharper as the fog of sleep lifted.

He had seen his sword turn into cherry blossoms. He had seen a tiger and a crane locked in combat. He had seen hordes of barbarian warriors, the river, the great golden dome, the typhoon. All of it more vivid, like painted images on the walls of his mind, than much of what he had done yesterday or the day before in the everyday world. There were no tigers in Japan, except perhaps in a court noble's menagerie. Tigers were a creature of fables and far-off lands. The campfire had been scattered, to be sure, but he could have done that himself in his stupor. Nevertheless, he circled the camp looking for tracks. The only tracks besides his and Shirohige's were the dog-like, four-toed, clawed tracks of a *tanuki*.

Ken'ishi moved to the wagon and sniffed the jar where the old man had kept his lotus supply. The jar reeked of piss. That part had not been a dream. But the *bokken*? He had seen stranger things, he supposed.

Shirohige rolled over, chomping back snores. Even in sleep, his face bore no kindness, no innocence, no calmness.

Ken'ishi felt a tightness in his shoulders, in his jaw, in his fists, as he looked at the old man. The world had squeezed Shirohige, drained him of life, left his spirit as shriveled and leathery as a fallen persimmon left in the sun. He now fed on the lives of others.

The thought of spending two more days in his presence as they rode to Hakata filled Ken'ishi with misgivings. He would not become this old man's personal thug. The way Shirohige had manipulated the potter's raw desire, the way he had treated the children in Hoshiya, his reaction to a boy who could be his son. So many ways that the old man could have let a spark of kindness emerge, but did not.

And yet, how could Ken'ishi leave before they reached Hakata? He could make his own way there if need be, but something told him that his and Shirohige's paths had intersected for a reason.

He took his *bokken* into the forest and found a quiet place on a large boulder to practice his sword techniques. As he breathed deep and sought the Void, he found his mind to be muddled, fuzzed by dust, like a ball of sticky *mochi* dropped under a table.

He moved through the series of practice movements he had known by rote for years, the same series that he constantly sought to perfect. Some days, flashes of perfection gave him joy; never had he performed every movement with complete perfection. He always noticed tiny errors in his form, tiny disruptions in his rhythm, tiny thoughts flitting into his mind and blocking his release into the No-Mind. His martial art had gone stagnant. It felt dead in him, like a rice field deprived of water. And even as he thought these thoughts, he knew they were intruding upon his practice. So much flotsam and jetsam of life and desires in his mind. Was it his mind or after-effects of the lotus?

Nevertheless, he did not stop. He struck and moved, struck and moved until he felt the warmth of sweat on his chest and back, going through the series over and over again, knowing that, as his master had once taught him, even in unsuccessful practice, there is knowledge, tiny imperceptible steps toward perfection.

Returning to camp, he found Shirohige in the wagon sourly sifting through the broken pottery and casting it onto the ground. He grunted at Ken'ishi's approach. "Filthy beast. It picked an opportune time, with my sole protector in the land of lotus dreams. Did you find your heaven?"

Ken'ishi recalled the incredible rush of pleasure and well-being. "With all the suffering in the world, I can see why people eat it. But today, my mind is too scattered. I don't like that."

Shirohige nodded. "You're a wise man for one of your years. Most people never figure that out. Besides, if you want any more, you'll have to pay me. Touching heaven costs money."

"And money is your reason for existence."

The old man stopped and glared. "Don't you dare judge me, stripling! I've seen more suffering in this world than you can imagine. Thieves, thugs, rulers who treat people as slaves. Don't you doubt that I'll take from someone weaker than me, and I'll enjoy it until the next foul bastard comes along who takes it from me. All the world is a hierarchy of taking, boy. Now, set your arse in the wagon and stop looking at me that way."

Roads and villages passed behind them with the incessant rattle of the wagon and inexorable undulation of Pon-Pon's hindquarters. Shirohige had been taciturn since their exchange in the early morning. Ken'ishi passed the time playing on his flute, something he had done less and less of in recent months. Nevertheless, he found that with a little practice his skill returned, and soon the strains of his own emotions flowed onto the air like birdsong.

He found his thoughts drifting to Kiosé as he played, and Shirohige soon grunted at him. "If you keep playing such music, I'll have to hang myself from despair. Play something merrier."

In the villages they passed, Shirohige peddled his wares with a beaming smile and an amiable demeanor, but on the road again, he grew sour and surly. His jaw chomped at something. "I don't like it when someone thinks he's better than me, boy."

"We have different paths. For now, our paths have merged."

"What are you doing here anyway? Why are you going to Hakata?"

"Something was stolen from me. I intend to take it back."

"And I don't suppose you'll tell me what that was. Who are you, anyway?"

"I am a *ronin*. That is all there is."

"You know, I did not ask to you to ride with me by accident. I saw you there. I heard about you. The man with the wooden sword. The man who laid some pain upon Green Tiger's men in Hita town."

Ken'ishi's hand slid toward his *bokken*. "Why did you invite me to come with you?"

"I wanted to size you up. Green Tiger is not the only boss around. I don't work for him, don't worry."

"Perhaps not, but perhaps he would pay handsomely for information about who defeated his men."

Shirohige looked shocked. "What kind of man do you take me for?"

Ken'ishi listened for the *kami* and heard no warning. "Who do you work for?"

Shirohige smoothed himself. "Myself, but I do know people."

"What kind of people do you know?"

"The Chinese gang that supplies me with lotus for one. Are you looking for someone?"

"Yes."

"The one who stole whatever it was?"

"Yes." The dream of a tiger and a crane.

"Perhaps Green Tiger would know. Perhaps you should talk to him."

"Or perhaps he is responsible."

Shirohige gulped. "Then you may as well give it up."

"Do you know how to find him?"

"I can help you find him, if you're in a hurry to meet your ancestors. But he may find you first if he hears you beat up his men in Hita. Even the other gangs give him a wide berth."

Ken'ishi thought about this for a while, and about the dream, and about the pebble-trail of fortunes that had led him this far. It seemed that Green Tiger and Silver Crane were connected somehow. "What do you want in return?"

"Why, just your kindness, of course!" Shirohige held a straight face for only a heartbeat, then roared with laughter until his eyes teared. He wiped his ruddy cheeks and said, "Fear not, I never forget debts owed to me. I may have need of your wooden sword someday. Perhaps if another *tanuki* comes around, you'll be awake enough to stove in its skull before it can do any damage."

Two days later, free of any further *tanuki* depredations or encounters with angry village boys, Ken'ishi and Shirohige arrived at the outskirts of Hakata. Ken'ishi immediately recognized the glimmering expanse of Hakata Bay. Strange to see it from a different perspective. The dark bulks of Shika, Nokono, and Aino Islands rising from the sun-drenched sea, the sailed specks of ships and fishing boats. The shore where Aoka village lay nestled was many *ri* to the east, lost in the blue-gray distance. From Dazaifu, the road had followed the Ox Horn River toward the north, eventually meandering between the congealing clusters of houses and shops and warehouses that formed the outskirts of Hakata, to empty further along into the bay.

Over the course of the journey, Ken'ishi often wondered what happened to Hage, of whom there had been no sign. He hoped the old man was well. Hage was a much more pleasant traveling companion than Shirohige, who flopped between a charming amiability, effective at times in his efforts to sell his wares, and a dark, bitter selfishness, where all the world lay poised to do him wrong. In every town and village, people knew who Shirohige was, and they either welcomed him or gave him wary glances.

Throughout the journey, he often listened to the birdsong and felt the frustration of being unable to understand, like trying to listen to a conversation through a door. If only he could find the latch on the door, throw it open, and reenter that world. He had never had wont of friends, or at least a conversation, when there were no other human beings around. Birds and creatures of the earth were everywhere and always surprised to encounter a human who could speak the tongue of their world.

The wagon descended into the thick of the city's labyrinthine streets and bridges. All rivers in northern Kyushu converged on Hakata, emptying into Hakata Bay, and the city lay astride those rivers with bridges and canals, using the waterways to divide itself into a host of districts and wards.

Dazaifu was a city, certainly, but it was infused with an air of old, stuffy authority, whereas Hakata was a bustling port filled with enterprising merchants and sailors, craftsmen and laborers, well-heeled samurai and scruffy *ronin* alike.

Shirohige reined up Pon-Pon before a house of respectable size, near a stone-banked canal smelling of sewage and moss. "You can stay at my house until you find what you're looking for. You're an honest sort. I don't expect you'll steal anything."

Ken'ishi silently wished that he could say the same of Shirohige. Nevertheless, he accepted the offer.

"Don't mind my sister," Shirohige said. "She's a bitter old hag, but she's a good cook."

Shirohige unlatched the gate and led Pon-Pon into the small

courtyard. The ox allowed himself to be unyoked and led into a small pen, where Shirohige dumped some millet from a sack into a narrow trough.

The respect, almost affection, that Shirohige displayed in his husbandry surprised Ken'ishi. "You seem to have more regard for that ox than you do for human beings."

"Pon-Pon hasn't a cruel or deceptive hair on his hide, unlike human beings. He's almost like a big, stupid dog."

Pon-Pon tossed his head and snorted at Shirohige.

Ken'ishi understood that appeal. He'd had such a friend once, with a red wagging tail.

Shirohige gestured for Ken'ishi to follow. "Come, let us go inside and revel in Junko's panic. She won't be expecting a guest."

The house was fine enough to warrant a tile roof, rather than a thatched one, but the tiles were broken in places, or perhaps peeled away by past typhoon winds. The exterior of the house looked dark and stained by time. The steps creaked and sagged under Ken'ishi's feet.

Shirohige called into the house as they stood in the entryway and slipped out of their shoes. "I'm home!"

"It's about damn time!" came a voice like a crow's. "I was expecting you days ago! Dallying with some whore, were you?"

Shirohige sighed. "Ah, a voice like a nightingale."

"Who are you talking to?"

"We have a guest, my dear sister."

"A guest! Are you out of your mind? Bringing a guest to this cesspit?" The sound of frenzied shuffling from some other room.

Moments later, an old woman stepped into the foyer, her cragged face split by a wide toothless grin. Gray-streaked hair was pulled into a tight bun, and her prominently curved spine bobbed as she bowed to Ken'ishi. "Welcome, sir, to this meager patch of ill-kept hell. You'll have to forgive me. I'm a terrible housekeeper. Shame on you, brother, for not telling me you were bringing a guest."

Ken'ishi bowed. "A pleasure to meet you, madam."

Shirohige stepped up from foyer to the raised *tatami* floor. "I

169

had not planned it, but … let us say we met on the road and have some mutual interests."

Her eyes glittered as she beheld Ken'ishi. "He's a handsome one. I can see why you brought him along."

Shirohige scoffed. "Don't mind her. She's never had a husband."

She countered, batting her eyelashes at Ken'ishi, "Don't mind him. I've never seen the need to settle on one man. But come in, come in. You must be tired from the road. I'll make tea."

That night, after a modest meal of fish soup, steamed cabbage, and rice, Shirohige smacked his lips over the tea. "Brought all the way from the old capital, this tea. Kyoto tea is still superior. I know a good tea merchant here."

Ken'ishi tasted it, considering the subtle differences in flavor from the tea grown in the mountains of Kyushu.

Junko sat nearby, leering at Ken'ishi, checking her hair, smoothing her old, stained robes as if they were court finery.

Shirohige said, "So, of course I would like to ask you what your plans are, but you're so damnably tight-lipped I don't expect you'll tell me anyway. But here's what I'll do. I'll go out tomorrow and talk to some people. If possible, I'll arrange a meeting."

Ken'ishi glanced at Junko.

Junko said, "Oh, don't worry about me, deary. You've no need to hide anything from my delicate feminine sensibilities. I ran a whorehouse near the docks for eighteen years. Perhaps I can help you. Of course, there's always a price, isn't there?" She waggled her naked eyebrows.

Ken'ishi swallowed hard and shoved away visions of what that might entail.

Shirohige said, "He thinks he's looking for Green Tiger."

Her face darkened. "Then I suppose he won't be staying long, what with such a death wish. No one has ever seen his face. One of my muscle boys ran afoul of him some years ago over some gambling debts. Granted, it was a boon for *me* that he lost his nose and ears—a face like that frightens people into line—but I doubt he much enjoyed it."

Ken'ishi sipped his tea. "I'll be careful."

She shrugged. "If you're not, you'll be dead, or worse. He's a hard man to find."

Shirohige said, "I have some ideas for that. The White Lotus."

Junko's withered lips collapsed into her face. "Filthy Chinese. A bunch of mongrel dogs. Be careful there, too, boy. A rough bunch, the White Lotus. But they might have a means of contacting Green Tiger. You'll have to keep your wits about you. I'm loath to see that pretty face of yours marred."

"I appreciate your concern, madam. I will be careful."

She rolled her eyes. "So says the stripling with no idea of what he's walking into." Then she sighed. "Well, you fellows enjoy yourselves. I'm off to wash my crotch. Ken'ishi, if you decide to avail yourself of it, my room is over there."

Shirohige flung a dismissive gesture at her. "Foul-mouthed witch! Begone!"

As she tottered away with her back hunched almost double, Ken'ishi took a deep breath, swallowed hard, and tried to sip his tea and ignore the loud sounds of bathing from the *ofuro*.

The uguisu sleeps in the
  bamboo grove,
One night a man traps her
  in a bamboo trap,
Now she sleeps in a
  bamboo cage.
      — *The Love Poems of*
        Marichiko

The naginata haft slid easily through Kazuko's hands as she flew through the practice movements. The arm-length blade glinted like a curved icicle as it spun and slashed at the end of the pole.

Master Higuchi scrutinized every movement with eyes as deep and glittering as the night sky, and just as impassive—that is, until she made a mistake. The naginata master could have been thirty-five or fifty-five. He kept his head clean-shaven, not like a samurai but in the fashion of a monk. When she asked him about it once, he gave her a faint smile and said that the sun reflecting off his bald head would blind his enemies. He wore his customary breastplate, greaves, and arm guards, naginata resting upright in his grip. He called out the names and cadence of the movements in sharp staccato syllables, and she responded in kind, using her voice to focus her spirit, body, and weapon into every strike.

Salty sweat moistened her lips and sheened her face, in spite of the cool morning air in the shadows of the castle walls. Sweat plastered her simple practice tunic and trousers to her body. She knew every scar and gouge on the practice post. She knew the heft and balance of her practice naginata, the feel of the oval-carved haft. Her father had trained her when she was a maiden, and now her husband had engaged Master Higuchi to train her. Tsunetomo had even given her exclusive use of his retainers' practice yard every day for as long as Master Higuchi required.

Nearby stood a dozen upright cylinders of fresh, green *tatami*, each about as thick as her leg, said to exhibit the same resistance to cutting as a human body. Her real naginata waited nearby, sheathed and freshly polished. Her husband had commissioned a naginata for her from Shintogo no Kunimitsu of the Awataguchi School, swordsmiths to the Hojo clan, and the smith's renown proved to be well-founded.

Her favorite part of daily practice was when she was given leave to unsheathe the real weapon, see the immaculate gleam of the blade and hear the unique sound as it sliced through air and imaginary enemies. How many imaginary *tatami* enemies she had slain she could scarcely fathom. She relished the power of the weapon. With the increased leverage of the long haft, a skilled stroke could cleave a man in two from shoulder to crotch. The only time she had ever used a naginata in real battle was against the horrid *oni* bandit, Hakamadare.

In the early days of her marriage, the training had given her respite from her despair over her longing for Ken'ishi, giving her a sense of power that she could find nowhere else. Nowadays, she found herself taking pride in her growing skill and strength.

Tsunetomo once said, "Some men prefer their women soft and meek, but I enjoy the spirit that martial training cultivates in you. I don't want my wife to be a meek little girl. I want a woman strong enough to stand up to any man."

Every day, Master Higuchi drove her to the limits of her endurance, every day the sessions growing longer and longer. It was as if he could see the verge of her collapse, and he let her reach that point before he ended practice. She had not reached it yet today, but she could feel it coming.

A deep, clear voice echoed through the practice yard. "Master Higuchi, enough for today."

Master Higuchi bowed low to the man striding across the practice yard.

Tsunetomo was dressed in his customary robe and trousers, garments of impeccable quality, fine silk and cotton, but not ostentatious, his high black cap atop his head, riding like the fin of a shark, his already broad shoulders extended by his stiff jacket. As always, he wore his short sword thrust into his immaculately wrapped *obi*.

Kazuko ceased her practice and bowed to him, careful to shift the naginata to her left hand and point it away from him. Carelessness with a weapon was disrespectful in his presence, even during practice. Her father, Lord Nishimuta, had once stripped a retainer of his rank because the samurai had carelessly allowed his sword to point at Lord Nishimuta during a promotion ceremony. Her father had said afterward that he had been lenient with the careless samurai. To do such at thing at court invited a death sentence.

With a moment of surprise, she found herself admiring her husband's strong, sure gait, a little bowlegged from much time spent in the saddle.

Tsunetomo and Master Higuchi exchanged pleasantries, and Master Higuchi bowed to her and excused himself. Then her husband came to her. "Your practice is going well, my dear. I have never seen a woman with your skill and dedication to martial matters."

She blushed. "You flatter me, Husband."

"Hardly. You are Tomoé Gozen reborn. Strong and beautiful, a warrior angel. Worthy of a shogun."

"Now you truly flatter me. Tomoé Gozen was an archer and skilled on a horse. I can do neither of those things."

He gave her a wry smile. "Perhaps. Nevertheless, you have but to ask me, and you shall have a horse and teachers."

"Thank you, Husband. Perhaps, someday. I'm sure Hatsumi would not approve. She already thinks I am too manly." She laughed a little.

The sparkle disappeared from his eyes. "She certainly would not approve. This is actually my purpose for speaking to you." He hesitated. "I know that she has been with you for most of your life. You are loyal to each other. Nevertheless, even now, she is wailing and weeping uncontrollably in her chamber, and the sound echoes like the sound of a hungry ghost through the halls. It is unseemly."

An old, familiar sick feeling resurfaced in her belly. "I will go talk to her, Husband. Immediately."

"There is more. I tried to talk to her myself, but she would not see me."

Kazuko stiffened. Refusing to see the lord of the domain was a grave insult, punishable by death by lords less kind than Tsunetomo.

"I can forgive her this, because she is dear to you. But my sufferance is not without limit. Her behavior shames her, and it shames you, and so it shames me. You must deal with this, or I shall have to send her away."

Kazuko swallowed hard. She could not imagine her life without Hatsumi in it, in spite of how difficult she was at times. "I will speak to her. Thank you for your forbearance, Husband. Such behavior will cease."

"If it does not, I shall have to find a new handmaiden for you. Perhaps one of Lady Yukino's nieces."

"I understand, Husband."

"I know you are sensible. I hear rumors as well that she still abuses the servant girls."

Kazuko's mouth fell open. "I know of no incidents since ..." Not since Hatsumi had thrown boiling tea in poor Moé's face.

"I'll trust you to look into it. Some of the servant families have served mine for generations. They deserve better treatment."

"I will, Husband."

"Good, now go and change into a lady's clothes. We have tea this afternoon with Abbess Mugai."

A cold hand on her spine. "Of course, Husband."

"I have asked her to say special prayers for us as we wish for a son. I have given a large donation to her temple."

A tightening of further discomfort in her belly. "You're very thoughtful, Husband."

"And you'll speak to Hatsumi right away."

"Yes, Husband. Of course."

"You're a good wife. Forgive me now, I must meet with Tsunemori." Then he turned and strode away, leaving Kazuko with a familiar hollowness in her belly that it seemed would only be filled by a son.

Hatsumi's distraught weeping echoed down the steep, narrow steps like the disembodied voice of a moaning wind. The upper floor of the castle housed the lord and his wife, with Hatsumi's and Yasutoki's quarters on the floor below.

Kazuko's heart grew heavier with each upward step. The anguish in Hatsumi's voice plucked at her heart like the strains of a melancholy *biwa*. Then anger surged forth. Such suffering, and all for a man who was not worthy to be spat upon.

Kazuko knocked quietly and announced herself at Hatsumi's door.

The sobs diminished to a sniffle. "Is that you, dear Kazuko?"

"Yes, please may I come in?"

Another sniffle. "Anything for you."

Kazuko slid open the door, letting a bit more light into the dim room. The shuttered windows clamped the room into shadow. Hatsumi lay in a cocoon of blankets and *futon* in the middle of the floor, only the back of her head visible.

Kazuko tried to be cheerful as she knelt beside the shuddering lump. "Still in bed, sleepy-head? It's almost mid-day."

"I cannot get up."

"Why not?"

"I want nothing more than to die. Let me lie here and starve."

"This is about Yasutoki, isn't it?"

A fresh sob, choked back. "He left for Hakata because of me."

"Tsunetomo says he is away on business."

"I must apologize to him for my shrewishness. I drove him away!"

"Nonsense! He is a foul, deceitful man! He is unworthy of your love. I know it is painful, but all this pining for him, this suffering, is hurting you. You must forget about him."

"He is—He—He is the only man who ever said words of love to me."

"I'm sure there will be other offers of marriage. Perhaps Tsunetomo could marry you to one of his retainers."

"I'm too ugly! No man will ever look at me!"

"What a foolish thing to say! There must be lots of men who would find you comely."

"I am too old! Men want young girls, beautiful, fertile, bouncy virgins. Girls like—" Hatsumi bit her lip and sniffled.

Some part of Kazuko twisted inside. "There are certainly men in Tsunetomo's employ who are looking for a good wife, and you would be a wonderful wife—"

"I hate men. I hate them! All of them! May *oni* take them and … and …" Her voice trailed off again into sobs.

Kazuko sighed and rubbed Hatsumi's shoulder. "Come, we'll have some tea, and we'll discuss who might make a good husband for you. Then I'll make some inquiries and—"

Hatsumi spun to look up at Kazuko. "*No!* I. *Hate.* Them." Her eyes were blood-red and wild, shadowed by dark circles, a spot of blood on her lip, teeth clenched so tightly she could have bitten through a steel bar. The face of a living *yurei*, a hungry ghost.

Kazuko gasped and shied away from the hellish chill of Hatsumi's glare.

Hatsumi turned her back again.

Part of Kazuko wanted to just leave Hatsumi to her suffering, but her husband's warnings sprang fresh into her mind. It might even be good to distract Hatsumi with some menial or invented task. It was time to end this. Kazuko shook Hatsumi's shoulder again. "Come, no more weeping for today. I have arranged a picnic with Lady Yukino, and you must help arrange the meal. Shall I await you in the dining hall?"

"It's too hot for a picnic."

Kazuko stiffened. Hatsumi's words were tantamount to refusing a request from the lady of the house. Another grave insult. "You're too distraught. You don't know what you're saying." She stood and moved toward the door. "I'll await you downstairs. Please don't be long."

As she shut the door behind her, she took a deep breath. It was unthinkable for a handmaiden to disobey her mistress. Such behavior was unacceptable. Perhaps her husband had been right. She did not want to take any more unpleasant steps with Hatsumi, but if Hatsumi did not get hold of herself soon, stricter measures or admonishment might be warranted.

Perhaps half an hour later, Hatsumi came down, her hair immaculately arranged, her clothes in perfect order. Two ragged, red eyes and the shadows of despair on her face were the only evidence of her suffering. Her sullen expression put Kazuko on edge. She looked more like a petulant child forced to do some odious chore than a noblewoman's handmaid. This tension felt all too familiar.

Kazuko gave Hatsumi a warm smile. "You know, now we have something more in common."

"What's that?"

"You spent three years telling me how bad a certain man was for me, how I suffered so needlessly because of him."

"Yes?"

"Now I get to do the same for you." She patted Hatsumi's hand.

Hatsumi's gaze remained on the floor.

Kazuko squeezed. "I hope it doesn't take you three years."

Hatsumi suppressed a sniffle. "I'll not survive that."

How many times had Kazuko thought the same, with her heart aching and her belly tight and sour? "Best to think about other things for a while."

"I apologize, dear Kazuko. I am an insufferable witch."

Something in Hatsumi's tone told Kazuko her handmaiden was just speaking the words. There was no contrition. Time to

178

take a firmer stance. "You need not apologize to me. But you should apologize to my husband. Your behavior was very rude." Hatsumi covered her mouth, eyes bulging. "Apologize for what? What did I do?"

"He requested to speak with you earlier and you refused him. You angered him."

Hatsumi seemed to collapse into herself a little. "Oh, no! I ... I must apologize! But ... I don't remember doing that!"

It was Kazuko's turn to be surprised. "Perhaps you just didn't hear him. Perhaps you were crying too loudly."

"I was crying loudly? I never do that! It's unseemly! If I weep, I do it quietly into my sleeves."

A chill went through Kazuko. She touched Hatsumi's hand again. "Oh, Hatsumi, you are not well. The whole house could hear you."

Hatsumi blanched and choked. "Jizo save me! They could?" Her eyes flared with panic.

Kazuko's mind fumbled for what to do. "Come, let us go for a walk. It has been a trying morning." She stood and gently pulled Hatsumi to her feet.

Silent and stiff, Hatsumi allowed herself to be led outside.

When facing a single tree, if you look at a single one of its red leaves, you will not see all the others. When the eye is not set on any one  leaf, and you face the tree with nothing at all in mind, any number of leaves are visible to the eye without limit. But if a single leaf holds the eye, it will be as if the remaining leaves were not there.

— *Takuan Soho, "The Mysterious Record of Immovable Wisdom"*

Ken'ishi sat on the ancient, moss-covered root of a massive tree, wondering about the purpose of the rope, festooned with carefully cut ribbons of white paper, looped around the tree trunk. The tree stood near the entrance of a temple, and the smell of incense wafted over the cool evening air. A bell gonged, calling the priests to evening prayers. People passed by on the nearby street in a bustling rhythm that never seemed to cease, oblivious to his weariness.

Exploring Hakata all day had left him footsore and thirsty. He had quickly learned to ignore the amused looks from passersby who noticed his wooden sword.

He had spoken to two moneychangers, four prostitutes, and

two street noodle vendors. Their reactions, averted eyes, and hurried excuses of pressing business, told him that they knew well the name of Green Tiger, but they also seemed shocked that he would ask such a question. It seemed that one either already knew the people of the underworld who would grant him an audience, or he would be an outsider trying in vain to get in, like a crow pecking at the outside of an overturned basket.

Assuming that the thief had been working for Green Tiger, and that Silver Crane was now in his possession, what would Ken'ishi do if he actually had the opportunity to speak to Green Tiger?

If Green Tiger had stolen Silver Crane, he had gone to incredible trouble to steal the sword, and if the thief three years ago was working for Green Tiger as well, the man also showed great tenacity. What could one samurai with a wooden sword do against such a gangster? Beg for Silver Crane's return? Laughable. Could he steal it back somehow? He did not know what he would do, but he had to try.

Earlier, Ken'ishi had even approached a constable, recognizable by the two *jitte* thrust into his sash, and struck up a conversation as they sat on nearby stools at a noodle vendor's counter. After discussing the weather and the quality of the vendor's pork *ramen*, Ken'ishi said, "In a city like this, you must have a lot of trouble with rough men. *Ronin*, gangsters, and the like."

The samurai stiffened. "Are you saying we don't run a clean city?"

"Not at all. But I'm new here, and I'm trying to avoid trouble."

"That's wise, especially if all you have is a wooden sword." The constable smirked. "Where are you from?"

"I've come a long way. Far to the north."

"You do have a strange accent." His eyes narrowed. "Why so far? Haven't you family there? A lord?"

Ken'ishi chose his next words carefully. "My family is dead. A man's path can lead many places."

The constable scrutinized him for a long moment. "What is your business in Hakata?"

"I came here with an acquaintance, but I've already had some bad fortune. I want to avoid any more."

"That's unfortunate. How so?"

"My sword was stolen, so I carry this one."

The constable's face twisted, and disdain crept into his voice. "It is a ... terrible thing for a warrior to lose his weapon."

"A disgraceful thing." Ken'ishi did his best to pretend it had just happened, and he found it easier than expected. The wound was still raw. "I cannot even ask you to help me, because it was stolen by some very rough men. And how does one find a lost weapon in a city like this?" Real despair laced his words.

The constable looked at him as if Ken'ishi should already have cut open his own belly. "Do you know who took it?"

"Perhaps some men working for someone you may have heard of. He seems to be infamous in these parts. Green Tiger." He scrutinized the constable's reaction.

The constable returned to slurping his noodles. "A terrible thing for a warrior to lose his weapon. You had best forget about it. Find another. Or maybe become a farmer."

"I'm fortunate that they didn't steal my money, too. What areas should I avoid if I want to stay away from Green Tiger's men?"

The constable grunted. "I wish I could help you. Where were you when your sword was stolen? Stay away from that place." He slurped his noodles faster.

"How much would it cost for such information?"

The samurai snorted and tossed his empty bowl onto the counter. "More than a man with a wooden sword can carry." He abruptly stood and walked away.

Sitting now against the bole of the ancient camphor tree, Ken'ishi thought about that conversation. He had tried to pretend he had Norikage's silver tongue, so masterful at gleaning information, often without the other person even knowing, but Ken'ishi could not do it. The constable had seen through his ploy and taken offense. He had not intended to bribe the samurai, but in hindsight he could see that his words might have been taken that way.

A swallow trilled somewhere in the dense canopy of leaves

overhead. Was it calling its mate home for the night, with a hint of warning that a man was nearby?

"Good evening, Mrs. Tsubame," he called up into the tree.

A querulous warble filtered down.

He sighed with a deep, shuddering despair, and put his chin in his hands.

More incomprehensible birdsong chattered down at him, each note raking frustration across his ears.

A scratching, shuffling noise led him to peer around the tree toward the outer perimeter of the temple. A darker shadow moved among the foundation stones, in the knee-high space between the earth and the floor. The light of dusk cast shadows deeper and turned colors to gray. There, among the shadows, two eyes reflected the light like tiny mirrors, looking at him.

A moment later, they were gone.

The way Junko flounced coquettishly and leered at Ken'ishi—as if he were a morsel of meat on a skewer—gave him shivers. There was a hunger in her gaze that went beyond the needs of the flesh, like a vast, empty chasm in her soul that could not be filled by any amount of coupling. She was an old woman, but much like her brother, there was nothing benign in her.

Upon Ken'ishi's dejected return, Shirohige greeted him with a grunt. "Thank your fortunes. And thank me as well. I spoke to my contact in the White Lotus this afternoon. They have dealings with Green Tiger. Gangs sometimes need a place to meet, either neutral territory or known points of contact. It occasionally keeps the bloodshed to a trickle."

"Will they tell me of such a place?"

"They might. For a price."

"What is the price?"

Shirohige snorted with a wry grin. "How much do you have?"

"I'll go there tomorrow. Tell me where."

"I must introduce you. The White Lotus is not much interested in talking to strangers."

"Very well. In the morning."

"In the evening. These men come out only at night. They're a bit surly if you encounter them in the morning."

"Very well, in the evening. And thank you, Shirohige."

"Oh, fear not. I never forget a debt."

Yasutoki wrapped his robes around him. "Who's there?"

"Masoku, Master."

A cool, moist breeze wafted in from the night-shrouded garden, curling through the ribbons of smoke rising from the burner of mosquito incense.

Yasutoki cast a long look at the naked girl kneeling beside him, the lamplight glowing on fine, smooth skin. A spattering of small moles lay among ripples of chicken skin in the center of the gentle swoop of her back. Whether from cold or fear, he did not care. Her gaze lay demurely on the floor. So lovely with a tear-streak on her cheek, and at fourteen the perfect age for initiation into the ways of pleasure; so soft, so ripe, so innocent.

"This had better be important," he called into the air, never taking his eyes from her flesh.

"It is one of your 'special circumstances,' Master."

To the girl he said, "Do not move, or you will regret it."

She pressed her forehead to the floor. "Yes, Master."

Yasutoki extracted himself from the bed of silken pillows, tying his robe as he crossed to the door. Masoku's bushy-headed silhouette rose against the rice paper door.

Yasutoki joined him in the hallway, sliding the door shut before the warrior could catch a glimpse of tonight's beauty. "Tell me."

Masoku knew better than to keep him waiting. "Constable Hiromichi and I were just having a drink at The Pink Orchid, and he mentioned in passing that a man had asked after you today. One does not simply bandy such a name as Green Tiger about lightly. So of course, his interest was stoked, as was mine."

Despite his interest in the story, Yasutoki's body tingled to return to the girl. "Cut to the bone."

Masoku cleared his throat. "He described a man of early years, perhaps twenty, who spoke with a strange accent, and carried a wooden sword."

"Yuto and his gang were laid low by a man with a wooden sword."

"I thought he said there were five of them."

"His tale does not match the tale of others." Yasutoki's mouth hardened.

"I told you Yuto was not to be trusted! A liar, through and through."

"An interesting condemnation coming from you."

"I know that you admire my truthful nature, Master." Masoku gave Yasutoki a wry smile, then cleared his throat and continued. "It's always better to talk to other witnesses, did I not say that? But listen to this, Master. This 'wooden-sword samurai' told our constable that his sword had been stolen from him by men who work for Green Tiger." He paused to let Yasutoki absorb the words.

"This certainly sounds like the man."

"But how could he know that?"

"He cannot." Yasutoki fixed Masoku with a cold scrutiny. "Unless he has found a leak in my organization."

Masoku's words spilled out. "I came here to tell you immediately. And I told the good constable that if he encounters this man again, there would be a substantial reward if he was taken into custody."

Yasutoki nodded. Almost half the constables in Hakata fell under Green Tiger's influence. That *ronin* had been a fool to think he could simply ask questions and imagine that Green Tiger might not hear of it. He rubbed his chin. How could he have followed the sword to Hakata? Kage would have left no evidence. No one except Kage, Masoku, Fang Shi, and Yasutoki himself knew that Silver Crane was in his possession. Practically no one knew of the sword's significance.

The possibilities turned his lips into a sneer. A spy within his organization who had seen the sword *and* knew its significance? One of his three trusted men had divulged this to someone? The *ronin* had powers that went beyond mortal perceptions? Shadow magic, perhaps? Had the *ronin* employed an augurer to divine the sword's location? But no, such a man would not be able to afford an *onmyouji*.

Yasutoki blinked as Masoku interrupted his reverie. "What shall I do, Master?"

Yasutoki worked the idea around behind his lips for another moment. "Instruct Constable Hiromichi and the rest to be watching for the man with the wooden sword. There cannot be many of those wandering around Hakata. I should have a word with this *ronin* before I kill him."

Masoku bowed and departed.

Yasutoki rejoined his trembling plaything. He sat beside her and stroked her hair. "You are very beautiful. A pleasure it is to look at you, to see your naked flesh. It is your destiny to give men pleasure, my dear. You will be famous in Hakata for the sweetness of your smile and the sweetness of your loins."

A few more weeks of hard work during the day and hard pleasure during the night, restricted to only one small bowl of millet and water to eat, and she would surrender to her new life, grow to relish it, in fact. She would all but forget her former life as a leatherer's daughter. The girl was too beautiful for life among the unclean in any case.

By all the gods and Buddhas, this delectable flower was a welcome relief from Hatsumi's jealous madness and her awful rigidity in life and lovemaking. Bedding her may have proven to be a mistake. Here in Hakata, Yasutoki felt as if he could breathe the air as his real self. Green Tiger was the real man; Yasutoki, merely a mask to hide from the eyes of the mortal world.

Yes, this lovely little flower would be well-used by morning, and the fear she felt would soon become pleasure. Not yet, but soon, and he would teach her. Besides, fear mixed with pleasure was a powerful combination.

The man with the wooden sword would soon kneel before him for some pointed questions. If the man was resourceful enough to come this far, he might make a powerful ally indeed. If he were properly tamed first, of course.

The mind is like the
moon on the water
Form is like the
reflection in a mirror
— *Yagyu Munenori, "The
Life-Giving Sword"*

The cacophony of languages dizzied Ken'ishi as much as walking through a forest filled with unintelligible birdsong. Hakata's

docks were overrun by Chinese and Koryo sailors and laborers, not to mention locals who spoke a smattering of related tongues. He even spotted one man with strange, brown skin; ugly, hawkish features; and a peculiar wrap of cloth around his head. His clothes were bizarre, but richly adorned with gold thread and colored stones, and he was flanked by two large men with features that were not quite Chinese, not quite as foreign as the brown man.

"Quit gawking," Shirohige said. "Act as if you are at home here as a fish in water, or else some pickpocket will likely sniff you out. The thieves around here can steal the jewels from between your legs."

Looking around at the hard eyes and grim features, Ken'ishi said, "There are sea monsters in this water."

"Indeed, and they're hungry for small fish. Best not to behave as a small fish. We're going to meet some sharks. Best to transact your business and then leave as quickly as we can." Shirohige cleared his throat. "Now, the leader is called Teng Zhou."

Ken'ishi tried to reproduce the name and found the syllables so strange on his tongue that he could not reproduce them.

"Keep practicing. And they're going to ask a price; I don't know what price. You might see only two or three of them at a time, but you can bet there are twice as many watching." Shirohige squinted and shaded his eyes at the sun, which was falling to the horizon. "At this time of day, the lotus eaters among them will not yet have indulged. They'll be alert, but perhaps a bit—don't look, but we're already being followed."

"Where?"

"There's a man wearing a white headband with a red stripe perhaps twenty paces behind us. The headband is their badge."

Ken'ishi tried to quiet his mind through the bustling activity all around him. Scores of ships, dozens of makes, a forest of masts and rigging, the incessant wash and gurgle of the sea at the feet of the piers, the thump of feet and the creak of wood, the stench of sweat and refuse, fish and brine.

A slash through his imagination.

A shining silver path into darkness, a black abyss without boundary. A path he was already walking.

He blinked at the power of the image, and his gait faltered at the tremor of pain behind one eye.

Shirohige paused. "What is it?"

Ken'ishi paused to steady himself. "Nothing. It's nothing."

"You look like someone just slapped you."

Ken'ishi composed himself. "What about the man following us?"

"He's just watching. The warehouse is near the last pier. And let me do all the talking until you're addressed directly."

The crowds thinned as Ken'ishi and Shirohige approached the warehouse. Its location kept it out of the way of the high-traffic central docks, on a rocky spit of land reaching out into

Hakata Bay. Two Chinese junks were moored at the nearby docks, surrounded by stacks of cargo, coils of rope, and piles of netting. The warehouse was a weathered structure of wood and bamboo, stained by years at seaside as only such buildings can be. Two small wiry men, bare-chested and wearing pantaloons—and white headbands with a single red stripe—lounged on crates near the entrance. Their eyes were flint-hard and as sharp as the large, wickedly curved knives thrust into their belts.

One of them eyed Shirohige. "Back so soon, old man? Business good?" The peculiar lilt and accent of his speech was unlike anything Ken'ishi had ever heard before.

Shirohige bowed and said, "I must speak with Teng Zhou."

"Who this? Bodyguard?"

"A friend with a problem."

"We no fix problem. We live harmony." The two men in the doorway grinned at each other over some hidden joke.

Shirohige said, "I would be in your debt if you took us to Teng Zhou."

"Why he got stick?" The man grinned like an eel at Ken'ishi's *bokken*.

"He is just learning. His master forces him to carry it around all day."

The two men exchanged gusts of gibberish and shot predatory grins at Ken'ishi.

Whispers of the *kami* crept over Ken'ishi's shoulders.

One of the men stood up and gestured for them to follow. His back was sun-bronzed and scarred by dozens of little white cuts. Some of the scars were still pink. The other man fell in behind as they stepped into the shade of the warehouse's interior. On each wall, crates and barrels were stacked almost to the ceiling. Moments later, a third man followed them through the entrance as well, dressed the same, carrying the same style of broad-bladed knife, as long as Ken'ishi's forearm.

From the shadows in the back of the warehouse strode a tall, broad-shouldered man, younger than Ken'ishi expected, with a cheek scarred by an old slash that bared half his teeth and distorted his words. "You come soon, old man. He your friend?" He carried not only the same style of knife, but also a long, straight sword on the other hip. The other three White Lotus thugs formed a loose circle around Shirohige and Ken'ishi.

Shirohige puffed out his chest and straightened his back. "Call him 'Mr. *Bokken.*'" He turned to Ken'ishi. "Mr. *Bokken,* may I present Mr. Teng Zhou. Teng Zhou, perhaps you can help him with his problem. Perhaps he can make it worth your while."

Ken'ishi bowed. "A pleasure to make your acquaintance."

Teng Zhou sniffed and licked moisture from the jagged lips of the scar that bared his teeth. "What you do with stick?"

"My sword was stolen," Ken'ishi said. "Do you know Green Tiger?"

Teng Zhou laughed, "Everybody know Green Tiger. And nobody. He take your sword?"

"Perhaps. I must find out."

Teng Zhou's chuckle almost reached genuine mirth behind the slices of his eyes. "You think he give back to you?"

"First, I must know if he stole it."

"Green Tiger want something, he take something. He give nothing."

"I must talk to him."

"You maybe talk his men. Nobody talk Green Tiger. Just like nobody talk my boss."

"Perhaps his men will see differently."

"Why want sword back? Find another."

"It was my father's sword. It belongs to my ancestors, not to a … criminal."

Teng Zhou smiled at the last word. "You say we know such criminals?" He gestured to his compatriots. "We all honest men!"

The White Lotus laughed.

Teng Zhou's scrutiny bored into Ken'ishi. "He not give back, what you do?"

"I will kill him."

Fresh laughter exploded all around him.

After a while, when the mirth subsided, Teng Zhou said, "You kill him with stick, Mr. Wooden Sword?"

"Perhaps, if I can. Or with my hands, or with my teeth, if need be. You share territory with Green Tiger?"

Teng Zhou spat. "We share nothing. He no cross us, or there is war."

"What would happen to your territory with Green Tiger dead?"

"We take more." Teng Zhou licked through his teeth again and crossed his arms, pacing. "I like you, Mr. Wooden Sword. Maybe hear stories of you die. Make me sad. I know place. Meet Green Tiger's man there. But you pay."

"What if I kill him for you? Would that be enough?"

Teng Zhou chuckled again. "You brave or you fool. Sure bet, Green Tiger cut out your guts. No, you want place, you give me something."

"I have money."

"You maybe need money, buy back your head."

"Perhaps I'll give you the lives of your men. I could take two or three." Ken'ishi kept his voice steady, but his *bokken* was in his hand.

The smiles among the White Lotus evaporated like smoke.

Shirohige seized Ken'ishi arm and hissed. "What are you doing? Trying to get us both killed?"

Ken'ishi stepped forward. "I am Ken'ishi the *Oni* Slayer. I slew the bandit chieftain Hakamadare. I slew Nishimuta no Takenaga in a fair duel. I took the head of his foul deputy Taro and left it on a spear. Not four days ago, I single-handedly defeated three of Green Tiger's men in Hita town, with this very wooden sword. And I challenge you, Teng Zhou of the White Lotus."

A cold solemnity settled over Teng Zhou. "You think you challenge me like samurai!" He spat. "I not samurai!"

"You understand a challenge."

"Maybe friends here kill you!"

"If you kill me, you have saved yourself the trouble of a gang war. You can still have things as they are. I have gold and silver in my purse. It is yours, if you win. If I defeat you, you tell me what I want to know."

191

Suddenly there were not four White Lotus men, but seven, and their knives were in their hands.

Shirohige snarled. "Idiot!"

Teng Zhou drew his sword, a long, straight double-edged blade. He spat a long string of incomprehensible vitriol at Ken'ishi, and then he assumed a strange stance that Ken'ishi had never seen before.

No matter. The Void was still the Void, a blade was still a blade, and a strike was still a strike. He took a deep breath and settled himself, forgetting thoughts and techniques and his opponent's strange stance. He raised his *bokken* to the middle guard position, the point of the sword aimed at Teng Zhou's throat.

Ken'ishi eased forward, slowly closing the distance between them.

Shirohige began to back out of the circle of White Lotus thugs, until one of them seized the scruff of his neck and held him in place. He released a gasping bleat and froze.

Without seeking to scrutinize, Ken'ishi took in his opponent. Teng Zhou's disfigured face was a reef, impervious to the thunder of the sea. He knew the closeness of death's door even more intimately than Ken'ishi, had opened it almost as many times for himself as for others. His thews rippled with movement and his sword was rock-steady. The blade was notched and stained, but its edge would cut. No sweat betrayed any fear. Arm extended, body sideways, one-handing the sword above his head, feet wide apart.

Their eyes met over the point of Ken'ishi's *bokken*. The eternity of the Void lay upon the world, infinite time stretching between eyes, souls in conflict. The steady poise of Teng Zhou's gaze bespoke a familiarity with the flow of intention, the inevitability of death. In every fight Ken'ishi had ever undertaken, his opponents had been coarse fools, flailing at life with their arms and weapons as if bluster, cruelty, and a sharp edge would always conquer. Ken'ishi's teacher had taught him well to seek the No-Thought, No-Time of the Void, because only in those spaces were extraordinary things possible. Everything else was only ordinary.

Not so with Teng Zhou. He was a rough, strong-armed

gangster to be sure, but he had not risen to leadership by flailing at anything. Teng Zhou knew the Void as well as Ken'ishi. He might call it something different, have discovered it on some other path in some far-off land, but he knew it. A flicker of recognition. In that infinitesimal instant, Ken'ishi envisioned Teng Zhou's strike and his own counter attack, or else his own attack and Teng Zhou's counter. In both possibilities, death for both men was inevitable.

The good side of Teng Zhou's mouth curled into a faint smile. As he lowered his blade, his eyes remained on Ken'ishi. "You find Green Tiger's men gambling house. Alley behind *Pink Orchid Dream*, whorehouse in Nakasu district. Find *ronin*, name Masoku."

Ken'ishi lowered his weapon, but allowed his awareness to encompass the room, Teng Zhou, and the other men.

Shirohige's mouth fell open. "That's all? You're giving him something for free."

Teng Zhou's contempt turned upon Shirohige. "No, old fool. You not understand, never. Now silent!" He turned back to Ken'ishi. "Green Tiger is sorcerer. He control shadow. He invisible sometimes. His face never see. And he *always* have weapon. Always."

Ken'ishi bowed. "Thank you, Teng Zhou. Perhaps someday we'll meet again."

Teng Zhou nodded. "Next time, you bring real sword."

The man who would be a warrior considers it his most basic intention to keep death always in mind, day and night, from the time he picks up his chopsticks in celebrating his morning meal on New Year's Day to the evening of the last day of the year. When one constantly  keeps death in mind, both loyalty and filial piety are realized, myriad evils and disasters are avoided, one is without illness and mishap, and lives out a long life.... Being resolved that a man may be alive today but not tomorrow, one will be aware that today may be his last chance to serve his lord and attend his parents.

— *Daidoji Yuzan, Budoshoshinshu*

"I'm not going with you," Shirohige said, kicking off his *zori* and stepping up onto the *tatami*. He fixed Ken'ishi with a stern gaze.

Ken'ishi practically vibrated with the urge to be off to the *Pink Orchid Dream*. Even now, he could feel the silken silver thread tugging at the fringe of his mind. "This is not your fight. You have already put yourself in enough danger for me."

"So, already you think there will be a fight."

"A fight is most likely."

Junko's voice echoed from the depths of the house. "Did you say 'fight'?"

Shirohige called back, exasperation emerging in his voice, "Yes, my little nightingale. Our young friend here was successful with the White Lotus. I still cannot believe what I saw, boy. I've never seen anything like that. And I don't even know what it was. He just gave in like that. It's unheard of!"

"There are things more valuable than money and favors."

"Such as? Bah! Some silly warrior drivel. Eh, you might as well come in for your last meal. I'm starving. Sweet sister, where is dinner?"

Her sing-song reply floated out to them. "In your arse, dear brother."

"Must I do everything?" he snarled. "I'll put you in the street, witch!"

A crow's cackling reply reddened Shirohige's face, and he wrapped his fingers around his beard and tugged, muttering, "Filthy useless old whore!"

"I'm old," she called back, "but I'm neither blind nor deaf. For that, you can go suck Pon-Pon's arsehole for your dinner."

Shirohige turned to Ken'ishi. "Come inside so you can stop me from killing her and think about what you're doing. No sense in doing anything more rash than you already have planned. Green Tiger will still be there in two hours. That part of Hakata goes to sleep with the rising sun."

Ken'ishi followed him into the house.

Junko sat with a bundle of cloth and metal scales in her lap, working at it with a needle and thread.

Shirohige noticed her work. "What is that you're darning there? Armor? Where in the hell did you get that?"

"I've had this for years." She held it up by the shoulder straps, a ragged, dusty shirt of black-lacquered steel scales woven together with black silken cords. The interlocking scales wrapped the back, chest, and lower torso. "It's light, flexible." She hefted it. "Made for wearing under your clothes. It won't turn a real weapon aside for long, but it saved my old doorman more than once from a dagger in the back." She looked at Ken'ishi. "I thought perhaps you could use this. You must bring it back to me of course, and I'll be sure to peel it off you myself."

Shirohige said, "Give that up, woman. You're making me ill."

"No one knows better than I that men have needs. Besides, he's not getting out of here without giving old Junko a little, stiff warrior."

Ken'ishi clamped down on his tongue.

She continued, "So where are you off to? Where is Green Tiger's current den of iniquity?"

Shirohige said, "A gambling house behind Pink Orchid. I've heard of the whorehouse, but you probably know better than I, my sweet, innocent dumpling."

"Pink Orchid, eh? I know the place well. And you're a bald-faced liar. I happen to know that you frequented that place when mother was still alive. I had a lovely brawl with the madam there once."

Shirohige chuckled and shrugged. "'Lovely', she says. Show him."

Junko opened her robe and exposed a pale, withered breast with a livid, white scar as long as a hand puckering the skin above a shapeless, brownish-gray nipple. "That pustule-ridden bitch tried cut off my teat! Well, she got the harder bargain, I daresay." She met Ken'ishi's gaze, then cupped the sagging end of the breast in her fingers and fluttered it for him with a lascivious grin.

He did his best to remain unperturbed.

She slipped it back inside her robe. "Anyway, the gambling house and the whorehouse are connected somehow. The Nakasu district is a maze of passages above and below ground. There is always at least one man, at night probably two, in a hidden alcove near the door, watching patrons come and go, making sure no one gets out of line. If there's any trouble, they'll be on you like flies around my brother's head."

Ken'ishi bowed. "Thank you, madam. You are most kind."

She grinned. "Such a silver-tongued young man! What else can you do with that tongue?"

"Hachiman's Balls, woman, give it a rest!"

"Oh, shut up and let me have a little fun, you old coot!" She sighed. "Well, I'll have this stitched up in no time, if you'll leave me the hell alone. Make your own supper. I'm not going to be around forever."

Shirohige grumbled and set to rummaging through cupboards for rice, putting fresh wood on the fire, fanning it to a larger flame, setting water to boil. He sporadically shouted questions at Junko about the hidden location of the pot, and the rice, and the ladle, and derided her for letting the wood supply diminish. She shouted back harsh retorts, and finally threw down the armor and went to prepare the meal herself.

Shirohige eventually sat back down beside Ken'ishi, concealing a smug grin.

Throughout all this activity, Ken'ishi sat quietly, thinking about what he would do if he found the *ronin,* Masoku. Shirohige did manage to make some tea without complaint, and they shared a pot while Junko finished preparing the meal. A pall of solemnity fell over Ken'ishi, and the tea tasted better than any he had ever drunk. During the meal, every kernel of rice burst with flavor and texture in his mouth, along with the sourness of the pickled plums, the crunch of the vegetables in the savory soup broth.

This could be the last meal he ever ate.

But could not the same be said of every meal? Fortunes could shift and crack and let loose like the ice melt of northern mountain streams. On any given day, he could encounter another *oni* ready to flay him and feast on his flesh. Tonight was a night like any other. The danger of the situation should lend itself to caution, but not worry.

Shirohige said, "You're very quiet tonight."

Junko said, "He's always quiet."

"I know that better than you do, hag!"

Ken'ishi washed down the last of his meal with a sip of tea. "I shall return by morning, or I'll likely not return at all."

Shirohige nodded.

Junko sighed. "Just make sure you come back. Your shoulders make me all juicy and tingly. And you owe me a tumble for the armor."

"Of course, madam."

Junko's directions to and around the Nakasu district proved accurate. Ken'ishi navigated the warrens of narrow streets and alleys filled with drunken men of all walks of life. The smells of *saké* and food, gusts of laughter, cries of surprise and pain echoing from dark niches, the hard-packed earth under his wooden sandals, the faint strains of a flute or a *biwa*. Sweat soaked the interior padding of the armor under his robe, plastering it to his body.

He stood under the large red lantern painted with the characters "Pink Orchid Dream" and he thought of Kiosé. Old Tetta the innkeeper had purchased her from a whorehouse in Hakozaki when she was very young. How would her life have been different if she had remained there? Paths of human lives intersected, woven together for a time before they unraveled and parted. Had she awakened from the dream Hage had given her? Would she ever?

Sounds of pleasure emanated from a window above. How different they were from Kiosé's little gasps and contented sighs. Louder, more energetic, but less sincere, hollow.

He let his awareness encompass the street, listening for the voices of *kami* or the silver tug. Two men lounged in a doorway a few dozen paces distant, muttering to one another, torn clothes sweat-stained and unkempt, swords in battered scabbards thrust haphazardly in their sashes—*ronin*. Down the street, under a different red lantern, sat a beautifully lacquered palanquin with two porters and two samurai bodyguards who were paying close attention to the *ronin*. A trio of drunken tradesmen singing a bawdy tune staggered past, lost in their own camaraderie.

Ken'ishi found the narrow alley that Junko had described and headed down it. The shadows lay deep between the shacks and walls, the light of a half-risen moon still insufficient to do naught but skim the thatched rooftops. The alley stank of refuse and dog shit, littered with debris that crackled and shifted underfoot. The soft-grunting bulk of a pig lay tied in a pen little bigger than its body.

Another red light appeared beyond the shifting curves ahead, and he soon found himself at a dead end, standing under another red lantern. Sounds of conversation sifted through the closed door. He opened the door and stepped into the lamplit hallway. The *kami* tingled over him as he heard the shift of a doorman's bulk in a curtained alcove beside the door.

Beyond another curtain lay a room filled with tables and men. Dealers brimmed with false joviality, shuffling cards or wooden placards carved with dots and slashes and other markings. Men groaned and cheered and hoisted cups. Greed and desperation thickened the closeness of the humid night air. Near a rear door stood a grim-faced *ronin*, arms crossed, beard unshaven. He chewed on a fingernail, his face slack with boredom.

A round-faced woman with the eyes of a fish approached him, brushing at strands of unruly hair. "Can I show you to a table, sir? What is your game tonight?"

"I have business with Masoku."

She sucked in a little breath and scrutinized Ken'ishi in a flash. "I'm sorry, sir. He is not here tonight. Perhaps you would like to try a round of Ya Pei. Fortunes are with the players tonight—"

"Where can I find him?"

She glanced over her shoulder. "As I said, he is not here."

"As I asked, where can I find him?"

She bowed. "I'm very sorry, sir. Please wait here." She disappeared through another door. He watched her go.

When his attention returned to the *ronin*, the man's bored demeanor was gone. His gaze lay full upon Ken'ishi, his expression unreadable. Ken'ishi held his gaze, feeling the *kami* hum to life behind his mind.

A short, thin man came out and approached Ken'ishi, his bald head fringed by wisps of hair, his eyes dark and hard as lava rocks. He carried no visible weapon. "Who are you? What do you want with me?"

His abrupt rudeness grated over Ken'ishi's nerves. "You are Masoku?"

"Yes, now what is your business?"

"I have business only with the real Masoku."

The man's narrow face soured, and his eyes flashed. He glanced at the wooden sword in Ken'ishi's sash.

Ken'ishi said, "I am not here to cause trouble. I don't even have a real weapon. I simply require a brief word with Masoku. It is an urgent matter. In private."

The man turned away. "Come with me."

Ken'ishi followed him back through the same door, down a hallway into a dim storeroom lit by only a single shaft of moonlight through a high, narrow window. The air smelled of the dust that lay heavy on the floor, decaying wood, and moldy *tatami*. Another narrow door stood closed on the opposite side of the room.

The man said, "Wait here," and left Ken'ishi alone.

Ken'ishi positioned himself with his back to the wall, both entrances in full view. He stilled himself into the Void, where the *kami* sang choruses of warning. His *bokken* could be in his hand in less than a heartbeat. An image flashed into his mind of standing in the mouth of a tiger.

The *ronin* entered from the opposite door, his face a block of unreadable stone. His hand rested on the pommel of his sword, a façade of nonchalance. "I am Masoku."

"So the last man said."

"Best to be cautious. Things are never what they seem, eh? What's this business you say you have with me?"

"I want to speak with Green Tiger."

The man's dark eyes narrowed. "You must have a death wish. Go home, kid."

Ken'ishi bowed, "I respectfully request an audience."

The man laughed, "This is not a noble's court! Take your pleasantries and plug them in a horse's arse!"

"There is no need to be discourteous. We are both warriors." Masoku nodded toward Ken'ishi's weapon. "Do you think this is a training hall?"

"All the world is my training hall."

Masoku snorted, and his gaze bored into Ken'ishi for several long moments, only to be turned away. Then he scoffed. "How can you call yourself a warrior with only a wooden sword?"

Ken'ishi said, "I have come here respectfully to request to speak to Green Tiger. You can, of course, deny that he is here. Across northern Kyushu, his name could be among the Bodhisattvas for the power people associate with him. He is clearly a busy man, but my business is urgent. Either take me to him now, or arrange a meeting."

"And if I don't?"

"I suspect that if I kill you, he'll find me himself."

Masoku burst into a harsh laugh. "And if I kill you?" He thrust out his sword hilt.

"Then I'm not worthy to present my message to him."

"Tell me your business."

"My business is between me and your master. Take me to him, agree to arrange a meeting, or draw."

Masoku's sword sprang into his hand, a curved ribbon of tarnished moonlight. "You've a dangerous overestimation of yourself, kid." He edged forward.

Ken'ishi's awareness encompassed the room, areas that might cramp his movement or hinder his weapon, floorboards that might give way under his foot, the exact distance between him and his opponent.

Masoku's free hand slipped out of sight for a moment, then blurred with motion. Something hissed through the air, flashing slivers of steel. Three small knives thudded into Ken'ishi's chest and belly, embedding themselves. One of the points found its way between the scales under his shirt and lightly pierced his flesh, but the armor held true. Ken'ishi swept the knives free and held his ground.

Masoku's eyes widened.

Ken'ishi said, "Take me to Green Tiger, or die."

Masoku's blade slashed through the dimness, glinting. Ken'ishi allowed it to pass him by, but he was out of position to counterattack, constrained by the size of the room. Another slash, and he slid aside. Another slash, and Ken'ishi attempted to redirect the blow with his *bokken*, but too late he realized that the attack was not meant to harm him; it had been aimed at his sword. The steel edge sheared neatly through the hardwood, and two hand-spans of *bokken* tumbled through the air.

A heavy foot creaked in the hallway behind him. A hulking shadow loomed over him, bare-chested. Heavy blunt features snarled. He spun. Great, thick arms wielded two clubs. He caught one attack on the clipped length of *bokken*, but the blow was so powerful that it sent jarring shivers up both arms. A splintering sound crashed through the room. The other club slammed into his shoulder, driving him sideways with a sudden flare of agony. His arm went numb.

Masoku's blade slashed toward his face, and he ducked, just in time to meet the second man's meaty leg sweeping upward. The kick plowed into his belly with shocking pain, lifting him off the floor. If not for the armor, his ribs might have been shattered.

He collapsed onto his knees, gasping for breath. There was a sound of club against skull, and Ken'ishi fell to the floor, his vision going white.

Another kick to his belly, and a thick voice rumbled, "Armor."

"Well, isn't he the resourceful one? Perhaps he's less willing to die than he let on."

"Master say no kill, yes?" A strange lilt and accent similar to Teng Zhou.

"That's right. He'll get his audience with the master, but I don't expect he'll survive it. Truss him up."

Existence and Non-Existence, Good and Evil, are sicknesses of the mind. If you do not expel these sicknesses from the mind, nothing you do will turn out well.

— *Yagyu Munenori, The Life-Giving Sword*

Pain brought Ken'ishi out of his stupor, starbursts of pain that tore through his belly and knotted his shoulders and numbed his arms. A strange, silver worm wriggled through his mind, inching through the parched earth of agony, delving, probing. Coarse ropes constricted his arms and wrists, lashing them to a timber crossed under his shoulder blades. A foul-tasting wad of linen filled his mouth; a gag pulled tight across held it in place like a horse's bit. He lay on his back, his own weight crushing his elbows under the timber. He tried to shift his weight to relieve the pressure, but white-hot pain gouged into his torso and the weight of the timber held him in place. His belly felt like an enormous, aching bruise. Each heartbeat brought a throb of agony through his arms, and his awkwardly hanging head pounded in perfect rhythm.

The silver worm shifted its form, growing wings, a regal, curving neck, a long beak. It spread its wings and took flight, but its eyes were upon him, and he felt its judgment. It felt so close, but out of reach.

An enormous mountain of a man sat on a barrel, watching him with massive arms crossed over his naked chest. Shaven head, lumpen, bestial features, beady black eyes. He gave Ken'ishi a wry grin. "You get wish. Master come."

Ken'ishi heard the words, but pain so disrupted his mind that he could not formulate a thought. He bit down hard on his gag, clamping back the pain as he heaved his back off the floor into a sitting position, fighting the weight of a timber as thick and heavy as his leg. He waited for the pain to subside, fought to resist gagging on the foul wad of linen, simply focused on breathing, but each inhalation opened a burning gash of agony under his ribs. His arms were immobile, lashed so tightly to the timber that they felt like so much dead flesh.

The square of moonlight crept like an inchworm across the dusty floor.

Ken'ishi caught himself bobbing forward, losing consciousness or falling asleep, but some interminable time passed before a globe of yellow light bobbed into the room, a lantern in Masoku's hand.

A third man entered, a man in a basket hat, with a cloth wrapping the lower half of his face and a bamboo sword case across his back. The man moved with the surety and grace of a serpent or a spider, and he stood before Ken'ishi with a gaze so intense that its pressure touched him like the point of a spear. Everything about the man's face was invisible, except those powerful eyes. Otherwise, he was a man of smaller stature, thin, but with a cultivated power in his movements, even swathed as they were in black silk and linen, as if he invited the night to swallow him into its embrace.

The man made a small gesture to Masoku, who stepped forward and untied Ken'ishi's gag.

Ken'ishi spat out the wad of linen, and it splatted onto the floor, leaving trails of spittle back to his dry mouth.

The ebon mask muffled the man's voice. "Who are you?"

"Are you Green Tiger?" Ken'ishi said.

"I am Green Tiger, Lord of the Underworld."

"I have met two men tonight claiming to be named Masoku. How do I know you're not simply another lackey?"

"You don't. And you won't, unless I will it so. You've interrupted my night with your impertinence. Now tell me who you are, or I'll simply slit your throat and throw you in the bay."

"I am ... a *ronin*. I have no name."

"What does a *ronin* want with Green Tiger?"

"I came here to ask you a question, but everything about the underworld and its lord is wrapped in mystery and deception."

Masoku said, "Don't forget death. Lots of death."

Green Tiger said, "I have no reason to lie to you, nor do I have particular reason to tell the truth. I may not even answer your question. Displease me sufficiently, and you'll watch bits and pieces of yourself go into a chum bucket. But you may ask."

"Did you send a man to Aoka village to steal a sword?"

Silence fell over the room. The two lackeys glanced at their master. Moments passed like drops of dew from a hanging leaf.

Green Tiger's voice was as cool and neutral as a gray, fog-bound dusk. "And you have come from Aoka village seeking the thief?"

"The sword belonged to my father, who handed it down to me before he was murdered."

"Give me your pedigree, samurai. Tell me your exploits. Show me you are worthy to live, or at least to die a warrior's death."

"I am Ken'ishi the *Oni* Slayer. I slew the bandit king Hakamadare. I slew the demon-*yoriki* Taro and mounted his head on a spear. I slew Nishimuta no Takenaga in a duel of honor. And, several days ago, I single-handedly defeated three of your men in Hita town, wielding a wooden sword." Ken'ishi took a slow, calm breath. "Did you send a man to Aoka village to steal my sword?"

"I did."

A rush of tingling sensations shot through Ken'ishi's body like a blast of typhoon wind. "Why?"

"Silver Crane belongs to my family."

"So you know its name. And you knew that Silver Crane was there. How?"

"I answered your question. It's my turn now. How did you come to possess the sword?"

"I told you. I had it from my father, and presumably, his father before him."

"Who was your father?"

"He was murdered when I was a baby."

"Who raised you?"

"My teacher."

"What do you know of the sword's history?"

"Nothing." The dream came to mind where he had seen Silver Crane in the hand of some samurai lord during a great sea battle, but his thoughts were too clouded by pain to recall other details. Was it only a dream, or was there truth behind it?

"You are a *ronin*. Have you never had a lord?"

"A teacher, but not a lord."

"Who is your teacher?"

"His name doesn't matter, only that he taught me, and I fear no man in a duel."

Masoku sneered. "I took you down fairly handily."

Ken'ishi nodded. "It will not happen again."

Masoku started forward. "Damned right! You'll be dead!"

Green Tiger raised a hand. "Those are worthy exploits for one so young. Most men reach their deaths with much less distinction."

"Will you give me back my sword?"

"It is not your sword, samurai. It is a far larger thing than one such as you can carry."

"And who can carry it? You? A criminal?"

"I have the blood."

"But not the honor!"

Green Tiger laughed. "Honor! Honor means as much as a pig's fart in the belly of the underworld, where men's base desires are indulged, their darkest longings pursued and experienced. Gold, secrets, flesh, and the power they grant. These things are real. But a bumpkin samurai with a wooden sword would know little of real power. As I said, secrets have power as well. I know you, little bumpkin samurai. I knew who you were before I stepped into this room, before you set foot in Hakata. I have known of you since you slew Hakamadare. Oh, don't look so surprised. I looked for you, but I could not find you."

"Yellow Tiger," Ken'ishi said.

"Oho! So he did find you!"

"I slew him."

"Well done, indeed. But Hakamadare, there was a feat worthy of legend. The *oni* was infamous, and stories are still being told about the mysterious *ronin* who slew him and then disappeared. What if I told you that I will return Silver Crane to you?"

Hope flared in Ken'ishi's heart.

"But I have one condition."

"And that is?"

"You will work for me. Swear your sword to me, and I will allow you to wield it again. There are dark times coming, and we will need a strong man to wield it, to be a light in the darkness."

"What dark times? How could a criminal like you offer a light while you stand in darkness?"

"Men wear many masks, some of them more brightly painted than others. The fortunes of the world sometimes turn toward darkness." He slid the sword case from his shoulder, pulled off the cap, reached inside, and withdrew the silver-chased hilt Ken'ishi knew so well, the battered scabbard with its mother-of-pearl cranes. "I see the desire in you. What would you be willing to do to get it back? Work for me, and it is yours. You could be greater than Hakamadare ever was, with more power and wealth than you can imagine."

Nearby, Masoku frowned and fidgeted.

Green Tiger continued, "The *oni* was a vile creature, but *powerful*. He carved his power and infamy from the world through sheer brutality and ferocity. Nothing could long sate his lusts, and none could stand against him. And yet, with this weapon, you defeated him." Green Tiger pulled the blade free, and it glimmered like a feathered mirror in the mix of moon and lamplight. "It can be yours again, and you can carve your own place in the world. All you must remember is that I am your master."

Something in Green Tiger's words and tone resonated in Ken'ishi's mind, something about Hakamadare. Images of that day over three years ago flooded through his mind, the melee with the bandit gang, the valiant stand by Kazuko's samurai bodyguards, Hatsumi's horrific rape, the *oni*'s monstrous form as it emerged from the bushes, the way it had feasted on human flesh and blood, its blood flowing as black and thick as molten pine resin, Silver Crane slashing again and again. Even Hakamadare's severed head had remained alive until they seared it in a fire until nothing was left but blackened skull.

And he remembered the way Kazuko's beauty and grace had hammered him harder, and left a deeper mark on his soul than the demon's iron club.

Green Tiger broke the silence first. "I see your eyes upon it, and I see the desire in them, the greed. If you think you could steal this from me, remember that I found you once. There is nowhere distant enough to hide from me."

Amid tumbling thoughts, a realization struck Ken'ishi like a stone. He gazed up into Green Tiger's eyes. "You knew Hakamadare. He was not your enemy." He saw a single flash of truth in Green Tiger's eyes before it disappeared like an ember in the sea.

The possibilities of the path that Green Tiger's proposal represented for Ken'ishi came like stepping stones, the tasks he would be expected to perform. Like Yuto and other thugs, pushing around helpless townspeople. Like Shirohige, preying upon the fear and need of the lotus-addled potter. Like Hakamadare, gouging a swath of rape and banditry across the countryside, striking fear into everyone. Could he do such things? Was it worth doing those things to have Silver Crane again?

"No."

Silver fingers in his mind, brushing the corners, feather-light. If he accepted Green Tiger as his master, he would no longer be worthy of a sword like Silver Crane. He would not even be worthy to be called samurai. He would be nothing but a bandit, a "filthy *ronin*" like so many had believed of him for so long.

Green Tiger's voice became a low rumble. "So, you refuse."

"I refuse."

The silver fingers seized his mind, and outside thoughts rang within his. *Destiny. Patience.*

Ken'ishi steadied himself and took a deep breath. The pain in his body was gone as if it had never been. He remembered well one other time when such a thing had happened, with a sword impaling his thigh, and Taro, the deputy-turned-demon, threatening to kill Naoko, Kiosé, and the newborn Little Frog. He took a deep breath and leveled his gaze at Green Tiger. "Release me, return the sword to me now, and I will let you all live."

All three men laughed.

The giant wiped at his eyes and clapped his hands. "You funny!"

Masoku said, "For a dead man!"

Green Tiger stopped laughing first. "Bold talk for a man standing at the precipice of hell. No one threatens me. You have no idea the suffering a man can endure. He can yearn for death for years. How long before you break? Every man does." He snapped his fingers, and the enormous Chinaman stepped forward, grinning, club in hand.

An explosion of pain and light in Ken'ishi's skull, then silence.

To depart while seated or
   standing is all one.
All I shall leave behind me
Is a heap of bones.
In empty space I twist
   and soar
And come down with the
   roar of thunder
To the sea.
     — Koho Kennichi, Death
              Poem

T he dank air smelled of seawater, sodden earth, rotting fish, and human excrement. Ken'ishi's arms ended in tingling stumps of agony at his shoulders. His hands and forearms, cinched in the coarse ropes, had taken on a dark purple hue. The weight of the timber still gouged into his back, and his head and neck were a constant, pounding ache.

A bone-thin man, taller than any he had ever seen, towered over him. Long strands of greasy hair hung to his chest, shadowing the deep brow ridge and nose that looked as if it had been mashed into his face. The man's words came thick through flabby lips. "It's all right to scream here. No one will hear you."

Ken'ishi smelled something else—blood. Gore so thick and

deep that it seemed to rise from the rough-hewn stone floor. "The Master has given you to me to play with. But don't worry, I won't kill you. You might wish me to, though. And when you reach that point, do ask. I like when my toys ask me to kill them."

Ken'ishi thought he should struggle, but his arms and shoulders were a massive insensate lump, crowned by a throbbing head. His vision swam. He kicked feebly at the man.

The man stepped forward and looped a rope around Ken'ishi's neck, slung it over a hook embedded in the small room's central wooden pillar, and hauled on the rope. It cinched tight, cutting off his breath, redoubling the pounding agony inside his head, and dragged him back up against the pillar. His legs flailed, but his feeble struggles accomplished nothing but to tighten the noose.

The man produced a dagger and sliced through the web of ropes binding him to the timber, which fell to the floor with a heavy thud. The sudden release of weight made Ken'ishi's body feel as light as a feather, but his upper arms were still bound back like the pinched wings of a butterfly. They were too dead to even reach for the noose choking his life away. He felt his face swelling, blotches of red and white shooting through his vision, then gathering at the edges and collapsing toward the center until he could see nothing except a spot of lamplit stone wall near the ceiling. His body fought to breathe, and no air would come.

The noose slackened, and he could breathe again. Great racking, coughing gasps sucked air back into his chest.

"A time to let your arms wake up. Oh, that should be some beautiful pain. It's been several hours, so I'll wager you've not felt anything in them for some time. That will return in fire."

The man worked at something out of sight while Ken'ishi recovered consciousness. He tried to flex his hands and fingers, but they were as dead stumps of useless, purple meat.

And then it happened. A small tingle became a rush, became a torrent of sensation. He gritted his teeth as swarms of voracious ants chewed through the flesh and bones of his arms. The purple in his arms turned to streaks of red and bands of white where the ropes had been tied. An agony of eternity later, he could move his fingers.

A wooden frame crashed onto the floor before him, startling him with the noise. Three wooden timbers held in parallel, planed smooth on the sides of triangular cross-sections, with the edge of the timbers pointing up.

The noose jerked upward again, but this time he had the strength to raise himself on his legs, sliding up the pillar to relieve the constriction.

The man kicked the lattice under Ken'ishi's shins and then released the noose again. Ken'ishi's shins collapsed under him and fell upon the three upright edges of the hardwood timbers. Excruciating pain such as he had never imagined possible, white-hot, exploded into his legs as the hardwood edges pressed across his shins, driven deeper by his own weight.

"This is my favorite," the man said.

Ken'ishi remembered all the times as a boy when Kaa had beaten him with a bamboo switch or pelted him with stones, but all of that collected into a whole was as only a candle to the sun. More ropes slithered around him and lashed him upright to the pillar, bound kneeling in a torturous *seiza* posture, supporting all of his weight on his shins, pressing harder and deeper onto the wooden edges.

A satisfied chuckle sounded from behind him as the man went about unseen business.

Ken'ishi gasped for breath and fought the pain for a time, each heartbeat an infinity. He sought the Void as refuge, and found within it a place to let the pain pass him by.

A sudden slap shattered the Void and brought him back to the world of pain. The man shoved a bony finger into Ken'ishi's face. "You pay attention! That's the best way. Love every second of the pain. It seems you've gotten used to it already. Fear not, we're just getting started."

The man disappeared behind the pillar again. Ken'ishi heard a grunt of exertion, the grating of stone on stone, and then the man came back into view carrying a square-cut stone slab as long as his leg, half as wide, a hand's breadth thick. The man maneuvered this stone over Ken'ishi's thighs and settled it flat over them. The pain exploded into a thousand suns as the wooden edges dug deeper and deeper into his shins under the stone's weight and his knees bloomed with the agony of tearing sinew. He bit back another cry. The man said, "It's always surprising. One thinks that the pain cannot possibly get better, and yet, it always—"

Ken'ishi regained awareness sometime later. The stone still rested on his thighs.

The world faded again into blood and night.

A dash of water in his face roused him. "No sleeping!" The man sat a few paces away and went back to sharpening slivers of bamboo. He sighed with contentment.

Another voice intruded upon the silence, "I told you, no permanent damage. He cannot work for me if he is crippled."

The man jumped up and bowed. "Of course, Master! Of course!" He squatted before Ken'ishi and lifted off the stone, muscling it back out of view. The release of pressure exploded through Ken'ishi's body like a climax of pleasure.

Green Tiger stood over Ken'ishi, an oily shadow in the dimness of the cave. "Give him water."

The man brought a bamboo ladle to Ken'ishi's swollen lips. Ken'ishi gulped at the water, tasting blood and bamboo.

Green Tiger said, "This can all end right now. You can rejoin the world of the living. You can wield Silver Crane again. Join me, and carve out a place among legends."

Ken'ishi looked up into Green Tiger's eyes, the cold, dead eyes of a serpent shrouded by the basket hat. "I will die first."

"Good." Green Tiger nodded. "But you'll change your mind. If you had broken so quickly, I wouldn't want you."

He stepped around the pillar and disappeared from view, leaving not a sound behind him.

The man gave him another ladle of water, chuckled. "You've some grit, I see. Ah, that's good news. These next few days will be glorious indeed. You'll come to see how merciful the Master is. You heard him. All you have to do to make it stop is to join him."

* * *

213

He was a boy called Antoku again, so small compared to all the powerful samurai rushing about the deck of the ship, compared to even his grandmother and the pretty ladies who waited on him. The flaming arrows came down, and the air was filled with the smoke of burning sails and other things burning that he did not like to think about. But he could see things so much more clearly now. It was all familiar.

The fluttering banners emblazoned with the butterfly *mon* of his grandfather's family.

Antoku wept with sadness for the ravaged corpses in the water, thrust aside by the passage of the ship's hull. Staring eyes, armored bodies thick with arrow fletchings, bobbing, sinking beneath the waves. All of them because of him.

The pursuing ships came after them with relentless fervor, their banners fluttering with the blue *mon* of bamboo leaves and gentian blossoms.

An eternity of pain stole his breath, his voice, his mind. In the interstices between tortures, Ken'ishi's consciousness disappeared. He must have slept, but even his dreams were filled with excruciations. His world became a dank, wet cave where a pale, waspy man beat him, embedded bamboo slivers into his flesh, under his fingernails and toenails, through his tongue, where he lay bound, hanged, trussed, deprived of water and food. When he was fed, he received only water and runny millet gruel. Bereft of the sun, he lost all sense of time.

Green Tiger visited many times, and Ken'ishi came to feel an immense wash of relief at hearing the master's voice, because it meant that the pain would stop for a while. Green Tiger admonished the torturer for his cruelty, always warning him not to cause permanent injury.

Ken'ishi wondered what was meant by "permanent." His nose was broken, his tongue was a hot, swollen lump after being pierced by the bamboo, and his fingers were searing, bloody messes from bamboo slivers under his nails.

Green Tiger's voice would become almost fatherly. "This

214

doesn't have to go on. You've proven your strength. No one has ever withstood it for this long. Our friend is running out of fresh tricks that don't leave permanent damage. I may come back soon and find you with your hands missing, or your feet, or your eyes. You can make it stop right now, this instant, and take your place at my side."

Ken'ishi would say, "Kill me."

And then Green Tiger would disappear, and Ken'ishi would fall into the Void once again, whether it was the Void of No-Thought, or the void of unconsciousness, he did not know. But he had a dream once, when his body had been most ravaged, of trying to swim through a lake of thick, molten fire, of his skin and flesh being seared away, layer by layer, one hand already reduced to a blackened stump, until the bones of his remaining hand closed upon something cool and vibrant, a silver rope, and the moment he touched it, a flash of cool liquidity shot through him, soothing the fire, and suddenly his hands had flesh again, and he snatched at the silvery rope with his other hand, now full and alive once more, and he clung to it as the fiery tides lashed over him. The silver rope throbbed in his hand like a vein, and something flowed into him. He felt the fire's heat, but the pain receded to a dream within a dream. In those moments, he wept with thanks.

A voice echoed from the edges of his dream. "What is this? Tears! Crying like a baby? Running out of that grit, perhaps?"

Ken'ishi had no connection to his body. For all he knew, the torturer could be cutting it into small pieces now. Perhaps he was already dead, and this was the afterlife. Perhaps he was simply waiting to be reborn, and these images in his mind were dreams of life, or dreams of dreams of life.

Antoku loved the whisper of bamboo in an autumn breeze, when the air was cool, and the whispers seemed to tell stories meant only for him. Gentian flowers were pretty, such a sharp blue. And yet, they were a symbol of the men coming to kill him.

His uncle stood beside him, his face pale and drawn, two arrows embedded in his armor or his flesh. His *tachi* was in his hand. He laid a hand on the boy's head, and spoke solemn words to the boy's grandmother. Grandmother nodded solemnly.

And the ships closed.

And the battle raged.

And his grandmother took him up, held him close, and leaped.

And the sea closed over his head like the cover over the candle flame of his life, rushing into his mouth, and he sank through the empty bodies of the dead samurai, toward the sea bottom. And the spirits of the dead swirled like silken shadows through the dark depths. His uncle sank like a stone with the anchor rope tied around him, silver sword glinting in blue sea. Before the boy's candle starved of life, he saw the sea bottom alive with crabs, and the anguished spirits of the dead flowed into the crabs, and the crabs rose up to accept the spirits, their pincers raised to meet the blood-trailing feasts sinking toward them.

And the sword fell to the sea bottom, where it settled among the silt and blood.

A freshet of cool water trickling into his mouth sent his arms thrashing in panic. He was lying on his back, a cloth pillow under his head. His legs lay stretched out. There were no ropes upon him. Jewels of water clung to the ceiling of the cave, glistening with yellow lamplight. The stench of his own blood, sweat, and waste filled his broken nose. His trousers were sodden and full of cold paste. His naked back lay upon cool stone.

The torturer leaned over him, the expression on his face a strange mix of madness and respect. "Knowing you has taught me that not all men are weak. For that, I thank you."

Ken'ishi's tongue was so hot and swollen that he could manage nothing more than a croak.

"You are getting your wish. Our time together is coming to an end." The torturer lifted Ken'ishi's head and poured more water into his mouth.

Ken'ishi coughed and gulped, but he swallowed as much as he could.

The torturer offered another ladle of water. "Yes, good, drink as much as you can. You're going to need it."

Then the torturer slipped a cloth bag over Ken'ishi's head.

By flowering pear
And the lamp of the
   moon
She reads her letter
         — *Buson*

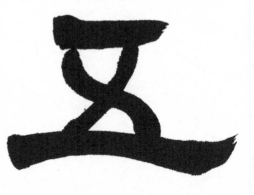

With the shrine of night sky sliding over the crest of the castle keep above her, and the immense earth and stone edifice of the castle below her, Kazuko slept between earth and sky. Lofted skyward by the light of distant ancestors, anchored by the solidity of the castle's fortifications, she floated between. Tsunetomo's quiet snores beside her, his seed drying against her thigh, his breath still in her nose, she floated between. Yearning for her womb to quicken and fulfill her purpose as Tsunetomo's wife, wishing that the seed belonged to someone else, she floated between.

A sound popped her bubble of slumber, distant and half-heard.

She sat up. The gauze of mosquito net whispered with the breeze through the window, a floating web of silver and shadow.

In spite of the night's warmth, she pulled her thin robe tighter around her. Something had left her with a chill across her back, over her breasts. What sound had awakened her? Her mind filled with a strange buzzing.

A moan rose like a specter, filtering through rice-paper partitions. The faint echo made Kazuko think that the sound had risen from the stairwell. Looking at her husband, she considered waking him. No. She could take care of herself.

As she slid from under the net, the moan emerged again, not a sound of physical pain, but of deep, deep despair. *Hatsumi*, whispered through Kazuko's sleep-fogged mind. But the voice had not sounded like Hatsumi's. It had been deeper.

Kazuko padded toward the door, looking back at Tsunetomo. He stirred, but did not wake. If this disturbance was Hatsumi, he might be inclined to send her away. Kazuko would handle this herself. But what kind of creature made such a half-human noise? She opened the door and slipped into the hallway, padding toward the narrow stairwell.

A guard would be at the bottom of the stairwell. Had he heard the noise?

The moan rose from the stairwell again, soft but insistent. On the floor below were Hatsumi's chamber, and Yasutoki's when he was not absent, and chambers for the lord to entertain guests.

Kazuko descended into the narrow black box, whispering, "Is someone there?"

No reply came. Where was the guard? The doorway below was a dim rectangle of light.

There should be a guard standing just to the side, so she repeated her call.

Silence.

Her slippered feet followed the stairwell with practiced ease. The nightingale plank sang under her foot.

A few dim candles lit the empty hallway below.

"Hatsumi!" she whispered.

Silence.

"Guard!" she said.

Silence.

She emerged into the hallway below. There was no guard. The man responsible for leaving his post at the lord and lady's bedchamber would face the harshest punishment.

She crept down the hallway toward the door of Hatsumi's chamber, taking down a candle as she passed a sconce.

A muffled thump, a shuffling footstep.

She raised her voice, "Who's there?"

Whispers.

"Hatsumi," she said.

She slid the door aside.

In the darkness she discerned two figures, one hunched on the floor, the other, taller, standing over the other, head bowed.

She held the candle aloft. "Hatsumi."

The figure on the floor looked back, eyes glowing yellow for just an instant in the candlelight, like an animal caught. The figure's hair was wild and unkempt. Kazuko recognized Hatsumi's robe. Hatsumi turned, and her mouth opened into another moan, blackened teeth around a stiff, pink tongue.

Kazuko stepped back.

The standing figure was the guard, head bowed. The lacquered plates of his armor turned the candlelight into a hundred dim flames, and his sword hung at his hip. He did not move.

"Guard!" Kazuko said. "What is the meaning of this?"

The guard's stance faltered for a moment, and then he shook his head, as if waking from a dream. His eyes widened like unpolished shells. After several long heartbeats, they focused upon her, and a look of horror dawned on his face as his gaze flicked between her and the figure.

Hatsumi turned away, her moan intensifying. Her claws raked and tore through her hair, tufts coming out between her fingers.

Kazuko ran to her side. "Hatsumi, it is a nightmare! Wake up!" She took Hatsumi's shoulders and shook them, but there was a strange strength in them that resisted for a moment. The moaning stopped, Hatsumi's face turned to Kazuko, eyes wide, fixing upon her, a storm of confusion.

Hatsumi said, "My lady, what are you doing here? Aren't you still alive?"

"I am, dear Hatsumi, wake up! I am alive, and so are you!"

Hatsumi blinked again, "I'm walking on the roof of hell."

Tears streamed down Kazuko's face at the pain in Hatsumi's eyes. "What?"

Hatsumi shook her head. "I am ... I was walking ... on the roof of hell. And here you were ... are."

"You were dreaming!"

Her voice came as if from a dream. "Dreaming."

The guard suddenly threw himself prostrate beside her, spewing apologies and tears of shame.

She turned on him. "Why did you leave your post?"

He pressed the plate of his armored headband to the floor, his voice halting, confused. "I do not know, my lady! I cannot remember! I heard a noise, I think.... Please accept my apology, my lady. I am disgraced. I will ... I will offer my life to my lord tomorrow!"

Kazuko wiped at her tears and straightened. "There is no need for that. There is no need for my husband to know of this. No need for anyone else to know of this. Anyone. Do you understand?"

"Yes, my lady."

"You may return to your post. Your vigilance is to be commended."

"Yes, my lady!" He jumped up and bowed his way out of the room.

When he was gone, Hatsumi said, "Why are you here?"

"I heard ... a noise. I found you here moaning pitifully."

"Moaning. I do not remember." She held up her hands, and long strands of dark hair trailed from her fingers. Sobs burst out of her.

"Oh, Kazuko, what is happening to me?" Hatsumi wept, collapsing against Kazuko.

Kazuko hugged her but bit back her thoughts. Was Hatsumi going mad? Was the person Kazuko had known from childhood falling into darkness? Hatsumi wept against Kazuko's shoulder, and Kazuko cursed Yasutoki's callous games for driving her to such bleak, black depths. They were depths that Kazuko knew well from her own heart. How long had she taken to emerge from them herself?

For a long time, Kazuko held her, until Hatsumi's tears seeped through Kazuko's robes. When Hatsumi's anguish had subsided, Kazuko put her back to bed, feeling the incipient dawn outside. An immense weariness washed over her as she trudged back upstairs.

As she slid back into bed, Tsunetomo's voice startled her. "It was Hatsumi, was it not?"

Something in his voice stirred her belly to dread. "Yes. It was just a nightmare." She lay on her side, facing away.

After a moment, his strong hand lay gently on her shoulder. "I know you love her."

The tears she had held back while comforting Hatsumi spilled out of her. When she could form words again, she said, "I fear she has gone mad."

"She has already all but destroyed her reputation. She should forget any thoughts of marriage. If word of more of this spreads, she will be shunned, or find herself a laughingstock at best. I want you to send her away."

A bolt of ice shot through her, directly into the space she had prepared for those words. "Please, Husband. Let me help her."

He removed his hand. "I will bow to your wishes for now. But when you find that she cannot be helped, it should be you who sends her away." Bedcovers flopped over her, and he rolled out of bed, leaving her alone again with her despair.

Half in a dream
I become aware
That the voices of the
    crickets
Grow faint with the
    growing Autumn.
I mourn for this lonely
Year that is passing
And my own being
Grows fainter and
    fades away.
        — *The Love Poems of*
        Marichiko

Blackness so empty that Ken'ishi could not distinguish the waking world from the Void. Rough stone cooled his back. He touched his eye with a ravaged fingertip and found it open. The cool, dank air smelled of the sea. His breath caught in his throat for a moment, and the gasp echoed sharply. Water lapped against stone, echoing in a small cavern. Distant surf thundered somewhere.

Willing his aching limbs to obey, he explored the dimensions of his black confines. One arm reached a rough-hewn stone wall; the other fell against a lattice of bamboo bars. He tried to heave himself into a sitting position and smashed his head against the jagged stone ceiling. Stars exploded in his vision, fresh pain and a trickle of warm blood running over his ear. The ceiling was too low for him to sit up, perhaps an arm's length above. He could roll, however, or lay on his side.

His mouth was as dry as an empty gourd. He could not remember the last time he had eaten. He was in too much pain to be hungry, but he knew he needed food. Even the thin millet gruel would be welcome. He could not eat much else. A moment of gratefulness that he still had all his teeth, even though two of them felt loosened.

For eternities, he lay there on his back, sometimes shifting to his side, endless pain washing through him like surf.

Then the sounds of the surf intensified. Seawater lapped into his cell. Before long, it began to slosh toward him, and the brine made his fingers, toes, and other wounds burst into searing flame. The incoming tide brought the water higher and higher in the blackness. Blind, he grabbed hold of the bamboo lattice and held his face above the surging seawater, even as it crept closer to the ceiling.

Animal panic exploded in his chest, bringing fresh strength. He thrashed and tore at the bamboo bars as best he could, weakened as he was, but they remained immobile.

And the tide rushed in.

His body floated until it bumped the ceiling of his cell. Seawater splashed into his gasping mouth, and he spat and fought for breath, striving to keep his nose and mouth above the surface. He found a rough-hewn corner of the cell opening with a higher pocket that allowed him to keep his nose above water.

Amid the rushing water, he caught the sound of coughing, gasping, echoing through the chamber. Another prisoner?

The jagged stone rubbed rough and cold against one cheek, the hard roundness of bamboo squeezed against the other, black water lapping into his gasping mouth, and he prayed to all the gods and Buddhas that the tide would come no higher.

More eternities passed in the blackness as the tide's advance halted, and then eventually withdrew. His hands and arms ached from holding his face above the water.

Many hours later, he lay upon the wet stone floor of the cell again, exhausted and shivering. His flesh felt burned and tender, wrinkled like a pickled plum, his limbs half-numb from cold.

A tremulous voice echoed through the cavern. "Is someone there?"

Ken'ishi opened his mouth to say, "Yes," but barely a croak issued forth. The seawater burned his tongue, but he licked his cracked lips.

"I can hear you," the voice said. "Please tell me someone is there."

Ken'ishi coughed and cleared his throat, then tried to speak. It had been so long. "I am here."

"Oh, thank all the gods and Buddhas! I have been here alone for so long."

"How long?"

"Twelve tides have come and gone."

"Who are you?"

"It doesn't matter who I am, does it?" The despair spilled from the disembodied voice.

Ken'ishi said, "You are not my enemy. It feels good to have another standing with me in this bowel of Hell."

A pause, then. "Yes, it does. I am Minamoto no Hirosuke."

Ken'ishi vaguely recollected that this was the clan of the Shogun. "Why are you here?"

A sob echoed. "It doesn't matter. One's deeds sometimes overwhelm the man himself. I am ... I was a scholar, a chronicler, in Dazaifu. I worked for the Shogun's government. I was good at what I did! And I am destined to die in a black, forgotten sea cave. Please, tell me of you. Who is my companion on the road to hell?"

"I am Ken'ishi, a *ronin*. I refused to submit to Green Tiger's will."

"As did I. I refused his bribes. I would not be his spy in the government's offices. I am sure that I have since been replaced by someone more pliable."

"Won't your family miss you? The Minamoto are a powerful clan. Won't they be looking for you?"

Fits of coughing interrupted the man's words. "The Shogun's court considers Kyushu little more than an unruly backwater, populated by fractious samurai lords who resist the *bakufu*'s edicts. Besides, the Hojo clan holds the balance of power these days."

"Your parents? Your wife?"

"My father is in the old capital. His influence secured a post for me in Dazaifu. My wife is there, too, and my sons. She is a good woman, kind and thoughtful. It was a good match my parents made. If only I could see her again." His voice fell into despair again. "I will be long dead before they know anything is amiss."

The despair in the man's voice brought up Ken'ishi's memories of Kazuko's quiet cries of passion on the only night they had been together, the intense beauty of her naked body in his arms.

Hirosuke continued, "I had a lover before her, a wealthy merchant's daughter whose husband had left her. She was the most beautiful woman I have ever known, but her blood ran so hot and cold, push and pull, that it drove me half-mad with trying to win her fully to me. But how I loved her, and how I despaired."

In other circumstances, Ken'ishi would have been uncomfortable with a tale so fraught with private emotion, but now he was simply exulted to hear another's voice. Perhaps Hirosuke was spilling his heart for the same reason.

"Part of me was relieved when her father found another husband for her and sent her away. A few months later, I met Yuka, so kind and sweet, and asked her father for her hand soon after. She made me forget the woman who had turned me into a shadow of myself."

Ken'ishi's rough stone cell became a soft *futon* against his back, and Kiosé's gentle, warm hands lay upon his chest, on his face, her face sleeping against his shoulder. A spasm of regret shot through him. Her quiet sighs of contentment as she fell asleep in his embrace. The gasps of passion as she pulled him deeper into her. The food she brought him, always without being asked. The cleanliness of his house, all her doing. He missed her so badly at that moment, wished to be with her.

He whispered to the darkness. "As soon as I have Silver Crane, Kiosé, I will come back to you, and we will take Little Frog and leave Aoka village forever."

"What's that you say?" came Hirosuke's voice.

Ken'ishi clamped back the lump in his throat, then cleared it. "I said, maybe they will let you go. Maybe they are just punishing you, frightening you. Maybe they will have mercy."

An empty chuckle. "Perhaps."

The sound of heavy footsteps splashing over stone broke the conversation. Yellow light swelled through the chamber, blinding bright even in its dimness. Ken'ishi squinted against the glare of the lantern as it came closer and closer. A massive figure loomed before the entrance of his cell, and the enormous Chinaman thrust a bowl of gruel through the lattice.

Hunger roared through Ken'ishi like a wildfire, but he did not seize the bowl and fall upon it like an animal. He would not give this creature the satisfaction. Instead, he called, "Water!"

The Chinaman looked back over a meaty shoulder with an expression of amused disdain as he went farther down the passageway and thrust another bowl into some unseen cell.

Hirosuke's frenzied slurping brought a smile to the Chinaman's face that Ken'ishi could just see, a smile and something else, something darker, as of a secret. The Chinaman went back the way he had come and took the light with him.

Ken'ishi devoured the pitifully small portion of gruel, licking the bowl, sucking at every last kernel of tasteless millet, every drop of moisture. His pierced tongue ached, but there was nothing to be done about it.

With the empty bowl in hand, he sagged onto his back.

After an interminable time, Hirosuke's voice brought Ken'ishi out of his dreams of Kiosé's arms and Little Frog's hoarse giggles.

"Beware the crabs."

"What?"

"I said, beware the crabs. They come out at low tide."

Ken'ishi imagined his cell invaded by an army of pincers and shells, pincers that snipped off bits of flesh to be stuffed into little chitinous mouths.

"Do you know the stories?" Hirosuke said. "Have you seen the crabs with the faces of samurai on their backs?"

"No, I'm not a fisherman."

"In the last hundred years, a new kind of crab has been found, spreading from the straits near Dan-no-ura, the gateway to the Inland Sea."

"You say 'Dan-no-ura' with much weight. I am not from Kyushu, so I don't know that place."

Hirosuke's voice brightened as if delighted to share his vast knowledge. "It is one of the narrowest gaps between Kyushu and Honshu. The tides there are fierce. Even experienced sailors approach that stretch of water with care."

"And what about the crabs?"

"Ah, it was a terrible day, but a glorious one, almost ninety years ago now. The most glorious day for the Minamoto clan. It was the day that we crushed the Taira clan. So many warriors died on both sides that day. Their bodies must have littered the sea bottom of the straits at Dan-no-ura as thick as fallen leaves, along with the false emperor Antoku and the rest of the Taira who wanted to use him. The sea was awash with blood. This battle ended the war, all but destroyed the Taira." His voice drew into a practiced cadence, precise, dramatic. "It was soon after the battle that fishermen began to discover crabs with the shape of samurai faces on their backs. It is said that the spirits of the dead Minamoto and Taira samurai went into those crabs. To honor the souls of all those fallen warriors, or perhaps to avoid angering any hungry ghosts, the fishermen throw these crabs back into the sea."

Ken'ishi found himself lost in the story, but something else scratched at his memory. "The 'false emperor Antoku', you said. Tell me about him."

"He was just a boy of six. Minamoto troops were about to take his vessel when his grandmother, Tokiko, a Buddhist nun, took him into the sea, along with all their handmaids and bodyguards. The boy's uncle, Taira no Tomomori, commander of the ship, followed them to the bottom by tying himself to an anchor. A sad thing for a child to die that way, a pawn of ruthless power-mongers who told him he was the Son of Heaven."

"Did Taira no Tomomori have a sword?"

"That is certain. He was an heir to the Taira clan, son of Kiyomori. Kiyomori's name is still spoken with awe in the old capital."

"I mean, did he have a well-known sword?"

"There were many relics the Taira had claimed for themselves, symbols of the false emperor's power, the Imperial Sword, the Mirror, and the Jewel. They threw the Imperial Sword into the sea, but we captured their ships before they could throw away the rest. Tomomori would have had the best of the Taira clan at his disposal. For over three hundred years, they controlled the Imperial Court. They had the most renowned smiths in their employ."

"Was the Imperial Sword a tachi-style weapon?"

"No, it was ancient beyond compare, handed down from the Sun Goddess Amaterasu herself to the first Emperor. It was straight like a Chinese sword, but with a shorter, broader blade. But now it is lost at the bottom of the sea. Tomomori and the others guarding Antoku would have had the best weapons Taira smiths could create. Why all this curiosity? There is more to it than an interest in history."

"I have seen dreams of these events, and the things you speak of ring truth for me."

"Dreams can be pernicious things, taunting us with our desires, torturing us with our fears, as if the best and worst of what we can imagine come to life when we sleep. I have had such ... such dreams in this place. After what I have seen coming in recent months, I have dreams only of war and death."

"What have you seen coming?"

"Dark days! The *bakufu*'s spies have learned that the Koryo have been building ships for Khubilai Khan, Emperor of China. Hundreds of ships, perhaps thousands, denuding entire forests. The shipyards of Masan and Pusan have been teeming with activity. The Koryo have no love for the Mongols, but they have been forced to submit. The might of the Golden Horde, as they call themselves, is too strong."

"But why cross the sea? Is the whole of China not enough?"

"Not for men like Khubilai Khan. The Khan has sent several emissaries to the Imperial Court and to the *bakufu* over the last few years. The last one to arrive in Dazaifu carried threats of invasion. The emissary was imprisoned for several months before he was expelled. The Shogunate has ordered the lords of Kyushu to maintain a state of vigilance and to build their troop strength. For three years the lords of the Western Defense Region have been building their armies. But such lords are a willful, fractious lot. If the Mongols do not come, war is likely to erupt among them."

Ken'ishi thought about having spent three years in Aoka village. "Perhaps when we get out of here, I will be able to find a lord to serve." What if he had just kept looking for a lord to serve? What if he had never saved Kazuko's life and found himself fleeing her father's grasp, forced to hide in a quiet backwater when he should have been honing his skills and cleaving to the Warrior's Way?

After a period of silence, he heard Hirosuke weeping. Ken'ishi said, "Brace up, Hirosuke. You have come this far with honor. Don't forget it now. Tell me about your life, and I will tell you about mine. Tell me what you'll do after we escape."

"Escape! Hah! You're mad. There is no escape from Green Tiger."

"Don't lose hope. Tell me." The bowl in Ken'ishi's hands was made of plain wood, its lip rounded.

Hirosuke sighed and spoke, telling tales of his childhood in Kyoto, spending his life in the circles of learning and scholarship, where he studied the Chinese classics, history, and poetry.

Meanwhile, Ken'ishi slammed the edge of the bowl on the stone, but he was too weak and the wood was too thick to shatter.

"What was that?" Hirosuke asked.

"Pay no attention. Tell me more." Ken'ishi's fingers explored the bindings of the bamboo lattice, finding them taut and fresh, the bamboo green and rigid. He listened to Hirosuke's tales, urging him on at intervals of silence. He began to scrape the lip of the bowl against the floor, wearing away the blunt edge to create a sharper one, in spite of the burning pain in his fingertips. "You are a good man, Minamoto no Hirosuke, to have stood up against one such as Green Tiger. Tell me what you will do after we escape."

"Ah, you are a dreamer, Ken'ishi. I harbor no illusion that we will escape, but if we do, I will go back to Kyoto and be with my wife and children. Kyushu will never see me again."

Ken'ishi continued scraping the lip of the bowl against the rough stone. An edge was forming.

"I have three sons, two of them bookish boys like I was, but the third will be a warrior, I think. Perhaps when he is grown, he will avenge my death." Hirosuke's voice cracked, and he wept for a while.

Ken'ishi continued scraping his bowl. His belly roared for food, and his throat yearned for water, but still he worked at the bowl until his hands could barely grasp it. After some time, he had worn the rounded lip into a crude edge, and he used it to saw at an inconspicuous corner of the bindings around the bamboo lattice.

Then the tide returned and turned his wounds to fire once again, and he was too weak to cling to the lattice and also cut at its bindings. He spent hours barely able to keep his face above water.

At one point, he called out to Hirosuke, "The tide is not as high this time."

"But what happens when it fluctuates higher than our ceilings?"

Clear water —
a tiny crab
crawling up my leg.
— *Buson*

When the tide receded again, the Chinaman's lumbering bulk broke the blackness to bring another bowl of gruel and demanded the old bowl back. Ken'ishi prayed for him to overlook not only the two sets of bindings that had been cut through, but also the ground edge of the bowl.

In the silence between the jailor's departure and the arrival of the next tide, Ken'ishi told Hirosuke of Kiosé and Little Frog, Norikage and Aoka village. As he spoke, he ground the new bowl's edge against the rough stone to create another edge with which to worry at the lattice bindings.

"We are lucky," Hirosuke said, "to have women who care for us, even if yours is not a human being."

Ken'ishi did not like to think about how the world did not see whores, or former whores, as true human beings. "For a long time, I didn't believe it, didn't care. I was selfish, lost in longing for another."

"But now things look different."

232

"Yes."

"And the girl you lost?"

"Married to another, a samurai lord."

"The world cares not for the yearnings of a boy's heart. Or a man's." Hirosuke said the next words tentatively. "If we can escape, if we ever see the light of day again, I will go back to Kyoto. You must go back to your village and take your woman and keep her with you. And your son."

Ken'ishi nodded to the darkness. "Yes, my son."

"Bring them with you to Kyoto, and I will see to it that you have a home in the Minamoto clan."

"You are a generous—Ah!" A sharp pain sliced into Ken'ishi's elbow. He jerked his arm away, scraping skin from his hand onto the ceiling.

Hirosuke said, "What is it?"

"Something just ..." He slid away from the source of the pain and touched his elbow, feeling wetness on his fingers. His back rolled over something crusty and squirming beneath him. Another sharp stab between his shoulder blades. He cried out in anger, lifted himself from the shape, felt it scuttle from under him. "Crabs!"

"They are fierce. A shame we cannot eat them."

Ken'ishi lashed out and swept the first horny shell, about the size of his palm, back out through the lattice. The second snipped him once more on the neck before he snatched it and crushed it against the wall. "When we get out of here, let us feast on boiled crabs!"

Hirosuke's chuckle echoed strangely. "Indeed—Away, foul little beast!" A scraping, rustling from Hirosuke's cell. "Their pincers are small but sharp. In enough numbers, they could strip our bones clean in a few hours."

In the silent darkness, Ken'ishi strained his ears for carapaced legs scuttling nearer. He periodically swept his arms blindly over the floor, but he found no more. Somehow, he sensed their presence hovering outside the bars, as if waiting for their chance.

His fingers sought the crab that he had crushed, brought it to his mouth and sucked at the foul paste leaking from its shell. His belly rebelled and forced him to spit it back out.

Its body was a pulpy mess of ooze and sharp edges. His fingers traced a ragged, broken pincer. With his tiny tool, he began to saw through the bamboo bindings.

Another tide came and went.

As the sea receded, the sound of sloshing feet echoed through the cavern, accompanied by even more light. This time, it was the torturer who passed by Ken'ishi's cell, carrying a lantern, followed by the Chinaman, who carried not only a lantern in one hand, but also some sort of stout wooden rack under the other arm.

Now in the light, he could see the level of his cell opening was perhaps half his height above the uneven floor of the outer cavern.

Ken'ishi pressed his face against the lattice, straining to see, a sick dread building in his belly. The men hung their lanterns on hooks embedded in the stone, and the Chinaman began to erect the wooden rack. Only one corner of the rack lay within Ken'ishi's field of vision.

Hirosuke's voice trembled. "What are you doing? What are you going to do to me?" He repeated this over and over as the Chinaman continued his work.

Ken'ishi could see ropes hanging from the rack. Some shifting, clattering sounds, and Hirosuke's voice grew higher, building level upon level of desperation.

The rhythmic scrape of a blade on a whetstone.

The sounds coming from Hirosuke's cell ceased. A limp dragging, scuffling sound, the slap of flesh against wood, the slither of ropes. Ken'ishi saw the Chinaman bind Hirosuke's clenched fist to the wooden rack. The rest lay out of view, but Ken'ishi surmised that Hirosuke was now tied to the rack with arms and legs outstretched.

The torturer's voice sent a bolt of ice through Ken'ishi's veins and clamped his teeth together. "Our friend Fang Shi here taught me this technique. Those Chinese, they are inventive." More scraping of the whetstone, the ring of expectant steel.

Hirosuke blubbered. "I have money. My family has money! Let me go, and I will reward you! Please!"

The Chinaman and the torturer laughed long and loud.

Hirosuke hung silent in his bonds, falling into shallow, quavering breaths.

Ken'ishi called out, "Don't! Take me instead!"

The torturer laughed. "Oh, don't be foolish. The Master may still have use for *you*. Ah, my noble friend," he said to Hirosuke, "I have been looking forward to this for days. You will give me such joy."

Fang Shi rumbled, "Ropes tight, pinch skin hard. Stop blood."

"Of course! In my excitement I almost forgot. With the ropes too loose, he may bleed out too quickly. You may do the honors, sir."

More slithering, tightening ropes. Hirosuke's grunting, gasping, his breathing becoming shallower, constricted.

The torturer purred, "Ah, lovely little gobbets of flesh now, so graspable, easy to cut. Well done, Fang Shi. Shall we begin?"

Ken'ishi's voice failed him, and hope drained away.

Hirosuke screamed.

Ken'ishi could not tear his gaze away from Hirosuke's outstretched hand as it spasmed and clenched. Something trickled into the sheet of seawater covering the floor. A little splash as of something tossed into the water.

The torturer grinned with satisfaction. "See, now that was just a little piece. That wasn't so bad, was it?"

Hirosuke screamed again, and again his fist clenched, but weaker this time, and the trickling grew, and something else plopped into the water.

"Ah, so lovely," the torturer said, "like twin red camellias on your breast. You will be one of my greatest works, my friend."

Ken'ishi closed his eyes and tried to block his ears against Hirosuke's screams. The torturer marveled over each cut, the beauty of the blood flow, speaking to Hirosuke as if they were long-lost friends, intimate confidants. The stench of blood and emptied bowels filled the cavern. Hirosuke's fist was no longer a

235

fist. It was just a bloody, fingerless palm. Then the palm was gone, shrunk to just an oozing wrist with the white bones peeking out through the trickling blood and sliced sinews. Bits of flesh pattered into the shallow crimson water, dozens of bloody morsels, fingers, knuckle by knuckle, toes, ears, all floated around the feet of the two executioners. The floor of the cavern was awash with blood and bits of flesh.

Hirosuke's ragged breathing sent shudders through Ken'ishi's body. Ken'ishi marveled at how the man clung to life. He clutched and tore at the bars, but his weakened bindings were not yet weak enough. "For the mercy of all the gods and Buddhas, kill him!"

Fang Shi and the torturer just laughed. And then the wet, meaty chopping sounds began. The glint of a meat cleaver in the torturer's hand. A severed piece of a foot splashed into the water. Then harder chopping, splintering of thick bones.

Ken'ishi lost the moment when the weeping stopped forever.

"He dead?" Fang Shi said.

"Not yet, but he seems to have lost consciousness."

The splash of water and a gasp of breath that wept.

Brine and blood painted the floor of the cavern, and hundreds of tiny pieces of flesh—skin, muscle, bone, entrails—floated on the surface or trailed across the bottom. The water rose.

The torturer said, "It seems our timing is impeccable. Let us go ahead of the tide."

More slithering of ropes, a little splash, and then Fang Shi collapsed the wooden rack. The torturer rolled up coils of blood-soaked rope. As they turned to retreat, the torturer knelt in front of Ken'ishi's cell. "And all you must do is say, 'Master, I will serve you.'"

Ken'ishi spat the words, one by one. "Bastard! I will kill you!"

The torturer and Fang Shi laughed. "That's the spirit!" Then they disappeared, but they had left one lantern hanging near the ceiling of the cavern.

And then the water rose, along with the black rage in Ken'ishi's belly. He tore and thrashed at the bars with his ruined fingernails, but the bindings were made of tough sinew and he was weaker than he could ever remember. The few he had managed to cut were not yet enough to break free.

Crimson water lapped into his cell, stinking of blood and viscera. Bits and pieces of Hirosuke washed in with the water. Ken'ishi clamped his teeth against the bile rising in his throat. The incoming tide foamed red, sloshing flesh and blood around the cavern. A triangular fin the size of his hand slashed up through the surface of the water. Gobbets of flesh began to disappear in sudden splashes.

As the water flooded into Ken'ishi's cell, the lantern's light diminished and finally disappeared altogether, plunging him once again into the familiar blackness. Again he struggled against the bars and then succumbed, clinging to them for life. Soft fleshy bits bobbed against his cheeks, and when he swallowed seawater, he swallowed blood, too.

With the tide at its full height, Ken'ishi's face was jammed into the tiny pocket of air between the cell ceiling and the lattice. Something bumped into the bamboo. Something alive. Another bump. A lithe rippling body brushed against his fingers, and he jerked them away. The body had not been scaly like most fish. A pointed nose thrust through the lattice into his cheek. He sucked a lungful of seawater as he flung himself away. His fingers closed around a blunt snout, and the hide felt rough like Silver Crane's ray-skin hilt. The snout jerked away. He held his breath as long as he could and then sought the tiny niche again for another breath. When he found the niche, he sucked at the air and then pulled himself back into the cell again to hold his breath. Dozens of times he repeated this, scores. Several times he stayed in the niche longer, hoping the fish had gone, but then he would feel a gentle bump against the bamboo and know it was still out there, probing, perhaps snapping up bits of Hirosuke as it found them.

Hours later, when he lay once again on the floor of his cell in the darkness, sodden, shivering, and seawater-logged, he heard a subtle conglomeration of scuttling and clicking against the stone out in the larger cavern. An army of crabs, drawn by the taste of blood in the water, scoured the floor for bits of flesh and tender viscera.

The light returned with Fang Shi's menace. He stood before the cell and held out his hand. "Bowl." Ken'ishi passed his bowl through the bars. Fang Shi slung the fresh bowlful of gruel through the bars. It splattered across the stone floor and into Ken'ishi's hair. "Clever," he said. This time he took the bowl and the light with him.

Ken'ishi seethed, but his hunger became so sharp, so biting, that he licked the watery gruel from the coarse stone, trying to ignore the taste of saltwater and blood. He had been so hungry for so long, so thirsty for so long. How many times had he envisioned taking long draughts of seawater to quench his thirst?

The blackness around him permeated his skull, driving black tendrils deep into his thoughts. All he must do to be free was serve Green Tiger. He could live. Perhaps he could even have the opportunity to exact revenge. Perhaps he could just pretend. Perhaps he could have Silver Crane in his hands, and then he could flee, and then he could retrieve Kiosé and take her away with him. Perhaps serving Green Tiger would not be so bad. He would have plenty of food, plenty of gold, perhaps enough to secure a sword master to teach him. As Green Tiger had said, Ken'ishi would have power in the Underworld. He would be feared, perhaps like Hakamadare. Would it not be favorable to make lesser men like Yuto fear him? Perhaps one day he would have opportunity to rid the world of Green Tiger and men like him. Perhaps then he could return to Teng Zhou and conclude their duel. Perhaps with Green Tiger dead, Ken'ishi could become a lord of the Underworld himself. Kiosé would want for nothing. Little Frog could learn the ways of the samurai. The boy would not have to be the bastard son of a used-up whore. Little Frog could be the son of a samurai, with a real name, a brave name.

All Ken'ishi had to do was swear to serve Green Tiger, and his suffering would end.

Would Little Frog want to be the son of such a man?

If part of Ken'ishi's service were to wrangle whores, frighten unruly gamblers, punish thieves, would he be worthy of Kiosé's affection? Would she want such a man?

As the seawater ate into his wounds and turned his clothing into sodden rags, as hunger gnawed at his belly like a frenzied wharf rat, as his body withered like a dry twig and his tongue became leather, he thought that the next time Fang Shi came with food, he would accede to Green Tiger's wishes.

And then Fang Shi came, threw the food at him through the bars, and departed, and Ken'ishi held his tongue.

Many times the tide came and went, Fang Shi came and went, and every time, he intended to succumb to Green Tiger's wishes, but every time, he kept silent. He just slurped up his food as best he could and kept silent.

Sometimes, he dreamed of things that brought him strength. A silver bucket lowered to him as he lay trapped in the bottom of a well, and he drank vibrant, shimmering elixir from the bucket. A crane brought him a silver egg that he took and clutched to his breast until it melted into him. A woman, standing in a shrine to Jizo to avoid the downpour of the world, invited him to take shelter with her and gave him a gleaming rice ball that he devoured. A silver net lowered him into some glimmering lake of cool, soothing water that bubbled with life and *kami*. After such dreams, the pain of his wounds, the ever-present ache in his back and neck, the maddening thirst and hunger, all diminished for a time.

He lost count of how many times the tide came and went, but as the days passed, the seawater became cooler with the passing season. Every day, his body took longer to stop shivering after the water receded.

Somewhere in the depths of his mind, he knew he would not last much longer. If winter came, he would die of cold.

Fang Shi's damnable, blessed light speared into Ken'ishi's eyes. He squeezed them shut, and his voice was a barely audible croak. "Take me to your master. I will speak to him."

Fang Shi laughed.

On the mountain,
Tiring to the feet,
Lost in the fog, the
   pheasant
Cries out, seeking her
   mate.
         — *The Love Poems of*
              Marichiko

"Stupid whore!" Chiba snorted as he watched Kiosé running after Little Frog. The brat kept glancing over his shoulder to see if she was about to catch him, oblivious to the column of horsemen riding down the village's central street. It would certainly be amusing to watch him pummeled into pulp by the oncoming hooves. Kiosé squealed with panic and snatched the boy by the arm, jerking him clear. Chiba felt a twinge of disappointment.

He stepped back between two houses and leaned against the wall, curious about what brought a column of Otomo clan warriors into the village. There had not been a war since his grandfather's lifetime. Aoka was part of the Otomo clan domain, but too far north along the rim of Hakata Bay to be near any well-traveled road.

Clan banners flapped over the heads of the mounted samurai, all bristling with spears and arrows. The leader of the column's ten men reined up in the center of the village and called out. "Headman, come out!" Horses stamped and fidgeted, tossing their heads and fighting their bits.

Chiba appraised the lead samurai, who looked to be hardly a leader at all, with the face of a baby and armor that was too big for him, its weavings of metal scales and silk cords too elaborate, and its shoulder guards too broad. The flared cheek plates of the helmet made the leader's face look even smaller. The armor of the others was less elaborate, simply breastplates with modest helmets.

Kiosé clutched her brat to her chest and hissed scoldings into the boy's ears. If she had kept her back turned for two heartbeats longer, the world would have had one less bastard brat soiling the land.

The lead samurai's voice was just a bit too high to warrant real command, especially over the more seasoned, fierce-looking samurai who rode behind him. "I am Otomo no Ishitaka. Headman, come out!"

Norikage finally emerged from his office and bowed to the horsemen. "Greetings, Lord. My name is Norikage. How may I serve?"

"Is not Hojo no Masahige administrator of this village?" the samurai asked. "Where is he?"

Chiba's eyes narrowed. Hojo no Masahige had been dead three years. Chiba's father had killed him in a drunken brawl over that useless bitch Kiosé. How had word not reached the government that Hojo no Masahige was dead?

Norikage hesitated an instant. "I am his assistant, and Hojo-sama has gone to Hakozaki on business, but he is due back shortly. Perhaps you would like to come inside and refresh yourselves until he returns."

The samurai frowned. "We have no time. We have come to deliver a message."

"I will relay your message," Norikage said.

Chiba raised an eyebrow. What game was Norikage playing at?

The samurai said, "Barbarians from across the sea have sent

threatening messages to our Shogun and the illustrious Son of Heaven. The Shogun's regent, Hojo no Tokimune, has ordered that all towns and villages across Kyushu be informed of this situation and to prepare for a possible attack."

Stupid, soft nobles, fearful of shadows. They could all go hang themselves and the world would be the richer for it. On Chiba's occasional trips to Hakata and Hakozaki, he sometimes heard news that the emperor of China, some barbarian horseman from the steppes, a usurper, had been threatening war for almost a decade. He had subjugated the Koryo over the last few years, and now seemed to have his greedy eye on Kyushu. The Imperial Court in Kyoto had wanted to pay him tribute, but the *bakufu* in Kamakura had blatantly refused. They had not even allowed the foreign emissaries to land in Hakata. Chiba snorted with derision.

Norikage said, "That is dreadful news, Otomo-sama. Is there anything Aoka village can do? We have no weapons except clubs and pitchforks."

Ishitaka's smooth brow furrowed. "If we are attacked, take everything you have and retreat south to Dazaifu. Men and boys will be conscripted as spearmen. Now, bring us water. We have ridden long."

Naoko came out from the inn, carrying a bucket of water and a wooden ladle. She let each samurai drink his fill. Then she offered them rice balls, which they snatched up and devoured with gusto.

Norikage said, "When might such an attack happen? Tomorrow? Before winter?"

"The barbarians have not informed us of their attack plans," Ishitaka replied.

Chiba imagined what it must be like to wear armor in the summer heat. Fortunately, the heat had all but faded into autumn coolness in the last few weeks. No more sweltering crotch or dripping brow for every moment the sun was in the sky.

Otomo no Ishitaka thanked Naoko for the refreshment, then said to Norikage, "Please give my regards to your master. We must ride on."

Norikage bowed deeply. "Of course, Otomo-sama."

The samurai spurred their horses and galloped with a plume of dust into the forest.

What game was Norikage playing at? The *ronin* had been gone for more than a month, leaving the village without a constable. Norikage kept telling people that the "constable" would be back soon, that he had gone to Hakata on business, but Chiba was starting to doubt. And now, it seemed, Norikage had not only failed to inform the authorities of Hojo no Masahige's death, but also intended to keep up the deception that the late village administrator was still among the living.

Across the street, Kiosé's brat squirmed and fussed until she put him down. As she leaned over, her robe fell open to reveal a soft, supple breast, a tender nipple hanging free.

Like a forgotten ember, lust roared to life in Chiba's veins, rushing through him like a wildfire. He watched Kiosé tuck a few strands of hair behind her ear, and his eyes followed her, noting the carriage of her backside, the delicate flesh of her neck, until she disappeared inside the inn.

For the rest of the day, the village buzzed with gossip about the warriors' visit. Apparently only Chiba had been close enough to hear clearly the exchange between Norikage and Otomo no Ishitaka. Chiba heard no mention among the other villagers of the Otomo asking after Masahige.

As the sun set, Chiba sat alone in the inn with a fresh bottle of *saké*. The sweet warmth of its kiss suffused his belly and set his mind to scuttling about like a loose crab. He needed the *saké* tonight, almost as much as his little warrior needed the wet kiss of a woman.

Norikage was hiding something, Chiba was sure of it. The *ronin* had been gone roughly a month and a half. Was it possible that no one outside of the village knew of the *ronin*'s presence here? Had the *ronin* been acting as "constable" all this time without any real authority? What scheme had he and Norikage cooked up?

He smashed his earthen cup down against the table, startling the other patrons with the noise. The blow left a dent in the hardwood surface. He squeezed the rim of the cup, throttling it as if it were the *ronin*'s neck, but the clay did not yield.

"All this time ..." he muttered.

Old Naoko bowed to him as she passed. "Another jar?"

He grunted and shook his head.

Kiosé steadfastly ignored him as she carried a basket of dinner dishes outside to be washed.

Chiba's gaze fastened on the delicate curves of her ankles, the sway of her buttocks, before they disappeared into the evening's darkness. He grunted and shifted where he sat, curling his fingers around the edge of the table and squeezing.

He filled his cup and drained it, filled it again, drained it. Boldness burgeoned in his veins. He filled his cup one more time, and the jar was empty. He tossed the last of his *saké* back and hurried out the front door.

Only the moon-drenched surf broke the night's silence. Even the frogs and crickets lay strangely silent as he stole around the inn toward the back.

The clatter of dishes reached him even before he saw her there, bathed in the light of a lantern. A chill sea breeze ruffled in from shore, and she shivered against it, rubbing her arms with wet hands. Her hair was pinned up with a chopstick, revealing the sensuous curves of her neck.

His boning knife was in his hand, gleaming with its fresh edge.

He stole up behind her, quickly, shoeless, silent. From behind, he clamped his left hand over her gasping mouth and pressed the cold flat of his knife against her warm throat. Her eyes bulged white, and he jerked her head back against his shoulder.

"If you scream," he hissed, "I'll gut you like a yellowtail. And then I'll cut your brat's head off and leave it for the crabs."

Her body stiffened against him for a moment, and then almost collapsed in his arms.

"Where's your filthy protector, bitch?" he grunted as he dragged her away from the light toward a small storage shed. "You think he's going to save you now?"

She looked back at him over her shoulder, her eyes wide, but not just with terror. Confusion as sharp and bright as a look at the sun. "Who are you talk—?"

A quick squeeze choked off her words. "Shut up! He's never coming back! You'll spend the rest of your days wondering why he ran away from you!"

He dragged her to the shed, up the steps, kicked the door open, and dragged her inside after him, glancing behind to see if anyone might have seen.

"If you tell anyone of this, I'll kill you. No one will believe you, and even if they did, you're just a whore, not even a person. I'll slit your whelp's throat first while you watch. And then I'll kill you. Do you understand?"

She squeezed her eyes shut and nodded, choking back sobs.

Lightning charged his veins, bursting through him like the power of ten thousand *kami*.

If he is able to gain this freedom, he will not be perplexed by anyone on earth. According to this, the martial artist who is able to gain freedom will not be in a quandary about what to do, regardless of who on earth he comes up against.

— *Takuan Soho, "The Clear Sound of Jewels"*

The interior of the barrel squeezed Ken'ishi's legs against his chest, constricting his breath, and the air inside was hot and stale with it. The barrel stank of old wood and salt fish. Delicate flickers of light seeped through the small hole in the barrelhead, the only aperture through which fresh air could enter. Otherwise, he lay crunched up in a darkness as black as his thoughts. The quality of the meager light and the relative silence outside told him that the world lay in the depths of night. He did not have strength enough to scream, and if he did, who would hear?

What was he going to do when Fang Shi brought him before

Green Tiger? Swear allegiance? Swear vengeance? So addled was his mind that the answer to that question changed with every bump and rattle of the barrel. He knew he should be steadfast, firm and committed to a decision even unto his final breath, but his mind felt as muddled and useless as the gruel he had been eating these many eternities of suffering.

When Fang Shi had dragged him out of the cell, his first moments upright in untold weeks drove a nauseating swoon through him, and his legs could not support him. When he regained consciousness, Fang Shi was dragging him by the arm through a wooden trap door in the ceiling of the cavern. He vaguely remembered some cavernous black structure, the sound of the sea, and his first breath of fresh air in untold, tortured lifetimes. Then he had awakened with his body jammed into this barrel, barely able to breathe, his arms and legs with room enough to shift barely a finger's breadth.

Throughout his captivity, Ken'ishi had imagined summoning some heroic burst of strength, subduing the Chinaman, and escaping, but he knew now that he could not even stand, much less harm a brute of Fang Shi's enormity. He could imagine now only having the strength to beg Green Tiger to kill him. Many of the wounds the torturer had given him weeks before were slow to heal and still pained him. His neck and shoulders felt like a knotted up fishing net, hopelessly tangled. His arms and legs had shrunk so that he must have looked like a sick, scrawny baby monkey, unable to even cling to its mother's back.

The barrel rocked and rattled in the rear of a clattering wagon, toward what destination he had no inkling. Fang Shi had been silent. Flickers of lamplight played across Ken'ishi's nose through the narrow aperture. The faint whisper of night air soothed his nostrils like cool water in his throat on a humid day. If he craned his neck just right, he could even see a couple of faint stars above.

A moment of delight coursed through him, and he laughed. How long since he had seen the stars? Or worse, how long since he had *noticed* them, paid attention? His thoughts went back to the birds and animals he could no longer speak with. The pang of that loss had dulled; soon he would be dead, and that loss would no longer matter. So much lost in a man's life, a man whose absence from this world would matter to no one.

The stars disappeared as if a blanket had been thrown over his barrel. Fang Shi's voice rose in confusion, and the cart halted so suddenly the barrel tipped for a moment, then settled back onto its base.

The wagon lurched as Fang Shi moved, lurched again. Bits of Fang Shi's frustrated expostulations in Chinese reached Ken'ishi's ears. Then Fang Shi roared a command in Chinese and jumped to the ground.

A skittering, snuffling, chittering, Fang Shi's feet shuffling, and whoosh of a club swinging, another confused outburst. A heavy blow thudded against the ground, then smashed into the side of the wagon, the force reverberating through the wood into Ken'ishi's barrel.

Not all the sounds belonged to Fang Shi, perhaps some kind of animal, little claws on the earth, scratching over the wooden wagon, a small voice that almost sounded like taunts, amused, playful. Fang Shi roared and swung, roared and swung. A momentary sniffing at the aperture of Ken'ishi's barrel.

A small voice whispered to him. "Rock the barrel! Do it now!"

Ken'ishi threw his weight from side to side. It was difficult in his weakness with so little room, but in a few heartbeats he had managed to build a rocking motion. Back and forth. Farther and farther, until the barrel tipped onto its side, bounced and rolled off the side of the wagon, over the rear lip, and crashed onto the ground. The barrel cracked like an egg against the earth, driving out the little air in his chest. He gathered strength enough to kick the bottom free, and that allowed him to shrug away the rest of the barrel. He lay on his side, gasping, his arms feeling like overcooked noodles.

But in it all, he could see nothing, as if the entire world was a pitch-black cave like the one he had occupied all these weeks. Yet he felt a gravel-strewn earthen path under him. Something small and furry brushed him.

A wad of fur found its way over his palm. "Seize onto this!" said the voice.

Fang Shi roared his frustration, his club whooshing through empty air.

With both hands, Ken'ishi grabbed the wad of fur and skin, warm and alive like the soft, bristly scruff of a rusty-brown dog's neck. The voice came like a child's, "Hold tight!"

Suddenly he was jerked out straight as his furry handhold launched away, dragging him over the earth with incredible speed.

The furry handhold seemed to roll out underneath him, expanding like a warm, living blanket, protecting even his feet from the gravel and stones of the path. Suddenly he could see the stars again, as if he had just burst through a bubble of utter blackness, and he was holding onto a gray-brown pouch attached to some animal's furry rump. Behind him lay a swirling mass of black shadow, like smoke, engulfing Fang Shi and the wagon. The clamor of Fang Shi's outraged frenzy receded behind them. The stars disappeared behind a canopy of foliage, and small leaves and branches whipped over Ken'ishi as his living sled dragged him through the night. The furry sled extruded from between the hindquarters of some lumpy hulk of a creature, and Ken'ishi's hands were clamped onto a fold of skin under the creature's rump. Two globules within the folds of the blanket, the size of ripe persimmons, bumped into his fingers.

A furry face, eyes wrapped in a black mask, glanced back at him as his furry sled sluiced between bamboo stalks and stones and tree trunks and undergrowth, bumping gulps of breath from his lungs. His hands and arms and shoulders ached from the strength of his grip. Had his grip been any weaker, the creature's wild flight would have sent him tumbling free to be left behind. When they had gone an untold distance through the forest, the creature slowed its pace and finally paused.

It looked back at him again, its shoulders and chest heaving with exertion.

Ken'ishi lay gasping as well. When he caught his breath, he said, "Thank you, Master Tanuki. You have surely saved my life."

"Think nothing of it, old sot," said the little voice. "I've been looking for you for weeks." The *tanuki*'s chin was shot with gray hairs. "Whew, I'm getting old. Time was when I could have run you all the way to Kumamoto."

"Hage?"

The *tanuki* grinned, and Ken'ishi's furry blanket rippled. "Still as dense as overcooked *mochi*, aren't you, old sot. Where in the world have you been?"

Ken'ishi's heart thundered louder and louder, each beat leaving a black afterimage in his vision. "Why didn't you tell me you were a *tanuki*?"

"It's not exactly *allowed*. What happened to you?"

Exhaustion, despair at what he had become, and elation pounded into him like a wave smashing him on a beach. "Green Tiger ..." was all he could manage to say before the blackness became too much.

Ken'ishi recognized the sensation of more movement, being dragged through the forest, through the outskirts of the city, through neighborhoods, engulfed in a warm, furry pouch.

He awoke to the sound of familiar voices and the feel of a *futon* under him. After so many weeks on his back in the cave, even a ratty old *futon* such as this one felt feather-soft, and he sighed at the luxury of it.

"If Green Tiger discovers that he's here, we're all worse than dead!"

"Oh, help someone else for once in your whole miserable life! How much more life do you really need?"

"Shut up, the both of you. You bicker like a pair of old swine. He chose to go with you, some pull toward destiny. Your fates have been intertwined from the moment he stepped onto your wagon."

A sheepish silence, then, "Are you really a *tanuki*?"

"Do you want me to show you again, you old fool?"

"I ... I suppose that's not necessary."

"Now, unless you want the rest of your miserable lives to be

250

plagued by misfortune, you'll do what I say. That little rescue venture chafed half the fur off my jewels. I daresay you don't want to chap them any further."

A throat cleared. "Of course, Master Tanuki."

"My name is Hage. And don't you forget it." He shifted where he sat, adjusting himself.

"There's no need to be disagreeable, Master Tanuki. My brother and I hold the young man in great affection. Can I offer you some tea? I have some smoked fish saved back."

"That sounds delicious. I'm famished. And *saké*, too, if you have it."

"Oh, look! He's already awake!"

Ken'ishi licked his ever-parched lips and croaked, "Water."

Junko hurried to bring him water, and as he gulped at it, she said, "He looks so awful, like he's risen from the grave." She laid a warm hand on his face.

"Half-pickled in brine, more like," Hage said. "He reeks of the sea and his own shit. Practically starved to death. Green Tiger was keeping him somewhere even I couldn't find him."

Ken'ishi opened his mouth to speak, but Junko cut him off, her voice full of pity. "The tale can wait until you're stronger."

Hage continued, "Without a particular chain of unusual events, I would not have found him at all. I have been searching the docks and hidden places of the city for weeks. A bit ravenous myself at one point, I was looking for some food when a rather unpleasant dog decided he didn't appreciate my presence in his alley. So I chose to change locale, and I happened down another alley, where I spotted a chicken running loose. I decided to avail myself of the chicken for dinner, and after I had caught it, the dog found me again. Since I was loath to share my dinner, I retreated with my chicken. To avoid a passing group of horsemen, I turned onto a path leading out to a shrine on the seashore northwest of the city. There, amid a pile of driftwood washed up the beach, almost at the tree line, I spotted a discarded *bokken*, or what was left of one. It had been cleft in two. I recognized the *bokken* as his. So I waited there until evening. I saw a very large, very rough-looking man come with a wagon and disappear into the shrine. When he appeared again, he had our friend here in a barrel. Never in ten thousand lifetimes would I have sought him there."

Junko said, "That is a long, twisting story. A stroke of pure fortune!"

Shirohige breathed. "It is the will of the gods that you found him."

Hage grunted. "It seems we cannot discount the possibility. It was as if I was following a carefully laid thread of happenstance."

"Well, he's safe now. I'll go and make him some fish broth. Seeing his ribs like that makes me want to cry."

Ken'ishi opened his eyes and blinked to be sure of what he saw. For the merest instant, the room seemed filled with hundreds of intricate silver threads, crossing and interconnecting, stretching through the walls, through Shirohige and Junko, coalescing on Hage like a pocket of spider webs glistening with moonlit dew. Ken'ishi blinked again, and the webs were gone.

Hage grinned at him. "Brace up, old sot. In a few weeks, you'll be right as rain." But the smile did not reach his eyes.

When one punishes or strives with the heart of compassion, what he does will be limitless in strength and correctness. Doing something for one's own sake is shallow and mean and turns into evil.

— *Hagakure*

"What do you mean, he's dead?" Yasutoki said. Night wind whispered over the walls of his garden, rustling the bamboo leaves and meticulously manicured pine trees. Beyond the walls of this house, pine needles whispered across the hillside and down into Hakata.

Fang Shi stood before him, head bowed. "He is dead. Bars broken. He not go outside. Maybe shark take him."

"Could he have swum out?"

"He is too weak. Couldn't walk now."

Yasutoki scrutinized him. Fang Shi's accent was terrible, and he was a savage brute of a man, but he was not dimwitted. How far did his loyalty go? All men lied, but Green Tiger did not suffer habitual liars in his employ. Fang Shi's only motivation for

253

lying would be that the *ronin* had escaped somehow, and after so long in half-starved confinement, the *ronin* would not have the strength to make a real escape. The Chinaman's story was not implausible. The cave was open to the sea, and sharks and other fish sometimes ventured inside to find themselves trapped when the tide withdrew. And yet ... "Is it not possible that he broke the bars himself?"

"He become too weak. He stronger before. Break bars then, not now. Very sorry, Master," Fang Shi said, keeping his gaze nailed to the floor.

Yasutoki eased back. The sound of agonized weeping from out in the garden distracted him for a moment, until he realized it was simply the man he had had staked out yesterday, a petty thief caught attempting to rob one of Green Tiger's gambling houses; now he was joining Green Tiger's garden. "Do you expect me to punish you?"

"Yes, Master."

"Good. But this time, I will not. Fate delivered the *ronin* to us, and fate took him away again. His death is one less loose thread that I must tie up." Besides, Silver Crane was still safely in his possession. Its loss would affect him much more than the death of some unknown *ronin*, even one renowned as an *oni*-killer. Regrettable that a man with such potential, however, should die such an ignominious death. But he had not broken; Yasutoki had expected him to.

His lovely new servant—he called her Tiger Lily—shuffled up to the door to the veranda, silhouetted from within, so dainty, incredibly poised for only fourteen. She had always submitted to his will, meekly at first, like a terrified kitten, but now she embraced it, spending every night fulfilling his every desire. Her own carnal desires now seemed to have no limits, occasionally bordering on ferocity, something he had never seen in one so young. A most welcome change to the odious task of bedding Hatsumi.

"Forgive me, Master," she said quietly. "You have a messenger."

"At this hour?"

"I am very sorry, Master. He was very serious about giving the message only to you."

"Then bring him in, my little swallow."

She withdrew from the door, and Yasutoki faced Fang Shi again. "You know full well, Fang Shi, that if you ever lie to me, if the *ronin* is still alive, if you let him escape, that our friend Goumonshi will be working his craft on you, like our historian from Dazaifu."

Fang Shi did not flinch. "Yes, Master."

Two silhouettes appeared on the wall, and the door slid open. Yasutoki stood to meet them, and Fang Shi moved forward to stand half-between the visitor and Yasutoki.

A dull-eyed Koryo sailor stood there with the girl, his gaze flicking back and forth between the two men. He smelled of the sea, his hair wildly bound within a sweat-stained scarf. "Are you Lord Yasutoki?"

"I am." Why would a foreign sailor be bringing him a message?

The sailor swallowed hard and held out a bamboo tube, stoppered with wax on one end. "My master say, give this to you. Only you." His words were strangely stilted, as if he had been practicing them over and over.

"Who is your master?"

"You read message, you will know him."

Yasutoki took the tube, whipped out a hidden dagger and cut through the wax, prying loose the stopper. A scroll slid into his hand. He cut the leather thong that bound the scroll and unrolled it. It was written in Classical Chinese, in a precise, well-cultured hand. "*The wise man will find business away from Hakata in the eleventh month.*"

A bolt of white heat shot through Yasutoki's body, and his eyes narrowed as he scrutinized the Koryo. The man did not look particularly bright, with his little rat eyes; tenacious perhaps, but not bright, a mere toady sent to deliver a message. But he had been directed to deliver the message to Otomo no Yasutoki's house, not through one of Green Tiger's usual Hakata channels.

The earth moved under Yasutoki's feet at the implications of this.

He gathered himself and said, "Thank you. You may tell your master that his message has been received and understood. Please wait while I prepare a reply. My sweet, prepare our guest some tea."

He removed himself to his study, his mind reeling, his hands shaking as he pulled out a sheet of paper and prepared a well of ink for his brush. As he ground the *sumi* stick into the moistness of the inkwell, his fingers blackened along with the cloud of fear in his thoughts.

Green Tiger's identity had been compromised. The Khan *knew*. And he wanted Yasutoki to know that he knew. Where was the leak that must be stopped? Who had compromised him?

He wrote, "*Your humble servant will endeavor to be wise in the eleventh month. I will rejoice on the day when I may offer you the hospitality of my house. Our efforts have been arduous but the rewards will match the beauty of heaven.*" As he set down the brush, he hesitated to place his seal on the letter. Should he call himself Green Tiger or Yasutoki to a man who somehow knew his greatest secret? In case the message was intercepted, he left the letter unsigned.

He inserted it into the tube, resealed it, and returned it to the Koryo messenger, who sat nervously with a teacup that he seemed unsure how to use. Fang Shi sat near him, eyeing him in enormous silence.

Yasutoki offered the sailor the tube. "You may return this to your Master."

The sailor stood to bow and accept the tube. Yasutoki delivered it into his hands.

"Before you go, tell me," Yasutoki said, "how did you find this house?"

The sailor blinked. "My master say, 'Give this to man named Otomo no Yasutoki in Hakata.' Many people know this place." He gestured about him to indicate the house. "Lord Yasutoki is easy to find man."

"Of course, I am a high-ranked retainer of the Otomo clan. Where are you from?"

"Pusan, Lord."

"A worthy place, Pusan. I saw it myself twice, when I was a boy. Tell me of Pusan these days."

The sailor stiffened, and his eyes narrowed. "Pusan is ... always Pusan. We fish, and we make ships."

"Yes, a wonderful, industrious city. And Koryo ships are so much better than Japanese ships, more suitable to the open sea."

"Yes, Lord."

"Better able to carry cargo, lots of it."

"Yes, Lord."

"Cargo, and men."

"Yes, Lord." The sailor squirmed.

"Is Pusan very busy these days?"

"Oh, yes, Lord, very busy. But almost finished."

"And relations with your horse-loving neighbors have bloomed like a field of chrysanthemums these days. The Koryo prince even married one of the Emperor's daughters, yes? So good to see your people getting on well with the Emperor of China and lands beyond. Bloodshed is a terrible thing, but necessary sometimes. Trade is so much better than war. Tell me, my friend, how many *trading* ships have you and your brethren built in the last year?"

The sailor hesitated. "I do not know."

"A hundred? Two hundred? Five hundred?" Yasutoki watched the man's eyes carefully. "A thousand?" The merest flicker in the sailor's eye, the faintest twitch in his lips, gave Yasutoki the answer he wanted.

"I do not know," the sailor said. "Maybe one hundred."

"I am sure they are all fine vessels," Yasutoki said smoothly, restraining the lightning in his veins. A thousand ships! "I am sorry for my rudeness, but the hour is late. I must retire. Fang Shi will show you out."

The sailor bowed, and Fang Shi escorted him out.

Moments later, Tiger Lily appeared, sidling up next to him, allowed her robe to fall open just enough to expose a supple breast and a tantalizing curve of throat.

"Ah, my little swallow, you bring me joy." Never before had he taken a young girl as a slave to prepare her for the life of a whore, and then kept her for himself. His efforts to mold her to his will had succeeded beyond his expectations. The difficult part for him, now that he had allowed her to behave more like a concubine than a slave, was that she knew both of his identities. She shared that knowledge with only two other people, Fang Shi and Masoku. It would be some time before she gained enough of his trust, but she gave every indication that she relished her new life of luxury and carnal pleasure. Of course, she knew full well the terrible price if she ever betrayed him. To lend mortar and foundation to her loyalty, he would have to make her complicit in his dealings, make sure that she had as much to lose as he did.

She purred in his ear. "I already see the joy in your face, Master. You have good news."

"Good news, indeed." The thought of a thousand ships filling Hakata Bay, all crammed with Mongol barbarians and their horses, thrilled Yasutoki, but also filled him with trepidation. He would have to withdraw to Lord Tsunetomo's estate or he would face the brunt of the invasion, along with the rest of Hakata. The barbarians would not care to distinguish friend from foe in that initial onslaught. He began considering plans to transfer, discreetly of course, many of his records and possessions. He would perhaps entreat Tsunetomo for a large house near the castle, rather than staying within the castle itself, which was far too close to Hatsumi.

"Lie back, Master, and let my lips and tongue give you more joy."

He did so, couching his head on his arm and looking up into the rafters, feeling her tugging at his robe. He stroked the back of her head and sighed as she took him into her mouth, imagining how he might take her with him to Tsunetomo's estate. He would have to find quarters for her in town, and conceal her existence from Hatsumi for as long as he could. Hatsumi's bitter jealousy would sour even the heavens if given free rein. Of course, if Hatsumi gave him too much trouble, she might encounter some sort of accident, and a welcome one for the entire household, to be sure.

He stroked Tiger Lily's hair, imagining Silver Crane in his hand

and a string of Minamoto and Hojo heads lined up reverently before him, and allowed her mouth to lead him to bliss.

Patting my empty belly
full of worms,
the clouds billow

— *Issa*

A cool cloth on Ken'ishi's face and the familiar scent of her hair in his nostrils as it brushed his cheek, her warmth hovering over him as the cup of fish broth touched his lips. A tingling wave of yearning for her caught up his hand and tried to raise it, to touch her, embrace her, but he was too weak. She hummed over him, a quiet lullaby in a dark room. He wanted the sun. He had not seen it in so long. The warm saltiness awakened his mouth and sent a trickle of life down into his stomach.

"Kiosé."

"Shh, drink. Then rest."

"Where have you been?"

"Right here, all along."

"You remember?"

"I remember."

"That's good."

He drank.

He slept.

He awoke to sunlight, creeping across the floor from an open window toward his face. The brilliant orange-gold light tore a hole in his emotions, and he wept.

Junko came in later with a bowl of rice porridge.

He said, "Where is Kiosé?"

"Who?"

"She was here."

Junko sat beside him and spooned a bit of porridge for him. "Who is Kiosé?"

A spike of bitterness drove through him. He took the spoon. "I can feed myself."

After a few days of broth, runny porridge and water, Ken'ishi's stomach was finally able to hold some fish and then a rice ball. It felt so alien, and yet so wonderful, simply to sit upright and hold himself with some decorum, however unsteady. And to eat. How many times had he licked and sucked every morsel and drop of that awful millet gruel from the stone floor of his tiny cell, sometimes mixed with detritus swept in with the tide? Or worse things.

Junko often told him with a wink, "Yes, those hollows around your eyes are going away. You'll be your old hale and virile self again in no time."

His first attempts at walking ended with waves of nausea and dizziness that turned the floor upside down and sent him crashing into it. His head was too far from the floor. His body felt so light, as if much of it was now missing, his limbs as weak and unsteady as the legs of a naked hatchling.

Hage had warned Shirohige, "You let that young man eat as much as he wants, after a few days. He'll need to eat like a herd of oxen to regain all the strength he's lost. Any complaining from

261

you, and I'll turn every drop of your *saké* as rancid as two-week old fish, and your tea will be filled with maggots."

Shirohige grumbled, but Junko bought great quantities of rice, vegetables, and fish. With the coming of autumn, pears and persimmons were coming ripe. The fall crop of beans, onions, and *daikon* radish had come, and Junko delightedly filled Ken'ishi's belly with fish and vegetable stews, boiled eggs, pork *ramen*, rice cakes, Chinese buns, pickled plums, and great bowls of steaming rice.

The sharp remembrance of his hunger made each bite a moment of grateful heaven. Even when he was not eating, his thoughts wandered often toward food, and he wondered if that would ever cease.

Dreams of silvery streams and moonlit ocean foam coursed through his sleep, infusing his body with strength he had not had the day before. Nightmares of cold savagery, blood and sliced flesh and chopped bone and whimpering pleas for mercy destroyed his sleep, filling him with more rage than he had felt the day before.

The rope of his trousers wrapped further around him now, but as soon as he could walk steadily, he found a piece of timber of roughly appropriate size and began to practice his sword drills. His arms felt like a child's, weak and quivering. He took his bow and meager supply of arrows into the alley behind the house and set up a straw target to practice.

Curving the bow forward around his leg to string it, his hands trembled at the effort to bring the loop of bowstring over the tip of the bow. Frustration seared through him. "Vengeance," he whispered, sweat beading his brow, but he finally managed it.

Junko hovered nearby. "Shirohige wanted to sell your things. He didn't think you'd be coming back. I told him I would cut his balls off if he did."

"Thank you, Madam Junko. You are very good to me," Ken'ishi said. "And I am sorry that I lost the armor you gave me. It saved my life."

"Then it served its purpose. Tell me. Why are you out here so soon? You certainly don't intend to go after Green Tiger again, do you?"

Ken'ishi nocked an arrow and sighted down it toward the target.

Junko watched him for a long moment, then sighed and left him to his practice. In the silence, snippets of conversation flowed around him from nearby houses, from the street. The neighborhood today felt alive, buzzing with activity.

He shot through his supply of arrows, retrieved them, shot them again. His arms grew shaky far too soon, but he kept going until his fingers bled and his forearm bore an angry red welt from the chafe of the bowstring.

Pon-Pon chewed placidly, watching over the top rail of his pen.

A small voice turned Ken'ishi's head. "I see you're up and about and ready to charge once again toward death, eh, old sot?" The *tanuki* watched him from the crawl space under a nearby house.

Ken'ishi took a deep breath, drew and fired another arrow. The trembling of his arm sent the arrow skittering down the alley, wide of the target. He sighed at having to retrieve it. "Not yet. My strength is far from recovered. But soon. And thank you for saving my life. I am forever in your debt."

"Since you owe your life to me, perhaps I should forbid you from spending it foolishly. But I don't suppose that would matter."

Ken'ishi fired another arrow.

Hage said, "What are you going to do?"

"I'm going to rebuild my strength. Then I'm going to kill his men, one by one. And then I'm going after Green Tiger himself. I know how to find them now." And even now, in the daylight, a tiny silver thread tugged at his mind, toward the west, away from central Hakata.

"And I don't suppose you can be dissuaded."

Ken'ishi frowned as another arrow went astray.

"Then perhaps you should ask me what I found in those weeks of looking for you."

Ken'ishi lowered his bow and looked down at the little furry face, a face that somehow resembled Hage's human countenance. The *tanuki*'s expressions and mannerisms were instantly recognizable.

Nearby, two shrill voices rose into a staccato quarrel, two women arguing over the trappings of their houses.

"What did you find?"

"I found several places frequented by Green Tiger's men—his gambling dens, his whorehouses, even a couple of moneychangers who skim the profits for him."

"So you'll help me find them all, and kill them."

"I didn't say that. If someone starts picking off Green Tiger's men, he'll likely disappear into a burrow where you'll never find him. You might make it harder to reach the sword."

"I have a plan."

"Care to share it?"

"Not just yet."

Hage sniffed. "What are you going to fight with, naked bravado? Arrows are weapons of war and bandits. If you go around shooting arrows into people, the constables are likely to take notice. In fact, if any of the neighbors see you out here, they might report it to the constables. You'll end up tortured and executed in somebody else's prison."

"I'll be careful to avoid capture."

The *tanuki* snickered, a light, wheezing chitter. "So you're a shadow warrior now as well! Let me tell you, this Green Tiger knows such people."

"I have faced them before."

"So you have said. But some of them may not be simply men. The shadows they manipulate may in turn come to manipulate them. It is said that Green Tiger himself possesses power over shadow. There are hidden schools in distant provinces where such things are taught, so I have heard."

Ken'ishi fired another arrow. "An arrow through the eye-hole of his basket hat will kill even a rumor dead enough."

"It may not be all rumor. I thought once that I had found him, Green Tiger himself. I thought I had caught him leaving one of his haunts, so I hurried to catch up. I was sure that I had him, but he melded into some shadows as if he were a hungry ghost. He disappeared."

"Perhaps you were ... imagining things."

"Of course, I was imagining things! I imagine everything all the time! That's how my magic works, dolt! Don't try to deceive a deceiver! But I saw what I saw."

Ken'ishi said, "I grow tired of everyone's assumption that I am no match for him. Green Tiger will die at my hands, and Silver Crane will be mine again."

The nearby quarrel between the two women rose to a strident fury. One accused the other of stealing the best thatch. The other screamed about the first's brood of young ones whose voices had interrupted her afternoon naps all through the previous spring.

Pon-Pon chewed contentedly, watching Ken'ishi's conversation with mild interest.

Hage said, "It's truly worth all this suffering? Perhaps you should just forget about it and enjoy life."

Ken'ishi turned on him. "Where does your magic come from, your power? Does it come from your jewels?"

"It comes from the earth, and the air, and fire and water, gathered in my jewels, yes. Waiting to be brought to life like seed in a womb."

"And how are those powers replenished? Have they a limit?"

Hage's whiskers twitched. "Same as yours. I eat. I drink. I pay homage to the *kami*, whose powers flow through me like water through a fish's gills. Some of that I get to keep, and use. But I cannot remain in human form too long, or else I become too attached to the human world, human thoughts. The longer I hold human form, the more I begin to think like a human, and my powers cease to replenish."

"What would happen if you were castrated? What would you become?"

The *tanuki's* body suddenly shrank to the size of a fox, a distressed expression striking his features. His voice was smaller now, higher. "I would rather die."

Ken'ishi nocked another arrow, raised the bow. "Exactly." His weak fingers slipped prematurely, and the arrow thudded into the thatch of Shirohige's roof, burying itself up to the feathers. His frown deepened.

"You're not concentrating," Hage said.

Another voice said, "Perhaps you should meditate first. Clear your mind, and your hindquarters will follow."

Ken'ishi looked around, wondering who had spoken. The voice had not belonged to Hage.

"One step at a time. One hoof in front of the other. Choices are simpler that way," Pon-Pon said, his mouth full of cud.

Ken'ishi's mouth fell open, and his bow dropped to his side.

Pon-Pon swallowed his cud and continued, "Needless complications are just complications. One task, one first step, then a second step. It is no good to get lost worrying about every blade of grass in the field. Better to think about just the field and your place in it."

"You can speak!" Ken'ishi said.

"Of course, I can speak. Forgive me for interrupting your conversation with Master Hage."

Ken'ishi could not find words. Tears burst from his eyes.

Hage said, "Master Ox here could speak all along. You just couldn't hear him. Too much noise in your mind, the noise of the human world." The *tanuki* waved a paw as if swatting at a swarm of flies. "You were raised outside the human world. In the human world, your mind became too concerned with human worries, human suffering, the endless wants that men subject themselves to. Perhaps you found a way to forget the noise."

Just then, Ken'ishi realized that the quarrel he had been hearing was not between two women at all, but between two small birds arguing over the quality of their nests. The two female birds abruptly spun away from each other with *hmphs* of disgust and flew away.

How long had he been consumed with thoughts that distracted him from his path? The suffering he had seen, the suffering he had experienced, his love for Kazuko and the agony therefrom, his denial of love for Kiosé, his fears, his yearning. And because of it all, he had stopped listening to the moments, to the flow of the *kami*; he had grown too attached to the past and the future.

His imprisonment and torture had been an endless series of black moments, but they were over now, and his mind felt clear. His *path* was clear.

Pon-Pon swished his tail at some flies. "And you are dropping your elbow. That's why your shots pull toward the right."

The sound of Junko approaching emanated from the house. "Who are you talking to out there?" she said.

"I am speaking to Hage-sensei," Ken'ishi said.

"Shirohige just returned. You should talk to him. He says he has bad news."

While you yet live, become a dead person. Then do as you like.

— *Bunan*

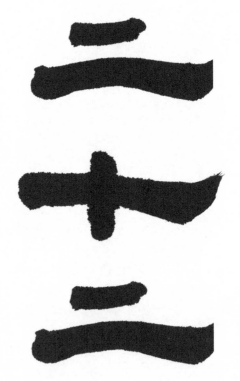

"Something terrible is going to happen," Shirohige said. Ken'ishi and Hage, taking his human form, sat with them while Junko made tea. Shirohige's hands trembled as he stroked his beard.

"All the world is calamity," Hage said wryly. "Explain."

"I have been expecting a shipment of … goods from Pusan, and I went to the docks again today looking for the ship. I have looked for the last week. The shipment is long, long overdue. If I have to wait much longer, Junko will have to go back to whoring." He clapped his hands together to pray. "And Jizo prevent such a calamity."

Junko shuffled toward him and kicked him in the back.

Shirohige cried out in pain. "A jest, foul hag! In any case, we won't be able to feed our warrior so lavishly for much longer."

Ken'ishi bowed. "I apologize for all the trouble."

Shirohige waved it away. "It's not just that. I started asking questions. Rumors abound that the Koryo have been building ships, whole fleets of them. The trade ships seem to have disappeared. Very few are coming into port now. I've never seen the docks so empty. There is no real news from Pusan. The docks are full of speculation that the Mongols are keeping the ships for an invasion fleet. They have been threatening to invade Kyushu for years."

Hage snorted, "Humans and their greediness. Monsters of pride and avarice. Thievery should be kept to a small but amusing pastime. Any self-respecting creature can only hope to amuse himself among all this nonsense."

"What do these barbarians want?" Ken'ishi said.

"Wealth. Expansion of their empire. Vengeance for a slight. It is said their empire stretches to the lands of the setting sun, so far to the west that the *ri* are beyond counting."

Hage raised a bushy eyebrow at Ken'ishi. "What happens to your plans if an invasion fleet arrives tomorrow?"

Ken'ishi had no answer. But when he quieted his mind, the tug of some invisible thread turned his attention toward the northwest, outside of Hakata.

For the next several days, Ken'ishi practiced, driving his body back toward the strength he had once possessed. Every shooting pain, every failure, every moment of aching exhaustion was tinged with the taste of desperation. Something told him he did not have much time.

He practiced the bow until his supply of arrows dwindled to only three. The rest splintered or lost their fletching from incessant use, and he had no money to buy more. However, as he centered his mind, turning it away from thoughts of constant hunger, aching want, and crippling despair, he found delight in listening to the conversations sprinkled around him in tongues that other humans could not understand. He learned the birds who made their nests nearby, discovered more of Pon-Pon's gentle wisdom, and then acquainted himself with neighborhood dogs; unfortunately, none of them were as wise, agreeable, or humorous as his old friend Akao.

Shirohige's demeanor grew ever more desperate, and the meals Junko cooked became ever smaller. One day he came home and announced that, until his shipment of trade goods came in, any further food he bought would put them into debt.

THE TIME IS NOW.

Ken'ishi's body sat bolt upright in bed. Cold sweat beaded his forehead. His heart thumped audibly against his rib cage. He cast around the dark room for the source of the shout. The air was cold in the depths of night, and silence lay heavy over the house, broken only by twin snores from Junko and Shirohige in another room.

The voice had been clear, powerful, direct.

He shook away the confusion, and the shout still echoed in his mind. His heart fluttered from the force of the echoes.

Then he knew.

No more scheming. No more practice. No more waiting for his strength to return. He was still weakened, but he could wait no longer.

He dressed himself, took up his bow and arrows, put on Shirohige's straw hat—he must conceal his features—and ventured into the night.

Hage caught up with him in the next district. Ken'ishi, having learned what to listen for, detected the *tanuki* snuffling up behind him, following his scent. "Where are you off to, old sot? A bit late for a stroll."

"It's time. Help me."

Hage sighed. "I suppose tonight is as good a time as any. I was growing bored waiting for you. But first let me make you a little less conspicuous."

The bow on Ken'ishi's back became a monk's walking staff and the quiver of arrows a light traveling pack.

"Now the next constable you meet is less likely to arrest you. Your weapons will resume their forms in the morning as the earth and air in them greet the Sun Goddess. What's the plan then? Some brilliant warrior stratagem? Charge in and kill them all? Die a resplendent death?"

"I'll tell you."

After Ken'ishi did, Hage said, "I like it."

The docks were deserted at this tiny hour, quiet save for the lapping of the waves against the pilings, the creak and thump of ships' rigging. Ken'ishi passed a drunkard snoring loudly against a stack of barrels. He hefted his staff, once a bow, swung it about him to test the feel and the weight. It would serve as a passable weapon even in this form.

A faint light burned within the warehouse. Unintelligible voices filtered into the night from deep in the warehouse. A White Lotus gangster stood against the door jamb, arms crossed, head bowed drowsily.

The *tanuki* disappeared into the darkness.

Ken'ishi clung to the shadows as he approached, and took a position around the corner behind the gangster. Gripping his staff, he stole up behind the drowsing guard. The gangster blinked himself into groggy wakefulness just in time to see the shadow of the staff descending toward his head. A heavy thud, and the gangster dropped without another sound. Ken'ishi knelt and tugged off the man's headband, thrust it into his robe, and picked up the long knife. He pulled out the jade bauble, carved in the likeness of a tiger, and placed it on the gangster's chest.

Creeping around the warehouse toward the back, he picked his way among rubbish, debris, and discarded crates until he reached the rear wall. The building was fashioned of wood and bamboo, weathered by decades, and dry as a pile of fallen leaves.

Hage stole up to him in human form, bearing a lantern and an impish grin. With the flame he lit a handful of straw, then opened the lantern reservoir and splattered the oil across the warehouse. With the look of a young boy about some mischief, he set the flame to the oil. A sheet of flame bloomed across the wall.

As Ken'ishi and Hage stole off into the shroud of night, they heard the shouts of consternation and surprise rising behind them. Teng Zhou's voice shouted orders.

"We've kicked the hornet's nest now!" Hage, a dark, loping hump now, hooted.

Ken'ishi ducked into an alley, a safe distance away, the *tanuki* close on his heels, and thrust the White Lotus knife into his sash. He peeked around the corner for signs of pursuit. His heart thundered against his breast from the exertion, and his breath burned with every gasp, his limbs shuddering from weakness. He was still weaker than he thought.

Hage said, "They won't be long. Once they put the fire out and gather their wits, they'll pay Green Tiger's place a visit."

As Ken'ishi and Hage moved through the night, Ken'ishi tried to familiarize himself with the knife's heft and balance, a chopping, stabbing weapon, a cleaver with a point.

"Are you going to wait for them?" Hage said as they stood at the mouth of a certain alley. At the far end of the alley lay a familiar red lantern at the entrance to the gambling den.

Ken'ishi secreted his staff and traveling pack near the mouth of the alley. He would come back for them. "You said yourself they'll be coming soon."

"I said they'll be going after one of Green Tiger's haunts. It might not be this one. I'm sure they know of several, any one of which could be a target. What if you have to do this alone?"

"No matter. It will be done. But you said they would most likely come here."

"I think they'll come here."

"Why?"

"I steal because I am lazy. Criminals are lazy. They steal because they are lazy. They would rather someone else do all the hard work. They will come here, because this place is the closest of Green Tiger's haunts to their own. They want a fight *now*.

Come, I'll show you the quiet way in. My weeks of snooping were not without reward."

The *tanuki* kept to the shadows under the floors and porches of shops and houses as they made their way around the block to another innocuous doorway, marked only with a wooden plaque written in a script too scrawled for Ken'ishi to read.

"Can you read this, Hage?"

"I've known chickens who can scratch a better character, but it says 'Dreams of the Pink Orchid' or some such nonsense. Why must humans ascribe such poetical drivel to the opening the younglings pop out of?"

Ken'ishi chuckled. "Perhaps because it's rude to speak of it directly. Nonsense? Sometimes it seems men spend their entire lives in search of it." How many nights had he spent yearning for one in particular when another lay so close to him? How many nights under the full moon had his thoughts waxed just so poetic? Yes, nonsense indeed.

"We can't have you tramping through a house of delicate ladies with your pig-poker in hand. You'll cause too much of a stir." The *tanuki* stepped out of the shadows and rose to his hind legs. Hage's furry jewel sack pulsed and swelled. "Grab onto these."

Ken'ishi hesitated.

"Oh, come now, old sot. You've already fondled them more thoroughly than any woman's ever fondled yours. You've even been wrapped in them like a blanket."

Ken'ishi could not help but nod, so he knelt and cradled them in one hand.

"Squeeze."

Ken'ishi squeezed, and tingles shot through his fingers. Suddenly Hage seemed taller, of equal size. The buildings around them reared skyward, towering above like mountainous parapets. But Hage had not grown. Ken'ishi stood now on all fours, one hairy paw cradling Hage's jewel sack, and the other three resting under the furred barrel of his own body. He wondered where his weapons had gone, but he did not have time to wonder long.

Hage said, "If you let go, the magic goes away. Let go while we're crawling through a crack, and you might find yourself stuck in a dreadfully unpleasant place. Best grab them with your teeth—but not too hard!—and follow me."

Ken'ishi did.

If the mind congeals in one place and remains with one thing, it is like frozen water and unable to be used freely: ice that can wash neither hands nor feet. When the mind is melted and is used like water, extending throughout the body, it can be used wherever one wants to send it. This the Right Mind.

— *Takuan Soho, "The Mysterious Record of Immovable Wisdom"*

Ken'ishi's *tanuki* eyes saw clearly in the narrow crawlspace under the brothel, even though his field of vision was filled with little else besides Hage's undulating rump. The darkness around him seethed with insects, worms, rats, even a tomcat on the hunt. Sounds of human revelry, both in groups and in private, filtered down from above. The folds of furry skin in Ken'ishi's teeth sent tingling waves through his tongue and lips. His sharp *tanuki* teeth ached as if he was eating too much snow. The two *tanuki* wriggled between wooden pillars and floor joists and slogged through slimy bogs, tearing holes through curtains of cobweb. Onward to a narrow, ragged hole in the wooden floor above, barely big enough for a *tanuki*'s bulk.

"Ouch! Not so tight!" Hage snapped to make Ken'ishi loosen his grip.

Upward through the hole into a tiny, musty storeroom where brooms and washcloths were kept.

"Here," Hage whispered.

Ken'ishi spat out Hage's jewel sack, felt the tingles draining out of him like a punctured bag of sand. He began to grow and shift, and his head swam with sudden dizziness. The ceiling of the closet came down to press against his head, cocking his neck at an uncomfortable angle. His shoulders were squeezed against the handles of the brooms and the wall. Hage's bulk was crammed between his feet. Ken'ishi's Chinese knife was in his hand.

Hage whispered, "A bit of a tussle to extract yourself from the closet, but you're inside. To the right is the house of ladies. To the left is a passage leading to the gambling house."

"I'll lead the way."

"And I'll guard your back."

Ken'ishi eased the door latch aside and swung the door open. The hallway was dim, but the sounds of pleasure grew louder. He shrugged himself out of the closet and gripped the long knife. "Can you hide us until we find the enemy?"

"My powers have been taxed, but I can manage this much." Hage wiggled his head, and the air whispered with glimmering motes that coalesced around Ken'ishi. He was now dressed in a woman's *kimono*, and his hair hung long in the style of a young woman.

Ken'ishi stiffened and tried to restrain an outburst. "What are you doing? A woman!"

"Hide in plain sight, fool. You're in a brothel, and you're pretty enough. Pretend to be the new girl."

"There is no honor in this!"

"You're right, not in any of this. Now shut up before someone hears us!"

"No, change the appearance of only my weapons. I can pose as a patron."

"Oh, very well. But my way would have been much more fun. What a waste of my powers!" Hage clucked his tongue, and Ken'ishi's appearance was restored. The knife became a folded fan. Strangely, he still felt like he had a knife in his fist.

"Only the air of your appearance has changed," Hage said, "what others see. The earth of your weapons has not. I cannot manage another transformation of your substance just now. You will have to leave by a door."

Ken'ishi stole down the hallway, passed an open door wherein a young woman was straightening a *futon* and rumpled bedclothes. She gave him a bow and smile that was pretty but wearied. The hour was late. She looked no more than fifteen. He bowed in return and continued down the hallway.

Behind him, Hage assumed human form and gave the girl a smile and a bow himself. "Pardon me, little sister, but my young companion here is looking for a friend of his, an enormous Chinaman. Is he here?"

Her eyes widened with fear, as if surprised that Fang Shi had any friends at all. "He is usually at the front door. I saw him there earlier. Shall I take you to him, Uncle?"

"No need, you have plenty to do. Much obliged."

She bowed again, and Hage took Ken'ishi's shoulder. "Come." Down the narrow hallway, Ken'ishi said, "Clever."

"Attitude, boy. Behave as if this is exactly where you belong, and there is no need to sneak. Why make this harder than it is? You'll have your hands full enough if you find him."

Another young girl, only slightly older than the last, dragged a drunken samurai behind her by the hand. Her robe was half open, a tender breast just visible. They were both laughing, but hers was forced, too enthusiastic. The warrior groped for her buttocks. Ken'ishi and Hage made way for them in the narrow hallway. They lurched past, leaving a miasma of *saké* fumes and lust in their wake. She had had a mole on her cheek similar to Kiosé's, and she looked so much younger. A sudden spasm shot through him. He could walk out of here right now, and go back to Aoka village, take Kiosé away from there, Silver Crane or no Silver Crane—perhaps he could even find a new sword—and he could make his way in the world. Kiosé would never have to even think about her old life in a place such as this.

A strain of *biwa* music and singing echoed from somewhere.

Ken'ishi and Hage stepped into a large room furnished with a multitude of brightly embroidered cushions, where cloying incense filled the air and patrons awaited their pleasure. Shadowed hallways and doors went off in several directions.

A middle-aged woman wearing resplendent robes of multicolored silk, the beauty of her features sharpened by predatory greed and cold, glittering eyes, her hair immaculately coiffed, face and hands powdered almost white, entertained a fat, nervous-looking merchant.

The madam glanced at Ken'ishi for a moment, then again. Her eyes blackened instantly from affable and merry to brittle suspicion. "Who are you?"

Ken'ishi said, "The Master sent us to find Fang Shi." He gripped his "fan," and wondered for how many more heartbeats it would look like a fan. He took a deep breath, felt for the Void, and settled himself into it, each moment becoming a discrete eternity of spaces between moments.

She nodded toward a rice paper door. A moment later, the door slid open, and Fang Shi loomed through the opening. His beady gaze swept over Ken'ishi, and his face twisted with a tumult of surprised recognition and then rage. He drew a curved, single-edged broadsword from the scabbard at his hip.

Ken'ishi charged.

Fang Shi's sword rose.

The merchant squealed like a child and scrambled away.

The madam hissed and slid back like a serpent, a dagger

appearing in her hand.

Hage clucked his tongue, and her dagger became a writhing serpent. She screamed and cast it away.

Ken'ishi grabbed Fang Shi's sword wrist with his left hand. It felt like grasping a thick tree bough. He stabbed with his right. The "fan" plunged into Fang Shi's belly. Ken'ishi twisted, thrusting deeper. Fang Shi's eyes bulged. Ken'ishi jerked the fan out with a gush of gore and entrails.

But Fang Shi still stood, and his fist came down on top of Ken'ishi's head like a hammer, driving him facedown onto the floor. Fang Shi's blood poured into Ken'ishi's hair, over the back of his neck. He heard the whoosh of a massive blade coming down, rolled through hot viscera and raised the blood-smeared knife to block Fang Shi's blow. A sharp clang amid the flashes of white in his vision nearly drove the hilt from his grip, but he held on.

The madam screamed again.

Fang Shi's sword swept around for another blow, a continuous movement, advancing, stumbling legs bumping his entrails. Crimson sheets spurted over the glistening ropes.

Ken'ishi scrambled back. Fang Shi was a dead man, but he had not yet accepted this as a fact.

Two samurai *yojimbo* burst through the front door with a gust of cool night air, blades at the ready. The merchant squealed, "Save me!"

Their eyes immediately took in the ensanguined combatants. They leaped to interpose themselves between the fight and the merchant, but they did not attack, unsure to whose side they should lend aid.

Fang Shi swung again, and the tip of his blade tore a deep gash in the tatami floor. Ken'ishi lunged forward, thrusting up under Fang Shi's ribcage, into his heart. Ken'ishi felt the rest of Fang Shi's life spill out in another hot gush over his hand. The giant sank to his knees.

Hage roared and cast an oil lamp at the feet of the two samurai. The lamp exploded into fire and sparks, which swirled through the smoke like fireflies of every color. Both samurai fell back, coughing and cursing.

Ken'ishi kicked Fang Shi onto his back, and a last breath wheezed free. Ken'ishi left the White Lotus knife embedded in Fang Shi's torso. Oily fire licked over the giant's twitching legs.

"Come!" Hage cried.

Ken'ishi's touch bloodied the white headband as he tossed it onto Fang Shi's face, then pried the curved Chinese broadsword from Fang Shi's dead, meaty fingers and took it with him.

"Come!"

Hage fled back down the hallway, with Ken'ishi close upon his furry rump.

If by setting one's heart right morning and evening, one is able to live as though his body were already dead, he gains freedom in the Way. His whole life will be without blame, and he will succeed in his calling.

— *Hagakure*

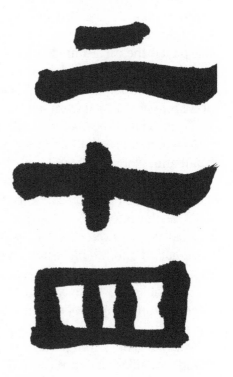

Yasutoki made sure his basket hat was in place before he stepped out of the palanquin and surveyed the scene. The street was dark at this tender hour, but several firemen stood outside the door of the brothel, and Madam Kuro kept the women herded and huddled together nearby. Any former patrons had long since vacated the area. Smoke hung thick; a few wisps still trailed from the open doorway of Dream of the Pink Orchid.

He strode toward the doorway. Firemen and others with their empty buckets made way.

Masoku approached him and bowed. "Master."

At that word, a hush spread through the crowd, and others bowed around him. They all knew who owned his establishment, and he might have taken a moment to savor their fear if someone had not just tried to burn down one of his most profitable ventures.

Yasutoki's eyes scanned the crowd, remembering faces, demeanors, reactions. Would the culprit have remained nearby to watch his handiwork? "The fire has been contained?"

"Yes, Master. But there is more. If you would come inside." Masoku gestured toward the door.

Inside, the walls of the entry room were blackened with soot, and the stench of smoke, ash, sodden *tatami*, and seared flesh sharpened the air. Runnels of soot-blackened water collected in puddles, and a great patch of *tatami* lay blackened and soaked. Amid the remnants of the fire lay Fang Shi's charred body, the hilt of a knife protruding from his chest.

Yasutoki had seen such a knife before.

Masoku said, "I found this near the body." He held out a headband, soot-blackened and blood-stained to be sure, but Yasutoki recognized its fashion, white with a single red stripe.

There were too many ears about to discuss this openly. Yasutoki led Masoku into a room deeper within the brothel. The smoke had permeated even this deeply. Would the entire building have to be gutted and rebuilt? Such an expense would erase his profits from this place for the entire year.

Yasutoki said, "Why would the White Lotus do this? We have done nothing to provoke them. The last war was too costly for them."

Masoku said, "Teng Zhou is ambitious. Perhaps they have found new allies, or new reasons to seek a greater share of territory. Perhaps they simply had a grudge against Fang Shi."

"He had many enemies. You have twenty-two sturdy fighters in your direct employ, yes?"

Masoku nodded, "Thirteen *ronin* and the rest commoners good with spear and club, and all hungry for coin. They'll fight."

"This insult cannot go unanswered. Take your men to—"

A scream from outside cut him short.

Yasutoki snatched his short sword from its concealment within his robes, drawing a handful of *shuriken* into his left hand.

Masoku drew his sword, and the two of them hurried back toward the street, where a clamor spread. More screams from the women pierced the night. The firemen flung down their buckets and fled. Voices rose in terror, others in rage. Masoku peeked out the charred doorway, then dodged back as a torch flew through the doorway into the entry way. It landed on charred wood that was unlikely to catch fire quickly.

A man in a white headband charged through the doorway with his long knife upraised. Masoku cut him down. "Master, run!"

Grim-faced men in white headbands, clutching vicious-looking knives, filled the street. Women screamed and tried to scatter, only to have their hair snatched in mid-flight. Three more men charged through the doorway, driving Masoku back, swinging their blades in deadly arcs. Masoku blocked and counter-struck, teeth gritted.

Yasutoki flung his *shuriken*, and one of Masoku's assailants fell with a gurgling scream and blades in his cheek, throat, and chest.

"Run, Master!" Masoku hissed, facing the White Lotus, bloody katana aloft, eyes wild.

Yasutoki slipped deeper into the brothel. Through a narrow passage he would emerge into the gambling house and could flee from there, making his way through the shadowy night to where others in his employ would be roused to vengeance. He ran through the smoky darkness, rage starting to boil within him.

Why would the White Lotus attack now? This put a severe crimp into his plans. Nevertheless, if the White Lotus wanted war, Green Tiger would give it to them.

"Are you sure this is his house?" Ken'ishi said.

The house was well-appointed from the outside, with a stone and plaster wall surrounding the compound, the gate emblazoned with the dual ginger-blossom emblem of the Otomo clan. At this late hour, the lanterns of the gate glowed surprisingly bright.

The surrounding wooded hillside filtered the lights of Hakata, which sprawled down the slope below toward the glimmering expanse of the bay perhaps four or five *ri* distant. The moon hung like a half-lidded cataract eye, misted by a film of silver-fringed clouds. Over the course of the night, a steady wind had risen, moist and strangely warm for this time of year.

The *tanuki* hunched in the shadows at Ken'ishi's knee. "Quite sure, old sot. That's what a nose is for, after all. If only you humans could use yours. Then again, perhaps you should be telling me whether your toy is in there."

Ken'ishi had indeed caught glimmers of the silver thread in his mind, feeling for its gentle tug, but the sense had been too ephemeral to give him more than a vague direction. Nevertheless, something unseen filled the air as if with silent hornets. He could still smell Fang Shi's blood and entrails on his face, in his hair. They had crossed through most of the city, clinging to alleys and shadows, lest his bloody appearance raise the alarm. His hand and arm were still sticky with it as he carried Fang Shi's heavy blade. He took a deep breath and tried to steady himself. From within the Void would come awareness of Silver Crane.

His body startled to tingle with anticipation.

Hage edged forward. "It seems we have missed some activity."

A dark shape stepped out of the gate, then another, guards with swords and light armor.

"The hour is too late for lamps and such alert guards," Hage said. "Perhaps your ruse is working, and the White Lotus have begun their reprisals."

"We had best find the sword before alerting the house," Ken'ishi said. "Can you not spirit us inside?"

"My powers have been taxed. I have little left tonight. Perhaps one last burst, and then we are left with just our wits and strength. There is a smaller rear gate for servants and deliveries, and a garden. We could sneak inside there."

Ken'ishi nodded approval.

"And cover your face. You don't want Green Tiger or anyone else to see your face."

"I'm not a thief!"

Hage had urged him to bring a cloth to conceal his face, but he had been loath to wear it. Such things were not the behavior of a samurai.

"Does stealing from a thief make you less of a thief? You mortals get so twisted up over labels and words, good and evil. If you don't want to listen to me, don't listen to me, but I'm telling you that if anyone, especially Green Tiger, sees your face, you'll regret it. You've been in his clutches once. Care to find yourself there again?"

Ken'ishi let out a long breath to release the bolt of fear that drilled up his spine. If by fortune or the favor of the *kami* and the gods and Buddhas he succeeded, he would live a life of renewed honor until the end of his days. He wrapped the cloth over the lower half of his face.

Hage led him into the shadows under the trees. Ken'ishi stepped gingerly on fallen leaves and sticks, but the noise drew a hiss from the *tanuki*. "You sneak like Pon-Pon!"

Ken'ishi's skills as a woodsman had gone rusty, like so many of his other abilities. On the faraway mountains in the north, he had developed great skills at forest stealth, even until he had successfully stolen upon Kaa, who had the senses of a cat. It seemed like such a long time ago. Nevertheless, as the memories came trickling back of all the times he had stolen through the forests of the northern mountains, he found the noise of his step diminishing. Sharp snaps and crackles became rustlings and brushings that could have been mistaken for the movements of small night creatures or the wind in the leaves. And the wind had become a stiff, steady breeze.

Suddenly the *kami* all but screamed a warning through Ken'ishi's flesh. At that moment, Hage hissed and froze in place, front leg poised, eyes fixed on something ahead.

Ken'ishi could make out nothing, and it came home to him how blind he was in this darkness. The *tanuki* seemed to function perfectly well, when all Ken'ishi could see was the dark smudge of the *tanuki*'s body moving among other dark smudges of forest floor, undergrowth, and deeper shadow.

Hage backed up a few small steps. A wiggle began in his haunches, passed forward through his body, to his neck, his cheeks, until a puff of golden mist erupted from him like a combination of sneeze and cough. The mist hung in the air and spread out before him like smoke in a faint breeze. In the path of the mist, a pale line emerged drawing across their path toward the base of a tree, then surreptitiously up the trunk, higher into the branches, to a spiked log poised to sweep down from on high and simultaneously impale and flatten anything in its path. The racket of its rampage would bring guards to mop up what remained.

A chill shot through Ken'ishi. The entire area could be a sea of traps like this one. Of course, Green Tiger's house would be protected in unseen ways. Why had Ken'ishi not considered this? What other traps lurked in the night? The roar of the *kami* diminished to an incessant murmur.

Hage changed course to circumvent the tripwire. A handful of steps later, the carpet of leaves collapsed under his feet, and he fell forward with a startled squeak. Ken'ishi snatched Hage by the tail, catching him before he plunged into the pit. A rug of burlap and leaves caught in the bottom on a snarl of shaved bamboo spikes, just visible as pale streaks in the earthy shadows below. Hage's legs sprang out stiff in all directions as Ken'ishi lifted him by the tail and carefully set him back upon solid ground.

For a long time, Hage simply stood and shivered. Finally, he looked over his shoulder at Ken'ishi with silent thanks.

The golden glow of the tripwire was fading, so he wrapped an arm around Hage, slung him underneath, and stepped over the wire. If the *kami* wanted him to live and he was wise enough to heed their warnings, he would live. Nevertheless, the earth might fall away at any step and send him plunging down onto a bed of spikes like a sea urchin's back. With each step, he wondered if it would be his last. He set his jaw and stalked through the forest. No more fear.

And then the plaster wall emerged from the darkness, a sheet of ghostly white across the forest.

"Put me down!" Hage whispered. "This is undignified!"

Ken'ishi put him down. "Like putting me in a woman's *kimono* perhaps? Seeing you hanging by your tail was enjoyable."

Hage paused, then sighed. "It's only fun when it's not *me*, fool. But your point is taken. Now follow me. There is a drain opening over there."

"Can't we go over?"

"The top is lined with iron spikes."

Ken'ishi followed Hage to a low opening that allowed a small stream bed to pass through the base of the wall. In rainy times, the stream would be alive and gurgling, a source of water and pleasure for the house and its garden. Iron bars filled the opening. Hage stuck his nose between them, held his breath, and started to wriggle through. The fit was tight, however, and he grunted and cursed with each finger's breadth of progress. Finally, he popped clear on the opposite side.

Ken'ishi dropped to all fours in the soft, cool streambed. The opening was so small that his human form could not have fit through even without the bars present. He reached his hand through, and Hage offered his bulging jewel sack for Ken'ishi to grab, which he did. A burst of hot-cold tingles and moments later, he had again taken the shape of a *tanuki*. He thrust himself through the bars after Hage. Perhaps he made a thinner *tanuki*, but he found himself passing through the bars with relative ease. Even as he did, he felt the tingle of the magic sputtering like a starving candle, until it faded completely and he found himself in human form again with one ankle still caught between the bars. Fortunately, he was able to extricate his foot with little difficulty.

"That's all of it, old sot." Hage suppressed a worried frown.

Lamps glowed on the house's garden veranda, turning bushes into hunched, half-human shapes, bamboo stalks into black shafts spearing heavenward, swaying in the wind.

Somewhere between himself and the glow of the veranda, Ken'ishi heard wet, labored breathing, accompanied by the stench of death.

The crane and the
    tortoise
on their playground —
a burnt field

— *Issa*

K en'ishi froze and listened, but the breathing did not change. The source was invisible in the lamplight and heavy shadows. The soft, moss-covered earth allowed him to slip closer to the sound. The stench of decay intensified, sickly sweet and ripe and wretched. A pair of bare feet, bound to fat stakes, twitched. The breathing was a wet rasp, labored, struggling.

Ken'ishi stepped closer and stood over a man's pale-skinned body. The man wore the well-proportioned, finely woven clothes of the well-to-do, but they were now stained and rumpled. He lay on his back with hands and feet splayed, staked to the earth. Each painful breath seeped in and out of a gaping mouth, in a face with eyes closed but features drawn taut by agony. From his right breast, a finger-length spear of bamboo shoot, as thick as a sword blade stabbing skyward, pierced the front of his robe, rooted in the midst of a dark, wet stain.

The man's eyes snapped open and fixed on Ken'ishi with the half-crazed glaze that meant he was not sure of his sight. His voice was a parched, ragged hiss. "Kill me!"

Ken'ishi knelt beside the man's head and raised a finger to his lips.

The man seemed only to half-see Ken'ishi. "Kill me, please, Master.... Three days ... three nights ... the bamboo grows." Sweat sheened the man's pale face, his haunted features, and his eyes gleamed like red-rimmed eggshells. He stank of filth and fever and infection.

Ken'ishi touched the point of the bamboo shoot. It was as sharp and hard as the point of a spear. He had long known that bamboo shoots could spring to great heights in a manner of days, but this ... He did not need to ask why this man had been staked out to die this way. The very act of torture was reason enough for Green Tiger. And yet, this was the house of a well-to-do retainer of the Otomo clan.

"Is he here?" Ken'ishi said. "Is Green Tiger here?"

The agonized rasp came again. "Kill me, Master!"

How many days to die, impaled with excruciating slowness by something simply looking for purchase in a harsh world? Might such cruelty corrupt the spirit of the bamboo?

Finally he could stand the gurgling and wheezing no longer. He raised the broadsword and severed the man's head with a single blow. The body spasmed once, then trembled for a few moments before subsiding.

Ken'ishi stood, anger rising in him even as he tried to push it down.

The smell of death made his eyes water, but the stench did not come from this man. Nearby, another bamboo stalk stood, more mature, with a half-rotted corpse impaled at its base. The bamboo now stood as thick as Ken'ishi's forearm, prying apart first one set of ribs, savaging a lung, then another set of ribs to emerge into the sunlight, and there to grow taller and thicker, nourished by the death it had caused.

A single thought crashed through his anger like the peal of a gong.

DESTINY!

The thought had been so powerful that he staggered for a moment. Silver Crane was here!

But so might be more guards. Gripping his weapon, Ken'ishi crept up onto the veranda, bathed in the light of the lamps, stilling his mind in search of the invisible thread that might lead him to the object of his quest. His senses drew taut, acute. Then he slid open the veranda door and stole into the house.

Tatami rooms decorated by painted scrolls, bits of lacquered furniture inlaid with gold and mother-of-pearl, beautiful but not ostentatious. The air was redolent with incense and fresh *tatami*.

Where would Green Tiger keep his prize? Hidden in the deepest, darkest corner of the house? Displayed for the world to see? Would Ken'ishi have to turn every room upside down?

He could only trust that Silver Crane wanted to be found.

Incense burned on a raised platform a hand's breadth above the floor, the house's shrine to the *kami* and family ancestors. An offering was there of a rice cake and a cup of *saké*. Near the incense, a wooden slat stood, painted with a magical charm, the nature of which he could not discern. The writing was too esoteric to be comprehensible.

Green Tiger would not hide the sword away. He would pay homage. The sword was here.

A piercing scream tore from the opposite side of the room.

A girl, stunningly beautiful, perhaps no more than fifteen, her eyes wide with terror and warning, naked under a loose silk robe.

Hage jumped up on his hind legs and charged her, waggling his jewel sack, leaving a trail of sparks in his wake.

She fled.

Hage chased her to the doorway then looked back. "Do you have it?"

"Not yet."

A coarse voice from beyond another doorway. "Is that you, Master?" The door whished aside. Silhouetted by lamplight stood a wild-maned figure with a curved splinter of flame-lit steel in his hand. The man's hair was matted with sweat and dust, his clothes and face shabby and spattered with dark stains. "It's you!"

Ken'ishi recognized the voice. "I'm glad you're here," he said. "You have spared me the trouble of hunting you down."

Masoku said, "This is it then." He raised his weapon.

Yes.

Ken'ishi raised Fang Shi's sword to high attack position, and the world was Void. Every breath, every heartbeat became an eternity of infinitely tiny moments wherein the possibilities of the universe unfolded.

"So it was you, not the White Lotus," Masoku said, a twist of surprise on his lips. "Clever bastard."

They circled each other, spiraling nearer, step by step. They shifted the positions of their blades, testing. Masoku feinted and retreated, testing for reaction, finding no opening, because Ken'ishi seemed to sense the action coming before it happened. He knew where Masoku would feint, knew where the attack would come, almost as if he were privy to Masoku's thoughts. When the strike came, Ken'ishi caught the blade, struck back, thwarted, slashed, clashed, struck, licked, snicked, clanged, retreated.

Masoku, too, knew the Void.

Ken'ishi's Chinese sword was bulky, clumsy, compared to Silver Crane's feather-light precision, but it was stout and razor-sharp. Fang Shi had kept his weapon well. The two combatants lunged again, closed with a clang, strained at each other's blades, nose to nose. Strength surged from outside through Ken'ishi's hands, arms, shoulders, as if his flesh drank the power of starlight, as if his thews were swelling to their former thickness and beyond with each passing breath, forcing Masoku to slowly, inexorably give way. They separated and struck and thwarted each other's attacks.

Ken'ishi sneaked a quick strike at Masoku's abdomen, and the tip of his sword struck something hard, unyielding. Armor. Without it, Ken'ishi's blow would have cut a rib.

Masoku's chest heaved with exertion.

Ken'ishi raised for another attack, a high one. Masoku's blade rose to meet it, as Ken'ishi had expected. But the focus of his attack was not Masoku's head; it was to bash Masoku's blade aside. The heavy Chinese sword struck just above the katana's guard, striking sparks and driving it from one of Masoku's hands. Startled by the sheer power of the blow, Masoku stumbled back, eyes wide, raising his off-balance weapon in feeble defense of the blow he knew was coming.

And it did come.

Ken'ishi felt no resistance at all, slashing through Masoku's shattered defense, then his neck, as if both had been mere scraps of silk.

The body stiffened and felt forward, and the head thumped to the floor, bulging eyes white in the lamplight.

Ken'ishi slung the blood from the blade and watched the *ronin*'s head bobble away. Should he feel more triumph? Elation? The dissipation of rage? He felt none of these things. This death was simply a tick on his list of things that must be done.

The stench of blood was thick in his nose, thicker than it should be, as if he were swimming in it. The *kami* of the air and earth buzzed with unease.

A river of death unto the end of the world.

Hage's eyes caught yellow in the lamplight. "Find your toy, and let us begone! Guards coming."

"Wait."

Ken'ishi knelt, rolled Masoku's corpse onto its back, and spread the robe open to reveal the armor that Junko had given him.

"What are you doing? It's ill fortune to play with the dead!" Hage hissed. "Get what you came for!"

Ken'ishi stripped off the robe and untied the armor.

A shout from outside the house.

Hage warned, "Haste!"

Ken'ishi donned the armor.

A trickle of liquid moonlight stole across the floor, falling across the house shrine. Ken'ishi knelt before the shrine. He found his fingers probing the edges of the wooden sides of the shelf. One of the boards stood apart, a seam that was too wide or ill-fitted. The board slid free into his hand. An invisible bolt of lightning shot through him. He reached into the black opening, half-expecting some hidden blade to spring out and sever his fingers. With excruciating care, his fingers quested, and encountered a wooden case, heavy enough, thick enough, long enough to house a sword. In a near frenzy, he yanked the case into view.

He opened it, his heart hammering like a smith's blows, and revealed a bundle of black silk. The moment his hand closed around it, he knew. A breath of ice rippled up his arm. He lifted it out of the box, and the silk fell away, and there revealed was the worn, stained ray-skin hilt that he knew like his own hands. The silver fittings gleamed. "I have it!"

Icy warmth shot through him, a deluge of strength that he had not felt in years. He could slay an army of *oni*. He almost felt his clothes tighten as his flesh seemed to rejuvenate.

Destiny.

"Then let's go!" Hage dropped to all fours and lunged for the door to the garden. "The rear gate!" It was just visible at the far corner of the garden.

Ken'ishi snatched up the Chinese sword as well—best to leave no evidence behind—and turned to follow Hage.

A sharp cry from behind spun him around. "Stop!" Two warriors burst into the room, swords drawn.

Ken'ishi whipped out Silver Crane and faced them. Instantly, he found the Void and charged. The sword was a glimmer of moonglow as it arced and sliced. The first man's thighs split open, deep and to the bone like a soft rice cake, at Silver Crane's passing, and the blade's continuation drove aside the second man's sword, creating an opening for Ken'ishi to thrust straight to the heart with the point like a crane's beak. The first man was still falling, his legs unable to support him, as Ken'ishi drew out his sword, spun, and took his head in a single swift stroke. Gore spewed across rice paper walls and new tatami.

The two bodies fell across Masoku's headless corpse.

Power surged through him. Strength. Ferocity.

And it felt right. As if it were meant to be.

He snatched a lamp down from its place on the veranda and dashed it against the floor, spilling oil and flame over wood and tatami. Then he grabbed another, throwing it against rice paper walls and wooden lattice. Orange flames rushed and licked and breathed. In the glow, Ken'ishi spotted the girl, her eyes bright with fear. Their eyes met, and then her face hardened. She retreated.

He sprinted through the garden, dodging stalks of bamboo, with fleeting thoughts of dead men feeding their roots. Hage waited for him at the rear gate, jumping up and down with the urge to be away. Ken'ishi threw open the bar, flung open the gate, and out they ran into the night.

My sword leans against
  the sky
With its polished blade
I'll behead the Buddha
And all his saints.
Let the lightning strike
  where it will
　　— Shunpo Soki, Death
　　　　　　　Poem

As they ran down the path toward Hakata, the flames of the burning house burgeoning in their wake, Ken'ishi flung the Chinese sword into the roadside undergrowth. His thoughts raced through possibilities of what to do next. He had not made plans beyond finding Silver Crane. He had not expected to survive the attempt.

Thoughts of Kiosé and Aoka village, his promise to return. In his imprisonment, he had imagined often going back and taking her and Little Frog away from the village. Would they remember him now? Could Hage undo the magic, awaken Kiosé from her dream of forgetting?

Then an unbidden thought: would his success gain Kazuko's attention if she knew? How would she feel if she could see him at this instant? Could his bravery and strength win back her heart if she knew? Would she approve of the man he had become? Would she have nursed him back to health?

The man has shown courage, strength. The man is worthy.

Ken'ishi stumbled for a moment with the sudden force of the voice.

The thief also showed strength and courage, but his spirit was steeped in even more blood than I. An ocean of it, frothing and limitless, spilled at his hands. The thief's hand sharpened my thirst for it, and the taste was bitter. Now, the man's hand brings sweetness and justice to the taste. It is good.

Ken'ishi's feet pounded the earthen road. The first hint of paleness rose behind the mountains on the eastern horizon.

I am old as the sea, young as the mountains. At moments of great destiny, I cut through barriers of possibility. I have lain at the bottom of the sea in a dead man's hand. I have been washed ashore and found. I have shaped the lives of powerful lords and simple warriors, fishermen and crafters. I am a shuttle moving in the loom among the threads of time and happenstance. And I am grateful to the man.

Ken'ishi's mind whirled with confusion. The voice thundered through him, leaving silver after-images of thought like lightning bolts.

What does the man regret most in all his life?

A swirl of thoughts exploded in his mind, a swarm of the regrets, and the first was that Kazuko could not see the man he had become, what he had accomplished, the justice he had done.

He shook those thoughts away. "Kiosé," he muttered. "I regret that Kiosé no longer knows me."

Words and thoughts so seldom align. The crane's feathers stir the winds of fortune. The man's destiny shifts.

Hage huffed as he ran next to Ken'ishi. "Who are you talking to?"

"No one," Ken'ishi replied. "One last visit to Shirohige and Junko, and I am going home." Even if Kiosé did not know him, she soon would again. He would see to that. He would take her away from Aoka village, carry her away on his shoulder if need be, and start a new life somewhere else, and he would find real service with a lord. Perhaps he would go to Kyoto and tell Hirosuke's family of his demise, and the Minamoto clan would reward him. And he would be a better man to her than before.

The glow of the flames over the treetops sent a spike of fear through Yasutoki, spurring him into a run. Rage boiled up in him. All his careful plans and meticulous maneuverings crumbling into ashes, imploding upon themselves too quickly for him to stem the collapse. One worthy henchman dead, the other missing, possibly dead. His enterprises savaged by a mindless gang of foreign thugs.

And now his house rose in a pillar of smoke and flame—the house of Yasutoki, not Green Tiger.

Silver Crane was still inside.

He charged up the hill again, his flagging vigor renewed by desperation. He had been all over the city of Hakata tonight. A heavy satchel of gold sloshed with great weight against his back. He had emptied the coffers of both of his moneychangers, lest the White Lotus know of those ventures and attempt to rob him. They even seemed to know where he lived! Had his entire identity been compromised? If Otomo no Yasutoki's identity as Green Tiger was revealed to Lord Tsunetomo or the bakufu's governor in Dazaifu, his punishment would make Minamoto no Hirosuke's death look like child's play.

A torrent of flames engulfed his house. Three of his guards stood in the road, with a handful of early-rising onlookers and three bleary-eyed firemen with their jackets stained by smoke. Piles of household possessions, artworks, boxes of scrolls and books, all lay in the road, well away from the flames.

Tiger Lily saw him first. Even with hair singed, cheeks smudged by soot, eyes streaming tears of sadness and relief, she was still breathtakingly beautiful. She almost threw her arms around him, fought with the want of it, and stopped short, throwing herself at his feet. "I'm sorry, Master!" Sobs thickened her voice. "I could not stop them!"

"There were five of you," Yasutoki said to the guards. "What happened?"

Kanehiro, the head guard under Masoku, pressed his forehead to the earth again and again. "I apologize, Master! Forgive us!"

"Tell me what happened!"

"Captain Masoku is slain. Sadamichi and Naiki are dead as well. We think someone killed them, but we did not see."

"How could you not see? Speak up!"

Kanehiro's mouth worked.

Tiger Lily slid forward. "I saw it, Master!" she said, "I screamed when I saw the intruders. They were after ... They took—"

Twin bolts of dread and elation exploded through his breast. Dread at what might have been taken, elation that it had not faced so ignominious an end as to be destroyed in a fire.

Tiger Lily glanced around at all the possible ears nearby. "They took *it*, Master," she whispered.

Yasutoki spurned Kanehiro with his foot, making space so that he could kneel close to her. "Who?" The White Lotus? How could they have known of Silver Crane?

"A man, he wore a mask, I did not see his face, and—"

"And?"

Her voice was a peep, fraught with trembling. "And a bear. I saw—"

"A bear!"

"Yes, Master. A huge, ferocious bear came after me, and I screamed and ran. A horrible, red-eyed beast with fangs like spear points!"

He considered this. She was too terrified to lie. "Did the man wear a white headband?"

"No, Master. He had a mask over his face. And he killed Masoku-sama. Then he *found it*."

He stroked her hair. Then with a deep breath, he approached the nearest fireman, a bald, gnarl-limbed man with eyes bloodshot and watery.

The fireman bowed deeply, sheepishly. "We are very sorry, Lord. We came as fast as we could, and there aren't so many of us in this district ..."

Yasutoki bowed in return and kept his voice admirably even, in spite of the seething tar pit his innards had become. "You have my gratitude. I commend you for your help, and I shall recommend you to the district constable for—"

"Hey! Look!" A voice from one of the onlookers rose in wonder and alarm. The man's arm pointed straight out toward the bay.

Yasutoki bit down on his annoyance at the rude interruption as his gaze fell upon the distant cause of the outburst.

Dawn reached over the eastern mountains, painting the smooth surface of Hakata Bay pink and orange. Speckling the colored tapestry was a profusion of black specks trailing foam streaks. Sails and masts.

Hundreds of ships, filling the bay, so many and so thick that a man could almost jump from deck to deck, ships in such numbers as he could never have imagined, all of them aiming for shore.

Yasutoki forgot all about his burning house.

PART 3: THE FIFTH SCROLL

"Battle! We are invaded! Ships! Hakata ... Hakozaki ... under attack! We will fall!"

The greatest joy a man can know is to crush his enemies, to see them driven before him ... to ride their horses and plunder their goods ... to  see the faces of those who were dear to them bedewed with tears ... to clasp their wives and daughters into his arms ... to ride from their burning villages to the lamentations of the dying.

— *Genghis Khan, grandfather of Khubilai Khan*

The shadow warrior known only as Kage crouched on a rock escarpment overlooking dawn-painted Hakata Bay. The sea and sky merged with the gray of early morning light, and small black islands in the distance seemed to hang suspended in the grayness. But there was something else in the mist. Dark hulks, sliding through the water toward Hakata and Hakozaki. Even a man as jaded and stoic as Kage could not fail to be awed by the sight of so many ships. He lost count somewhere after six hundred, and the endless fleet just kept coming.

The ships were of Koryo make, their decks swarming with more men than were required to crew the ships. Armor and weapons glinted in the gathering sunlight. The breeze bore the scent of horses. The ships rode low in the water, frothy wakes licking at their gunwales.

So this was what Green Tiger had worked toward for so long. There had been no large-scale war since a catastrophic rift between the Emperor's court and the Shogunate in Kamakura, a rift that had only been healed by the defeat of the clans loyal to the Emperor. Aside from the usual squabbling and skirmishing between rival samurai lords, the country had been at peace for almost half a century.

In the last three years, Kage had supplied Green Tiger with counts of troop strength from every domain on Kyushu, from the Otomo lords in the north to the Shimazu in the south, and the smatterings of the Nishimuta, remnants of the Taira, and other, smaller clans in between. He had stolen a Taira clan relic from a bumpkin samurai. He had disrupted communications and sabotaged fortifications. The oncoming horde would have solid knowledge of what opposed them, and they would tear through Kyushu like a butcher's cleaver.

Kage was not worried about the coming storm of war. A man like him, with his talents, could thrive amid the chaos of conflict. Knowledge of the enemy could be valuable, and he did not care which side employed him. These would be ... interesting times.

Kage knew enough about Green Tiger's past, through their mutual ties to the Taira clan, to know that he would stop at nothing to see the Minamoto and Hojo clans destroyed, even if it meant opening the door to barbarian invaders.

As the ships passed, he saw many of the decks laden with strange, mechanical contraptions. By now, the Golden Horde's empire stretched far to the south and west into distant unknown lands, and their mastery of warfare was spawning legends. No one had been able to stand against them. No one.

Khubilai Khan's relentless belligerence had put the Shogunate and the samurai lords on their guard. The Mongols would not find the warriors of Kyushu completely unprepared. Nevertheless, the information that Kage had provided to Green Tiger would be priceless in the hands of an invading general.

Hakata was the chief trading city on Hakata Bay, and the

wealthiest city on Kyushu. It lay within striking distance of Dazaifu, home of the offices of the Western Defense Commissioner, the hub through which most of Hakata's trade was distributed, and the seat of the Shogun's government on Kyushu. Beaches perfect for landing encircled much of Hakata Bay. Construction of stone fortifications to protect against attacks from the sea had begun last year, but were still in the early stages, and therefore useless.

Thanks in part to Kage, their construction had experienced numerous unforeseen difficulties.

The flap and snap of bamboo-ribbed sails reached him on his promontory, the slice of the hulls through the waves, and weeping. Realization of the sound dragged his thoughts from the majesty of spectacle and imminent chaos.

On numerous passing ships, bound with coarse ropes looped around necks and limbs, threading *through* bloody punctures in pierced hands, bound to the outside of the ships' gunwales, were scores of women, naked or half-stripped, bleeding, old and young and little girls, their faces contorted with suffering. Tied around one of the women, fluttering in the wind and salt spray, was the slashed, stained standard of the Taira clan governor of Iki Island.

Hell had come into the world on the decks of Mongol ships. Even a man as cold of heart as Kage was moved by such wholesale cruelty. In war, men fought, but women suffered.

By now, riders must be galloping southward across Kyushu to spread the word of the invasion. Within two or three days, every samurai on the island would be marching, like rival packs of wolves on a mission to defend their territory, and the gates of all the hells would be flung open to receive the dead. But would the wolves of Kyushu arrive in time, and would they be enough to stem the barbarian onslaught? These would be interesting days indeed.

He returned to his horse tied below. Best to put as many *ri* as he could between himself and Hakata Bay, and lay low until the blood stopped flowing.

Dew evaporates
And all our world is dew
   ... so dear,
So fresh, so fleeting.
    — *Issa, on the death of his*
                    child

Norikage looked out his window at leaves blowing in the steady morning breeze. The weather this autumn had been strange, both unseasonably warm and cold within a few days of each other. Typhoon season was over, but such strange weather sometimes brought unseasonable storms. High gray clouds gave the morning a dull, colorless hue, and the wind was stiff and moist. Even inside his office, with a smoky brazier of hot coals in the corner, Norikage huddled in his robes. Hanging in the window, the straw effigy of a monstrous octopus, crafted and blessed to ward off *kappa*, swayed gently in the wind, tentacles waggling.

Aoka village went about its business, even without a warrior to enforce the peace. Disputes were settled peaceably, if not always amicably. The vicissitudes of friendships in such a small place were Norikage's only real source of amusement. But like most days, he did miss Ken'ishi's naïve intelligence and his earnestness. Earnestness and honesty were so difficult to come by in this world.

Something small and hard struck the straw octopus, bounced and clattered off the shutter. He was reluctant to leave his place by the brazier to go look. Then another one, bouncing off the bulbous straw head with its fierce pebble eyes, through the window onto the floor. An acorn, followed by a hoarse giggle of delight from outside.

"Little Frog!" Norikage called. "That is not polite!"

Another scratchy giggle that quickly receded.

Norikage smiled, reached over and picked up the acorn, turned it around and around in his fingers, squeezing the all but impenetrable shell. Like the hearts of human beings, sometimes. Little Frog would grow up the same kind of outcast as his mother. Poor little thing, to be born so low in the world. Norikage sometimes wondered what sins Little Frog had committed in a previous life to be born under such bad kharma, the bastard son of a common whore. Kiosé could afford to clothe him only in the cheapest, most threadbare rags. His bare legs were usually filthy up to the knees, and his hands were always dirty from playing on the ground, but his eyes were bright, inquisitive, and intelligent, unlike many of the adults in the village. How would his life be different with a father to carry him on his shoulders, as Ken'ishi had done on occasion?

Norikage's own father had never carried him on his shoulders. His father was not a physically strong man, nor inclined to any sort of play that would distract from the dark, deadly world of court politics.

Kiosé's voice echoed through the window, calling for her son, threaded with concern and exasperation. Another distant, mischievous giggle. Norikage could imagine Little Frog enjoying the game of hiding from his mother, watching her seek him from whatever shadowed niche he had hidden himself, still too young for malice to have ever shadowed his heart.

The inventory report of the village's winter food stores looked like so much gibberish amid his distraction. How strange that Kiosé and Little Frog both seemed to have forgotten Ken'ishi's very existence. The rest of the village remembered, but Norikage had observed many times when Ken'ishi's name came up—more and more seldom these days—she simply looked puzzled at how everyone seemed to know this man except her. Since Ken'ishi had left, her spirit had closed up again. The sparks of life in her eyes had diminished again under the crush of daily toil and the demands of motherhood. How hard Kiosé's years had been on her. She was so pale these days. She was not more than twenty, but her features bore the weight of the misery of an old woman. She coughed a lot since the weather had turned colder.

Since Ken'ishi's departure, Norikage had neglected his own enjoyment of old Chinese poetry. As frustrating as it had been to teach a man so unschooled, to the point where Norikage had found himself reading the poetry to Ken'ishi, he did miss it. He took down a book and thumbed through it. The ancient words of Meng Jiao and Li Bai—Ri Haku in Japanese—reached out to him. Ken'ishi had been impressed to learn that Norikage knew Classical Chinese. Ken'ishi had likened it to mastering two weapons in a single lifetime, something most people could not do. Norikage appreciated the comparison. Growing up in Kyoto had given him a thorough education in the Chinese classics. Although Chinese culture and education had been out of favor in the imperial court for many years, many schools in Kyoto still taught Chinese literature, philosophy, and language.

An hour passed as he descended into the pages of Ri Haku and Li Yangbing, until a sound brought him back to the world.

Horses?

A distant scream of warning.

The rhythmic pounding of horses' hooves, growing louder. Many horses. Then another scream, closer.

Norikage jumped up and ran to the window.

Then another scream. Much closer this time. A man's gurgling death rattle.

Something whispered through the air, too quick to see. The pounding of horses' hooves, a rough war cry. Then he jumped as something struck the window frame. An arrow!

A handful of villagers fled down the street as if pursued by *oni*. He crept to the back door of his office, then into the back alley. The sounds of violence and chaos moved and shifted, difficult to pinpoint. He peered around the corner of a nearby house, catching a glimpse of a horse's rear, short and shaggy. Then he spotted two corpses lying in the street, the carpenter Taka and his son Hiroki, lying in puddles of deep-red mud, their bodies pierced by arrows, terror-stricken faces frozen in death.

A horse skidded to a halt not five paces away, snorting and frothing, so close that he could smell its hot breath. He cowered at the hairy, wild-eyed nightmare on the horse's back.

Fear of things is not rare. One is often filled with feelings of dread by the unknown. In large-scale battles, it is not visible things alone that induce fear in the enemy. One can probably frighten  him with noise, or by making a small force appear to be a large one, or by attacking suddenly from all sides. These are all ways of inducing fear into one's opponents. One can win by taking advantage of the enemy's confusion and loss of rhythm.

— *Miyamoto Musashi, The Book of Five Rings*

By the time Ken'ishi reached Shirohige's house, the city of Hakata roiled with chaos. A strange succession of intermittent thunderclaps had sent hundreds of people scurrying in panic through the streets, fighting through masses of samurai warriors and peasant spearmen on their way toward shore, where strange ships were sliding up onto the sand, disgorging their cargo of barbarian warriors and horses. Smoke tinged the air. The din and screams of battle wafted like ghosts from the docks, from the beaches, from the streets.

Running from Green Tiger's house, Ken'ishi had glimpsed the massive fleet choking the bay with masts and sails, and stopped to stare for several long moments. He had never imagined that so many ships existed in the world. In spite of the impending danger, he had to see Shirohige and Junko to safety; they had been kind to him. After that, he had to somehow make it back to Aoka village and take Kiosé and Little Frog out of there.

Hirosuke, the historian and scholar in that dank, briny cell, had told him of the terrible wars of decades ago, when the Minamoto clan seized ascendancy and created the Shogun's *bakufu* at Kamakura, how the land and the peasants suffered when armies clashed. Armies fought, but the common people suffered.

Against a force of invading barbarians, Aoka village and everyone in it would be wiped from existence. He had to get home.

Home.

As he and Hage ran through the city—Hage in his human visage—their progress was impeded by throngs of wild-eyed townspeople clogging the streets, struggling to flee the fighting. As mounted samurai struggled to reach the lines of defense, they barked orders and screamed curses at the peasants or ran them down.

Ken'ishi heard dozens of wild rumors spreading like ripples in a pond, growing more fantastic with each retelling.

"—a hundred thousand barbarians coming ashore—"

"—horses snorting fire—"

"—a thousand samurai already slaughtered—"

"—ships crewed by *oni*—"

"—defense fortifications were useless—"

"—eating children—"

"—Hakata's defense forces driven to rout—"

"—explosions blowing people to bits—"

He could make little sense of any of it in that first hour after dawn, except that the noise of battle waxed and waned with the distant clash of blades and the scream of horses.

With the coming of daylight, Ken'ishi's staff had reverted to the shape of a bow, and his mere handful of arrows clattered in the quiver on his back. Silver Crane still thrummed with power at his hip. Part of him yearned to charge toward the battle and fight the barbarians, but first he had to see to ... his family.

When he and Hage finally reached Shirohige's house, they found the front gate locked, the house empty, and Pon-Pon gone, along with Shirohige's wagon.

Ken'ishi said, "Apparently they wasted no time."

Hage said wryly, "There was the whiff of danger in the air. The old man is not the brave sort."

"They could be anywhere now." Ken'ishi imagined the throngs of people packing tighter by the moment, all fighting to get clear of the invaders, and Shirohige and Junko in the wagon behind Pon-Pon, mired in the mob. "Could you follow them, find which way they went?"

Hage pursed his lips. "I might be able to discern their general direction, but even the old hag's scent would soon be lost in the crowds."

"Can you find them? Will you protect them?"

"Are you truly so attached to those sour old villains? They hardly seem worth the effort. Souls as black as charcoal, both of them."

"They saved my life, brought me back from the land of the dreaming dead. I owe them a debt. Please do me this favor."

"What about you?"

"I must get to Aoka village."

"I thought there is nothing there for you now."

"Kiosé has forgotten me, thanks to you—"

Hage frowned and spat, "Don't blame me for giving you what you wanted!"

"I was a fool. But I will still save her. And Little Frog."

"I cannot reverse the enchantment. Those memories have left her mind like sand through fingers."

"I would not ask you to reverse it now. Perhaps it is better that she not remember all the ways I treated her so callously."

Hage scratched his white beard, then sighed. "Very well. I shall try to find the old villain and the old hag."

Ken'ishi bowed to him. "Thank you, Hage-sensei."

Hage puffed up at the honorific title, then bowed in return. "Farewell, old sot. Perhaps we shall meet again in this life."

Makeshift barricades choked the thoroughfares, spearmen and archers crammed behind the barricades, awaiting the enemy. No one paid Ken'ishi the slightest attention as he fought through crowds and ran down vacant streets interspersed with patches of determination and desolation. Great veils of gray-black smoke rose up to be torn by the stiffening wind. Fires raged through the harbor and nearby districts. The cacophony of battle rumbled and chafed through the city, echoing nearer and farther.

He had yet to catch a glimpse of the invaders. Nevertheless, he saw evidence of their passage: earthen streets torn up by hundreds of horses' hooves, a splatter of blood across the face of a vegetable shop, a scattering of hacked, trampled corpses, bristling with cruel arrows, an armored samurai trampled into wreckage.

Ken'ishi emerged from a narrow side street onto one of Hakata's major thoroughfares, Hundred Stone Bridges Street, named for the succession of bridges that crossed Hakata's many canals, which flowed toward the bay like the spokes of a wheel. At mid-morning, the street lay empty and desolate except for the dead, but a smoky tension still hung in the air, as if the next wave of invaders could come charging into view at any moment.

This street ultimately merged with the most traveled road to Dazaifu. A hundred paces down the street lay the wreckage of a barricade and the warriors who had defended it. If the invaders had broken through here, their path lay open out of Hakata.

Investigating the wreckage, he found only blood and death, shattered bodies and shattered weapons. He did find several quivers still filled with arrows, as if the samurai had barely gotten off a shot. In contrast, barbarian arrows bristled over the ground, the nearby buildings, the remnants of the barricade, and the remnants of the defenders, thicker than the spines of a dozen sea urchins.

He was replenishing his quiver when a step caught his attention.

A horse wandered from an alley into the street, a muscular chestnut stallion. Its saddle was empty, except for a Mongol arrow embedded in the gilded, black-lacquered wood. The horse's head hung low, sniffing the ground, then it spotted Ken'ishi and shied away from him.

"Wait!" Ken'ishi said.

The horse stopped, confusion showing in the white of its eye. Blood spattered the stallion's hooves and legs, slicked the saddle.

Ken'ishi stood. "Are you injured?"

The horse tossed and shook its head, nostrils flaring. "Who are you?" it asked.

"My name is Ken'ishi, and I am trying to get home to save my family. Are you injured?"

Sweat sheened the stallion's breast. "My master is dead. There was battle. Blood." Its voice was deep, quavering.

"Are you hurt?"

"I ... I do not know." The flesh of its breast shivered.

"May I see?" Ken'ishi edged forward.

The stallion tossed his head and stamped a sharp hoof. "If you try to ride me, I will kill you."

"I have never ridden a horse before," Ken'ishi said, but if this beast could carry him back to Aoka village with the speed he knew it possessed, he would take the chance. "You have much blood on you." He approached cautiously.

"It belongs to my master. He is dead."

"Were you able to kill any of the enemy?" He reached out and touched the stallion's taut shoulder. It was hot and moist, trembling with restrained power. He had never felt such physical strength before.

The stallion jerked away. "No, there were too many. My master shouted a challenge, and they shot him like a dog."

"How many?"

"As many as the needles of a pine tree."

Ken'ishi's fingers brushed over the stallion's coat. The animal eyed him skeptically. He moved alongside. "I'm going to pull out the arrow." He wrapped his fingers around the shaft and worked the head free, then tossed the arrow aside.

"Do you have water?" the stallion said, chewing at the bit. "I am thirsty."

"No, but I can take you to some. If I take you to water, will you carry me home?"

"Is it far?"

"For a powerful, noble beast like you, not far at all. And my family is in danger."

"And if we meet the enemy?"

"We will fight them."

The horse tossed its head and snorted again. "Very well. Mine was a good master, kind to me, a fierce warrior. He deserves vengeance."

Ken'ishi took the stallion's reins. "Very well, Sir Stallion. We will find water, and then we will run like the wind."

Now in sad autumn
As I take my darkening
   path ...
A solitary bird
              — *Basho*

With her body wrung out from an extra long training session, Kazuko sat down to eat. The rice was freshly made, the pickled plums were tart, and the apples were sweet. Sweat still dampened and stiffened her hair, but the weariness was pleasant. Today during practice, she had sliced clean through three rolled *tatami* mats, which Master Higuchi said was equivalent to cutting through an entire human torso. She had never made the cut so cleanly before. The rush of satisfaction at her growing skill and strength buoyed her heart.

As she savored the texture and flavor of the rice, she became aware of a gathering noise in the castle, like the furor of a crowd. Loud voices echoed in the courtyard below, reaching up to the window with the surprise and alarm still intact.

"—who is he?"

"—call Captain Tsunemori!"

"Hey! Get some help! He's alive!"

She leaped to her feet, gathered her robes, and ran down through the house. By the time she reached the courtyard, a large crowd had already gathered around a lathered, trembling horse. The shaft of an arrow protruded from the rear of the saddle, embedded like a strange, feathered spike. Blood ran in an encrusted, rusty-red swath along the horse's belly and flank.

As she approached the crowd, she raised her voice, "Move aside!"

Wide-eyed commoners and taciturn samurai alike suppressed their surprise and allowed her through, bowing low. Tsunemori was already there, kneeling beside a man clad in blood-soaked heavy armor. The bent or broken shafts of three arrows protruded from his body, one from his shoulder, one from his lower back, one from his side.

Tsunemori removed the man's dented, battered helmet.

Blood reddened the man's lips, his eyes rolled back and fluttering.

Tsunemori tried to hold him up, to prevent him from falling against the arrows. "Who did this? Who are you? Why have you come?"

The man's family crest painted on his armor was Hojo.

The man struggled to speak, his voice an all but unintelligible gasp. "Battle! We are invaded! Ships! Hakata ... Hakozaki ... under attack! We will fall!"

"Under attack!" Tsunemori exclaimed. After studying the unfamiliar craft of the arrows, a look of comprehension spread on his face. "Barbarians!"

The man coughed wetly. "I was sent from Hakozaki ... but they caught me! We must ..." The man sagged in Tsunemori's arms.

Tsunemori eased him down, and noticed Kazuko. "Milady! Do you know where he is?"

She nodded, still shocked at the implications. "I think he is in the practice yard."

"No," said a deep voice from behind her, "I am right here."

Her husband strode toward them, wearing only his practice trousers, naked to the waist, still sheened with sweat. His broad chest and shoulders were strong and hard, especially for a man of his years. His swords were thrust into his sash, as if he were already prepared for battle.

317

Tsunemori bowed to his elder brother, and Kazuko was struck for a moment by their resemblance. Tsunemori, the younger and more handsome; Tsunetomo, the elder, more muscular and swathed in an aura of command.

Tsunemori repeated what the man had said.

Lord Tsunetomo's eyes narrowed as he listened, and his lips hardened into a thin, dangerous line. "So," he said, "the Great Khan did not receive his tribute. The day we were warned of has come."

He raised his voice to the assembled throng. "The Khan thinks we are soft, like the Koreans and the Chinese. We must show him that his judgment is in error. We march in one hour!" His gaze swept over the surrounding warriors.

Tension stiffened the crowd. Tremulous murmurs spread through the crowd of commoners, along with numerous cries of "Yes, Lord!"

Tsunetomo faced his younger brother. "Send a patrol on horseback to scout the road to Hakozaki."

"Yes, Lord."

Lord Tsunetomo spun on his heel and stamped back toward the house, his back straight and his step sure.

Kazuko felt a sudden burst of pride in her husband as she watched him go, then gathered up her robes and hurried after him.

In their chambers, he called for servants to help him into his great armor. His *o-yoroi* rested on its tree. Servants buzzed around him like bees, preparing the undergarments.

She did her best to direct them, even though her belly fluttered and her neck tightened. Her face flushed at how the servants knew how to help her husband into his armor, but she did not.

He took her hands. "Kazuko, my dear."

Her eyes teared. "Yes, Husband."

"After I leave, only a few warriors will remain behind for the castle's defense."

"I know, Husband. I understand."

He lifted her chin and gazed into her eyes. "You are a good wife, a true samurai woman. You know that today may be the end of our time together."

She nodded and fought back the tears.

He raised his arms to the sides as the servants brought forth his under-robes and began to dress him. "I am leaving you in charge of the castle. You must command its defense if the enemy comes. The men are loyal, but you are a woman. If there is a man who refuses to obey your orders, you must kill him immediately. I know you have the skill. A sudden display of force will keep the rest in line. At a time like this, you must countenance no disobedience. Do you understand?"

The hard bluntness of his words shocked her, but she nodded. "I understand."

"Good. You are a smart girl." Then he seemed to study her face, as if for the first time. "You are so beautiful, my dear. I pray to the gods and Buddhas that I may see you again after today."

She threw herself against him and pressed her cheek against his breast, and he hugged her back. His breathing was deep and warm in her ear. She said, "Maybe it is not as serious as it seems. Maybe it is only a large band of Koryo pirates."

Lord Tsunetomo shook his head. "This has been coming for years, and the Mongols do nothing by half-measure. Those were indeed Mongol arrows. We do not yet know the size of the force, but I fear that things might actually be worse than they appear. Hakata and Hakozaki may already have fallen." He raised his arms again as the servant brought forth the lacquered breastplate. "The barbarians must not gain a foothold on Kyushu. If they defeat us here, their armies could sweep all the way to Kyoto, to Kamakura. Shed no more tears, my dear. Don your armor and take up your naginata. Defend our home."

She stepped away and wiped her eyes. "Yes, Husband."

Laugh lines formed at the corners of his eyes. "Good! I regret that I have not taught you the ways of battle strategy and defense. I have a book on my desk, a treatise on the art of war by a Chinese general. If you have time, read it. You may find it useful. It is a man's book, but you have a good head. You will understand, I think."

"Yes, Husband. I will read it."

"If Yasutoki were here, the duty would fall to him. I can only hope he survived the initial onslaught. Perhaps he might make his way back here."

The very thought of Yasutoki in charge of anything repulsed her. These last few weeks of his absence had lifted the mood of the castle considerably, as if his very presence brought gloom and distrust with him.

She stopped all but a single tear. "Be careful, Husband."

He nodded and stroked her cheek with his callused finger. Then, he raised his voice to the servants, "Bring Lady Kazuko her armor. Immediately!"

Kazuko stood on the steps of the central keep, armor-clad, newly sharpened and polished naginata in hand, surveying the ranks of foot troops, archers, and mounted samurai.

Lord Tsunetomo sat astride his glossy black steed, clad in his great armor, with its polished lacquered plates, broad rectangular shoulder guards, intricate embroidery and rainbow of silken cords and laces, plus his massive helmet, two swords tied to his belt, plus a bow and quiver of arrows, and a *nodachi*—a greatsword that stood taller than him—slung behind his saddle. He was a born general, appraising his troops as they formed up for departure.

A small contingent of fifty warriors would be left behind to defend the castle. The thought of asserting command over them still made Kazuko nervous. She believed they would obey because her husband had made it clear that she was in command, but many of them wished to be in the main force, chafing at being forced to remain behind. She dreaded that moment of having to assert authority over such a pack of barely tamed wolves.

Lord Tsunetomo gave a signal, and Captain Tsunemori ordered the troops forward. The drums began to pound, and the ranks of warriors started forward, the curved blades of the spears and naginatas glinting in the iron gray light, all swathed in the brilliant scarlet of Tsunetomo's domain. It was a solemn procession that marched out of the castle, down toward the town. As soon as the last of the column had passed through the outer gate, Kazuko ordered the gates closed.

Standing at the fortifications, she watched the troops march out of sight down the forest road.

What would happen to her if her husband were killed? Since she had not yet given Tsunetomo an heir, Tsunemori could claim his brother's title and lands. Tsunemori already had a son, an heir to continue the family line. Perhaps Kazuko would have to return to the Nishimuta clan to live out her days as a widow in her father's house, or shave her head and become a nun. If that was to be her fortune, so be it. Tsunetomo's wealth and power meant nothing to her.

With a deep breath, she summoned the officers who commanded the remaining troops. She had heard her husband say once that wise leaders take advantage of the wisdom of their subordinates. Captain Nobuhara was a seasoned veteran. He would know the immediate details that needed to be addressed.

As her mind whirled with imagined horrors that might be coming, her thoughts turned toward Ken'ishi. She had so often tried to expunge his name from her mind, a memory too painful to allow a name, but there he was again, at the forefront of her worries. Where was he amid this growing turmoil? Was he still alive? Had he been killed in some ignominious brawl, or had he found someone to serve? Had he found someone else to love? Yes, love, flashes of tingling, gushing ecstasy, and then the old longing to feel that searing flame once again, even though she knew that if she touched it she would be forever scorched.

"No," she whispered.

"Milady?" Captain Nobuhara said.

She dragged her mind back to the task at hand—a castle defense to organize, even though she as yet had no inkling how. Nevertheless, her husband trusted her. Hakata Bay was a half-day's ride, perhaps a day on foot at hard march. Perhaps the enemy would be crushed before they got this far. Perhaps fortune would smile on her, on her husband.

"Captain," she said, "let us discuss the defenses."

In a world of grief and
  pain,
Even flowers bloom,
Even then ...
  — *Issa, on the death of his
                child*

Norikage squealed as the horse reared above him, thrashing the air with its hooves. The ferocious, hairy rider laughed in a voice like gravel and raised his ensanguined sword. Norikage darted for the narrow gap between buildings, too narrow for a horse, so tight that he could not turn his body or kneel. He scrambled like a rat for the other side and emerged into the street. Or maybe it was a hell.

Arrow-pierced bodies lay pounded into the bloody, hoof-beaten dirt. Three riders crowded their mounts around one of the fishermen and his wife, forced them into a huddled pair, then hacked them to pieces.

Where was Hana? Was she safe for the moment within his house? Had she gone out on an errand? He had grown fond of her since he had taken her into his bed, and she him.

Little Frog wandered out of the inn and into the street, looking to see what all the noise was about. Norikage stared in horror, unable to move.

Where was Kiosé?

The look of curiosity on the little boy's face changed to fear at the sight of the thundering marauders. One of the riders spotted him. The boy froze.

"No!" Norikage cried, as if to draw the rider's attention away from the boy.

The barbarian spurred. Norikage wanted to close his eyes, but he could not. Little Frog started to cry. Kiosé appeared in the doorway of the inn, eyes wide and searching, fixing upon her son with growing horror. The short-legged, hairy pony broke into a gallop as it bore toward Little Frog. The rider leaned down and snatched the boy off the ground by the back of his neck.

Kiosé screamed, a wild, ragged, helpless sound.

The rider paused and turned, holding his squirming prize up high for his compatriots to see. They cheered him and laughed, eyes filling with cruel glee. They spurred toward the man holding the little boy high in the air, as if this was a familiar game. The man grinned like a shark. He charged away from his comrades, still carrying Little Frog by the back of the neck. The child wailed. Then the man spun his horse and charged back toward his comrades. Just before passing them, he lobbed the child high into the air.

The boy tumbled as if time had stopped.

Norikage closed his eyes.

When he opened them again, Kiosé flailed out of the inn, her mouth opened into a shriek of madness, pelting toward the small, bloodied figure on the ground. She threw herself down beside it, unaware of the rider behind her, the blood-smeared glint of cruel steel. Her scream ceased and she fell forward, a crimson gash across her back. The barbarian rode past. She thrust herself up onto her elbows, gathered up Little Frog's mangled form, fought herself upright, staggering toward the inn, lips of the monstrous gash drooling crimson down her back.

Norikage's heart clenched. Another rider turned toward him. He dashed into his office, praying the barbarian would seek a more available target.

Moments later, he peeked outside, until a flaming torch arced through his back window, crashing onto his desk, flames licking at the stack of documents, his records, his histories, his poetry. In moments, his office would be engulfed in flames.

He rushed out the back again and sprinted toward his house. The distance was only perhaps a hundred paces, but the moment he stepped outside, it became the longest hundred paces he had ever encountered. On one end of the street, a horseman crashed outward through the door of a house, dragging a woman by the hair. Yumiko—her name was Yumiko. Her scream ripped the air and lent wind to Norikage's heels. He had forgotten his shoes. Pebbles tore at the bottoms of his pounding feet. His breath wheezed and gasped. His robes fluttered around him in his flight.

Not Hana. She would not be dragged through the street by the hair to be raped to death.

Somehow he reached his front gate and flung himself inside, lurching into the house, gasping her name.

Hana burst out of a closet and flung herself weeping into his chest. He held her for a long moment, feeling her cling to him with something aside from desire. Trust. Comfort. She looked to *him* to protect her. The thought landed on him like a sack of rice. He could hardly protect himself!

His heart clenched. The last time a woman had looked at him that way, she had been with child, and soon after that, he had been banished from the capital.

Their only hope was to flee. But to where?

A crash sounded at the front gate.

Ken'ishi knew of a well and water-trough near the outskirts of Hakata, at a shrine where carters and riders often took their animals. He led the stallion by the reins. Before he rounded the last corner before the well yard, a strong warning from the *kami* stopped him. His senses snapped alert, his entire body tingling. A group of gruff, unintelligible voices echoed around the buildings with the clatter of weapons and horses' hooves.

He crept to the edge of a building and peered around. Ten barbarian horsemen clustered around the well, watering their mounts. He had never seen their like—except in a lotus dream. They were almost bestial, riding shaggy ponies that stood so short the riders' feet almost brushed the ground. The warriors wore fur-trimmed hats—no, helmets—with conical tops of dull metal and leather draping the ears and neck. Scruffy faces, pointed beards and mustaches, and strange, blunt features. Metal scales glinted on their arms and chests. Their clothes and boots were dun-colored or gray, trimmed with fur. In spite of the horses' small size, they appeared to be heavily laden with equipment, bags, pouches, even cooking pots. Each of them also carried a thick, strangely curved, symmetrical bow, three quivers of arrows, and a sword. They stank of unwashed bodies and horse dung.

Ken'ishi knew some Chinese from his lessons; their speech did not sound like Chinese. One of them barked a command, and the group of gnarled, knotted men turned their mounts away, trotting up the street. They rode as if they had been born in the saddle; each rider and horse moved almost as one being.

As their sounds dwindled into the distance, his ears caught something else coming from the direction of the sea. More thunder crashes, dozens of them, faint and echoing with the hazy distance. The horse shied and stamped at the sharp reports. Ken'ishi had never heard thunder crashes so abrupt yet repetitive.

The Mongols were gone, so he hurried the horse to the trough. The enemy had gone down his intended road. Somehow he would have to find—or fight—his way through them if he was to make it back to Aoka. The village might already be under attack, or destroyed.

Ken'ishi asked, "Are you swift?"

The stallion tossed his head and sniffed. "I am swift as a typhoon wind."

"We may have to outrun pursuit."

"My legs are alive again," the stallion said, "and the day is young. Vengeance awaits us. Climb up, Warrior."

"I don't know how."

The horse snorted in contempt. "I'm not going to wait for you. You may have helped quench my thirst, but I'll let no coward upon my back."

"Very well, Sir Stallion." Ken'ishi grasped the reins with one hand, and the saddle with both, and pulled himself up, throwing his leg over. He reminded himself suddenly of Little Frog's first attempts to climb steps—clumsy, ungainly, but determined. He hoped the boy was all right.

Now astride the hard saddle, Ken'ishi adjusted himself to get a feel for it under his backside.

The stallion said, "Put your feet in the stirrups, fool."

He slipped his feet into the cumbersome boxes that dangled on either side. They did help him feel more balanced in his seat, however. It was a peculiar sensation to sit so high above the ground upon a living creature.

He did not know what to do next. He tried bouncing on the saddle. He tried flicking the reins.

The horse looked back at him. "Well? What do you want?"

He kicked the horse's flanks, and the animal reared. As it launched into a gallop, Ken'ishi nearly tumbled backward out of the saddle, but he snatched its front and managed to right himself. The unfamiliar rhythm of the horse's movement flopped him about like a fish held by the tail. Struggling for balance, he stood in the stirrups, using his legs to dampen the violence of the horse's movements. As if by magic, the ride smoothed, like the difference between violent whitecaps on the water and gentle ripples. A broad grin stretched his lips as he leaned into the horse's run, bending over the animal's neck, feeling the wind in his face, synchronizing his rhythms with those of his steed.

As the horse charged down the empty street toward the countryside, he hoped he could make it stop more easily.

Chilled through, I wake
 up
With the first light.
 Outside my window
A red maple leaf floats
 silently down.
What am I to believe?
Indifference?
Malice?
I hate the sight of coming day
Since that morning when
Your insensitive gaze turned me to ice
Like the pale moon in the dawn.
— *The Love Poems of Marichiko*

Perhaps two *ri* into the countryside, Ken'ishi and the stallion came upon a corpse in the road, a lightly armored samurai, a single arrow protruding from the back of his skull.

The stallion snorted. "Another horse without a master."

"Another *ronin* steed, like you," Ken'ishi said.

He cautiously dismounted and approached. The man lay face down. Tied to his *obi* was a wooden message box bearing the seal of the Office of the Western Defense Commissioner, who had his office in Dazaifu, about ten *ri* to the south. This man was a messenger. Ken'ishi grabbed the box and jerked it free, snapping the cords. Inside was a letter, addressed with hasty scribbling to Hojo no Masahige.

Ken'ishi's predecessor had been dead some three years, slain by Chiba's father. He considered opening the letter, but a nearby noise stopped him, more horsemen coming, this time from ahead. He threw away the box and stuffed the letter into his robe, then snatched the horse's reins and tugged him toward the bushes.

The horse resisted. "You run from a fight?"

"I'll choose my moments to fight, now come!"

The horse followed him into the undergrowth, where he looped the reins over a branch, then readied his bow.

The barbarians rode into view, looking even more fearsome up close. Their stench was even worse. Five of them passed within a few paces of his position, but riding too fast to spy him and paying no attention to the corpse in the road.

When the barbarians had gone, he pulled out the letter and tried to read it. The hurried, scrawling brush strokes made understanding all but impossible. The only sentence he could understand fully was the last one, which was a request for all able-bodied men to assemble immediately at Dazaifu.

Norikage would be able to read the rest of the letter. He only hoped that Norikage still lived. But why was the letter addressed to Hojo no Masahige? That thought troubled him as he continued toward the village.

Chiba waited for as long as he could after the last barbarian had left before squeezing himself out from under the floor of his family's house. The dark hollow beneath the floor where he had often hid as a child to outwait his father's drunken rages had served him well once again.

Young Shota stood nailed to the wall with arrows. Ryuba lay in the street, arrow-riddled and trampled. Chiba tried not to look, but he could not take his eyes from the corpses for a long time. Cold, empty blackness settled into his belly.

He knew he should be thinking about what to do, but his mind was too muddled. He should dart off into the forest like a rabbit and hide. He should take all the food and water he could carry. Such thoughts roiled forth, but then disappeared again with each new horror he saw. Houses roaring with flames. Corpses strewn like shredded straw dolls. Memories of the screaming. The stench of burning flesh, of blood, of smoke.

He knew them all, this throng of the dead. He had liked very few of them, and even fewer had liked him, but he knew them. They were as much a part of his home as the houses and the docks and the shore. There was no one left to bury them. No one left to chant sutras or burn incense. Chiba certainly was not going to do any of that. As soon as he could think straight, he was going to gather some food and water and get out of here.

Movement caught his eye from near the inn.

He shambled toward the shape, a woman, dragging herself painfully toward the doorway of the inn, pulling something bloody behind her. Chiba's eyes were not good enough anymore to distinguish details. Drawing closer, he saw the deep gash across her back. Through the crimson-soaked lips of her robe, a streak of white bone was visible. With one hand she was dragging the ravaged body of a small child.

A quavering laugh came out of him.

Kiosé gasped and looked back over her shoulder. Recognizing him, she rolled onto her back, eyes wide and hollow, her face and lips as pale as the belly of a fish. She dragged Little Frog's remains close to her, hugged them against her side.

For long heartbeats Chiba and Kiosé looked at each other.

Her breath came in wet, ragged gasps.

Then he stepped over her and went into the inn to search for food.

The whore would soon join her whelp. Perhaps there was justice in this world after all.

The unnatural silence hammered on Ken'ishi's ears as he paused at the outskirts of the village, wary of danger. Flames engulfed several buildings, one of which was Norikage's office, belching smoke into the gray sky. With the nearness of the surrounding structures, the fire was likely to consume most of the village, but he saw no villagers trying to quench the flames. He saw no one at all, except scattered, arrow-riddled corpses. For several long moments, he waited for any sign of the marauding horsemen. Only when he was certain none were coming did he urge the horse into the village.

His lips tightened, his throat clenched as he passed the corpses lying in pools of muddy gore on the dirt street. All familiar faces, now frozen into grotesque masks of death and terror, smeared, spattered with blood, arrows sticking out of them like feathered spines. Men and women, young and old. He searched the faces for two he most did not want to find among the dead.

His eyes and nose burned from smoke and grief. Outside Norikage's office, he tried to shield his mouth and nose as he peered into the roaring flames. The stallion snorted and stamped at the inferno's proximity. If Norikage was in there, he was long dead. This village no longer needed a constable or an administrator—only gravediggers.

He called into every house, every shop. Not a single soul remained alive. Some faces he knew were not among the dead; perhaps they had fled into the woods or been taken prisoner. Most of the buildings had been sacked, including his house, with clothes and other belongings strewn into the street. The storehouse appeared to have been raided before it was set to burn, judging from the rice grains and bits of smoked fish strewn about the entrance.

A figure in tattered, bloody clothing lay in the doorway of the inn. A deluge of sick dread flooded his guts. Flinging himself off the horse, Ken'ishi ran across the street. Not one bloody figure, but two. He recognized Kiosé's robe. The child's dirty hands and feet, the scrap of topknot, were unmistakable.

A choked sound of rage and grief escaped Ken'ishi's throat before he clamped it off.

Blood stiffened the back of Kiosé's robe around the long gash from her neck to her hip. The blood trail and marks in the dirt told of how she had dragged the remains of her son this far. But now her eyes were closed as if sleeping, and her open mouth sagged onto the floor, her stiff hand clawing at nothing.

His torso became a cavern of ice, numbing the rest of him. A terrible trembling swept through him.

The stallion said, "You were too late to save your mare or your son."

"My son?"

"He has your scent, even in death."

Ken'ishi's chin fell, and he struggled to control the grief that howled up within him like a typhoon wind. He knelt beside Kiosé and, with infinite gentleness, scooped up her body and carried it to his house, then returned for the remains of Little Frog. He tried to ignore her cold, gray flesh; the last time he had held it, it had been steeped in warmth and life. He placed them both on his *futon*, child on his mother's breast, wrapped them in his best blanket, clapped twice and said a prayer to the *kami* to help them on their way.

Then he scattered oil and tinder and set the house aflame.

He knelt on the ground and watched the house burn, trying to convince himself that it was the smoke that made his eyes water so.

The stallion said, "You did not know that he was your son."

Ken'ishi shook his head. "Kiosé knew. She tried to tell me, make me believe it. But for a long time, I didn't want it to be true."

"A strange thing to deny one's progeny the comfort of the herd. Of course, when they grow, they must be cast out to gather their own herd, but until then it is a joy to be surrounded by the cavorting of one's colts. I have a great many strong sons and swift, beautiful daughters."

"I was a fool."

"But you are alive, and vengeance awaits."

Ken'ishi's grip tightened on the reins as he prepared to mount. "Yes. But first I hope to find one last friend."

Deepen, drop, and die
Many-hued
  chrysanthemums ...
One black earth for all
  — *Ryusui*

Hatsumi sat in her chambers, dressed in her rich, feather-soft robes, wringing her hands, waiting for news. Lord Tsunetomo had departed with his troops. Soon, darkness would fall.

Kazuko was off somewhere in the castle, pretending to be a man. The girl's father had always suffered her to play with sharp things, and now her husband allowed the same. Kazuko was too fragile a flower to risk her beauty in manly ways. Now she seemed to fancy herself a true warrior, dressed up in all that armor and acting like a man.

Hatsumi wanted someone to bring her tea, but there was no one. All the servants were hard at work preparing for a possible siege, gathering wood and hauling vast quantities of food and supplies into the castle, intent on saving the fruits of the recent harvest from the enemy. So Hatsumi was forced to venture toward the kitchen to warm some water. Making tea was beneath her, except to make it for her mistress, and even then she had other servants bring her the water and the tea leaves.

This waiting for news was the worst part. What would be her fate if Lord Tsunetomo was killed? She scowled. Tsunemori would probably claim his lands and castle. What would happen to Hatsumi and Kazuko in that event? Would Tsunemori allow his widowed sister-in-law to remain here? Tsunemori and his wife, Lady Yukino, that selfish old busybody, would take over the lord's chambers, relegating Hatsumi and Kazuko to smaller, more modest rooms. The new lady of the house might even throw them out entirely. What would happen to them then? For that matter, what would happen if Tsunemori was killed, too? Perhaps then Kazuko could maintain her claim to the castle. Perhaps not. Some of Lord Tsunetomo's relatives might try to assert their claim on his lands. Even the Shogun might step in and award the lands to someone else. So many possibilities for ill fortune.

Hatsumi had grown accustomed to the opulence of life in the house of a great lord. To have it snatched away now ...

She did not reach the doors outside before she saw Kazuko and Captain Nobuhara approaching. Absorbed in their own conversation, they did not see her. Kazuko looked worried. No, she looked terrified. She concealed it well, but Hatsumi knew the signs, like the way she clenched her fists and tilted her head.

Captain Nobuhara bowed. "This changes nothing, milady. Our preparations must continue for as long as possible, until the enemy is in sight."

Spotting Hatsumi coming down the hallway toward them, they both stopped. Kazuko turned to the armored samurai and said, "Please see to it, Captain."

Captain Nobuhara bowed again. "As you wish, milady. Do not worry. The enemy will never see the inside of these walls." The captain went back outside.

Kazuko turned toward Hatsumi, her mask beginning to crack.

Hatsumi knew she must sequester her mistress before the mask shattered completely. It would not do for Kazuko to weep in front of everyone. She hurried forward and took the young woman by an armored elbow. "Come, dear. You can tell me all about it in your chambers."

Kazuko allowed herself to be led. Her gait was stiff with the effort of self-control.

Hatsumi had held her arm many times before, but the difference in how Kazuko's body felt after all the martial training and while wearing armor was startling. The womanly softness that made her so beautiful was now encased in layers of lacquered plates and silken cords. She almost felt like a man. They climbed all the way to the upper reaches of the castle keep.

Behind closed doors, Kazuko sank down onto the *tatami*, and her shoulders sagged as if her armor weighed upon her like a cartload of iron ore. Her face was not powdered. Her hair was in disarray. She almost looked like a young man.

"Now, what is it, dear?" Hatsumi said.

Kazuko's mask shattered like porcelain. She buried her face in her hands and wept.

Hatsumi held back a stab of fear, but hugged Kazuko's shoulders and waited patiently until the first gush of sobs subsided.

Kazuko shuddered out the words, like the beat of a drum. "There was a messenger. He brought word from Tsunemori. We have been defeated. The enemy force numbers in the untold thousands. Our defenses were crushed and scattered. Our troops have fallen back to Dazaifu, where the other lords gather their forces. My husband was wounded by an arrow, and was unable to write the message himself. The enemy fights like demons, and ignores all honorable ways of battle. Our samurai could not stand against them."

Hatsumi's fear deepened, but she would not show it. How long before her own mask of control would shatter? Did Yasutoki still live? Had he gotten away from Hakata in time? The thought of him coming to harm filled her with fear and regret. She regretted that she had never been able to enjoy him fully, too lost in her own suffering.

Kazuko said, "This is not a pirate attack, or peasant rebellion, or a war between samurai lords. These are not just barbarians; they are *oni*."

Their eyes met, and a rush of revulsion and terror swept through Hatsumi's body.

Kazuko's voice hardened, and her eyes sparkled with brittle

ferocity. "They will not take us alive. Do you understand, Hatsumi?"

Hatsumi gulped down her fear. "I understand."

A beautiful woman sobs
in a shabby inn
   surrounded by
   bloodgrass —
with a deer's voice
         — *Buson*

Ken'ishi searched for any signs of hoof prints on the forest path, but saw none. The quicker he traveled, the easier it was to drive out the memories of Kiosé's dead face, the feel of her lifeless body, the savaged remains of Little Frog. Perhaps Norikage was dead, too. Everyone and everything he knew, dead and gone. He would never know Kiosé's gentle touch again, nor the pleasure he felt when she gave him a rare smile.

The forest held its breath, and the pond where he had once faced the deadly *kappa* lay just ahead. Suddenly, a blood-smeared apparition erupted from the bushes with its mouth agape. Pale, thin arms flailed at him. Silver Crane jumped free into his hand, rising to strike.

Norikage's voice stayed his blow. "By all the gods and Buddhas, Ken'ishi, it is good to see you! You're alive!" The little man ignored all sense of propriety and decorum, throwing himself against Ken'ishi's stirrup.

Ken'ishi could not help feeling relieved as well. He slid his sword back into its scabbard. "And you as well!"

"You have been gone so long! All this time! But I knew you

would come back and—"

Ken'ishi dismounted. "What happened to you? Are you wounded?"

Norikage scrutinized the gash across the top of his shoulder. "I think an arrow nicked me. They rode into the village, killing everyone, looting houses, the inn…. Everyone just ran. Some of the villagers escaped, I think."

Ken'ishi said, "How did you escape?"

"I ran like a *tanuki*." Norikage's haunted face filled with shame. "And poor Kiosé. And …"

"They are dead."

"Yes, I saw. Oh, my friend—"

Ken'ishi pulled the letter out of his robe. "I found this on the body of a dead messenger. I cannot read it all."

"Show me!" Norikage took the letter with two quivering hands, opened it, and read. His gaze flicked up and down the crumpled page. Norikage's hand sank to his side as if the letter had suddenly become a tremendous weight. His face drained of color.

"What does it say?" Ken'ishi asked.

Norikage's normally rich and well-controlled voice was now tight and quiet. "The islands of Tsushima and Iki, between Hakata Bay and the Koryo peninsula, have already fallen to the enemy, their entire garrisons slaughtered. The town of Imazu on the western side of the Bay is under attack, likely to fall before night. Hakata and Hakozaki are lost. This letter is a message to summon all men to Dazaifu, where the government is gathering an army to defend Kyushu."

"Then we must reach Dazaifu. What do you know of these barbarians?"

"When I lived in Kyoto, I heard quite a lot about them, none of it good. They are demons, said to drink blood! And they wear the skins of their victims." His face twisted with revulsion. "They conquered all of China under the leadership of a great general known as Genghis, who became their Khan. Their dominion has spread to lands as far as the gods can reach. Now their emperor is Khubilai, grandson of Genghis. When I was still in Kyoto, there was a great panic when the Imperial Court received a letter from Khubilai Khan, demanding that the emperor submit to his rule and pay a huge tribute, or else face invasion. The court thought it best to suggest a compromise, but the shogunate refused to allow it. They sent the Khan's emissaries away with no reply at all."

"Is China a big country?"

Norikage's voice grew more fevered. "Ah, Ken'ishi, China is larger than you have ever imagined, and the Mongols were able to conquer it with little struggle. They are barbarians of the steppes, practically born on horseback, with bows no one else can pull and armies so vast and potent that no one can stand against them. We are doomed!"

"Tighten up your courage, Norikage." Ken'ishi's voice was cold and grim, thick with unspoken warning. "Or the enemy has already beaten you."

A rustling in the bushes tightened Ken'ishi's awareness and he spun, hand on his sword.

Norikage raised a hand. "Do not worry." He glanced over his shoulder into the bushes. "You can come out."

"Who is with you?" Ken'ishi said.

Wide-eyed and trembling, Kiosé emerged from the bushes, clothes torn and disheveled, her hair in wild strings.

He gasped and reached for her.

But it was not Kiosé.

Hana flinched back. After a moment to compose herself, she bowed to him.

He stared for a long moment, then swallowed the lump in his throat and returned the gesture. The lump in his throat became a hot spear through his heart. Hana moved close to Norikage, as if taking comfort in his presence.

The hot sizzle in Ken'ishi's breast flared, but he tried to suppress it. Kiosé had often done the same with him.

He cleared his throat. "There is something else. Something that has been troubling me."

Confusion flickered in Norikage's eyes at Ken'ishi's tone.

"That letter was addressed to Hojo no Masahige."

Norikage looked away. "Yes."

"You never told the government or his family of his death."

Norikage looked away. "That missive must have been lost somehow."

Rage boiled up in Ken'ishi's breast, threatening to explode into violence. He snorted and turned his back on Norikage, reaching for the stallion's reins. "Even now you lie!"

"Why are you angry about this now? You have been gone all this time. Almost everyone in Aoka village is dead and—"

"Idiot! We are lucky Masahige's spirit does not haunt us!" The rage grew. Or Kiosé's spirit. Some small voice told him his anger at Norikage was misplaced, but the strength of it exploded past any thoughts of its injustice. "He never had a proper funeral! You had me assume the identity of a dead man?"

Norikage's confusion deepened. "He had a funeral! He was cremated and buried in the village cemetery! And a priest from the temple in Hakozaki said prayers over his body."

Ken'ishi turned on Norikage. "What of his swords?"

Hana cowered behind Norikage.

Norikage's voice trembled. "His family is rich! They do not need them! I sold his swords long ago."

"Lies and corruption! You have dishonored me! Three years of a false life! Three years of lies! Three years of ignoring—"

The truth ...

Then something appeared to shift in Norikage as well. "You are *ronin*! In the eyes of the world, you had no honor to lose!"

"A man's honor lies within himself, not in the eyes of the world!"

"Wrong! Honor comes from the power other people grant you, based on who they *think* you are! Who is the fool, Ken'ishi? The deceiver, or the man who allows himself to be deceived?"

"You took advantage of my ignorance!"

"And you took advantage of my position! No legitimate constable would ever have allowed you to be a deputy. A legitimate constable would have had you tortured and executed for killing Nishimuta no Takenaga."

Ken'ishi's jaw clenched. "Get away from me, coward! Liar! Perhaps the barbarians won't catch you." He threw a leg over the saddle.

Norikage shook his head. "Wait, please! Ken'ishi, this quarrel is absurd!"

"You didn't protect her! Someone should have protected her!"

"It all happened too swiftly!"

"They are dead. Everyone is dead. Little Frog was my son, and you did not save him." Kiosé's slack, gray face. Little Frog's poor, pulped head. "If you try to follow me, I will kill you." Ken'ishi's voice was as cold as the ice of Hokkaido. He turned his mount back down the path, spurred the stallion into a run, ducking branches and snarling back tears. But even as he let the stallion have its head, he knew it would never be able to run fast enough.

It is said that, in all things, if you would know a man's good and evil points, you should know the retainers and underlings he loves and employs, and the friends with whom he  mixes intermittently. If the lord is not correct, none of his retainers and friends will be correct. If this is the case, he will be despised by all, and the neighboring provinces will hold him in contempt.

— *Takuan Soho, "The Mysterious Record of Immovable Wisdom"*

As darkness fell in Dazaifu, Yasutoki trudged through the samurai camp, footsore and bone-weary. He counted himself lucky to have gotten away from Hakata ahead of the Mongol advance, but it had been a long walk to Dazaifu after an exhausting night; he was no longer a young man. Tiger Lily limped beside him on blistered feet, shivering in the stiff, autumn wind.

Among the tents surrounding the city, brooding warriors saw to their weapons and injuries. In the light of the campfires, haunted, beaten faces did not acknowledge Yasutoki's passing. Many of them lay with bloody bandages covering arrow wounds. None of them had wounds of any other kind.

Along the road, he had heard tales of samurai trying to join in combat with the enemy, calling out their challenges in the traditional manner, but all of them had died under sleeting arrows. The Mongol ponies were small, but they were swift, and huge units of horsemen could move with the precision and unity of a school of fish.

But then, Yasutoki had long known these things. The samurai defenders would be routed again and again because they were too stubborn to adapt to the ways of war the Mongols employed.

Despite the despair the defenders must be feeling, they bore it with their characteristic samurai stoicism. Their encumbering tenets of honor notwithstanding, Yasutoki respected the prowess of professional warriors. They endured incredible trials and years of training to hone their martial skills to perfection, just as he had. Nevertheless they were the pawns, unwitting or not, of a corrupt and useless government, one that must be swept away by cleansing fire. In time, after the invasion was successful, the samurai lords would regroup and revolt. They might even rethink their battle strategies to better combat the invaders, and then they might drive the Golden Horde back to China. By then, however, the Shogunate would be gone, and with it the Minamoto and Hojo families. Because of the imperial line's divinity, the emperor would likely remain and perhaps even reclaim some of his rightful power. Perhaps he would see to it that the Taira clan, whose blood was woven so tightly into the Imperial line, would be restored to their rightful prominence.

Dazaifu swarmed with activity. Thousands of samurai had converged on the city after numerous defeats the previous day. The streets were still choked with men and horses.

The loss of his house in Hakata had turned his belly to a vat of acid, but at least now he had a conveniently plausible reason for its destruction, and his lamentation at its destruction would be real. Nevertheless, the anger would fade quickly. As with all things, the house was simply a tool, a convenience. He would adapt, as he always did. He would find new tools, new advantages. He had learned long ago to cling to nothing in this world except power and riches, and even those must sometimes be relinquished for future gain.

The weather had grown dismal and gray by evening, with warm, wet winds blowing in from the sea. Samurai and peasant alike had been looking at the sky and grumbling. Yasutoki had seen days like this before. A sky like this one had the potential to settle either into a mild rain or a full-fledged typhoon.

He walked through the campsites to the government offices along the Bamboo Hat River, which flowed through the center of the city. Near the government offices lay the festival grounds, which were now packed with tents and cookfires. It was there he spotted a familiar tent and banner.

The red-striped tent of Otomo no Tsunetomo stood with a light inside and two burly warriors at the entrance, whom he recognized as some of his lord's trusted bodyguards. He had been away from Tsunetomo's service for so long, he took a moment to compose himself into the identity of Yasutoki, the trusty chamberlain.

As he approached the tent, the burly *yojimbo* blocked his entrance.

Yasutoki took off his basket hat. "Out of my way!"

The whites of the guards' eyes glowed with recognition. "Of course, Lord! Welcome!"

They had been slow to recognize him. Did he look so different now?

Stepping inside, he saw Lord Tsunetomo lying upon a mat near the fire, with more armored, taciturn bodyguards on either side. His armor had been removed so that his wound could be tended.

One of the guards followed him inside.

Yasutoki trained his gaze on each of the warriors in turn. "Report."

The guard kept his voice admirably even. An arrow had slipped between Lord Tsunetomo's shoulder guards and breastplate, lodging deep in his shoulder. It had been removed, but the removal had caused more damage than the entry. The healers had given him powerful medicine to put him to sleep. In spite of the blankets covering him, he shivered with fever.

Yasutoki felt an uncustomary twinge of worry. If Tsunetomo died, Yasutoki would lose the legitimacy of his disguise, and a real source of wealth. Part of him respected Tsunetomo's martial prowess. Tsunetomo was honorable, just, brave, and strong, and his retainers adored him. They would follow him to their deaths. But it was those qualities that gave Yasutoki the ability to enact his plans without detection because Tsunetomo assumed that others were just as honorable. Indeed, they had known each other since they were young men, and Yasutoki sometimes enjoyed Tsunetomo's manly company, but he never forgot that the man was merely a tool.

The lord needed his rest. Yasutoki withdrew. At least he felt some measure of comfort at rejoining the company of friendly forces.

Outside, he spotted Captain Yamada on horseback, a man whose services Yasutoki had occasionally employed. Yamada knew Yasutoki was a schemer and sometimes enjoyed the bits of intrigue his lord's retainer tossed his way, but he did not know of Green Tiger or the true depths of Yasutoki's plans.

Yamada bellowed at the crowd as his stallion shouldered through the masses. "Out of the way!" More than once he used his riding quirt against a sluggish peasant.

Yasutoki waved to him.

Finally Yamada reached the tent, dismounted, and knelt before Yasutoki. "Yasutoki-sama. I am happy you have found us. I heard that Hakata had fallen."

"I am hale and hearty, Captain. What news?"

"Tsushima and Iki Islands have fallen. Imazu town is burning. Pockets of Hakata and Hakozaki hold out, but they have been surrounded. The barbarians have broken through our lines. Their patrols are scattered across the countryside, and there is talk of a much larger force gathering to strike Dazaifu."

"How large?"

"Ten thousand, but only one scout claimed to have seen it, and he has died of his wounds."

344

"And our lord's castle?"

"Under Captain Nobuhara's command and the authority of Lady Kazuko."

"Lady Kazuko?"

"Yes, my lord. Lord Tsunetomo left her in command."

Yasutoki rubbed his chin. Much had changed in the short months he had been absent. Perhaps little Kazuko had come to fill the clothes her title granted her. "Thank you very much, Yamada. You may go."

"But, my lord, would you like something to eat and drink? What about your ..." He glanced toward Tiger Lily, then let his eyes linger over her charms.

"My servant shall prepare some food for us."

Yamada bowed again, remounted his horse, and departed.

A breathless messenger ran up moments later. The messenger had the harried, stricken look of a man with the world riding on his shoulders. He knelt at Yasutoki's feet, gasping for breath. "Message for Lord Otomo!"

"I shall receive it," Yasutoki said.

"I beg pardon, my lord, but I was ordered to give it only to Lord Otomo or to Captain Tsunemori."

"Lord Otomo is wounded, resting. I am Otomo no Yasutoki, his chamberlain. Give it to me."

The messenger reluctantly produced a message case and gave it to Yasutoki.

Yasutoki snatched it away. "I shall see that Lord Otomo reads this at the first opportunity."

The messenger bowed again, then dashed off.

Yasutoki opened the seals on the box and held the paper near a lantern. As he read, he could not contain his amazement.

The general in Imazu, Hojo no Yoshimasa, was no fool. Contained in the letter was a detailed description of the Mongol battle tactics, numbers, and some of the terrifying siege weapons they had used against the city. Their use of strange siege weaponry that "roared with thunder and smoke" had confounded the defenders at first, but the defenders had regrouped and held on for now. The general made some astute observations and included comments on how to fight against the Mongols more effectively. "Let our failures be your guide to victory," the message said.

The general's judgments were sound. The Mongols were not simple horsebowmen or mindless barbarians. They were all, every one of them, as tough as the steppes that spawned them, and their generals were formidable strategists, else they would never have conquered China and spread their dominion over lands west.

He considered destroying the message, but then realized that by the time Tsunetomo awoke, it might already be too late.

Tiger Lily sidled up to him. "I am frightened, Master."

He patted her forearm. "We are in the hands of the gods and Buddhas. And never call me 'master' again. In the world above, better to call me 'lord.'"

"Yes, Lord."

"Good girl. Now, let's find some sustenance, shall we?"

"Perhaps I can help, Lord."

"Oh? How?"

"As beaten down as these men are, I saw many of them with food. Please allow me to ... try something."

He could not suppress a smile. "Very well."

"Wait here, Master. I will be back soon with food." She bowed, then dashed away into the night.

Of course, he could hardly let her play unsupervised, and he was curious about what she had in mind. Sticking to the shadows as she made her way into the encampment of warriors, he watched her from afar as she wove through the pools of firelight, her step dainty, her demeanor that of any frightened fourteen-year-old girl.

She sat beside two weary-looking samurai, bowed obsequiously, and spoke, clasping her hands to her chest, eyes glimmering with hunger in the firelight. She was too far away to hear, but he noticed that by the time she was done speaking, her robe had somehow fallen open to expose—almost expose—a soft, nubile breast. Lust glinted in the warriors' eyes, but tempered by some real concern at the suffering of so lovely a creature. Each gave her a rice ball and a piece of smoked fish. She thanked them profusely and departed.

Yasutoki was surprised at how quickly she managed it, and never once did she expose the wanton, lascivious nature that had awakened in her under his tutelage. No, these men were simply giving food to a hungry, beautiful, innocent girl. Fools. He met her on a side street.

Her smile was wicked. "That was easy, Master! Far easier than I thought. And you were watching."

"Well done, my sweet. Your perceptions are keen."

Her eyes glittered like a steel edge in moonlight. "Those fools were so busy trying to glimpse my nipple that I could have shoved a needle in each of their ears before they moved to stop me."

"Indeed." He took the food she offered and ate, studying her. "Indeed." He had taught her well enough that he would have to watch her now, closely.

Even if one's head were
to be suddenly cut off,
he should be able to do
one more thing with
certainty....With martial
valor, if one becomes
like a revengeful ghost

and shows great determination, though his head is cut
off, he should not die.

— *Hagakure*

Ken'ishi and the stallion traced their way around Hakozaki,
eluding four enemy patrols and circumventing two sentry
posts. Apparently, the entire town now lay in the hands
of the enemy. The precipitous danger of their travel allowed his
quarrel with Norikage to settle into the back of his mind, where it
merely simmered. Finally, they reached the road to Dazaifu, their
ears always alert for the sounds of hoofbeats.

An hour after nightfall, the glow of a fire ahead gave him pause.
This close to enemy lines, only they would be so bold to build a
fire here. He dismounted and left the stallion hidden behind some
undergrowth near the road, where he readied his bow and stole
towards the light. He nocked an arrow as he crept, hugging the
bushes to mask his advance. The wind, so steady and moist since

the night before, bespoke a coming rain, but its noise would cover his footsteps. He heard the barbarians' guttural voices and their strange tongue before he could see them. A mounted sentry stood in the road beyond where they had made their camp.

Through the trees and bushes, three tents glowed with flickering firelight. The black silhouettes of ponies were tied nearby.

Ken'ishi slid nearer, using the dancing shadows to conceal his approach, until he could see the Mongols' heads as they sat around the fire. Five of them. Hairy, beastly looking men they were, drinking from gourd bottles, gnawing leathery strips of meat. Dark, ruby-red wetness glistened on their lips as they drank.

One of the Mongols took the last drink from his bottle, then got up and approached the horses. The Mongol's gait was bow-legged and ungainly, as if he was unaccustomed to walking with his own legs. He led one of the ponies closer to the firelight, then drew a small knife and handed the pony's reins to one of his comrades. The second held the pony's head still as the first made a quick, deft slice across the side of the pony's throat. The pony flinched once, then stood still, trembling. Blood poured from the wound, and the Mongol raised his bottle to the catch the blood. When the bottle was full, he stoppered it and put it down, then pinched the wound shut with his fingers, pulled out a needle and thread, and carefully stitched up the cut.

These ... creatures actually drank blood! They were not men at all! They were *oni*! Ken'ishi's belly heaved at the thought of drinking blood. Which would be worse, warm and fresh, or cold and half-congealed?

Ken'ishi reached for the emptiness, driving down the revulsion churning in his guts. His consciousness settled into the Void. Heartbeats became their own eternities. He drew his bow and brought the sentry into his aim. His arrow toppled the sentry from the saddle like a sack of meat. The others leaped to their feet like wolves. Ken'ishi let fly another arrow, which pierced a Mongol's upper arm, pinning it to his side. The Mongol fell onto his side with a harsh grunt, out of sight behind the bushes. The remaining three scanned the darkness, snarling. One of them pointed at Ken'ishi, barking a warning. Ken'ishi dropped his bow, and Silver Crane leaped into his hands. He loosed a sharp *kiai* from the depths of his belly and charged.

The first Mongol managed to cross blades, but Silver Crane hummed with power. The force of the blow shattered steel, cleft the Mongol's helmet, then his face from pate to chin.

Another lunged at Ken'ishi, but he sidestepped the blow, pivoted behind the Mongol's movement and slashed across the base of the man's neck, neatly severing his enemy's spine.

The last one bawled like an enraged bear and threw himself at Ken'ishi, locking his arms around the *ronin's* body and pinning his arms to his sides. Beneath the Mongol's coarse, smelly clothing, his arms were solid as trees, and his grip, iron. The Mongol threw him hard onto the ground, forcing Silver Crane from his grip. One hand released him, and Ken'ishi heard the slither of a drawn weapon. Just in time, he caught the Mongol's wrist as it swept around with a wicked, broad-bladed knife. He redirected the stab into the earth, a finger's breadth from his side, then cracked the Mongol across the cheek with his elbow. Once, twice, three times, but the hideous, blunt features of his enemy only spread a bloody, gap-toothed grin. The Mongol raised the knife for another stab.

Ken'ishi grabbed the knife wrist again, and then struggled to throw off the knotty weight, managing to writhe free. He rolled to his feet, facing his leering, demonic enemy. Silver Crane lay a few paces away. The Mongol grinned and kicked the sword further away.

Then the Mongol with his arm nailed to his torso groaned and clutched feebly at Ken'ishi's foot. Ken'ishi snatched the Mongol's short sword from his belt, hacked open his throat, and faced the last enemy with the unfamiliar blade.

The Mongol circled cautiously, feinting, taunting, but Ken'ishi did not move, did not even look at him.

Ken'ishi merely waited.

The Mongol charged.

Ken'ishi allowed the incoming blade to slide past and slashed as the Mongol stumbled off-balance. The Mongol's enraged gurgle told Ken'ishi that his slash had struck home. The Mongol fell into the dirt, blood spurting, clawing at the earth.

Ken'ishi retrieved Silver Crane and took the wounded man's head.

Norikage had been right. They were demons. They drank blood. They were as tough as hardwood wrapped in leather and iron, but they could be killed.

He could reach Dazaifu in an hour or two. But before he left the campsite, he slashed the throats of the Mongols' demonic steeds. The shaggy ponies could be little else than monsters themselves if they allowed these barbarians to feed upon their blood. The horses squealed and shied and struggled against their tethers, but they could not escape his blade.

Speed is not the true way. Speed is the fastness or slowness that occurs when the rhythm is out of syn-chronization. ... What a master does seems to be done with ease and without any loss of tim-ing. Anything which is performed by someone who has experience does not look busy.

— *Miyamoto Musashi, The Book of Five Rings*

A few hours in the saddle with no prior experience turned Ken'ishi's backside and thighs into a mass of chafed bruises. The steady moan of the night wind chilled him, and he was grateful for the sweaty warmth of the stallion beneath him. A veil of swift-moving clouds obscured the moon, casting darkness so dense that Ken'ishi had to trust the stallion's eyes to see the road. The horse maintained a steady trot, and his breath puffed out of him like the steam of a rice pot. As he felt the noble power of the stallion under him, he could not fail to compare it to the short, shaggy ponies the invaders were riding, nor could he free his mind from the images of the barbarians drinking their blood.

They must be nearing Dazaifu by now, having passed through two deserted villages, but the night was so dark he could discern few details.

Suddenly, he heard the distinctive *twang* and hiss of an arrow, the wet thud as it embedded in the road at his steed's feet. The stallion reared and neighed a warning.

A bark sounded from the darkness ahead. "Halt! Announce yourself or die!"

Ken'ishi squeezed the reins and called out as he had heard other samurai announce themselves. "I am Ken'ishi. My father was a great swordsman of northern Honshu. Tonight I single-handedly slew five of the barbarian invaders. Their bodies lie dead and cold on the road from Hakozaki. I heard news that a defense force is gathering at Dazaifu, and I have come to lend my blade. Now, I have announced myself. You do the same!"

There was a moment of pause, then the man in the darkness answered. "I am Ota no Nobusada. My family has served the Shogun since the days of Yoritomo. My great-grandfather was with the first Shogun, Yoritomo, when he crushed the Taira. You are welcome here, samurai."

Pride bloomed in Ken'ishi's chest.

A dark shape emerged from the deeper shadows. The sentry bowed, and Ken'ishi returned the gesture. "I am at your service, Master Ota. May I speak to your commander about joining the defense?"

"Of course, I will take you to him. Sergeant Masamori, stay at your post. I'll be back soon."

The grunt of acknowledgment came out of the darkness from another location on the opposite side of the road.

The sentry led him down the road at a brisk trot. After a few hundred paces, they emerged from the forest above the city of Dazaifu. Unlike the dark, desolate villages Ken'ishi had passed through, Dazaifu was alive with activity. Lanterns, torches, and campfires danced in the darkness. All available open spaces were crammed with tents or warriors sleeping on the ground beside flickering campfires. A dark chill raced through him. The faces of these warriors were the faces of weary, beaten men. He smelled the blood, saw the dark stains on their bandages and the haunted looks in their eyes.

Nobusada led Ken'ishi to a teahouse that had been commandeered as a command post. Ken'ishi took stock of his guide. Slightly older than Ken'ishi, Ota no Nobusada was dressed in a fine suit of heavy armor, well made and practically sparkling in its pristine condition. From the man's uneasy demeanor, Ken'ishi wondered if he had ever seen war or battle firsthand.

Nobusada went to the door and announced. "My lords, another samurai has come to join the defense."

A voice came from within. "He may enter."

Nobusada stepped aside.

Ken'ishi bowed to him and went inside. Seated around a large table were three armored warriors. Their helmets rested on armor trees behind them, dusty and scuffed. All three looked as if they had not slept for days.

The man in the center appraised Ken'ishi. He was middle-aged, handsome, with sharp, wide-set eyes that mirrored a well-honed intelligence. He wore elaborately decorated armor, but scuffs and scratches bespoke a seasoned martial history.

Ken'ishi placed his sword on his right side as he knelt before them and pressed his forehead to the floor.

The man in the center spoke. "I am Otomo no Tsunemori, officer in charge of emergency recruitment. You wish to join the defense forces?"

"Honored commanders, my name is Ken'ishi. Until recently, I came from Aoka village. Earlier today the village was destroyed by the barbarian invaders."

Tsunemori said, "Aoka village is north of Hakozaki."

"Yes, Lord."

"The enemy holds that area. Do you mean to say that you came through the enemy lines?"

"Yes, Lord."

The three officers glanced at one another. One of them said, "You were not captured." The words stopped just short of being an accusation.

"No, great lords. I killed five of them on the road here, a scouting party."

Their eyes widened.

Tsunemori said, "Five, you say! We could not get close enough to fight them like honorable men. They just shot their arrows at us and ran away on their ugly little ponies. Clouds, storms of arrows. I have never seen so many. Our men were shot to pieces before they could even issue challenges. How did you manage it?"

"I came upon their sentry post and surprised them. They are demons. They are tough, but they can be killed. I saw them ... drinking the blood of their steeds."

The officers' faces twisted in disgust.

One of them said, "You did not bring us any heads."

Ken'ishi shook his head sternly. "They were too ugly. And carrying the heads of five demons this far might have tainted me beyond all hope of purification. But I do have this." He reached into his pack and withdrew one of the Mongol swords, with its broad, curved blade and simple wooden hilt. He offered it to them with both hands, head bowed.

The sour one took it, examined it with a warrior's eye for steel. "Crude craftsmanship. Our swords are infinitely superior." He passed it to Tsunemori.

Ken'ishi said, "That is true, my lord. My blade shattered one of their weapons in the fight."

Tsunemori nodded thoughtfully. "But we must find a way to fight them. Right now, they outnumber us. Their ponies are quick and agile, and their bows have a longer range than ours. They never walk on their own two legs." He took one of the scrolls and turned it around to face Ken'ishi, pushing forward a brush and inkwell. "Ken'ishi, sign your name to the roster. Fight well tomorrow."

Ken'ishi felt a flush of pride and vengeance on his face. He had much blood to repay. With determined movements, he took the brush and signed his name.

Tsunemori said, "Have you any armor?"

"A light breastplate, my lord."

"That will have to do for now. Report to Kono no Kiyonaga. He is the captain of one of our scout units. You can find him in the white tent at the end of the street. At dawn, we march."

"We will be ahead of the main force." Captain Kono's gaze swept over the group of twenty kneeling men. Most wore armor of varying types; some wore helmets, some did not. All around them, the encamped troops were coming to life with the growing dawn. "We will observe the enemy and report back to the main force. All of you know your duty. You, Ken'ishi."

Ken'ishi bowed. "Yes, Kono-sama."

"Have you no armor?"

"I have a light *do-maru*." He tapped his chest with a knuckle. "It might turn aside an arrow or two."

One of the other samurai standing in the group laughed brusquely. "Then you will have the honor of being the first among us to die!"

Several of the other samurai laughed.

Ken'ishi failed to see the humor, but he did not take offense. If he died, who was there to pray for him? He had no one, no family, no clan, and no lord. With no family or priest to pray for his soul, his spirit might be trapped in this world as a ghost. The only one in the world he could call friend was not even a human being; Hage was unlikely to pray for anything, ever. "If it is my destiny to be the first to die with honor, then so be it, but I would not seek to hold anyone else from claiming that honor themselves."

This brought another gust of gruff laughter, and he allowed himself a small smile.

Kono said, "Ken'ishi, you have a horse?"

"I have a horse."

"Where does a *ronin* find a horse?" said a man.

Ken'ishi fixed his narrowed eyes firmly on the man who had spoken. "The same place you did. The gods granted one."

More laughter. The man held his gaze for only a moment before looking away.

Captain Kono said, "Save your blood for the enemy. May the Buddha grant us victory." He stood, and the other men followed suit. Servants led their horses forward.

One of the samurai approached Ken'ishi and said, "I am Otomo no Ishitaka." He clapped Ken'ishi on the shoulder. "I like your spirit, Ken'ishi! You will fight well today." He had a broad, round face, a flat nose, and eyes that sparkled with vigor and intensity. Only up close did Ken'ishi realize how young Ishitaka was, perhaps no more than sixteen.

Ken'ishi bowed. "I'm sure you will take many heads today."

The young warrior smiled wanly and stood straighter.

A servant brought Ken'ishi's stallion forward.

"A fine animal!" Ishitaka said.

"He is indeed," Ken'ishi said. "He saved my life yesterday." Then he said to the horse, "Vengeance today. Battle."

The stallion snorted. "Are you ready to die, Warrior?"

"I am ready. But perhaps death will not come today."

"Perhaps you will live to gather your own herd, and sire many more strong sons."

Destiny.

Ken'ishi suppressed a flinch at the power of Silver Crane's resounding thought.

Ishitaka said, "What are you saying? It almost sounded as if you were speaking to the horse."

"I was. He is a strong, fierce steed."

Ishitaka gave him a puzzled expression. "You are an interesting man, Ken'ishi."

Ken'ishi tied his bow and quiver to his saddle and made sure that his scabbard was tied securely to his sash. Some of the other warriors had swords that were considerably longer and stouter than his, some so long that the point of their scabbards almost dragged the ground. Most carried bows, some lances, but all wore faces of grim determination.

Captain Kono spun on his mount and called out to his warriors. "Ride!"

I have only one
   possession —
My life, so light,
Like this gourd.
        — *Basho*

The road flew past under pounding hooves. The new day was cold and dreary and gray, with darkening clouds. The air was moist and heavy, a cold, wet washcloth across Ken'ishi's face.

After half an hour of hard riding, his already weary legs felt like limp seaweed.

They paused where Ken'ishi had slain the five Mongols. It lay just as he had left it, but the road was dappled with fresh hoof prints. At the next crossroads, the dirt was so freshly pounded by the passage of riders that discerning which direction they were going was impossible.

Captain Kono said, "We must watch our backs now as well."

The day had warmed like a balmy, late summer afternoon, but it made the air seem thick, like a damp, smothering blanket. The tops of the trees waved and rippled in the warm wind. Dark clouds roiled above.

One of the men said, "Perhaps the gods will favor us with a rain to ruin their bowstrings!"

Another said, "Yes, and ours as well."

Ishitaka pointed. "There!"

Down a branching side road, several Mongols stood, staring at the samurai. With lightning speed, the invaders spun their stunted ponies and galloped away.

"After them!" Captain Kono shouted.

Without hesitation, the samurai spurred down the road after the barbarians. Kono and the other leading warriors readied their bows for shots at the fleeing Mongols. The longer-legged Japanese horses gained on the ponies. Kono and some of the others attempted bowshots, but shooting directly over their mounts' heads was difficult on a winding road with branches that dipped low enough to sweep a man from the saddle. None of their shots found a mark.

One of the Mongols raised a long horn and blew it as they fled.

Ken'ishi and his comrades pounded down the forest road. Perhaps a *ri* down the road, the forest receded, and the pursuers barreled into a patchwork of harvested rice fields filled with low-cropped, golden-green stubble.

The far end of the valley swarmed with horsemen.

On either side of the road, large groups of enemy riders closed on them like the pincers of a crab.

Ken'ishi shouted a warning, but Kono had already seen their peril. Kono hauled on his reins and spun his horse back the way they came from. The rest of their band followed him. If they could clear the tips of the pincers, they might escape.

Ken'ishi glanced over his shoulder and saw perhaps a hundred riders peel off from the larger swarm and charge in pursuit. They drew their bows and loosed. A cloud of arrows hissed into the air, and Ken'ishi could only watch as they arced high, hung against the gray sky for long moments, then fell toward him. The air around him hissed and buzzed with the falling arrows. Horses screamed and stumbled as the arrows sank into their haunches or shoulders. A samurai ahead of Ken'ishi fell out of the saddle and under the hooves of Ken'ishi's stallion. His horse stumbled, but kept his feet. Another horse and rider went down together into a flailing heap. Ken'ishi kicked the stallion's flanks. Its eyes bulged, and its breath huffed as it summoned a fresh burst of speed. Two of the other men ahead had arrows protruding from their armor, but stayed in the saddle.

The pincer-tips reached thirty paces between them when Ken'ishi and the others galloped past, back into the forest. Just as they did, the snap and pop of another flight of arrows tore through the branches above. A few shafts trickled ineffectually through the canopy.

The enemy horsemen gathered in pursuit.

Captain Kono rolled out of the saddle, falling heavily to the dirt, snapping the arrow embedded between his neck and shoulder, eyes wide and staring and dead.

Ken'ishi galloped down the narrow, winding road, hemmed on both sides with trees and undergrowth. A flash of silvery web brushed over his face, through his thoughts. The enemy would not be expecting a handful of scouts to turn and fight, and the road was too confined for flights of arrows. He hauled on the reins, bringing his steed to a skidding halt.

"Enough running!" he shouted. "Fight!" He whipped Silver Crane out of its scabbard and turned to face the oncoming pursuit.

His comrades heard him. They reined up.

Otomo no Ishitaka drew his sword and unleashed a high-pitched war cry, spurring his mount back toward Ken'ishi. The others, not to be outdone, did the same. The rumble of the pursuit rose. Ken'ishi and Otomo no Ishitaka stood side-by-side, blades in hand. Wielding his sword one-handed would be difficult enough, but he had never fought from horseback before.

The Mongols thundered into sight.

"Vengeance," he said to the stallion.

"Vengeance!" the stallion snorted back.

Ken'ishi charged, building a long *kiai* from the depths of his belly. A grim smile stretched his lips when he saw the surprise on the faces of the lead Mongol riders. The first rider's sword was only half out of its sheath before Ken'ishi was upon him, slashing as he rode past, severing the man's arm.

Ishitaka piled into the second Mongol rider, his larger horse pummeling the pony into the dirt.

Oncoming Mongols plowed into the fallen. Horses and men screamed.

Another horse crashed into Ken'ishi's stallion. The stallion screamed with rage, bowled sideways, and the collision flung Ken'ishi into the underbrush. The undergrowth snagged his clothing, preventing him from extricating himself. He struggled and hacked until he had freed himself, then charged back into the melee. The closest enemy's armored leather coat blunted most of the force of his first blow, but Silver Crane came away stained with more blood. The wounded Mongol slashed, but he ducked away. A writhing, flailing chaos of horses and men screamed and thrashed on the road. He deflected the next blow, turning the parry into a lightning cut that sliced the pony's throat wide. The animal gurgled a scream as it collapsed. The wounded rider fell with it, and Ken'ishi easily dispatched him.

Ishitaka extricated himself from the mass of fallen horses and men, stood weaving, blood pouring down his face. He pointed at the nearest unengaged Mongol and roared, "I am Otomo no Ishitaka! I challenge you!"

The Mongol sneered and brandished his sword as if to accept the challenge, but the savaged mass of groaning men and fallen horses kept the two of them apart. One of the tangled horses thrashed free, righted itself, and limped toward the samurai. Its front leg, splintered and bleeding, flopped horribly as it moved.

Ishitaka charged, his blade raised to attack the Mongol who had accepted his challenge. The Mongol, astride a well-trained horse, had the advantage of height, but Ishitaka had the advantage of mobility. Ishitaka leaped in close and struck the pony squarely in the forehead. The pony dropped like a stone, spilling its rider. Ishitaka's katana lodged in the pony's skull, however, pulling him into range of its hooves' death spasms. A rear hoof slammed into his belly, doubling him over. An adjacent Mongol hacked downward, and his blade clanged onto the crown of Ishitaka's helmet. Ishitaka crumpled.

Ken'ishi leaped to his defense, severing the Mongol's sword arm near the elbow. The man screamed, and a gush of hot blood blinded Ken'ishi. A horse plowed into him, and the war cry of a samurai told him that one of his comrades had filled the gap. He wiped at his eyes and blinked the stinging blood away, hot copper on his lips, in his nostrils.

More samurai horsemen surged forward, pushing the Mongol line back, leaving Ken'ishi among the dead and wounded. He could not see the stallion anywhere.

The melee shifted forward and back, both sides bellowing war cries, grunting with exertion, blades clanging and ringing, bodies tumbling to be trampled into the blood-soaked earth. Ten of the original twenty-one samurai remained, fighting shoulder to shoulder, larger horses straining against the Mongol ponies.

The Mongols in the rear let fly a few bowshots past their comrades. One of the samurai rolled backward and landed on his back with an arrow embedded in his eye socket.

Ken'ishi cast about for some way to aid his comrades. He snatched up a bow and quiver from a fallen samurai, then shoved into the thick bushes beside the road. Circling the line of engagement to about twenty paces from the melee's flank, slightly elevated by the rocks of the hillside, he found himself with clear shooting.

He drew and fired. His first arrow dropped an enemy from the saddle, and so did the second. He killed or wounded three more before the rearward ranks saw him. They returned fire. Ken'ishi ducked behind a tree, arrows hissing around him and skittering between the branches and trees. The samurai pushed the Mongols further back, until Ken'ishi was forced to shift his location to regain a clear field of fire. More arrows blasted into the trees.

The samurai gave one more powerful surge against the weakened line of Mongols, and the enemy broke and fled. The elated samurai charged after them, roaring like tigers. They chased their prey for about fifty paces, until they appeared to remember how quickly the hunters could become the hunted, and let their quarry go.

Ken'ishi returned to the road, and seven remaining samurai joined him.

One said, "Well done, Ken'ishi! It was your archery that turned the tide in our favor."

Several of the others grunted in assent and looked at him with respect. His chest swelled.

"What now?" the samurai asked Ken'ishi.

Ken'ishi's mind raced. They were looking to him for leadership! After a few heartbeats of internal frenzy, he pointed to two of them and said, "You two, ride back to Dazaifu and report."

"We obey!" They spurred their weary, blood-spattered steeds away.

Ken'ishi said, "The rest of us will return to the crossroads where we first saw the enemy. There we will set up an ambush. If they wish to follow us, we will make them pay."

"Master Ken'ishi, where is your horse?"

Ken'ishi said, "I lost him in the melee." He cupped his hands and called, "Halloo, Sir Stallion!"

Something stirred in the tangled mess of the dead. With a great heave, the horse rolled onto his side, snorted, and struggled to his feet. He approached Ken'ishi on wobbly legs, blood pouring down his face from a severed ear. "I am ... here, Warrior."

"You are hurt," Ken'ishi said. "You cannot fight."

"It is but a flesh wound," the stallion said. "I still have one good ear." He blinked and shook the blood from his eyes. His legs steadied with each step.

Two of the samurai whispered to each other. "He talks to horses!"

"Let's check for wounded," Ken'ishi said to the warriors. "You two, go about fifty paces up the road and watch for the enemy."

The two samurai obeyed.

The others slid off their horses to examine the bodies. There were Mongols still alive among the fallen bodies, but not for long.

Ken'ishi examined the stallion's ear. Blood poured down the

stallion's face, but the cut had been clean. The ear was simply gone. "Perhaps I shall name you 'One-Ear.'"

The stallion snorted, "That sounds like a mongrel dog's name. Besides, I already have a name. My former master called me Thunder."

Ken'ishi examined the horse for other injuries but saw nothing. "A fine name. Rest here."

Ken'ishi approached Ishitaka's body. The Mongol's sword stroke had opened a finger-long cleft in the crown of Ishitaka's *kabuto*. Ken'ishi turned him over. His face was a mask of blood, but he still breathed. "He lives." Ken'ishi scooped up Ishitaka's limp form and dragged him free of the tangle.

The other warriors finished their examination of the bodies. "The barbarians are all dead."

A groan came from the pile of dead.

A Shimazu clan warrior, the man who had fallen with an arrow in his eye, groaned again and stirred. His face was a mask of blood, but his lips were moving, fighting to breathe.

They ran to help him.

The wound was hideous. The eye was nothing more than wet, bloody wreckage around a cruel wooden shaft. The arrow point had glanced off the brim of the helmet, leaving a deep dent. Perhaps that was why it had not penetrated deeply enough to kill him outright.

Ken'ishi said, "We have to take the arrow out."

The others stared. "He is as good as dead."

"Not yet," Ken'ishi said.

"We have to get out of here!" another said.

Ken'ishi looked at him. "If this was you, what would you have us do?"

The man stiffened. "Leave me to die. A one-eyed warrior is useless."

Ken'ishi should have expected that response, but it was true. Nevertheless, the thought of leaving this man behind to die slowly, in agony, filled him with disgust. With the arrow removed, he might live.

Ken'ishi fixed the man who had spoken with a hard stare. "Do you have any bandages?"

The man shook his head.

Ken'ishi tore a long strip from his own robe, then knelt down beside the wounded man, untied the chin strap of the man's helmet and eased if off his head. "What is his name?" he asked of the men standing around him.

"Shimazu no Hironori," said the man.

Ken'ishi said to the wounded man, "Master Shimazu. Shimazu, can you hear me?"

The wounded man whispered. "Yes. Am I dead?"

"No, but you have an arrow in your eye. Do you understand?"

"Then I will die."

"I think we can take it out. Do you want to live?"

"Yes ..."

Ken'ishi realized that the wounded man was hardly a man at all. No older than sixteen summers, maybe even fifteen. "Very well, I will try to remove the arrow." Then, to the men standing around him, "Someone hold his head."

The man who had spoken knelt down and held the boy's head with both hands. The boy screamed the moment Ken'ishi's fingers touched the arrow shaft. Ken'ishi took a deep breath, grasped the arrow and pulled. The boy screamed more, and the man holding his head gripped it tighter. But the arrow did not come out.

Ken'ishi's guts tightened. He pulled still harder, and the boy screamed louder. The wooden shaft creaked with the force of his pull, but the arrow held fast. The barbed point was firmly lodged in the boy's skull. If he broke the arrow shaft, he would never get the arrow out.

"Hold his head tighter," Ken'ishi said. "Someone hold his arms."

Two more men came forward and knelt to grasp the boy's arms. Ken'ishi marveled that the boy was still conscious. He looked at the three men holding the boy down, and they looked back up at him, signaling their readiness.

Ken'ishi braced his foot against the boy's cheek, grasped the arrow with both hands, and pulled. The boy screamed. The arrow came out with a wet squelch and a sound like it was pulled from the trunk of a stout oak tree. Ken'ishi sighed with relief and tossed the arrow away. The boy's roar of agony turned to rage. The men released him, and he lurched to his feet.

"Bastard!" he shouted. Blood still gushing from his ruined eye, he drew his short sword, his good eye aflame with rage. "I would rather have died than suffer the disgrace of having your foot in my face!"

Ken'ishi could only stare. The boy stepped forward on wobbly legs, raising his sword to slash. Ken'ishi jumped back, and two men moved forward to restrain the boy.

Then he collapsed again, sagging against the men holding him until they eased him back to the ground.

Ken'ishi shook his head in puzzlement and wrapped the bandage around Shimazu no Hironori's terrible wound. "Can you carry him?"

The first man nodded.

"Then take him. My horse is too weak to carry two. You, go and bring back our sentries. We've lingered here long enough. Back to the crossroads."

The mightiest gods
Loom naked in a black
  wind
Laughing at demons
            — *Soseki*

From Ken'ishi's vantage point in the rocks above the open crossroads, the road lay visible in every direction. Around him, the others lay hidden at other favorable locations. They picketed their horses deep within the forest.

A few of the men had been displeased by the idea of waiting in ambush; it was not honorable, they said. They should fight in the traditional way, by issuing challenges and fighting man to man.

Ken'ishi had answered them, "Is the enemy honorable? No. They are demons who drink horse blood! They have no honor, so they fight with none. We must fight as they fight, or they will simply shoot us from afar. Dying needlessly, uselessly, is not the way."

His words were apparently sufficient to assuage their discomfort.

The enemy did not come. An hour passed with no sign of them.

A tremendous weariness emptied all the strength from his limbs. The battles with the White Lotus, with Fang Shi, with Masoku, seemed so long ago, almost as if they had been in another life, as if his life had resumed the moment he had recovered Silver Crane. He fought against sleep, but his exhaustion would not be denied. His vision became hazy and indistinct, as if he were in a lotus dream. The branches around him took on a strange, silvery cast, as if coated in iridescent dust.

A strange bird sat on a branch above. It was larger than a hawk, with fine, silvery gray feathers, a bright crimson beak, and beady black eyes that seemed to glisten with mischievous intelligence and scrutiny.

Ken'ishi felt a tingle of recognition that he could not name. "Good day, Mr. Bird."

The bird's eyes closed in silent laughter. "Good day, Monkey-boy."

Ken'ishi's voice caught.

"Come now, nothing to say?" The bird preened its wing feathers.

Finally Ken'ishi managed to speak. "Sensei!"

"So you finally recognize me! How perceptive."

Ken'ishi bowed deeply. "I am sorry, Sensei. You do not look like yourself."

"I never did. How do you think I should look?"

"Well, as I remember you."

The bird laughed silently again. "Sometimes you are such a fool."

"I am happy to see you again, Sensei. It has been a long time."

"Hardly an eye blink to me, but not so long as you might think. And it seems that a new band of monkeys wants your territory."

"You speak of the barbarians?"

"Yes, but you are all barbarians, aren't you?"

"We are not like them! They are vile, evil creatures. Demons!"

"Demons lurk in every one of your race, Monkey-boy. They only require the necessary circumstances to be given reign. Do not be so quick to think your people are any better than these 'barbarians.' You have not seen the capacity for brutality your people conceal in their darkest corners. You slice off heads and disembowel yourselves and cut each other up into tiny pieces with your beautiful swords. Swords, I might add, that you stole from my people in the beginning."

"But I have seen it, Sensei." The memory of a thousand agonies shot through every fiber of him.

The bird studied him for a long moment. "Perhaps you have at that."

"These barbarians have no honor!"

"Ah, but they do. They hold many things as dear as your people. Those things are merely different from yours."

Ken'ishi felt the anger starting a slow burn in his belly. "Creatures who drink blood and slay little children have no honor! They cannot!"

"I have traveled the steppes of Mongolia, Monkey-boy. I saw how these men live, long before the man born as Temujin ever dreamed of uniting them, changing his name to Genghis and conquering an empire. They drink blood for food, Monkey-boy, because their homeland is a far harsher place than this one. They quench their thirst with mare's milk because there is little water. Endless tracks of dry earth and open sky, with nothing between them and starvation. The land is a harsh teacher."

"You sound as if you admire them! They killed—" A sudden vision of Little Frog strangled off the rest of his words.

"Of course, I admire them! And so should you! If you turn them into mindless monsters in your mind, you make them less than yourself! Down that path lies failure because, if they are less than you, there will come a time when you underestimate them. And that will be your death. You must respect your enemy *while* seeking his weaknesses."

"They have no weaknesses."

"It certainly appears so on the surface. Each of them is as tough as an oak tree. But what will fell an oak tree?"

"Chopping it down."

"No, you fool!"

Ken'ishi suddenly had the feeling that a pebble was hissing toward his head, and he ducked instinctively.

The bird's eyes closed again, and his feathers shook with mirth. "It is good to see you still have some awareness. You remember my lessons." The bird sighed. "So when is it easiest to fell an oak tree?"

"When it is rotten."

"Why does it rot?"

"Because it is dead."

The bird shook its head in disgust. "Roots, Monkey-boy! Roots! The tree draws its power and life from the roots. Starve the roots, and the tree will die!"

"But, Sensei, I am sorry. I did not know that."

The bird blinked, then launched into a fresh tirade. "Then you must have been sleeping during that lesson! Nevertheless, it is true. The Mongol army is like a tree, incredibly tough and resilient, with leaves uncountable, but if it is attacked below ground, at the roots, the tree will starve and die and rot."

Ken'ishi pondered this.

"Since you are so thick-skulled, I will explain it to you. The roots of the Mongol army stretch all the way back to China. They are like a tree growing on a rock escarpment. Their roots are exposed. Ah, I see that you finally understand! That is good!"

"Sensei, is this why you have come? To tell me how to defeat the enemy?"

"I don't care who wins. I just became sidetracked by your chattering. Nevertheless, I would dislike seeing you die so soon."

"Then why have you sought me out now, after all this time, with the enemy bearing down upon us?"

"Because I only just discovered the things I have to tell you. And they could not wait."

"What is it? What have you come to tell me?"

"I have seen your future. There is a day coming when you will learn the history of your family. You will learn who your father was—"

Ken'ishi leaned forward in excitement. "Tell me!"

"—But that day is not today. And what's more, that knowledge will cause you pain that you cannot imagine."

Ken'ishi looked away, trying to control his anger and growing frustration. But he could not rise up against his former master. "Why have you told me this? To taunt me?"

"To warn you! But, my efforts will probably be fruitless." The bird sighed. "Like all your kind, you will probably ignore my warning and charge forward like a bull into your destiny. Monkey-boy, you have triumphs and pain ahead of you like you cannot imagine now. I have looked in on you from time to time. You have done well, Little Acorn."

"Little Acorn. You have never called me that before."

"Haven't I?" The bird winked. As the Raggedy Man had winked.

The thought of Kiosé lying down with Kaa stoked Ken'ishi's heart to anger. "Were you looking in on me when I was starving? Were you protecting me when I was imprisoned? No!"

"Petulance! You have grown too big for your trousers. Perhaps I owe you a lesson in swordsmanship. But not today. Of course, I saw you when you were starving! There was a day when you were trudging through the rain, and you came upon a woman taking shelter in a shrine."

"I remember. She gave me a rice ball."

"She was there because I guided her there."

"What happened to her?" Ken'ishi asked. That was long ago, but he still thought about her sometimes.

"She was strangled to death six months after that by a jealous man."

Fresh grief squeezed his stomach. "She was so kind ..."

"That is the cruelty your race inflicts upon itself, no matter what land you come from. Someday you will all be dead, and we *tengu* will still be around to reclaim our places in the world, but alas that is many, many lifetimes away. In any case, mostly I have left you alone to find your own way, even when you lost your precious toy, even when you were Green Tiger's prisoner. Too much help from me, and you would not be as strong as you are today."

"You knew I was there and did nothing to help me!"

"For a time, even I could not find you. You were lost in the underworld. There are things driving your destiny that are beyond me, deft little touches shaping the events all around us."

"What do you mean?"

"I mean that there are forces beyond you that are shaping your destiny. And not just yours. But never mind about that. I have told you what I came here to tell you. Your trials this day are not yet over. And you would do well to forget that woman. Your tangled-up mind is the cause for forgetting most of what I taught you in the first place!" Kaa shifted on his perch, unfurled his wings, and leaped off his branch.

Ken'ishi could only watch him wing off through the canopy.

Moments later the sound of marching caught his attention. The others heard it, too, and prepared their bows.

He breathed a sigh of relief when a line of shadows emerged from the forest road, marching from the south. Horsemen. Behind them marched a column of spearmen and naginata samurai. As the column of troops neared, he recognized one of the lead horsemen.

Ken'ishi jumped down from his hiding place into the road. "Otomo-sama!" he called.

Startled, the horsemen reined up and stopped the column. The order to halt echoed and repeated back.

Otomo no Tsunemori rode up before Ken'ishi. "Master Ken'ishi."

Ken'ishi bowed deeply. "Did the messengers arrive safely?"

"They did," Tsunemori said. "Have you seen the enemy since then?"

"No, Lord." Ken'ishi pointed down the fork to the west, then reported the day's events in full. When he finished, he said, "Otomo-sama, we have two wounded men."

"They'll be taken care of. Ken'ishi, take your scouts in the direction you last saw the enemy. Find and observe the larger force, and report back. We will be following you."

Ken'ishi bowed again. "Yes, Otomo-sama." He couldn't help swelling with pride at finding himself in command.

From dark windy hills
Voices driving weary
   horses ...
Shouting of the storm
       — *Kyokusui*

Tsunemori ordered Ken'ishi's band of scouts reinforced to a total of twenty, and then he led them back toward Hakozaki.

As the scouts neared the bayside town, the forested roads and valleys spread out into rice fields and rocky meadows, and the incessant wind tore at the ribbons of smoke rising from it. The sky looked as if it were about to clear. Perhaps there would be no storm after all.

Countless hooves had pounded the roads and once-golden stubble of the rice fields into oblivion. But where had the enemy gone?

Ken'ishi scanned the tree lines and hilltops but saw no sign of the invaders. Hakozaki lay ahead, perhaps one *ri* distant.

An arrow took the man beside him out of the saddle.

Like a coming rainstorm, the arrows fell faster and faster. Ken'ishi whipped out Silver Crane and slashed an inbound arrow from the air.

Then he saw them, as if an entire tree line three hundred paces long had come to life. Hundreds of hairy, armored horsebowmen emerged from the trees and loosed another swarm of arrows as they advanced.

For less than a heartbeat, Ken'ishi watched the arc of the incoming swarm. "Ride!"

The arrows went up.

He kicked the stallion hard, and the horse sprang into a gallop, turning perpendicular to the arrows' path.

At their apex, the arrows seemed to pause with dreadful slowness, then arced down again. The scouts barreled forward to clear the incoming volley.

The fringes of the swarm sleeted over the rearmost two scouts, turning horses and men into a tumbling, skidding mass.

Ken'ishi spun his horse to retreat, but he heard the thunder of hoofbeats coming up the road behind them. Moments later, they came into view. Another pack of ravening Mongol wolves.

The remaining seventeen scouts galloped for Hakozaki, and the masses of horsemen fell into pursuit. The ambush had been well-executed, herding them toward the town and the bay, where more of the invading forces would be concentrated. He and his meager band were back between the pincers of the crab. They could not hope to stand against endless swarms of arrows. They must get behind walls, find some sort of fortification, or else be shredded with nothing to mark their passing but the screams of the dying.

An arrow hissed past his ear and embedded itself in the foundation of the house just ahead, where the road became a town street.

The scouts flew into the abandoned, smoking town, flying hooves trampling scattered corpses and wreckage as they went.

Rounding a corner at a crossing street took them out of immediate archery range. Just ahead lay the shattered remnants of a makeshift barricade, bristling with arrows and manned by six samurai corpses.

Ken'ishi hauled on the reins, and the stallion skidded to a halt. "Here! We fight here!" The others plowed into a disarrayed halt around him, horses snorting and whinnying.

The barricade consisted of overturned carts, barrels, crates, and livestock fences.

He swept a gesture over eight of his men. "Rebuild the barricade and take cover!" To the others, he said, "We will hold them off."

"They could come from the rear!" said one.

He whirled Silver Crane, and its glint flashed in their eyes. "Perhaps, but that will take time. This way we will have a fighting chance! Do it!"

Eight of the men jumped down and scrambled to reconstruct the barricade.

Ken'ishi sheathed Silver Crane and unslung his bow. He had never shot from horseback before, but there would likely never be a more pressing time to learn. He nocked an arrow. The other scouts lined up around him, bows readied. Moments later, the pursuers hove into view around the corner perhaps fifty paces distant.

The stallion's remaining ear lay flat against his head.

"Loose!" Ken'ishi drew and released.

The meager handful of arrows hissed across the distance, and five Mongols fell from the saddle, setting their charge into momentary disarray.

"Hold position!" Ken'ishi nocked another arrow, and the line of samurai drew their bows. "Loose!"

Two more Mongols fell, and the rest leaped over their fallen comrades and drew their bows.

The clatter and drag of the barricade reconstruction intensified behind Ken'ishi.

"Hold position!" he shouted, looking down a Mongol arrow shaft into the hard, cold eyes of his enemy directly before him. "Loose!"

His arrow speared through the Mongol's cheek and nose, and the barbarian tumbled from the saddle.

But he had not been aware of the enemy's return volley. Only he and three of his men were still on horseback.

A voice from behind him, "Captain! Take cover!"

The barricade stood once again. His archers spurred their horses back through the narrow gap that remained. He fired one last arrow, then followed, and others rolled a cart into the gap behind him. Still others drew their bows and sent more arrows at the knot of remaining enemy horsemen gathering itself to charge.

The street was narrow, perhaps wide enough for four horsemen abreast, with close-packed, single-story houses on both sides, walls of wood and rice paper, thatched roofs, bare earthen street between.

Arrows thudded into their barricade. A samurai hissed in pain as one enemy arrow found a chink and pierced his thigh.

Four of the men snatched up spears from the dead samurai who had once defended here. Their faces were grim, frightened, and steadfast. This would be their day to die, and they would ride a torrent of enemy blood into the afterworld.

At a guttural command, the Mongols charged, ponies deftly leaping over the bodies of the arrow-pierced fallen, picking up speed as they came. Gray steel against a gray sky.

The samurai cheered and hurled taunts at the thundering mob. Voices rose, summoning courage, focusing strength, gathering fortitude as the oncoming mob gathered momentum. Shaggy manes of horses and men flew. Eyes bulged. Nostrils flared. Steel edges poised. Hooves pounded up clouds of gritty, moist earth.

Spear points met the onslaught, and the bodies of horses and men impaled themselves, plowing into the makeshift barricade, shoving it back against the defenders. The samurai thrust and stabbed. Horses screamed and fell.

Over the heads of the spearmen, Ken'ishi and the others loosed arrow after arrow. The wall of enemy flesh stood so thick that they had no chance of missing either horse or Mongol.

The meager line of four spearmen could not stand for long against the overwhelming numbers pushing against the barricade. The air filled with the stench of blood and punctured guts. Dying horses and men fell into the barricade, tangling with it, crushing it, hooves shattering wood in their death spasms. Ken'ishi fired his last arrow, and another Mongol fell.

Break them! The voice of Silver Crane pealed through his mind.

"What?" he whispered, conscious that a one-sided conversation might cause more confusion around him.

Destroy their will, and the man will be victorious. Strike from the rear.

His glance trailed along the close-packed rooftops.

The man was born for this day.

An easy leap from horseback to rooftops.

Destiny.

Silver Crane hummed in its scabbard, yearning for release.

Ken'ishi dropped his bow, leaned forward and said into the stallion's remaining ear. "Be careful. You have been a brave and noble steed." Before the horse could reply, he jumped up with both feet on the saddle and leaped onto the nearest roof, snatching and clawing for purchase at the thatch, dragging himself to the crown of the roof.

Eyes trained upon him; bows swiveled toward him.

He ran, leaping from rooftop to rooftop. Silver Crane leaped into his hand. He became the Void, the No-Mind, the Nothingness between instants.

Arrows sliced toward him, and he slashed aside any that came near.

Strength and celerity such as he had never felt flooded his body. His blood roared in his ears, and his voice roared its defiance. He leaped off the last house, into the intersection, amid the ranks of enemy horsemen. Silver Crane came down, and a helmeted head soared free of its shoulders.

Cut them all!

Silver Crane swept a cold arc of death. Men roared and horses screamed. Men and beasts fell, cut deep, spewing hot gore.

Elation surged through him. Power surged through him. He severed limbs of man and horse alike, and in the chaos of death and thrashing hooves and brandished steel, men and horses injured themselves trying to escape his deadly reach.

Awash in a rain of blood, Ken'ishi slashed and cut and thrust, through forests of wet bone, mountains of straining muscle, rivers of putrid entrails. Blood dripped from his hair, slicked his palms, filled his nose, wet his lips.

The air grew dark.

He vaguely sensed blades coming near, lances thrusting toward him, the feather-soft brush of razor-edges against his flesh, but tiny cuts were as nothing against the monstrous, roiling thundercloud of power that rose through him and turned his body to steel. He became a single edge, cleaving, slicing.

Drinking.

The ring of slain men and horses grew. His toes squelched deep through crimson mud.

A droplet of rain licked through the blood on his cheek.

He leaped to the top of the chest-high ring, toward the barricade. Pale faces watched from behind the barricade. Fear took root in the Mongol faces.

His vision became a black-fringed scarlet haze.

A river of blood unto the end of the world.

Ken'ishi heard a guttural howl of assault that resembled his voice, and the droplet of rain became two, which became four, which became a pattering, plopping, spattering, mixing with the rain of blood falling to the earth.

Wind rose into a sudden howl across the rooftops. The sky darkened.

Forward and back, he slashed, he slew. Heads and arms and shoulders flew, and a long, savage cry *wrawled* from his throat. Another distant roar of defiance rose from somewhere beyond his enemies, the distant clash of blades and spears.

Drinking.

For infinite eternities, he fought, and the rain came down in thickening sheets. Lightning crackled overhead. The wind snarled and whistled, driving the rain nearly sideways, so hard it stung his face. He waded through oceans of adversaries, and the crash of surf pounded harder and harder on the distant shore like the fists of the gods. The enemies nearby sought only to flee, a chorus of screams.

Broken.

Ken'ishi found himself alone. None of the enemy remained.

And the power thrummed through him, waves of fortune crashing over the world.

A lightning bolt struck in the distance, and he felt its white-hot birth.

Dim voices, probing through the roar in his ears.

"Captain!"

"They have fled!"

Distant horns blew commands, borne upon the wind, passed along the rim of the bay, echoing over the dark, huddled rooftops of Hakozaki.

Rain sluiced the blood from his hair, from his arms, cleansing Silver Crane. Watery scarlet dripped from his chin.

The surrounding street was awash in rain and blood, corpses and pieces of corpses piled to window sills, to eaves.

His chest burned. His heart thundered with fierce heat.

He sank to his knees, gasping for breath.

He fell forward onto one arm.

Silver Crane pierced the earth, supporting his other arm.

Lightning and thunder coursed through the clouds, through his blood.

Vast cyclones of wind tore across Hakata Bay, tearing through sails, whipping the brine into frothy mountains. All of it rippled through Silver Crane, into him.

Destiny.

The taste of blood was still in his nose, in his mouth.

"A typhoon, Captain!" someone said.

"It came up so quickly!"

"Let us find shelter!"

He did not know how many of his men were left, but they helped him to his feet, into a nearby house. His right hand ached from its grip on Silver Crane's hilt, but he could not relinquish his hold.

In the darkness, their unease crowded over him. What had they seen? He began to shiver, kneeling alone, propped on the point of

Silver Crane.

They built a fire and watched him, muttering in hushed tones, reverent tones.

"I have never seen anything like that."

"I have never heard of anything like that."

"Such courage!"

"Such strength!"

"Such ferocity!"

Ken'ishi let his eyes close, allowing the conversation to ebb and flow around him. The storm outside roared and howled and slashed the rooftops with rain.

"But what about their main forces? All those ships in the bay …"

"Perhaps they took shelter in Hakata, or withdrew to Imazu."

"Most of their ships were of Korean make. Koryo sailors know the seas, those devils."

"They would not want to be trapped in the bay with this *taifu* blowing in. They'll be dashed to pieces."

"Perhaps they will flee for the open seas."

"Perhaps, but will they take the barbarians with them?"

"Would the barbarians want to be trapped on a foreign shore with no means of retreat?"

"They must know that we will eventually outnumber them."

"It came on so quickly!"

"Fortunately, we are on higher ground here."

Someone lit a lantern.

Twelve of his men remained, and he felt a moment of satisfaction. He said, "You have all accounted yourselves well."

"It was you, Captain!" someone said. "A hundred dead barbarians litter the street outside!"

Ken'ishi's torso still buzzed like the wings of a wasp, vibrations that traveled unknown distances, touched unknown possibilities. He sat up and finally sheathed his sword. His hand throbbed.

The wind moaned in the rafters like a mournful ghost. The entire house shuddered and rattled with each gust.

Ken'ishi tried to move nearer the fire, but collapsed from the fresh wave of weariness. He finally eased himself against a wall, resting his dripping head against the wood. His drenched clothing clung to his skin. Cold rivulets of water trickled down his body, dripped onto the floor, into the *tatami* ...

Both the victor
And the vanquished are
But drops of dew
But bolts of
  lightning—
Thus should we view
  the world.
— *Ouchi Yoshitaka, death*
poem

Hugging his knees,
the boy without
a name squatted
beside the mountain lake
where the waters were so
clear he could see the tiny darting fish, the tadpoles, the insects
skipping across the top of the water, far out into the dark depths.
His master was far away, on some trickster's errand. The sky was
an empty gray that reached down and obscured the mountaintops
and crowns of the pine forest. He knew this lake where he had
learned to swim, knew that its currents were fierce and capricious,
as *kami* of the deep earth rose up from beneath and warred with
the *kami* of the water.

The surface of the lake was smooth, flawless, reflecting the
forest and the mountains and the gray. And his face, which he

found to be a mask of blood. He was not hurt; the blood was not his. But he felt its heat, smelled it, as if heart's blood were pouring from his skin like sweat.

A drop of blood fell into the water and swirled into a beautiful pattern, and tiny ripples spread outward in rings across the lake. Tadpoles and insects and tiny fish scattered or changed course at the disturbance, some finding themselves within striking distance of a predator, only to be eaten. The ripples rebounded from distant rocks.

Another droplet of blood. Another set of disturbances, ripples that merged with the first wave, infinitesimally higher now.

Another droplet, and another, until the water under him assumed a scarlet cast, and waves of ripples echoed out across the lake, building and reflecting in ways he could not see.

The boy watched this, forgetting that his face was somehow bleeding, fascinated by the interplay of action and reaction. The waves were coming back now, higher, lapping over his naked toes. He giggled.

But in the deep, unseen, unnoticed, the waves coalesced. Something moved.

Ken'ishi awoke shivering. His clothes were still wet, and his hands and feet were numb. His entire body ached. The air was stale and thick with the smells of sweat, clothing that had been wet for too long, and smoke from the fire.

One of the men brought him a basin of clean water. "Here, Captain," the man said. "To wash your face."

Outside, the storm raged unabated.

Taking handfuls of water, he washed his face, and immediately the water looked like blood.

Sleeping men clustered around the fire pit for warmth. For a long time, he stood shivering over the coals, rubbing sensation back into his hands. He lay down again.

Night had long since fallen, and he felt the violence of the utter darkness outside pressing down upon him, driving him closer to the fire.

* * *

Ken'ishi's ears rang from the silence.

He opened his eyes and listened. He was warmer now, even though his clothes were still damp and the fire had burned to ashes. The noise of the rain on the roof was now a gentle hiss, not a pounding deluge.

He stood up and approached the door, trying to stretch some of the aches out of his muscles. The cuts that criss-crossed his flesh burned. He slid open the door, and his eyes met with hellish carnage.

Under the dim sky, rain-soaked death reeked and oozed. The morass of hacked bodies reached as high as his chest in some places. His knees buckled, and he clutched the door jamb.

When he gathered enough steadiness, he ventured outside. The light rain moistened his face, dripping, runnels flowing through mountains of dead flesh.

The street led down toward the sea, and for as far out as his eyes could reach, he saw wreckage. The shore was choked with shattered hulls, splintered masts, shredded sails, surging up and down with the low, groaning rumble of the waves. There was even a smashed ship nesting in the collapsed roof of a warehouse near the shore.

A strange mixture of elation and disgust washed through him—happiness that the invaders had been dealt such a deadly blow, but as he imagined how they died, trapped in rickety, leaky boats amid the black tempest, he felt a shiver that was not from the cold. The ripples of destiny.

Making his way toward the shore, he found the hulls of the ships were cracked open like eggs, spilling their limp, drenched contents onto the ground like rotten yolks. Waterlogged corpses choked the water around the shattered ships, thousands of them, men and Mongol ponies. Corpses draped the wreckage of masts and smashed hulls, bodies thrown up on shore in great, reeking piles, tangled in seaweed and flotsam, surging back and forth in the wind-blown froth. Gray, lifeless faces twisted by expressions of helpless terror, mouths filled with seawater. The waves pressed the half-submerged ships together against the land, again and again. The wreckage bumped and tore and ground against itself in the ocean's inexorable rhythm.

Had Silver Crane done this? Had *he* done this?

Most of the buildings near the shore had been demolished by the wind and sea. Dozens more had been stripped of their roofs. And before long, the air would be choked with the stench of thousands of brine-soaked corpses.

He spotted Otomo no Tsunemori and one of the other commanders on horseback, surveying the damage, and walked toward them.

Tsunemori said, "A fearful sight, is it not, Ken'ishi?"

"Yes, Lord."

"It seems that what we could not accomplish, the gods did for us. The barbarians have been destroyed."

The other commander said, "The gods and Buddhas were watching over us, it is certain."

Ken'ishi said, "Yes, Lords. The *kami* favored us." A cold tremor in his belly.

Tsunemori looked at Ken'ishi with an appraising glance. "Ken'ishi, you did well yesterday."

Ken'ishi's face flushed with pride, and with something else. "It was nothing, Otomo-sama. There were others who fought better than I, others who suffered more than I."

"Nevertheless, you should be rewarded."

Ken'ishi wished he could put aside the creeping dread in his belly.

"I serve my brother, Lord Otomo no Tsunetomo," Tsunemori continued. "When the enemy first attacked, we were regrettably not prepared for their dishonorable tactics. We suffered great losses. Lord Tsunetomo was wounded, and I was nearly killed, too. But now that the invaders have been destroyed, we can all go home soon. Enough death and horror for a hundred lifetimes." Tsunemori rubbed his chin thoughtfully. "I will need good fighting men to replenish our ranks. Would you fight for my brother? Or do you prefer the life of a wave-man?"

Ken'ishi remained silent for a moment. He remembered his elation when he had reached Lord Nishimuta no Jiro's castle with Kazuko so long ago, with her assurance that he would be offered service. Even more clearly, he remembered the shocking, heartbreaking moment when it was ripped away from him like a chunk of his own flesh. "If Lord Tsunetomo finds me worthy, I would serve him with all honor and loyalty."

Tsunemori nodded. "Very well. The castle guards do not normally admit *ronin* inside the gates, so when you arrive, show them this." He slid the small *kozuka* blade from its tiny sheath in the side of his scabbard and handed it to Ken'ishi.

Ken'ishi accepted it with both hands, his head lowered. "Thank you, Lord! I am in your debt!"

"It is nothing," Tsunemori said and lightly heeled his mount's flanks, moving away down the street. The other commander followed him, and they turned their discussion to other matters.

Ken'ishi looked down at the knife, slightly shorter than his extended hand, about as wide as a finger. Tsunemori's name was engraved in gold on the *kozuka*'s tang, gleaming from a recent polish.

He had never held such a beautiful thing before.

Ungraciously, under
a great soldier's empty
  helmet,
a cricket sings
                — *Kyoroku*

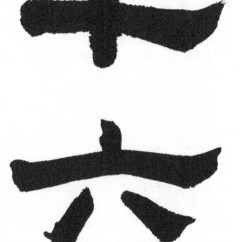

Yasutoki stood on the shore of Hakata Bay, holding his sleeve over his nose and mouth, staring at the remnants of the invasion fleet and the Mongol army. The stench was worse than anything he imagined this world could produce, worse than the most abysmal hell. He had spent all night camped in Dazaifu, near his wounded lord. After the messenger had arrived with news that the enemy was gone, all Yasutoki's hopes were dashed on the rocks, along with the splintered bones and shredded flesh of the invading army. The effort of many thousands of men, hundreds of ships, years of preparation, tens of thousands of lives snuffed out in one night, at the whim of the gods. The carnage staggered the imagination.

He wanted to spill blood to assuage his pain, kill something. His house in Hakata was gone, his underworld empire in ruins.

It would take him weeks to even take stock of what remained, perhaps years to recoup his losses. He still had a sack full of gold, but could be sure of little else.

Red foam stroked the shore. Bodies entangled in seaweed bobbed and rolled in the surf, shredded against the shattered wreckage of countless hulls. The water was thick with body parts, bits of flesh, splintered wood. Triangular fins knifed through the waves, feasting, and smaller fish clustered around the floating bodies to gnaw on the softening flesh. Crabs swarmed on the shore, their pincers tearing. A pile of corpses lay thrown upon the wreckage of a pier some fifty paces away. Even from this distance he could see the rats swarming over the pile, crabs sliding through cracks, crows hopping from splintered wood to splintered bone. All gorging themselves.

He cursed the gods for their capriciousness. *Why?* he demanded silently.

All of it gone.

All of it.

Gone.

Gone, gone, gone.

All of the danger to which he had subjected himself, all of the painstaking effort, all of the hopes, all of the gold.

Why had the Mongols retreated to their ships? They would have been safer on land! The Kyushu defenders had been shamefully unable to stem the Mongol advance. Perhaps the Koryo sailors who manned the ships had betrayed their masters in the face of the coming storm and threatened to leave them stranded. Perhaps the Mongol generals had not wanted to remain alone on a foreign shore with their supply lines cut.

The Koryo had acquiesced to the Great Khan's will, but their full hearts had not been in this invasion. Only the Great Khan's power had driven them to obey; perhaps the power of the typhoon had proven more persuasive.

Or perhaps this attack had been just a warning, a glimpse of the size of the sword that the Great Khan held poised over the heads of the Emperor and the Shogun. Perhaps this attack had never been meant as a full-scale invasion. Perhaps it was just a test, a feint to determine the true capabilities of the defenders.

Khubilai Khan was a stubborn, ambitious man. This might be only a minor setback in the Khan's eyes. Perhaps he would plan another invasion. Perhaps these thousands of dead men were but a paltry few, a drop in the bucket compared to the vast armies of the Golden Horde. To be sure, even with such horrendous losses as this day, the Mongol Empire had lost little of its fighting strength.

Green Tiger would send the Khan a message, informing the Khan of his well-being and of his readiness to continue his services. If the Khan was not amenable, then Green Tiger could find other ways to cause pain to the Shogunate, the Hojo and Minamoto clans.

There was still the matter of Lord Tsunetomo's recovery. If Tsunetomo died, Tsunemori stood to inherit Tsunetomo's holdings. Many of his chief retainers would commit *seppuku* to follow him across the river of death. Yasutoki would not, even though he would make a great show of the decision's difficulty. Then Tsunemori would most likely throw him out.

It would be best for Yasutoki if Lord Tsunetomo maintained his hold on life, at least for the time being. Lord Tsunetomo's estate was a secure base for Yasutoki, a den for Green Tiger to lick his wounds and rebuild his empire.

Fortunately, Lord Tsunetomo, a man of surprising strength and vigor, looked as if he would survive his wound.

Yes, even this terrible despair and disappointment would end. For now, he would help nurse his lord back to full health and return home with him as if nothing were amiss. He still had pleasant diversions there—Tiger Lily chief among them—to keep his mind occupied while he devised new schemes.

Scratching his head, Chiba wondered how he would ever fix his fishing boat alone. He had just spent the better part of the morning grieving for his brothers and burying their arrow-riddled corpses. There was no woodcutter to help him build a funeral pyre, no priest or monk to chant sutras, no gravedigger to dig the hole.

He was alone now, fallen so far that he must do the work of the unclean. Aoka had become a village of ghosts. And the storm had thrown his boat far up onto shore and impaled it upon a tree stump.

If everyone else was dead, however, perhaps he might find another boat still seaworthy, and the owner would surely not mind his appropriation of it. But first, one more look through his house for anything the invaders had not stolen or burned. The house belonging to him and his brothers had somehow escaped destruction, but its contents had been tossed and looted. He managed to gather the remnants of a few tools, net-making materials, an old rusty gaff hook, a robe of his brother Ryuba's that he had long coveted, and one last jar of *saké*, and bundled it all into a net.

As he thought about it, he realized there might be a few valuables scattered around the remnants of the village, perhaps a few things the barbarians had missed. And if the owners still lived and were foolish enough to return, any missing items would be ascribed to theft by the barbarians. He spent the rest of the day combing through empty houses for coins, jewelry, trinkets, anything that might be of value. Perhaps he would travel south to Kumamoto. At least it had escaped the invasion. He might make his fortune there, if he could find a boat. Aoka had never been a rich village, and the pickings were poor. Nevertheless, all told, he might be able to sell everything for a piece of silver or two.

He snarled with disgust at the charred remains of the *ronin's* abode. "I hope you're dead, bastard!"

There among the ashes he spotted a few spears of blackened bone, the curve of a skull. Who would have died in there? Curiosity aroused, he stepped gingerly into the water-logged wreckage, making his way toward the bones. He bent and extracted the skull from its place in the crook between two fallen ceiling beams. Most people would have been horrified at him soiling his spirit with the touch of the dead, but he had already been tainted by hauling his brothers to the village cemetery and digging their graves.

He examined the skull, turned it around, imagining whose face this might once have been, smaller slightly than a man's.

Then a sound turned his head, a woman's cry of pain, of anguish, of hurt and rage, sounding from a distance.

He froze. Could the barbarians still be about, ravaging one of the village women? The voice had been familiar somehow.

Then he saw her, shambling out of the forest some hundred paces distant. She wore a pale, tattered robe, colorless, hanging over her feet. Long, bedraggled hair obscured her face, hanging below her waist, tangled with things too small to see at this distance.

She stopped there, just at the edge of the wild forest, and the slight cant of her body suggested she had noticed him. Her shoulders bore the stooped curve of a woman beaten down by either age or the suffering of life.

The wail came again, closer now, sending a chill down through his feet into the ground, a sound so harsh his eyes watered, and he blinked away the tears. Somehow in those instants she had crossed most of the distance between them, but she was not walking. She simply stood. The glimmer of eyes regarded him from beyond the veil of unkempt, black hair.

With a gasp and strangled cry, he dropped the skull back into the ashes, and scrambled out of the wreckage. Stumbling over the last tangled, blackened debris, he found himself suddenly face to face with her. She swayed slightly, as if weak.

Only two paces away now, he could see that her hair was wet with blood, beslimed by the afterworld, crawling with beetles and maggots. The tips of her fingers were claws, reddened as if by her own dried blood. Her head tipped back, allowing her face to emerge from the black torrent of hair, and Kiosé's face rose toward heaven and unleashed another screech of such rage and despair that Chiba felt a burst of warmth spew down his leg.

Her face swiveled toward him, and her gaze flamed orange-red, boring into him like red-hot spear blades as she launched herself at him.

Chiba covered his face with his arms and fled like a lunatic, screaming. Her shriek filled his ears, his brain, and his legs pumped as he dashed blindly into the countryside, arms flailing, forgetting his stolen trinkets, forgetting any thought of stealing a boat, forgetting all but to run for his very soul. He ran until he collapsed from exhaustion, but the screech forced him up again and drove him on, to run until he collapsed again, then again, then again, until his limbs could no longer support his weight, and his mind could no longer support the weight of Kiosé's rage.

When he awoke, somewhere alone in the wild mountains, the scream was gone, but he sensed the presence still, hovering just out of sight.

He sat on a rock and wept.

That night, deep within the thick of the woods, with a mountain rearing at his back, he built his fire high, and hunched close in the circle of light, hugging his knees, his eyes catching smudges of black hair emerging from every shadow. Drifting embers became eyes like coals. He wished for the jar of *saké* he had left behind. He wished for some food to fill his belly. He wished for a bed and a safe place to sleep.

The typhoon clouds shredded themselves against the sky. The moon rose, and the stars drifted between the treetops.

His heart jumped into his throat at the brush of a robe against his elbow and the stench of death filling his nose. She hovered beside him, loomed over him, and the hem of her robe floated a hand's breadth above the ground with no feet visible beneath.

He scrambled back like a crab, a wild ululation tearing from his throat, but she followed, reaching down, down, her claws coming for him, snatching at his shoulders like knife points, falling down upon him, those eyes like coals burning into his, bearing him down against the earth, the breath of the grave in his nose, cold, scabrous lips closing over his, stifling his scream. He tried to tear himself away, to breathe, but cold tendrils of black hair snaked around his head, cinching, writhing, squeezing his lips onto hers. Her claws pierced deep, grating across bone.

Eventually, somewhere near morning, his screams died.

Norikage had almost starved to death by the time he found his way to Hakozaki. He had not eaten in days while he hid with Hana in the forests and mountains. His clothing hung like a sack on his already spare frame, and his legs wobbled. He had a small sack of coins hidden in his now filthy robes, and he needed to spend some of them on food. Every time Hana stumbled from weakness, he felt a pang of guilt that he should be providing for her.

A lonely, deserted mountain shack had been their shelter from the typhoon. They had been cold and hungry, but dry. When the typhoon was over, they had ventured back to Aoka village, found it ravaged, burned, deserted. Hana's fishing boat had been tossed far up onto shore, even though it still appeared seaworthy. It would take the work of several men to carry it back to the water.

Distant wreckage peppered the glimmering expanse of sea. Was the battle over?

Finally, on the road to Hakozaki, they encountered a group of woodcutters, and he had tightened up his courage enough to ask them for news.

When they told him that the invaders had been destroyed, the immeasurable relief brought him to his knees. His stomach had ceased growling days ago, but now with new hope inside him, the hunger raged like a living beast, dogging his every step. Water was easy enough to find, but he could not drink enough to satisfy his hunger. He tried to find berries or other fruits in the forest, but he could find nothing at this time of year but a few half-rotten persimmons. He did not know how to live off the land like Ken'ishi. And Hana depended on him.

Where was Ken'ishi now? Was he alive?

Norikage had spent much time thinking about what had transpired between them. What right did a *ronin* have to be self-righteous? Norikage had once told Ken'ishi that he himself was a sort of *ronin*. Now it was true. He could never go back to Kyoto, to his family. He had nothing. No one except Hana. No way to feed either of them, except for the paltry few coins hidden in his robes. When those coins were gone, they would starve, and the coins would run out far too soon.

When they arrived at Hakozaki, the devastation took his breath away. Much of the bayside had been flattened by the storm. The stench crept across the land far beyond the bounds of the town, clinging inside his throat as he breathed. At the edge of town, huge graves were crammed with countless thousands of ripened corpses. Other similar graves had already been covered over, forming great earthen mounds, while others sat half-empty. Steady streams of wagons and carts hauled piles of rapidly decaying corpses.

Around the shops of swordsmiths and armorers were piles of Mongol weapons and equipment, untold thousands of Mongol swords and armor plates, all of it destined to be melted down and reused. But as he shuffled through the city, he overheard people saying that some smiths would not touch the tainted foreign steel. Perhaps it *was* tainted with the demonic fury and brutality of the former owners. A Shinto priest performed purification rites over a neatly stacked pile of foreign weapons. Could the steel be purified to receive the soul of a samurai?

Samurai were keeping order, preventing looting and lawlessness. Every time he saw a lone warrior, he looked to see if it was Ken'ishi. He yearned to make amends. They had been friends for three years, and they had been through trouble and danger together.

Norikage finally found a shop selling Chinese noodles, mobbed by hungry people. Hana clutched his arm with a gasp. Only at close range did the smell of pork broth overpower the stench of death and decay that hung so heavy in the air. He mustered all the self-control he possessed to be calm and collected as they waited their turn, almost two hours. But when the bowl of noodles came, he could stand it no longer. He practically buried his face in the steaming broth, taking the chopsticks and shoveling into his mouth, burning his tongue, but he did not care. He began to feel ill, probably because he had eaten too much too fast, but he did not care. He had eaten.

As he sipped hot tea, waiting for his belly to calm itself, Hana was a quiet presence next to him. She was a woman of few words, which was one thing he liked about her. She allowed him silence.

He had initially thought that her silence meant she was simple-minded, but when she spoke, her words carried weight.

She said, "Perhaps you could find a way to manage an establishment much like this one. You have enough money to make yourself a credible businessman."

"Me? Become a merchant?" Merchants were mostly a dishonorable breed, but did that really bother him? Death was preferable to living as a penniless beggar. "Perhaps." He gave her a little smile. Yes, the idea began to swirl in his mind. But he could not start such a venture in Hakozaki. He would have to go to Hakata, where there were more customers and more profit. Besides, Hakozaki was still a bit too close to Aoka village. He wanted to be far from there.

Another patron ordered two bowls of noodles and pushed his straw hat off his head, letting it fall across his back. The old man slid onto a stool, bald and portly with a sprout of white beard poking from his chin and a tuft of white hair sprouting over each ear.

The old man looked at Norikage askance. "You look as if you have a story to tell. Did you lose your post as a scarecrow?"

Norikage smiled. "I suppose so."

"How's Aoka village?" the old man asked.

"How did you—!"

The old man waved a hand. "I've passed through there a few times. It's not a big village. I had an acquaintance who was trying to get back there. I'd like some news of him."

"Who?"

"A young warrior. Perhaps you know him."

Norikage could not conceal his surprise. "I saw him!" Then he scratched his head. "How many days ago ...? Since the day of the invasion."

"Does the old sot yet live?"

"He lived when he left me."

The old man nodded and sipped his tea. "Then perhaps still."

"Perhaps. How do you know him?"

"I have stories to tell about that myself. But you first."

Did a cuckoo cry?
I look out, but there is
    only dawn and
The moon in its final
    night.
Did the moon cry out
Horobirete! Horobirete!
Perishing! Perishing!
    — *The Love Poems of*
        Marichiko

While Hatsumi and Kazuko awaited Tsunetomo's return, Hatsumi combed Kazuko's long, beautiful hair, something she had always enjoyed when Kazuko was younger. She had pitifully few opportunities to do it these days. Kazuko had taken to doing many such personal tasks for herself. She said it was because she should ask no one to do anything for her that she could not do herself. Hatsumi had found this sentiment incomprehensible, and perhaps a bit offensive, but she did not press the issue.

Hatsumi yawned widely. She had slept poorly last night, a sleep fraught with increasingly awful dreams.

Today was a good day, however, in spite of her sleepiness. Lord Tsunetomo was coming home. Her fears of impoverishment could be put aside for a while. Kazuko's old, tiresome melancholy seemed to be gone forever. Her spirit had risen and opened once again.

Hatsumi was also happy that Yasutoki was returning, too. She had even written a poem for him, suggesting a liaison, and she would send it to him discreetly.

As the sounds of the gate opening reached their lofty window, Kazuko said, "They are here!" She jumped up with excitement.

"Oh, my dear, run along. I'm not dressed yet."

"Please come when you can!" Kazuko wiped tears and ran out of the room.

Hatsumi sighed and went to the window. If Yasutoki accompanied the entourage, she would stay here. She was not ready to see him yet. Ranks of troops began marching through the gate, spear tips glinting, next several ranks of mounted samurai and officers. There were many fewer now than when they had departed.

Next came Lord Tsunetomo's palanquin. Servants and samurai alike knelt at its passage. She could not see Kazuko below, but a ripple of reverence and joy spread through the courtyard at Tsunetomo's arrival.

The line of troops stretched down the hill and through the town. Near the end of the line, just ahead of the trains of riderless horses, were groups of scruffy-looking *bushi*.

Hatsumi sneered, "They look like filthy *ronin*!" A stab of hatred in her belly as she looked out over the new recruits, with their strange mishmash of weapons and threadbare clothing. That *ronin* who had ruined her life and Kazuko's. Her face tightened. She often wished she would have died at the hands of the *oni* rather than live with all the agony she had suffered since.

The images in her dreams the night before slunk back into her mind, the black, terrible dreams that had driven her out of peaceful sleep into the cold abyss of midnight wakefulness. Last night had been particularly vivid.

Drowning in a lake of sticky, black pitch in some vast underground cavern. And she, alone in the vast abyss, struggling to stay afloat, listening to her own screams echoing endlessly in the cavern. The tar clung to her arms, sucked her down, and she was weary unto death, gasping for breath. Her arms flailed and her legs kicked in the black muck, but she was lost. And there were eyes in the blackness. Beady, yellow eyes that drilled into her and laughed, enjoying the spectacle of her suffering. The more she fought, the more the tar felt as if it had a life of its own, moving across her flesh like an octopus or a squid or a mass of worms, but she could not see in the blackness. Thousands of black, slimy worms, wriggling, squirming, undulating. Searching. Seeking openings to burrow into her. She screamed and screamed again as the worms found their ways inside, wriggling, sliding into her nether regions. She squeezed her thighs together, clenched her buttocks, but she could not stop them. Burrowing. Biting. Gnawing! They were chewing through her skin, slowly, with their tiny, tiny teeth and vicious, sucking mouths. Burrowing into her legs, her arms, her belly, her back. Crawling up her face to slide into her mouth, her nose, her ears. The beady yellow eyes hovering above her, like fireflies in the deep, thunderous, familiar laughter that haunted her every day of her life. The worms tore, wriggling through her flesh, and she screamed and screamed, with no one to hear except the eyes and the worms.

But the deeper the worms dug, the less she felt their presence, as if their forms were dispersing within her flesh like juices in a stew. A strange calm settled over her. All of her flesh began to quiver, as if her body was being reshaped until she became a worm herself. Or worse, as if she were being remade from the flesh of the black worms.

That was when she always awoke, cold and sweating.

But what troubled her almost as much as the dream itself was that she sometimes awoke in strange places. Once, she had returned to wakefulness standing in the middle of the audience hall. Another time, she was in the hallway outside Kazuko's chamber. Another time, she was lying on the floor outside of Yasutoki's room. Another time, outside the servant quarters, and that time she had awakened to find a dagger in her hand. What had she planned to do with it? For that matter, whose dagger was it? She did not have one of her own.

A stabbing pain doubled Hatsumi over, tearing through her lower belly, through her womb. She gasped and clutched her belly. She pressed her forehead against the floor. The pain was like a hot knife stabbing into her womb. No, more like the rape by the *oni* ... She bit back a scream.

Then, suddenly, the pain was gone, like the flame on a snuffed candle. The shock of its departure was almost as great. She slowly straightened up again, her breath returning to normal. She took a deep breath and released it.

As she stood, she felt moisture between her legs, but she had not had her woman's bleeding for three years. Not since the rape. She had told no one this. Not even Kazuko. It had filled her with a sort of shame and fear. On the contrary, she had continued to talk with Kazuko as if her moon's blood still came. The thought of its return filled her with elation. She would be a whole woman again! Not a ravaged, soiled, wounded thing. She hurried out and returned to her chambers.

In the privacy of her own chambers, she searched within the layers of her robes and undergarments. She did not want to stain them with blood.

But blood was not what she found.

There were only a few droplets of a strange black ooze, oily and viscous, soaking almost reluctantly into her garments. Her breath froze in her throat and she tore off her clothing, engulfed in a miasma of fetid stench.

For a long time, she sat naked and alone, trembling in the middle of her chamber.

When she looked down at the small white pile of soiled under-robes, a retch leaped into her throat. A wave of dizziness washed over her, her belly threatening to purge.

She awoke what must have been moments later, lying on her back, looking up at the ceiling. Her body was ice cold and covered in sweat. Her first thought was that the robes had to be destroyed immediately. No one must ever see them. But they already lay half-burned amid the coals of the brazier.

Since the storm abated, Kazuko had waited, near breathless, for some word, any word from Hakata, but there was nothing. Her body felt like a sodden, wrung-out scrap of linen. Her eyes burned from lack of sleep. She had stayed up through two nights to keep watch with the rest of the warriors. No one had expected it of her, but in doing so, she had gained a modicum of their grudging respect. Their obedience, which she already had, was one thing; however, their respect was quite another, and it filled her with pride.

When the messenger finally came with news that the invading army had been destroyed by the typhoon, relief had flooded her with tears of joy. But what of her husband? Was he alive? Dead? Had his wound been a mortal one?

Later, another messenger arrived bearing a letter from her husband. He was alive, and he was coming home.

Throughout the time when Hatsumi was brushing her hair, she could hardly sit still.

The procession of warriors filed through the castle gates. Tsunetomo rode in a palanquin near the head of the column. Kazuko smoothed her robes. They were her best, exquisitely woven and painted with vines and pheasants. Her face was freshly powdered. She waited patiently, quietly, as a proper wife should, for the bearers to set down the palanquin before the doors of the house, for his men to help him out and to his feet.

The pain on his face was evident as he tried to straighten, but his jaw hardened and he shrugged it away. His smile spread like warmth when he saw her, and her face flushed beneath the fresh powder. He climbed the steps, hiding his unsteadiness. His face was pale, and dark sacks hung under his eyes as he concentrated on the steps, one by one. Then, his face rose again, his gaze lifted to her, and some of the color returned. Some of the pain lines around his mouth disappeared.

When he reached the threshold of the house, she bowed low and said, "Welcome home, Husband. I am so happy you are safe."

"I am happy to be home, my dear."

"Your journey must have been difficult. Please come with me so that you can rest."

He nodded, and she took his arm to support him. By the time they reached their chambers, his breathing was heavy with weariness. The air in the room was warm from the braziers of coals.

She said, "I have prepared a bed for you."

"Be careful, my dear. I am not used to being treated like a child. You will embarrass me."

Out of the mouth of another man, those words might have sounded harsh, but from him they were good-natured and playful. At this moment, she wanted to do everything in the world to make this man happy, comfortable, and well. She wanted him to recover and to live a long time. She helped him to undress and put on more comfortable robes. She helped him lie down on the *futon* she had prepared, propping him up on a large pillow. She winced along with him when every movement of his arm caused him pain. She poured him special healing tea.

As the steam rose from the teacup, its pungent aroma wafting into her nostrils, she was reminded of another time, long ago, when she had smelled another healing concoction. She drove thoughts of Ken'ishi from her mind immediately.

He said, "The warmth of one's own house is a wonderful thing when a man has been lying in a cold tent for days. When I saw that arrow coming, and I knew that it would hit me, I thought I was going to die. I was glad that I was not afraid. Only a coward is afraid of death. But I was also sad, because I feared I would never see you again."

He looked at her with a deep, searching gaze, and she gave him what he wanted. "I feared I would never see you again as well." And it was true. "You are a strong man, Husband. Many people rely on you, and you never let them down."

"I fear I will not be strong again for a long time."

"It will come, but first you must rest. Here, drink your tea." She gave him the teacup, and he took it with his good hand, sipped it

401

gingerly.

His face grew serious and thoughtful. "The Mongols are a terrible foe. If the gods had not lent their hand to help us, we would have been defeated. We *were* defeated! It is shameful to think about."

"You mustn't trouble yourself about it now, Husband."

"But these are the things that must be considered before the enemy regroups and comes again. Their ways of battle are foul and dishonorable, but effective. It was a slaughter." He took another sip of tea and stared into the glowing coals.

She slid closer and placed her hand on his forehead. "You look so pale."

"Do not worry, my dear." He smiled for her. "The fever broke yesterday. I will mend. I thank you for your kindness."

"It is you who has been kind to me, Husband. I regret my unhappiness when we were first married."

"Your feelings are common among young brides. I know that you have come to love me."

She smiled at him again, then leaned over and kissed him.

Even in castles
I have felt the
  searching breath
Of the wintry wind
             — *Kyoroku*

Ken'ishi spent several days with the army, searching northern Kyushu for any Mongols that had escaped. They captured nearly three hundred of the enemy, including Korean sailors who had either managed to swim ashore after their ships sank or missed their ships' departure altogether. All were summarily executed, their severed heads carefully cleaned, powdered, and mounted on boards for viewing by the Shogun's representatives, who arrived a few days afterward.

Winter arrived a few weeks later, making the massive cleanup and rebuilding effort even more difficult. Snow was never likely in northern Kyushu until after the New Year, but the days were still miserably cold and wet.

Rumors and stories of the invaders' atrocities filled every conversation, the slaughter of whole villages, the use of black magic to frighten and disrupt the defenders, riding their demon ponies across water, killing people with volleys of arrows from impossible ranges. Some said the invading army numbered in the hundreds of thousands. Ken'ishi could not fathom a number that large. Many of the stories sounded wild and incredible, but he had seen the Mongols drink blood, and he could not have imagined such a thing before.

When the Shogun's regent, Hojo no Tokimune, and his entourage finally arrived, the entire region was buzzing with rumors and preparation. The Shogun's representatives surveyed the destruction, listened to the reports of the commanders, viewed the heads of the enemy, and distributed writs of acclaim and reward for the lords and high-ranking samurai who had fought with success. With the surveys complete, the defending armies disbanded to return to their domains. Many of the lords of Kyushu squabbled about who would receive the richest rewards from the *bakufu* for successfully repulsing the enemy invasion.

Ken'ishi thought this was unseemly, but he could say nothing. Meanwhile, prayers and offerings of thanks to the gods filled the countryside.

Let them think the storm was the gods' making. The silent, silver whisper interrupted his meditations one night as he prepared for sleep.

From the warm, sensationless abyss of the Void, Ken'ishi answered. "How could you have done such a thing? How is it possible?"

The man's mind is too simple to encompass the enormities of time and existence.

"Did you bring the storm?"

I was once lost at the bottom of the sea, away from the sight of men. Through tides and time and long chains of fortune, I was found again. Is this not the nature of destiny?

Ken'ishi's mind reached out with more questions, but Silver Crane fell silent. The more he thought about what it had said, the more questions arose.

One day, Ken'ishi was walking through the market square, where a few brave merchants had returned and worked at rebuilding their trade, and he spied a familiar face. "Otomo no

Ishitaka!"

The young man turned to look and smiled with recognition. "Ken'ishi! I thought I might see you around here."

"I am happy to see you up and walking around," Ken'ishi said as he approached. They bowed to each other.

"As am I. I thought I was dead. Father always told me I had a thick skull. I guess this is the first time it has served me well."

They laughed, and Ken'ishi said, "I know a good saké house that is open for business."

Ishitaka smiled. "Lead the way, Ken'ishi. I am thirsty." He leaned over and pointed at his pate. "I have a crease in my skull running from here to here." His voice was proud.

The two young men spent the rest of the afternoon in the Spring Snow *Saké* House, but they did not drink enough to become disgracefully drunk. Ken'ishi had no wish to bring public dishonor upon himself, or for any tales of vulgar conduct to reach the ears of the lord he had never met.

As the afternoon turned into evening, Ishitaka said in an abruptly serious tone, "Ken'ishi, I have a confession. I know something about you."

Ken'ishi tensed. "What is it?"

"I know that you were a *ronin*."

Ken'ishi stiffened.

"Some say," Ishitaka continued, "that being a warrior without a lord is a dishonorable thing, a disgraceful thing. They say that a *ronin* can be nothing more than a cowardly bandit. His lord cast him out, or he failed to protect his lord with his own life, or did not follow his lord into death, so he must be a worthless man. I say that is wrong! Because I have known a *ronin*, and he is one of the bravest men I have ever met. The tales of your fight with the enemy in Hakozaki are spreading. Did you really slay a hundred Mongols single-handedly?"

Ken'ishi's face warmed. "I don't know how many it was."

"In any case, my father has heard of it, and is looking forward to welcoming you at my uncle's castle."

"Your father?"

"Otomo no Tsunemori."

Ken'ishi's mouth fell open.

Ishitaka laughed and pointed. "The look on your face!"

Ken'ishi's ears flushed again.

"You saved my life and the lives of your men that day."

Ken'ishi could not speak. How many other thousands had he slain by his actions?

"You will do well as one of my uncle's retainers!" Ishitaka raised his bowl and took another drink.

Ken'ishi smiled wanly and did the same.

"My uncle is an honorable man, and he treats his retainers fairly."

"I'm glad to hear it. I will serve him with all the honor and loyalty that he deserves." As he took another sip, he tried to distinguish if the warmth he felt in his belly was from the *saké* or from something else.

Destiny....

So ends the Fifth Scroll

GLOSSARY

ayu – *Plecoglossus altivelis*. Fresh water fish indigenous to Japan and Korea, often called "sweetfish" because of the sweetness of its flesh.

bakufu – lit. "tent government", but came to mean the dwelling and household of a shogun, or military dictator. Generally used to refer to the system of government of a feudal military dictatorship, equivalent in English to the term 'shogunate'.

biwa – short-necked fretted lute, often used in narrative storytelling, the chosen instrument of Benten, goddess of music, eloquence, poetry, and education in the Shinto faith.

bokken – wooden practice sword, designed to lessen damage. Sword master Miyamoto Musashi was renowned for facing fully armed opponents with one or two bokken.

bushi – synonymous with "samurai", military nobility, warrior gentleman.

daikon – variety of large, white radish with a mild flavor.

do-maru – lit. "body wrap", style of armor constructed of leather and metal plates, lacquered, lighter and closer fitting than the *o-yoroi* style.

futon – padded mattress flexible enough to be folded up and put away during the day.

Go – a board game for two players, originating in China more than 2,500 years ago, noted for being rich in strategy despite its relatively simple rules. Players place black and white "stones" on the intersections of a 19 x 19 grid, the object being to use one's stones to capture a larger total area of the board than the opponent.

hara – the belly or stomach, believed to contain the soul or the "center of being."

jitte – lit. "ten hands", also called a *jutte,* weapon consisting of an iron bar and U-shaped guard, designed to catch and hold sword blades, often used to disarm unruly samurai, typically 12-24 inches long (30-60 cm).

kabuto – helmet, comprising many different styles, secured to the head by a chin cord, often adorned with crests.

kami – sometimes translated as "god" or "deity", but also referring to the ubiquitous spirits of nature, the elements, and ancestors, which are the center of worship for the Shinto faith.

kappa – supernatural river creature or spirit, about the size of a child, with a turtle-like shell, a beak for a mouth, a flat saucer-like indentation on its head that must remain filled with water when it is on land, or else it loses its power. Their behavior and feeding habits range from pranksterish and lecherous to predatory and vampiric.

kemari – an ancient game wherein the players strive to keep a leather ball in the air using various parts of their bodies.

ki – spirit, life, energy.

kiai – battle cry or sharp cry meant to focus technique, awareness, and fighting spirit, sometimes to startle an opponent or express victory.

kimono – lit. "thing to wear", traditional garment worn by men, women, and children, typically secured at the waist by an *obi.* Straight-lined robe that reaches to the ankle, with a collar and wide sleeves.

komadori – *Erithacus akahige*. Japanese robin.

kozuka – small utility knife fit into the side of a katana scabbard.

menpo – metal armor covering the face from the nose to the chin, often fashioned into fearsome shapes.

miso – a thick paste made by fermenting soy, rice, and/or barley, used as seasoning. Very healthy. Miso soup is an excellent hangover cure.

mochi – rice cake made from pounding short-grain glutinous rice into a thick, sticky paste.

momme – unit of weight, approximately equal to 0.13 ounces (3.75 gm).

mon – emblem in Japanese heraldry, similar to coats of arms in European heraldry, used to identify individuals and families.

naginata – a polearm with a stout, curved blade 12-24 inches (30-60 cm) long, with a wooden shaft 4-8 feet (120-240 cm) long.

nodachi – also called *odachi*, lit. "great/large sword", averaging 65-70 inches long (165-178 cm).

obi – sash used to secure robes, of a myriad of lengths and styles. Typically men's *obi* are narrower than women's.

o-furo – a deep, steep-sided wooden bathtub, but also sometimes referring to the room where bathing is done.

oni – supernatural creature from folklore, translates as demon, devil, ogre, or troll. Hideous, gigantic creatures with sharp claws, wild hair, and long horns growing from their heads, mostly humanoid, but sometimes possessing unnatural features such as odd numbers of eyes or extra fingers and toes.

onmyouji – practitioners of a form of divination based on esoteric *yin-yang* cosmology, which was a mixture of natural science and occultism.

oyabun – lit. "foster parent", but most often used to refer to the boss of an organized crime family.

o-yoroi – lit. "great armor", heavy, box-shaped armor, used primarily by high-ranking samurai on horseback, consisting of an iron breastplate covered with leather, lacquered iron scales, woven together with silk or leather cords, and rectangular lamellar shoulder guards.

ramen – noodle dish consisting of wheat noodles served in broth, often with pork, *miso*, green onions, pickled ginger, or other toppings.

ri – unit of length or distance, equivalent to 2.4 miles (3.9 km).

ronin – a samurai with no lord or master, having become masterless from the death or fall of his master, or after the loss of his master's favor or privilege.

saké – fermented beverage made from rice.

seiza – lit. "proper sitting", kneeling position with legs folded under, sitting on calves and heels.

shuriken – lit. "hand-hidden sword", any small, concealed bladed object, used for throwing, stabbing, or slashing. Common types include weighted spikes and thin, bladed plates.

soba – buckwheat.

sumi – traditional ink, made from soot, water, and glue.

tachi – style of sword, earlier design than the *katana*, with a more pronounced curvature, usually worn with the edge hanging down, in contrast to the *katana,* which was worn with the edge facing up.

taifu – lit. "great wind", hurricane, root of the English word "typhoon".

tanuki – *Nyctereutes procyonoides*. Mammal indigenous to Japan, sometimes translated as "raccoon dog", member of the dog family (Canidae). Resembles a raccoon in having rounded ears, dark facial markings, and brown coat, but its tail is not ringed. Its limbs are short, brown or blackish in color, and its body heavy and low-slung. In folklore, *tanuki* are tricksters, said to possess magical powers and the ability to change shape. *Tanuki* are said to keep their magical powers in their scrota.

tatami – mat used for flooring, made of a core of rice straw wrapped in soft rush straw.

tengu – supernatural creature from folklore, having both avian and human characteristics. *Tengu* were long believed to be disruptive demons and harbingers of war. However, this image evolved into one of protective, if still dangerous, spirits of the mountains and forests.

tsuba – round or square guard above the hilt of a bladed weapon.

uguisu – *Cettia diphone*. A song bird known as the Japanese bush warbler.

yojimbo – bodyguard.

yoriki – lit. "helper, assistant", in the case of this story, the deputy to a provincial constable.

yurei – lit. "dim spirit", supernatural entity from folklore, analogous to Western ghosts. A person who dies in a state of extreme negative emotion, such as revenge, love, jealousy, hatred or sorrow, may be trapped in the earthly realm as a *yurei*.

zori – flat, thonged sandals made from straw or wood.

CONTRIBUTORS

This book would not have been possible without the generous support of this amazing army of people.

Archer
Daniel Cowling
Emily Normile

Spearman
Karen
Rhel
Matthew Boroson
Shawn Carman
Dantzel Cherry
A. Dorrance
Gintaras Duda
David Farnell
Thomas Albert Fowler
Regina Glei
Scott Grayson
Matthew Griffiths
Jeff Hartsell
Philip Harris
Jason Holtschneider
Scott Hughes
Aren Jensen
Mur Lafferty
Joe Maurantonio
Amanda McMurtry
Nayad Monroe

David Murphy
Robert Ness
Matthew Rotundo
John Rudd
Richard F. Sheehan
Christina Stiles
Michael R.
   Underwood
Derek Williams
Frank Wuerbach

Ronin
Bob Applegate
Don Arnold
Blake Badders
Michael Beddes
Eytan Bernstein
Guy Anthony De
   Marco
Rob Dake
Catharine Dixon
Olivia Do
Julia Dvorin
Melissa Fabros
Robert Fraass
Patrik Haraldsson

Jason Heller
William Hertling
Rich Howard
Mark Innerebner
Elaine Isaak
Zach Jacobs
Al Kallhoff
Korey Krabbenhoft
Tina Lindell
Peter J. Mancini
Tyler Mierholtz
Sheila Mosig Bond
Matt Mueller
Joseph Narducci
Theresa Oster
PowrSteve
Daniel Read
Aaron Michael
   Ritchey
James Sams
Lani Santos
Kyle Simonsen
Christa Smith
Susan Spann
Meagan Spooner
Suzanne Stafford

Harley Trimble
Mary Villalba
Josh R. Vogt
Amber Welch
Jon Zenor

Bandit Chieftain
Gerard Ackerman
Maggie Christensen
Craig
Kimberly Dahl
    Vandervort
John Evans
Jonathan Finke
Dianne Hradsky
Fantomas
Megan McGuire
Pretentious Moniker
Jonathan Reyes
R. Schuyler Devin

Samurai
Maria Anderson
    Knudtson
Nicci Bellmyer
Rachel Brewer
Dawn Christensen
Shelda Cline
Robert Corder
Paul Duncan III
Sean Eret
Amanda Ferrell
Kelsie Gardner
Guyver
Christine Hardy
Susan Malsom
    Holland
Norajane McIntyre
Ann M. Myers
Michael Nave
Paul Nelson
Mistina Picciano

Josh Seybert
John Shoberg
Emerson Small
Amber Toler

Infantry Sergeant
Kent Barker-Steen

Cavalry Sergeant
Cody Heermann
Chanel Helgason
Dorothy Heermann

Captain
Rich Chang
Gary Emenitove
Joel Gilbert
James Hollaman
Steven Rief
Jason Sperber
Patricia Vandewege

Chamberlain
Todd Ahlman
Megan Hinrichs

General
Jason Burns

Lord
Scott Baldwin

Minister of the Left
Casey Heermann

Ninja
Joe Aliment
Sean Crow
Nathan Davis
Darcy Duerfeldt
Michael Reed
    McLaughlin

Rimun Murad
Andrew Rasmusson
James Vnuk
Sally Wright

PERMISSIONS

414

ABOUT THE AUTHOR

Author, freelance writer, award-winning screenwriter, poker player, biker, roustabout, and graduate of the Odyssey Writing Workshop, Travis Heermann is the author of numerous short stories appearing in such places as Fiction River's hard SF anthology *How to Save the World*, and others such as *Weird Tales, Cemetery Dance's Shivers Vol. VII*, and *Historical Lovecraft*. He is the author of the The Ronin Trilogy, *Rogues of the Black Fury, The Wild Boys*, and *Snakes*. Aside from his fiction work, he has contributed to almost thirty roleplaying supplements, including *Legend of the Five Rings* and *d20 System* products, plus game content for White Wolf/CCP's MMORPG, *EVE Online*.

He spent three years living in Japan, where much of this story was researched and conceived, and now lives in a much larger world than before.

Find the author online!
Email: travis@travisheermann.com
Web: http://www.travisheermann.com
Blog: http://www.travisheermann.com/blog
Twitter: @TravisHeermann
Facebook: https://www.facebook.com/travis.heermann

Made in the USA
Las Vegas, NV
12 March 2021

19484203R00246